SEEDS IN T

First Published in 2004 by
Serendipity
Suite 530
37 Store Street
Bloomsbury
London

British Library Cataloguing-in-Publication data
A catalogue record for this book is available from the British Library
ISBN 1-84394-102-3
Printed and bound by Antony Rowe Ltd, Eastbourne

Seeds in the Black Earth

ELLEN THOMPSON

SERENDIPITY

To my daughter Eunice, my grandson Graham and my great-grandchildren Jenna and Ryan

Thank you to friends and family who have helped and encouraged me over the years with my writing.

If seeds in the black earth can turn into such beautiful roses, what might not the heart of man become in its long journey towards the stars.

G K Chesterton

The sound of swishing brooms and clanging buckets gradually diminished as Lottie Hanson's unexpected appearance made full impact upon a painfully familiar scene. 'My God!' shot through an anguished mind but the words stopped short of utterance, enormous effort was required to keep on walking, into the lions' den as it were. She could have kicked herself.

Born and bred in the place how did such a long established weekly ritual slip her mind, handing the onlookers a glorious opportunity to vent their spleen upon her? Dozens of curious women watching every step she took with speculative eyes, ill feeling immediately aroused and definitely out for blood. It was the wrong day to choose for a well overdue meeting with her brother, self-inflicted punishment and no mistake.

Her name began to fly like wildfire from one vicious tongue to the next, the entire assembly soon alerted to her presence, all ready to give voice to their strong disapproval. More satisfying in her hearing, naturally, but these same tongues had been wagging for days on end, now prepared to subject their hapless victim to more verbal abuse, the slating they truly believed she deserved. Judge and jury rolled into one, the verdict already in: guilty as charged.

Since the tender age of ten, Lottie had taken part in this Friday afternoon routine, considered old enough then to fill buckets for her mother, soon able to perform the whole tiresome task unaided, eight years of it to date. Bessie Hanson out of the picture when, after months of suffering, a terminal illness took its toll, her teenage daughter was left to carry on alone until two weeks previously when that brief letter arrived announcing her elder brother's imminent homecoming, Ralph an only sibling. News which sent the lass into instant panic and her hasty departure to an aunt's home in Quarry Cottages, Upper Meldon, half an hour's journey on foot, all uphill. Not the wisest of moves, her dead father's eldest sister was totally unpredictable, it was never known how Maude Elliott would jump in any situation. She was just a port in a storm but only delaying the inevitable, soon to be experienced to its full extent.

It couldn't have been much worse weatherwise, a prolonged spell of heavy rainfall ceased at last but the cold, capricious wind which accompanied it still tormented those obliged to be out of doors in the mining village of Saltersgate, just one among many of its kind on the Northumbrian coal field, less attractive than usual today, definitely no beauty spot but somewhere for folk to live and eke out an impoverished existence, almost totally reliant upon Polrigg Colliery, nearly three miles distant, to make work for its male population and the meagre wherewithal to keep body and soul together.

Lottie's destination lay well down Maria Street, a terraced row of two up, two down dwellings similar to others in the village, all with outside dry 'closets' open 'middens' and several taps at equally spaced intervals to provide running water; gallons of it already swilled down the drain on this particular Friday afternoon. A day Lottie deemed bad enough to qualify as an unlucky thirteenth of the month, which it wasn't. Most of its womenfolk, unfortunately out of doors, were attacking the communal gutter, the combined din of working utensils and raised voices echoed through chill October air, sure sign of an early winter, with food and adequate clothing much more of a problem to those already far below the bread line. Folk from whom transgressors like herself could expect no mercy, never before had she been on the receiving end but she was well aware of what they were capable of dishing out on such occasions and she was directly in the line of fire.

About time Ralph made an appearance, Lottie niggled as she quickened pace, too late to see their mother before she died, broken hearted by her only son's prolonged absence. And now, she seethed, condescending to come home at last with a south country wife in tow, a stuck up madam if village gossip held any credence. Ralph's choice of wife was latched onto for leaving the family abode in undue haste, her aunt's prejudice easy to arouse. Maude Elliott's animosity against all 'forriners' was no secret thereabouts. She must have heard the gossip, her father's younger sisters would see if they were on speaking terms, which wasn't very often. Should they not be, the scandal surrounding their young niece would surely bring them together in condemnation.

Lottie had no fond remembrances of the three women who had made her mother's life a misery after John Hanson's fatal accident at the pit, almost five years previously. For what reason nobody ever understood, Bessie was one of the easiest persons in the world to get along with. But if Maude Elliott heard any tittle tattle, the old besom chose to make no comment, money left after her sister-in-law's funeral expenses were paid was sufficient incentive for this grasping relative to keep mum, the work Lottie did around the house an added bonus.

Scared, no doubt, the eighteen year old was not without courage. With a bright auburn head flung back in defiance and her young back straight as a ramrod she steeled herself to take on the whole world, as it were, albeit a very insignificant part of it but all she had ever known, with very narrow boundaries. Narrow boundaries and even narrower minds.

Agitated and miserable but determined not to show it the poor lass plodded on, a grey woollen shawl hugged closely around her slender frame, stepping onward to brave fastly closing ranks, looking neither left nor right. Village women thrived on such situations, scurrilous tongues used to great effect, believing themselves quite justified in witch hunting, enjoyed in a macabre sort of way, with little else to enliven a frightfully dull existence. Lottie Hanson's fall from grace made her an ideal target, they were fully determined to squeeze every last ounce out of this dramatic situation.

Maria Street, in common with all other streets in Saltergate, took its name from a former coal owner's family, one row called Lizzie and another Elizabeth, which did seem rather odd. There was a James and a John, after two male members, among a predominance of female offspring, definitely a sore point with the father, sons were of more value than daughters. A long suffering mother kept on bearing children until she got the pattern right but few survived into adult life, the scourge of consumption not being confined to the lower classes. John Starrett, the present gaffer, inherited from his father, James, the elder son, dead before the older man passed away. Needless to say this super stud outlived his wife, who gave up the ghost after the birth of her last child, another girl, Agnes Maria. Her second name was bestowed upon the street, now hostile territory to one of its former occupants.

The harassed girl struggled to keep her cool but bristled inwardly, her brother once again the source of deep resentment. With the Boer War over now for two years and among the first to be demobbed, Ralph should have been home much sooner but, reluctant to return to the pit, he had tried his hand at other jobs in the London area, his wife's home ground. At last, out of his depth in the big city environment and homesick for the life he was once glad to leave behind, he came north again, his wife and two year old son with him, the former most reluctant to journey into the dreaded northern wilderness.

A man about the house may have spared Lottie the dubious attentions of the local village Lothario, a real snip for a chap of Jake Snowdon's reputation to take advantage of such an innocent abroad, much too naïve to see beneath the wiles of an experienced womaniser, Jake was no novice in the art of seduction.

Lottie's face flushed even more at the memory of the soft touch she proved to be, he could have told her black was white and been believed. She had been an absolute idiot to fondly imagine herself so different from his other conquests, completely taken in by such a smooth operator. Ralph could have saved her but when it really mattered her brother wasn't there, a sad fact which rankled in an addled young mind.

Maude Elliott had given her some suspicious looks of late, morning sickness in a chamber pot, on the floor above the old witch's head, a right give away, as she was not always able to reach the privy at the bottom of the back garden. 'Me catarrh's playin' up somethin' awful,' she popped into conversation on one occasion, careful not to labour the point, and hoped this might allay suspicion for a while, her voluminous skirt and baggy jumper continue to hide a multitude of sins. But being in the family way had a sure way of making itself known and time was fast running out. On the odd mornings she did reach the outside 'netty' she often speculated on the need for two round holes side by side in the wooden seat. Hardly a place to be shared for those necessary bodily functions, essentially private and not to be performed in tandem.

Once her condition showed itself, Aunt Maude would definitely give her the order of the boot. A bairn without a wedding ring on her finger was much against strong Methodist principles, Jake being Catholic another big issue. While Maude Elliott could never lay claim to being a true Christian she was a regular chapel goer, a sanctimonious old so and so, continued asylum under her roof was definitely ruled out and the other options somewhat low in the reckoning.

The aforementioned voluminous skirt and baggy jumper were the same working class uniform as her contemporaries but Lottie had unconscious style, an air of femininity the shapeless garments failed to disguise and other attributes likely to do her no good when the chips were down. A bonny young face, good bone structure and glorious hazel eyes, enhanced by striking auburn hair, did nothing to endear her to those less fortunately endowed, women whose youth had vanished all too soon and jealousy a great spur to aggression. A stormy session lay ahead, not only from folk such as these but her brother's anger yet to be faced perhaps a couple of weeks too late.

From an allotted space further down the lane, one terraced house up from her final destination, a tiny woman of indeterminate age monitored Lottie's approach in some dismay, sadly reminded of Bessie Hanson, a former neighbour and friend. Wise enough to keep her mouth shut, she fretted inwardly.

'A fine carry on when her an' that bull headed brother o' hers meet, the sparks sure t'fly. God knows why'ee had t'bide away s'long. His poor mother dead an' buried months ago.' She was better acquainted with Bessie than most, around the whole time to watch the losing battle against cancer. 'And fetchin' a Cockney wife with'im,' she scorned, possessed of the same sort of prejudice as Maude Elliott, although already reasonably neighbourly towards the newcomer. She was a kindly soul who considered Lottie's delayed contact with her brother an absolute waste of time, no forbearance likely.

Anyone unacquainted with this nondescript little body would have added ten years or more to her age, thirty-seven looking nearer fifty. Youth was but a fleeting experience, soon whittled away by the rigours of their tough lifestyle, the female sex its worst victims. Not that men went unscathed, coal dust played havoc with the lungs and fatal accidents occurred only too often down the mines, safety measures came a poor second to getting out coal. Mourners straggled behind the hearse and mourning coaches at funerals, more concerned with the traditional ham teas at the end of it all, insurance payments ensured a good send off, whatever poverty the dear departed left behind.

Ralph Hanson's enlistment became a great talking point after his departure, condemnation rife among womenfolk, male contemporaries secretly envious of a bachelor state which made such a move possible. Still a breadwinner their wives never ceased to remind them, no excuse for such irresponsible behaviour.

Janey's mind still continued to question. 'An' what else has him, bidin' away s'long, fetched t'the Hanson door?' Wondering if rumour had it right and Lottie was in the family way. It was not yet confirmed but Jake Snowdon's cocky manner and loaded remarks suggested it might well be true. Lottie's sudden flight only added fuel to the fire. Despite a strong feeling of moral indignation, her dull eyes softened in sympathy. Just to have her name linked with Jake's put her right beyond the pale, his reputation a byword in the village and, in that present day and age, the least touch of scandal was pure disaster.

* * *

But gossip, given full rein, was not confined to Maria Street on this dismal October afternoon, nor to adult members of the community. Not too far away, in the top class of Saltersgate Board School, Janey Wilson's thirteen year old son sat at a well scuffed desk, initials of former pupils carved into the woodwork, many a good caning had been received for such wilful defacement. Now, well into the afternoon, Pop Ainsley's monotonous voice delivered the final lesson, scarcely a single word of it digested, his pupils all ready for the pit or domestic service, school learning was not considered necessary for either of these workaday pursuits. A pair of dark eyes were fixed in fascination on Sally Greenhaugh's matted head, a filthy breeding place for a number of lice. His mind was elsewhere, occupied by thoughts of spicy conversation overheard the previous night, when his parents believed him fast asleep in bed. The lice were a painful reminder of that small tooth comb awaiting his own unruly mop later in the day. A weekly torture, endured at his mother's none too gentle hands, a stickler for cleanliness. 'Keep well away from them mucky Greenhaughs,' she constantly reminded him, an absolute impossibility with the eldest of the clan directly in front of him in class and well represented in every form throughout the school. A larger family in a place where big broods were the norm, except for such as the Hansons and Wilsons, a small minority with one or two apiece, probably more by good luck than good management.

The door at the bottom of the stairs, wide open, had allowed his father's voice, loud in anger, to reach the upstairs room Tommy shared with his elder sister Mary, their trundle beds separated by an old Japanese silk screen, which had seen better days. A flimsy barrier regarded as quite adequate to provide a measure of privacy for brother and sister, luckier than those who slept cheek to jowl in the same bed, never mind overcrowding, sex or age. Complacency would surely be shattered if it was known how often the teenage lad peeked through the hinged apertures when Mary dressed or undressed, suddenly conscious of the female form and already beginning to feel his oats. Heaven help him if he was ever caught in the act, Tod Wilson was a dab hand with his thick leather belt, another use for it apart from supporting filthy pit britches. Tod's husky voice boomed forth in righteous indignation.

'Fancy Lottie Hanson lyin' on 'er back i' Batey's field fer that no good son o' Satan, a bloody Cath'lick inta the bargain. Aa'd sharp o' fettled'er if sh'was mine,' he roared, quite incensed.

Janey did what was expected of her and endorsed these fiery sentiments. 'Shame on the lass,' she mumbled, convinced Lottie was more sinned against than sinful, never known to step out of line before.

Tommy waited for his father to get his second wind, easy to envisage the familiar scene downstairs. Tod in a flannel night shirt and his mother fully enveloped in her usual bed attire, obliged to listen while her husband shouted the odds between spasmodic puffs on a badly stained clay pipe. Sucking air until next Pay Friday if his ounce of twist had run out, a small luxury they could ill afford but never begrudged. 'A man has t'have somethin,' Janey insisted, the breadwinner's needs of paramount importance, her own never even considered.

The mere mention of 'lyin' on 'er back' brought lurid pictures into Tommy's mind, gained from snippets of information passed on by lads of his own age. Saucy tit bits gleaned from older brothers, smart ass youths anxious to present a macho image to their siblings, who absorbed it like a sponge, often well off beam in the urge to impress.

'A bloody Cath'lick inta the bargain,' his father repeated for extra measure, Methodist and not supposed to use bad language but he relished the sound of this particular phrase on his tongue. 'Let me catch that lass o' mine hobnobbin' wi' one o' them and aa'll tan the hide off'er,' he threatened Tommy, sadistic to the core, gloated at the idea of his sister on the receiving end of that dreaded instrument of torture, its sting felt on many occasions, rough medicine but not undeserved, he was a wayward laddie.

'A bonny lass our Mary,' Tod puffed out in pride. 'Plenty Protestant lads t'pick from, too good fer any damned papist,' astride one of his favourite hobby horses, not alone in this respect. The same feeling existed in the opposite camp, pictures of The Sacred Heart above bobble fringed mantelpieces. These and other symbols of faith were in full view of all who crossed their doorsteps, Tod Wilson was never likely to be along this number but he worked alongside Catholics in the pit, where they fought the same enemies.

Tommy listened, rather miffed that the name of the man involved with Lottie Hanson had not been mentioned, he had visions of imparting the news at school the following morning, while his classmates hung on every word, himself the centre of attention. One trait inherited from his garrulous father.

The morning had come and gone, beaten to the post by Billy Smailes, who had the whole story, name and all, decidedly chuffed to put one over on Tommy, no love lost between these teenage show offs. Smarting at being thwarted, Mary bore the brunt of of his displeasure, which boded ill for the lass, no match for her rascally brother. 'What if Aa blow the gaffe on'er fer sweetheartin' Paddy O'Neal,' as Irish as the name suggested. 'Serve'r right,' his mind grunted but the thought didn't linger, an ace in the hole when he cared to use it. A few coppers had already been extracted to keep his mouth shut, there could be more. He had no qualms in taking them, motivated by an innate sense of greed, a sorry trait his whole family had good reason to deplore. 'If that little buggar fell in a midden he'd come out smellin' o' roses,' his father said on more than one occasion. 'Jewish blood in 'im from somewhere,' he usually added, inclined to repeat himself and attach labels to everyone, ready to hold forth whenever an opportunity presented itself, well known for his soap box tendencies. 'All wind an' watter like the cobbler's cat,' was how Janey referred to such over the top behaviour, well aware of his shortcomings just as she was of their son's, a complete enigma to his uncomplicated mother.

'Mebbe th'broke the mould when we got 'im,' her husband said hopefully at one time or other, bringing a wry smile to his wife's lips. A mother who loved her son but didn't really like him, still anxious that the thirteen year old was ready for the pit although already warned by seasoned miners that underground work was no bloody picnic. Not that it dampened Tommy's enthusiasm, eager for this important leap into manhood, illusions soon to be dispelled when reality closed in upon him, as it did with every young greenhorn.

But now, the home time bell was almost due, a signal to galvanise the youngsters into action, ready for a head on clash with Catholic counterparts, teeming out of St Joseph's Church School, in the centre of the village, a regular occurrence, every day apart from Sunday, and ignored by authority on both sides unless real blood began to flow. These skirmishes had always taken place, expected to carry on 'ad infinitum', no big deal, the would be warriors were only interested in the heady excitement of a really good scrap, kissin' kind the minute it was over, the differences of their elders were not so easily solved. Any serious involvement with the opposite faith was severely frowned upon.

* * *

Some latecomers to the arena sighed with relief, let off the hook themselves, spared the embarrassment of saucy innuendoes and sly nudges, their belated arrival noted but not acted upon, the reason for it well known fact. Shift work was not allowed to interfere with the urges of sexually active men, broad daylight no acceptable deterrent. Such advances were suffered in silence by most wives, who lay on their backs and 'thought of England' always disturbed by the possibility of undesirable consequences. Quick to grasp the existing situation they joined the witch hunt, no sympathy for the errant lass now nearing her final destination.

Lottie took a deep breath as a familiar brown door loomed before her eyes, fighting hard to stem the flow of tears which threatened to undermine her courage, decidedly on the wane. What did it matter if Ralph showed her the door, after a good telling off? This was quickly banished as a totally dishonest claim, it mattered a lot. Quarry Cottages would cease to be a refuge once the truth was out, another fracas on the cards after the one ahead of her now. Maude Elliott's tongue was guaranteed to be in fine fettle when the news reached her, however soon that might be. Her brother was first on the list, who had to be faced whatever, both of them with fair share of the Hanson temper. Janey Wilson's prediction of sparks likely to fly was not to be dismissed.

As the distance narrowed, she prayed hard for control, humility and contrition, key words in the situation, neither of which came easily where she was concerned, well aware of her own failings. Damn Ralph for being 'holier than thou' but God knows she had provided plenty of ammunition to give this sorry tendency full airing. A bastard bairn who bore the Hanson name was certain to be the final straw without which her foolish dalliance may have been glossed over after a good dressing down and what he considered suitable penance. But this sort of disgrace was too much for him to swallow, her brother's intransigence known only too well from past experience.

On the doorstep at last, trembling in every limb, icy fingers wrapped around the heavy knocker, Lottie took a deep breath and let go. Its message echoed throughout the old, familiar house, filled with an ominous sense of foreboding as she waited for the door to open, conscious of a sudden hush in the lane and so many watchful eyes boring into her back. The mixed assembly of women, young and not so young were all agog, tense with anticipation, eager to be in at the kill.

* * *

The basement kitchen of Number Four, The Poplars, was Mary Wilson's undisputed domain, a four storey terraced house in the middle class district of Branton, a growing village which flanked The Great North Road on both sides, Newcastle on Tyne three miles to the south of it. It boasted shopping and residential areas in close vicinity, vastly different from Saltersgate, its near neighbour.

The young domestic held a tiny mustard spoon up for inspection before it joined the rest of her employer's silver on the big kitchen table. A detested chore finished and done with for another week, she was justifiably proud of the shining display in front of her, knowing Mrs Boyle would be hard pushed to find any fault. Not that the old besom wouldn't make a noble effort to do so, good reason not to be too enamoured of the woman who gave her employment.

Physically occupied for some time with a task which allowed her mind to wander, deeply concerned by her hush hush affair with Paddy O'Neal, she was amazed it had managed to stay secret for so long. A pity her blabbermouth brother knew of it, which completely altered the whole situation. Affair was scarcely the word, except that recently she had allowed her teasing to go a mite too far, the sure road to disaster but for Paddy's strength of will. There had been a few narrow squeaks when it took him all his time to cry halt. What love was all about, she supposed, and they were in love, head over heels. For all the good it was likely to do them, Roman Catholic and Primitive Methodist were not supposed to step outside their respective faiths for marriage partners.

'Roll on four o'clock,' she muttered. Bella Cosgrove arrived then to prepare the evening meal and wash up afterwards. She also made the bedtime drinks and slept overnight, on hand for early morning fires, herself there again at six to make breakfast for the Boyle family, seven in all and, from youngest to oldest, almost impossible to please. Thank God the weekly wash went out, called for Monday morning by a Saltersgate laddie and returned washed and ironed two days later. No wet clothes hung around this house, day in and day out except for Sunday, as they did at home. The Boyles were not upper class but well heeled, and domestic servants were ten a penny, dirt cheap and regarded as such.

Mary's mind flashed back to thoughts of Paddy and made a solemn vow to keep her feelings under control, no more teasing, suddenly reminded of Lottie Hanson and the mess she was in. 'No blinkin' fear!' came in heartfelt denial, even if she did love the big Irishman to distraction. 'Who wants t'pay t'the blessed priest anyway?' she scorned, irked that the O'Neals believed all Protestants would go to hell fire on the Day of Judgement, her own father just as bigoted. Far better if everyone followed the same faith, Protestant naturally, Primitive Methodist like herself. More of her male parent's teachings rubbed off on her than ever the poor lass imagined.

Janey Wilson's daughter was a comely lass, Tod's proud claim quite justified. Maybe not in Lottie Hanson's class regarding looks but she would have no bother finding a lad of her own religious persuasion, a good housewife into the bargain. The Boyle residence bore evidence of this fact, its kitchen a prime example of Mary's worth, radiated cleanliness and care. Everything that could shine did so, not only the fine collection of silver, painstakingly polished, nor the huge black leaded grate but also the leaves of a healthy looking aspidistra on the windowsill below street level, which shut out the natural light. Two gas lamps were already lit, as they were most of the time in this basement kitchen. Mary was definitely no slacker where domestic chores were involved, her mother an excellent example to follow.

At that precise moment, this particular mother's eyes were only one pair of many, fixed upon Lottie Hanson's rigid back, as Number 24 Maria Street echoed with the vibration of that heavy door knocker, the air already warming up again, impossible to keep the wagging tongues quiet for any length of time. 'A fine start,' Janey sadly bemoaned, 'Enough t'bring the house down.' Blissfully unaware of what could come to her own door if Tommy shopped his sister. She admired Lottie's guts for braving such hostility with more to come, about to do so when the door opened and a sweet anxious face appeared above the lass's right shoulder, Ralph Hanson's wife, a head taller than her visitor, obviously apprehensive when she realised who it must be. Apart from that distinctive auburn hair, brother and sister bore strong resemblance, especially around the mouths and determined chins.

A few moments of assessment by both women before a male voice bellowed forth, ordering the caller indoors, no matter to Ralph Hanson that, his feet ensconced in a tin bath of water, he was sitting at the fireside stripped to the waist. Margaret hesitated and Lottie quailed at the well remembered sound of her brother's voice but steeled herself to cross the threshold. At which point the whole lane erupted, angry hunters about to be deprived of their prey. Janey pulled a long face. 'Just like dogs after a bitch in heat,' she muttered in disgust, an opinion crudely expressed, soon on the receiving end of one caustic tongue. The temporary loss of the chosen victim left room for another and Janey Wilson's long association with the Hanson family made her the ideal replacement.

'Mind ye keep t'yer own stretch of gutter. Let that stuck up bitch get'er hands mucky fer a change. Ye've swilled hers fer the past two weeks, time y'stopped,' the woman snapped in accusation, foolish to cross swords with Janey, more than her match on a number of occasions, a self imposed silence brought to a sudden halt, ready to do battle.

'Ralph Hanson's been back at the pit fer varnigh a fortnight, Aa reckon'is missis has had 'er hands in plenty o'muck by now,' Janey carried on in full flow. 'It's tongues like yours that bother 'er not hard work,' she ranted. 'Anyway, what Aa do wi' me bucket an'broom's my affair, Florrie Gillespie. Ye wouldn't do good fer God if the devil was dead.'

Their female audience cackled in chorus, the temperature cooled by laughter until raised voices echoed from inside the house and the women drew nearer, two of them heard and recognised, a third not in evidence. Ralph's wife obviously a silent onlooker, a refined young woman, right out of her depth amid such conflict.

The plaintive cries of a child soon added to the din. 'The poor bairn must be out of'is wits,' Janey commiserated, a motherly soul. No holds barred if brother and sister ran true to form, often known to clash in earlier days. Angry words escaped into the lane, absolutely indecipherable, which didn't go down at all well with the listening women who resented exclusion from the whole intriguing business.

* * *

In the meantime, Mrs Boyle's usual inspection was over, surprisingly little fault to be found, a few words exchanged between Mary and Bella Cosgrove and the younger woman left for home, completely unaware of the afternoon's happenings, just in time perhaps for the tail end of it all with Lottie shown the door. No doubt she would be amazed to find the regular routine upset for once, buckets and brooms standing idle.

Although tired after a heavy day's toil, Mary felt on top of the world as she trudged along, her little chain purse jingling, Pay Day with the prospect of a few coins to call her own, most of the money destined for the household kitty. A euphoria which soon evaporated when her personal problems returned to the fore. What if Tommy demanded more to keep quiet? Time maybe to finish with Paddy before the whole thing erupted, but she was unable to visualise taking up with someone else and horrified by the possibility of him finding a lass of his own faith. Oddly enough outright defiance never occurred to her, Mary and Lottie were poles apart when it came to backbone but rebellion was unlikely in either case. Women were considered second class citizens when decision making arose, whatever their station in life, definitely a man's world.

About this same time the controlling genius in the Wilson household was making his way out by with the rest of his shift, travelling single file towards the wooden cage waiting to lift them to the surface and what was left of daylight. A ghostly column of bobbing Davy lamps, carried by chattering men indulging in ribald laughter and a lot of bawdy remarks passed along the line as they walked, not giving Lottie Hanson the lickings of a dog, the bit well and truly between their teeth. No better than the female contingent gathered in the lane.

'Let it rest,' Tod muttered, too quiet to be heard, resentful of John Hanson's daughter being labelled whore, his former work mate's name always beyond reproach. This reaction was completely alien to the man's nature, reduced thereafter to a most unusual silence. A big surprise awaited Tod when he arrived home, there to be regaled with the up to date gossip. A stormy encounter still raged unabatedly in the Hanson kitchen, both contestants in excellent form and the third party present absolutely dumbstruck.

When Ralph's open fist connected with his sister's astonished face, his wife kept silent no longer, although neither antagonist pulled punches verbally this was inexcusable, nothing to condone it, even those scarcely veiled hints that her son was conceived out of wedlock. A boy who howled unrestrainedly, impossible to pacify, his mother's agitation was strongly felt, her appeal for it all to stop soon denied.

'Let it be lass,' her husband raged, 'This has nowt t'do w' you,' he threw at her, red in the face, totally out of control. Margaret gasped and fled the room, no further than the long walk-in pantry at the far end. A swift flurry of skirts alongside as Lottie grabbed the opportunity to escape further harassment. Anxious to avoid even more confrontation in the lane, she hurried towards the front of the house and Margaret's sympathies went with her. The handsome soldier who swept a young girl off her feet had suddenly become a monster. Nursing both physical pain and mental anguish Lottie left the house.

Ralph's equally distraught wife heard the door slam, rattling on its hinges to reverberate the whole length of the row both up and down. She grieved for her sister-in-law's plight and wondered what Lottie would do, but was unable to offer assistance without incurring her husband's rage, made painfully aware of an uncontrollable temper for the very first time and rather afraid.

With her back against the closed door for support, totally enraged by Ralph's physical attack and relentless attitude, the bewildered lass began to vent spleen upon the women in the lane, pleased to deprive them of more satisfaction. 'If that racket doesn't tell them Aa've had me marchin' orders nowt will!' she spat out amid scalding tears. No room for her under her brother's roof not actually put into words but only too clear. She strongly contested this fact when half of everything should be hers by right but there was nothing down in writing. Bessie Hanson could never have envisaged such a confrontation ever taking place.

'Amen,' she sighed in resignation as the anger started to drain away, saddened by the thought that from now onwards this would be forbidden territory. If only the slate could be wiped clean of the past, few disastrous months, full retribution was yet to come. She was neither first nor last to be pregnant and unwed but marriage with Jake Snowdon was not even contemplated, dismissed out of hand, and no way would she grab just anybody to fill the role of father to her unborn child, as some lasses did, and lived to regret it.

'Make it go away,' she silently pleaded, filled with a cold, empty feeling that nobody was there. How could she expect the Almighty to take heed? There was always a price to pay for wrong doing and no turning back the clock. It was a much troubled young woman who stepped out into a future impossible to fully predict, almost blinded by the volume of her own tears.

* * *

Batey's Field, a small area of pasture land at the bottom end of Saltersgate was not the most private of venues to choose for Lottie Hanson's seduction, although completely surrounded by a thick, hawthorn hedgerow, then in full leaf; the sort of spot young couples might seek for a bit of harmless necking, there were more secluded places elsewhere if couples were into something rather different.

The lessee of the property, only into farming in a small way, eked out an existence with milk from the cows that grazed there, free range hens and a potato crop raised on another acreage of land in nearly Rawdon. As an extra there were always the pigs he fattened up for Christmas, neighbours were glad of a buckshee joint for swill they helped to provide. Money seldom changed hands, a barter system very much to the fore for certain commodities. Of course the owner knew of the many trysts that took place on his ground but turned a blind eye, having been young himself once.

Privacy did not rate high on Jake Snowdon's list of priorities, this sexual coupling anticipated longer than any other in a licentious career, still wet around the ears when he started. Twenty-five now and more than that number of used and discarded females behind him, he was a bachelor and determined to stay that way. Not into celibacy his courtship of Lottie had been three months of sheer frustration. It wouldn't bother him in the least to be caught with his pants down, his latest conquest beneath him, the calculated wooing of this particular lass a right pain in the butt. Jake liked his women experienced and willing, preferably married to somebody else, shrinking young virgins not his type.

This doomed relationship came to a sorry end on a sultry July evening, when the hum of bees merged into a symphony of bird songs to fill the summer air, soporific effect on bemused senses, a lamb to the slaughter. The culmination of a scheme cooked up in the spring of that same year when two companions in crime sat on the brick yard fence, gazing out across the pit heap towards Saltersgate. Brick making was carried on in abandoned surface buildings of an old mine, long since worked out.

Jake Snowdon was having one of his usual 'idle shifts' from the colliery, his close mate Cud Matthews dodging work on the small holding he ran with his wife Annie, who did more than her share of the graft. A case of no work, no pay for the former who lived by his wits on whatever he could beg, borrow or steal, not possessed of a single scruple and somehow he got away with it.

Their conversation, as it had done on a number of occasions recently, centred around one particular young woman in the village, Cud amusing himself immensely at Jake's preoccupation with Lottie Hanson. 'So ye think sh'wants takin' down a peg or two? Better watch yerself me lad, Aa reckon she's got under that thick skin o'yours. A bit out o'yer league isn't sha?' Treading on dangerous ground but choosing to ignore the baleful look cast in his direction.

'Aye, go on, have yer bit o'sport. Them bloody Hansons think they're a cut above the rest o' us mortals' Jake grunted, Cud was not wise enough to leave well alone, himself usually on the end of his mate's sarcastic tongue.

'So –' he drawled, 'It's that time i' the carriages that's buggin' ya, when'er old man put paid t'yer braggin' about layin' that lass from Bogg's Lane.' Deliberately rubbing salt in an old wound, watching Jake's face darken at the reminder of John Hanson's interference. Still a sore point although the man in question was killed at the pit shortly after the incident and over four years in his grave. His friend soon erupted into a tirade of real venom.

'It had nowt t' do wi' the psalm singin' hypocrite, a right Holy Joe!' he blustered, furious when their fellow workers put an end to his filthy talk out of respect for a well liked man.

'Holy Joe alright an' singin' wi' angels now Aa reckon,' Cud sniggered. 'One thing sure, the pair o' ya winna meet again.' This sick humour greeted with raucous laughter, there was not an ounce of decency in these two rogues, both tarred with the same brush ...

Good humour restored, Jake flung a head of tightly curled black hair in the air, cocky assurance in every line of his body, which was fast going to seed. Too much of everything, beer, women and self indulgence of all description but still handsome in a coarse fashion and often called a 'good lookin' nowt' Cud was always around to hero worship and boost an already inflated ego.

But he wasn't far out, Jake's interest in John Hanson's daughter was aroused as the means of settling an old score with her dead father, her innocence a decided challenge. 'That's where the straight laced bastard should be,' he said at last in response to Cud's sick attempt at wit. 'A shame, mebbe, in one way,' followed by an exaggerated sigh. The other man completely lost off and not exactly chuffed.

'What sort o' mischief are y'thinkin' of now?' he ventured to inquire, that certain look in Jake's eyes easily recognised, his companion soon into full throated laughter. 'Aa've just had a champion idea but, as Aa just sayed, it's a shame John Bloody Hanson isn't around t'see what Aa'm up to,' pleased with his own outrageous thoughts, which he seemingly wasn't prepared to divulge, making Cud sweat it out.

'Keep it t'yerself, see if Aa care,' he was told but his pal cared quite a lot and sulked because of it, so easy to wind this oppo up. 'Hold yer horses lad, Aa reckon it's too good t'keep t'meself,' Jake admitted and dropped his bombshell. 'What about me gettin' Lottie Hanson on'er back an havin' it off with 'er?' he announced and chuckled as Cud almost choked in disbelief, his big mouth agape … 'Fat chance y'have o' layin' that lass,' he blurted out at last. 'Well warned against your sort Aa guess,' he muttered smugly, coming out of the sulks, certain that for once Jake was out of his head. Jake not in the least perturbed oozed confidence. 'Aa daresay,' he shrugged, 'It might take a bit more time than usual but she'll go the same way as all the rest, mebbe further. What if Aa get 'er laid up?'

Cud hooted derisively, 'Half a crown says ye'll not get past first base,' he challenged, ready to put his shirt on a strict Methodist upbringing, carrying on to add further weight to his argument. 'Ye pay t'the priest an' all, she's not likely t'give ye the time o'day, never mind owt else.' Jake was incensed by this reference to his Catholic faith. Not that he kept it up, just the odd confession on a Thursday evening and the same sins over and again.

An enormous fist lashed out, only missing Cud's unshaven chin by a hair's breadth, the movement forceful enough to send them both toppling to the hard earth, a tangled heap of arms and legs. 'Canny on,' Cud roared, 'Aa couldn't care less if y'light candles or sing hallelujah,' adding ruefully, 'the last time Aa was in any church was at me own weddin', an' that wasn't my idea, Aa can tell ya.' A backsliding Anglican married in the local mission, his wife Annie said all the prayers for both of them.

Jake was first to extricate himself, rubbing off the dust and laughing heartily at his pal's woeful expression, now mollified. 'Yer on,' he accepted magnanimously, 'Half a crown it is then but no rush. This young filly'll take special handlin'. An' watch that big mouth o' yours, no blabbin' t'your Annie when ye've had a skin full or the lass'll get warned off fer sure.'

'As if Aa would,' Cud protested, rather peeved Jake should think along such lines but he often had a loose tongue under the influence, as his companion knew only too well.

The two men began to cross the pit heap towards Saltersgate's bottom streets, their hobnailed boots striking sparks on hard ground, Cud was first to find his tongue after a short spell of silence. 'Ye'll be seein' Lily Collins the night Aa suppose?' he queried idly. Jake's amorous escapades were always relayed to his friend in detail, most intriguing to someone whose movements were rather more restricted.

'Lily'll have t'keep,' Jake replied, so sure of himself, this woman a faithless wife with a husband easy to cuckold. He just laughed and basked in Cud's envy of his sexual provess. 'Yer a cool customer,' he was told, his mate suitably impressed but ever hopeful. 'Mebbe Lily'll fancy me i' yer place.'

'Only the best fer her, hot stuff under the blankets. Alec Collins is in fore shift. Fancy Lily all by 'erself in that soft feather bed!' Accompanied by a suggestive laugh and Cud did think, seeing it as such a waste but basked in Jake's obvious elation at the scheme he had just thought up. One miscreant believing his half crown quite safe, the other certain Lottie would be an easy conquest, especially with no man around to put a spoke in his wheel.

They plodded on, side by side, Jake's strides much longer than his shorter companion's, himself just over six feet in height, eventually arriving at Cully's corner where they parted company. The rest of Cud's route took him past Number 24 Maria Street, where Lottie made this oaf's day by stepping out of doors as he approached.

'Nice day,' he threw at her in cheeky rejoinder, her trim figure an immediate target, a real eyeful and no mistake, delighted to see her flinch at his greeting and a sensual mind alive at the thought of such a shapely body coming to grief in Jake's experienced hands.

Glued to the spot by this uncouth lout's keen regard, the sort she had been warned to avoid at all cost, she soon shook herself free and hurried off, causing him to yell after her retreating form. 'Stuck up little madam, canna even be civil,' he spat out and forged ahead, shoulders hunched and hands dug deep into his trouser pockets, full of hell and mouthing a stream of obscene oaths. 'An' ye shut up!' he flung at his astonished wife when he crossed his own doorstep to find her, arms akimbo and grim faced, obviously ready for battle but any expected reprimand was effectively silenced. Annie Matthews was much too flabbergasted to utter a single word.

Wise enough to quell her curiosity and leave any probing for information until later his wife fed him, her feelings of resentment at being left with a morning's chores successfully stifled, his obvious ill humour hard to understand, usually so easy to read, but terribly disappointed when nothing was forthcoming. Jake's anger was more to fear than the backlash of Annie's tongue. The half crown bet didn't figure high in the equation, he was more interested in the success of his pal's malicious scheme, cock-a-hoop at being taken into the other man's confidence, quite accustomed to getting most of his kicks second hand.

* * *

Now, six months later and three months pregnant, Lottie hurried away from the scene of conflict beset by feelings of all description, vivid memories of Batey's Field and the drastic results from what happened there on that fateful July evening. She knew now to her sorrow why Jake had wanted to be so open about their relationship and her own reluctance which meant clandestine meetings in out of the way places, although somehow or other most folk in the village seemed to know about it, no doubt he made sure of that also, the whole affair so hard to understand, a hotch potch of uncertainties.

On the evening in question they met in the field, slipping surreptitiously into it where he already awaited her coming and, before long they lay stretched out on the grass among the perimeter trees, where it all started, harmlessly enough, with some kissing and cuddling, totally unconscious that he was taking it slowly not to scare her off. This evening was the deadline Jake had given himself, fed up with waiting.

After a while he started to toy with the buttons on her black cotton blouse, she was only slightly disturbed when probing fingers played with the nipples of soft young breasts, a strange but not unpleasant feeling. The curious melting in the lower region of her body went unrecognised for what it was, never having been given the knowledge to deal with such, a true innocent. The first real twinge of fear came when her seducer lost his head and impatience took over. He pinned her with his weight to unyielding earth, his male arousal hard against her, quickly released from containment by one free hand, a searching tongue allowed entrance when she gasped involuntarily at this sudden onslaught of passion. There was no finesse from then onwards, open drawers no effective barrier and an end to any sort of foreplay. Lottie was wholly unprepared for swift and inconsiderate penetration. Robbed of virginity eventually in one savage thrust, more to follow until, grunting like a pig, his seed spilled into her and he rolled away in satisfaction. A lack of sensitivity which fully deserved the name of rape, she was absolutely defenceless in face of such brute force, it was an horrific sexual awakening for Jake Snowdon's eighteen year old victim.

Later, in the sanctuary of her own home, the violated girl sat, knees up to her chin in a tin bath full of water, almost hotter than she could bear, scrubbing furiously at every part of herself she could reach, her flesh red and angry looking from a merciless flannel and blue mottled soap, convinced she would never feel clean again. The makeshift washcloth was unable to erase that painful initiation into womanhood but was nothing compared to the degradation etched deep into a distressed young mind.

* * *

Lottie had no real sense of direction when the door of Number 24 Maria Street slammed behind her and banishment changed from possibility into painful reality. A pitched battle was taking place in the front street, no bloodshed but lots of shrieking and name calling, Catholic and Protestant youngsters in the midst of conflict. The bairns were much too occupied to take any notice as she pushed her way through an unconsciously made a left turn, deep down aware of where she was going.

Even if Maude Elliott did issue marching orders, Quarry Cottages had to be the next port of call, the few possessions salvaged in haste two weeks before were there and maybe, just maybe, there might be a slim chance of staying. There had been barely enough time for news to have reached her aunt, she had another night's asylum at least, time to collect scattered wits and decide what to do. Not that any other options came to mind, her father's younger sisters were not even considered for obvious reasons. Besides they both lived within a stone's throw of her former home, much too close for comfort.

Lottie badly needed to lay blame for her present predicament at someone else's door, things she ought to have been told about those strange sensations in a female body that Jake certainly knew how to arouse, knowledge of which might well have saved the day. But this was an age when such talk was a taboo, revelation left to green young fellows who performed initiation rites on their wedding night, often a terrible awakening which tended to colour relationships thereafter. Sex was regarded as something to be endured not enjoyed and never a subject for frank discussion, even between man and wife.

Saltersgate had its share of so called loose women, whose goings on provided a topic of conversation around mat frames on winter evenings, when small groups of housewives gathered at the firesides of friends and neighbours, their men on back shift. Social occasions when fingers and tongues worked overtime, gossip strictly for adult ears. But Tommy Wilson wasn't the only youngster prone to eavesdropping in the village and with houses not exactly sound proof, it was easy to listen in, and sometimes they got the wrong end of the stick.

What Lottie did manage to glean, which wasn't much, came from Aggie Bennett, a girl of her own age whose mother had the reputation of obliging any man for a glass of gin. Some of what went on obviously had an effect upon her young daughter. 'Right in front o'the clock' was how folk described this forward young miss. Bessie Hanson was horrified to find Lottie in Aggie's company on one occasion. 'Yer father'll take his belt t'yer backside,' she warned but failed to explain why, the association was made more intriguing than ever and still carried on in hole in the corner fashion.

The two lasses slipped in an out of friendship until school days were over and Aggie became embroiled in her mother's dubious way of life, dying in childbirth at a very young age, the infant also, a blessing maybe considering the family background.

Lottie's memory soon began to play tricks as she hurried along, an impish face before her mind's eye and a hissing voice close to her ear, accompanied by a sharp dig in the ribs. 'She's gone t'bed t'make a bairn,' the astounding announcement as Aggie gestured towards a red faced woman who hurried indoors, a burly, middle aged chap standing on a nearly doorstep, clad only in trousers and vest, his braces dangling.

'Davy's i' fore shift, that's why Maisie's getting' called in. He wants' er in bed an'Aa've told ya what for,' Aggie explained, quite taken aback when her words were challenged. Lottie usually open mouthed all agog, but not this time, quick in reply.

'A fine lot o'twaddle,' she scorned, 'W'all go t'bed, stupid!' making her informant cluck contemptuously. 'It's ye that's stupid, Lottie Hanson,' Aggie argued strongly. 'It has t'be a man an' woman in the same bed and if they're not wed it doesn't work.' Obviously she was not yet acquainted as to what 'it' was or she would have said so to have proved the point.

Now in the midst of all the present upheaval, Lottie's smile was rueful. A definite fallacy disproved by the girl herself in such tragic circumstances. 'Y'were wrong, Aggie, dead wrong,' she murmured in sorrow as that pert face returned to the past where it belonged. An apt expression, no doubt, but time had proved Aggie Bennett not to be the only misguided lass in those parts.

The recent episode in Batey's field finally endorsed that neither wedding ring nor comfortable bed were necessary to conceive a child.

It took enormous effort to pull herself together and take stock of her whereabouts, now in the vicinity of St Joseph's, rid of its pupils until Monday morning, the weekend devoted to religious instruction and worship. The sight of Theresa Street corner, slightly further ahead, brought her swiftly down to earth, several men were already congregated around the street lamp, collarless necks protected by a varied assortment of hand knitted mufflers, worn to keep out the cold. 'God give me strength' the fervent plea as her footsteps drew nearer, sure of another unpleasant experience, womenfolk not alone in pursuit of gossip. She was none too certain of the Almighty's indulgence, with dozens of unanswered prayers over the past few weeks, first waiting anxiously for that revealing red stain on the back of her white nightie which failed to appear, the painful conclusion accepted in great dismay.

Every eye turned in her direction, as expected, and the hub of conversation ceased, Jake was just the sort to kiss and tell, more than kissing in her case and doubtless bragged about. She was still at a loss to understand the reason for such persistent wooing and the final outcome. Impossible to decide what disturbed her most, Jake's betrayal, Ralph's rejection or her own stupidity. Full of natural loathing for the rogue who seduced her, a brother who denied her shelter and understanding and absolute disgust for the senseless behaviour which made her such an easy conquest.

Lottie had been warned, right enough, Janey Wilson quick to have her say when she got wind of the situation. 'Don't get yerself tied up wi' that black hearted villain,' she said, never one to mince words. 'Yer mother an' father didn't fetch y'up proper all them years t'fall foul o'the Jake Snowdons o' this world. No good t'any decent lass.'

'It would behove some folk t'mind their own business,' was the angry retort. 'It might pay ya t'watch what's goin' on closer t'home.' A strong hint at Mary Wilson's secret liaison, she was ready to bite her tongue as the words rushed out. Mary's dalliance had not yet spread abroad, strange but true, only a chance encounter made Lottie aware of it. 'Let it bide that way,' she decided at the time, only too conscious what harm gossip could do, brought home to her now more so than ever, sorry when she remembered the puzzled look on Janey's homely face. She felt pleased that the gossips hadn't got hold of it, a well kept secret.

Soon she was alongside the men, her battered cheek discreetly averted but not the face that drew attention, glad nothing showed as yet. Crude remarks came from lads of her own age but she was more disturbed by the silence of older men who knew and respected her dead father, whose disappointment in her would have been hard to bear.

Once out of earshot, Lottie released the air from tight lungs and rushed into a spate of self condemnation. 'Damn me for bein' such an idiot!' she choked, unconscious of having spoken aloud until a scavenging dog yelped and scuttled off out of danger. 'Talkin' t'meself now,' she muttered then chortled at the poor beast's antics but not for long. The gravity of the situation soon returned to torment her, still alive to the utter contempt on Ralph's coal blackened face and the scorn that whipped her ears. 'What on earth got inta ya?' he yelled. 'A good, chapel goin' lass beddin down wi' Jake Snowdon, scum of the earth. Thank God me mother an' father aren't here t'witness yer shame,' almost past himself with rage. It never entered this righteous man's head that but for this latter fact and his own prolonged absence from the scene, none of this would have happened. He was quite prepared to lay full blame at Lottie's door, who in his opinion should definitely have known better.

'Thank God!' she echoed thankfully, reminded of that great show of bravado, the ridiculous accusations thrown at her brother delighted to see him wince. 'Aa'm not the first lass i' the place t'have a bairn without the blessin' o' the church. And if ye've got any ideas in yer head about man t'man talks wi' Jake Snowdon ferget it. Aa'd sooner bide the way Aa am, bairn or no bairn.' She taunted wildly. 'Damn his rotten soul t'hell!' she spat out now in the aftermath of it all, reminded of this unscrupulous rogue and forgetful of any Christian principle taught at her mother's knee. No forgiveness in her, just hatred and an ocean of that to drown in, an overwhelming force.

There were no more upsetting encounters before she left Saltersgate behind, taking only front streets, womenfolk all congregated in the back lanes, most of them strictly to time, only Maria Street with still more to do. Thankful indeed for the absence of waspish tongues and determined to keep an optimistic frame of mind she gathered pace and hastened towards the foot of Fencers' Hill, there to begin the slow, uphill climb to Upper Meldon and the home Maude Elliott shared with her quarry worker husband. Billy Elliott, an only son, sailed on colliers to and from the Tyne, her cousin only home for brief spells. Uncle Robert, a kindly chap, wouldn't say boo to a goose, he was putty in the hands of his strong minded wife who definitely wore the britches. Her aunt was no mean adversary when it came to conflict of any description, not a heartening thought.

That same icy wind, up and about since early morning, took capricious fancy to the girl's bruised cheek and chafed it unmercifully, but barely conscious of the pain, her mind was already on to the next battle if there were to be one, the uncertainty most disturbing, any physical discomfort of far lesser concern.

Sustained by nothing but her own courage she struggled against the wind, in the hope of some reward at the end of her journey, and prayed Maude Elliott would continue to give her shelter, a last resort. 'An unpaid skivvy, that's what Aa'll be,' she recognised with regret, a grim outlook perhaps but infinitely more acceptable than the idea of ending up in Preston Workhouse, the biggest spectre on her immediate horizon.

* * *

One look at her aunt's face when she walked into an overheated kitchen told Lottie that any hopes she may have nurtured were about to be dashed. It was an expression seen so many times in the past and usually meant trouble for someone. No prizes for guessing who that someone would be on this occasion.

'My, it's a right pull up that blessed hill,' she said by way of small talk and waited for the balloon to go up which it did in the matter of seconds, Maude Elliott well and truly primed for this particular meeting, soon into verbal action.

'Aa didn't reckon ye'd be climbing it so soon,' thin lips twisted into ugly lines as they wrapped around the words. 'But mebbe ye've just come t'fetch yer belongin's. A grand reunion at Maria Street, or so Aa'm told. Jinny Roberts was seein' 'er aunt in James Street an' sayed ye'd been visitin your Ralph. A fine thing when a body gets t'know things second hand.' Very much affronted.

Lottie's heart plummeted, forced to wonder how much Jinny managed to glean on this supposed chance visit. Nothing chance about it if she had these two cronies sized up correctly. Probably she was no sooner out of her aunt's house en route to Saltersgate than the woman was hot on her tail. Come to think of it a pony trap did pass on the way downhill but she took little heed of its passengers, her mind otherwise engaged, this conception soon confirmed.

'Jinny got the offer of a lift down the hill wi' Joe Cuthbertson an' he brought'er back the short cut through the fields. Aa reckon you took the road.' Which Lottie had done, anxious to avoid Saltersgate's back lanes and the gossiping women in them. 'Aye,' she answered and waited for the next onslaught, sure of more to come.

Maude Elliott stood, arms akimbo, her back to the black leaded range, almost part of it, dressed as always in the same sombre colour, never out of mourning for somebody or other however distantly related. Lottie didn't reckon it to be out of any respect for her own mother, Bessie Hanson and her husband's three sisters could hardy be called soul mates.

The miserable old baggage, Lottie thought, but not so old really, only two years between brother and sister, John Hanson in his mid forties when he died almost five years ago. Maude was the eldest of the family and expected to be treated as its matriarch, regarded it as no more than her due, an attitude which often rubbed the others up the wrong way. Not surprising in the least but completely brain washed into uneasy acceptance of her superior role in their lives, both Ethel and Lizzie Ann dug their toes in at times, cold war periods which never lasted long. 'It beats me what sort o'bairns our John brought up,' Maude sneered. 'One o'them bides away over three years wi'hardly a scribe o' the pen, an' look what'ee fetched with 'im when'ee did condescend t'come back.' A nasty dig at her nephew's 'forrin' wife, who for some strange reason Lottie wanted to defend but deemed it wiser to curb the impulse.

'As fer you, me fine lady,' that sharp tongue ranted on, the implication only too obvious. The shrewd old bitch knew the lot or imagined she did. But who better at adding two and two together t'come up wi'the right answer. But she ignored the inference, far too much at stake and hopefully all might not be lost.

Now under full steam, Maude barged on relentlessly determined to get it off her chest. 'Well me little madam, will y'be shiftin' back t'Maria Street or not? Aa reckon Aa'm entitled t'that much infermation, seein' that Aa've boarded an' bedded ya fer two weeks,' she snorted, making Lottie seethe. 'And got well an' truly paid for it,' she wanted to throw in that twisted face but somehow managed to hold her tongue, still hanging on to a glimmer of hope. When she did speak it was placating fashion much against the grain.

'No, Aa'll be bidin' here if you an' me uncle's willin'. Ralph an' me never did hit it off an' nothin's changed. Y'know what'ees like.' The less Maude Elliott knew of their recent, bitter encounter the better for all concerned.

'Oh aye,' came the sarcastic reply, beady eyes alight in anticipation of more to come. 'Aa suppose the cuddy kicked ya an' all,' Lottie was totally unprepared for a vicious poke at her bruised cheek as if Maude knew Ralph's fist did the damage and revelled in the thought of it.

Out came the first thing to pop into an addled mind. 'Aa wasn't lookin' where Aa was goin, an' bumped inta the front door.' Not the best explanation to come up with and carried on to make things even worse. 'Ralph an' me were only on about family matters, anyway,' these latter words like a red rag to a bull. Maude Elliott's nostrils flared and the veins in her scraggy neck bulged alarmingly. 'God help me,' her niece panicked, 'the old bag is gonna have a stroke or somethin,' and wondered what to do if such a terrible disaster did occur.

But no need to worry, her aunt was made of sterner stuff and was soon into action again spitting fire. 'Yer uncle an' me aren't family, Aa suppose. Good enough t'take y'in when y'had nowhere else t'bide,' she said accusingly, Lottie's unwillingness to be more forthcoming was a great source of frustration for someone of her ilk, who enjoyed pushing her nose into anybody's business. The final stroke was not long in coming, deliberately withheld for most effect. 'Y'wouldn't be in the family way, Aa suppose?' Lottie was appalled to hear her condition actually put into words for the very first time.

But Maude wasn't finished by any means. 'Aa just sayed t'Jinny the other day that somethin' was up. Close as the grave y'are, just like that smarmy mother o'yours.' John Hanson's gentle wife was always a thorn in the flesh and she now felt free to release this long held feeling of resentment.

Restraint flew out of the window. 'Keep me mother out o'this, let'er rest in peace. God knows y'gave 'er little enough when sh'was alive, the lot o'ya.' The whole Hanson family was linked in this strong reprimand. 'If they aren't on speakin terms, they soon will be,' she silently predicted. The sisters' on and off relationship was a well established fact, usually Maude who stirred things up, the other two seldom in the running when it came to battle. 'A right lot o'blossoms,' as Janey Wilson often called them. She had no room for any of her former neighbour's tormentors.

Retaliation came thick and fast, Maude's eyes nearly popped out of her head. 'Neither yer mother or father'll be restin much wi' all that's goin' on around here. Bringin' shame on such a well respected name,' making Lottie gasp in utter disbelief. The sanctimonious old so an' so, talkin' as if butter wouldn't melt in'er mouth. She would soon prick that bubble of self righteousness that she would and proceeded to do just that, caution gone with the wind.

'Judgin' by juicy bit o'gossip Aa once heard when Aa wasn't supposed t'be listenin',' she stated pointedly, immediately rewarded by the hot flush on her aunt's astonished face, the barb had reached its mark as intended, thus encouraged to carry on. 'Aa guess Aa'm not the first Hanson t'blacken the family name,' her young voice was ripe with suggestion and she inwardly exulted as the words struck home. A sweet moment of triumph but destined to be very short lived, she was well and truly in the soup with her hasty tongue. Talk about fouling her own nest.

'Get out o' my house y'little slut!' the mortified woman shrieked purple with rage, greatly affronted by this unexpected reference to her own youthful indiscretion. Only six months wed when son Bill came into the world, Robert Elliott was not his father but willingly accepted responsibility, truly smitten with Maude Hanson, reckoned to be quite a looker in her time. 'Aa'll not be harbourin' you or yer nameless brat!' his wife shrieked in fury. There was no comparison in their situations or so the woman deluded herself. Marriage the magic word to erase this long ago transgression, her son was no bastard. She was more than capable of smoothing over the cracks in her own wrongdoing to consider herself blameless.

From then on the knives came out, thrust and parry no quarter given. Loittie cried halt, sick of so much aggression in the course of a single day, not yet over. She fled the field of battle to seek sanctuary of her attic room, fed to the teeth with a surfeit of back biting, Maude Elliott still hurling abuse. Once there, she threw clothing and other bits and bobs into an old bass bag in feverish haste, cursing her wayward temper all the while. Crazy to imagine her aunt would remain in ignorance of her condition when she retched morning after morning in this very room, above that wily old head.

Reluctant to waste any more time, Lottie dragged the cumbersome load across the linoleum covered floor and manoeuvred it down a crudely fashioned ladder to the landing below then tackled the main stairway to ground level where silence reigned, her tetchy relative nowhere to be seen. 'Hobnobbin' wi' Jinny Roberts, fetchin' that old witch up t'date,' was the calculated guess. 'Signed the pledge, both o'them, an' likely t'be sittin, next door downin' ale.' Fully resolved to shop them to the chapel minister, she was soon reminded that in this very reverend gentleman's estimation she would be doomed to hell an damnation from now on.

Deeming it wiser not to linger, unwilling to risk another painful session with her aunt, she left the house and immediately felt the fierce impact of cold air, glad to snuggle under her thick woollen shawl, a legacy from her dead mother, wanting those loving arms to enfold her in its stead. The outer chill was nothing compared to that feeling of emptiness inside a body first cruelly violated by Jake Snowdon, then to crown all, Ralph's punishing blow, the final humiliation.

She took a deep breath to contain screaming nerves and tried to concentrate on her next move. Where could she go? Who would take her in, if only for one night at least? Time to consider other options, not that any came to mind. A terrible dilemma, what might be termed total disaster and mostly of her own making, she was honest enough to admit her fault.

Then the thought struck. If there were to be any sort of salvation, where would she find it except among her own kind? But she was forced to acknowledge the disturbing fact that one lone voice, crying in the wilderness of social and moral prejudice had little chance of being heard.

Notwithstanding, Lottie Hanson began to wend her way downhill, drawn irresistibly to her place of birth, severely hampered by a strong wind and the heavy load she carried. This same road travelled for the third time in the course of one harrowing day, a sadly dejected figure, all the fire gone out of her. She had never felt so dreadfully alone in the entire eighteen year span of her young life, a mountain of woes fast closing in upon her.

* * *

Alice Ruddick wielded a pitchfork with the skill of a born navvy, simple minded maybe but worth her weight in gold to John Coulter, owner of several fields of arable land between Saltersgate and upper Meldon, even more further on, towards the main Newcastle to Jedburgh road. Some of his property lay adjacent to Fencers' Hill. One field in which Alice was now working, was situated near a rambling farmhouse occupied by Alec Messenger, the wealthy landowner's farm manager.

This gawky creature, seemingly all arms and legs, didn't care how hard she had to graft or how dirty the job, she was presently engaged on a dung heap which reeked to high heaven but might well have smelt of violets where Alice was concerned. She was an incongruous mess in a non matching assortment of clothing, only fit for the rag bag, her mousy hair not combed for days and obvious signs of scant use of soap and water.

Alice's spirits took a sudden lift at the sight of Lottie slowly trudging towards her. Here was the chief topic of Saltersgate's latest gossip, whose uphill climb had been noticed less than an hour before but, despite frantic waving, had chosen to ignore the greeting thrown across the road, or so it seemed. Lottie was too much obsessed with her own troubled thoughts to even be aware of it.

Alice thrived on the sniffing out and passing on of information, fresh snippets of news eagerly awaited by folk in the village, the only means of keeping contact with other women, ignored most of the time because of her simple ways. She was spoken of by young and old alike as 'daft Alice' but was not so stupid as they all imagined, sharp as a needle in some respects, a trait made good use of when it suited their purpose.

Lottie drew alongside and reluctantly slackened pace. Work came to a standstill, Alice straight into action, no wasting time. 'Aa shouted across t'ya on yer way up but y'took no heed,' she said accusingly and Lottie quickly pulled herself together, a meeting she would have fain done without and needed all her wits to cope with. Anything let slip was sure to reach eagerly waiting ears in no time at all.

'Aa didn't hear ya, Aa must have been miles away.' The truth, actually, but Alice soon abandoned the preliminaries and got straight to the point, eyeing Lottie up and down in obvious speculation. 'They tell me ye might be in a spot o'bother?' A question really not a statement, which didn't receive an answer. 'Say nowt's a good thing,' Lottie told herself but this simple lass was single minded with no intention of being diverted.

'Ye've had words wi' your Ralph the day so the farm lads say, an' they get t'know everything that goes on. Did he do that t'yer face?' No dissembling, Lottie's composure was gone in a flash swift to react.

'Them blessed farm lads should have more t'do wi' their time,' she rapped out in anger, absolutely incensed by this latest development. Alice was not in the least perturbed. 'Aa'll be sure t'tell them what y'sayed,' came in answer to the outburst.

'Aye, you just do that,' Lottie snapped and made to move on but her companion realised she had struck a nerve and prodded further. 'One o' them was deliverin' taties an' he sayed the fur was flyin'atween ye an' yer brother. The whole place is on about the carry on wi'Jake Snowdon.' There was no beating around the bush, Lottie was knocked completely off balance at the mere mention of that detested name. Her brave façade began to crumble, temper to the fore as usual, hell bent on her own destruction.

'Y' can tell them nosy parkers me Aunt Maude's sent 'is packin', that should please the miserable sinners, the whole damned lot o' them,' eyes brimming with tears, her flimsy defences shot to pieces.

Alice stared in amazement, her gleeful expression changed to one of real concern. 'Here hinny, take this,' a dirty rag fished from an apron pocket. 'If y'let them see y'care they'll torment ya all the more,' well experienced in this sort of cruel behaviour, pushing the makeshift hankie towards the weeping girl, who drew back in disgust when told to give her nose a good blow.

'Not wi' that mucky thing,' Lottie spluttered and used the sleeve of her jumper, much cleaner. Too thick skinned to take umbrage, Alice tucked the offensive article away, apparently deep in thought. 'So yer aunt's chucked y'out, that means ye've got nowhere t'bide,' At such unexpected sympathy, Lottie gave a loud sniff. 'One o'the orphan's o' the storm,' Lottie choked out between even more audible sniffs, seated now on her big bass bag, ready to indulge in an orgy of self pity. 'Well now,' Alice began, somewhat tentatively, 'Y'could stop wi' me father an' me. But only if y'have a mind,' she hastened to add, prepared to be rebuffed. She had no illusions about the way she was regarded by a whole village, more or less inured against such treatment.

The sniffs came to an abrupt half as Lottie gaped, completely taken aback. An offer of help at last and from this very surprising source. 'Just till y'get fixed up wi' somethin' more t'yer likin',' Alice chipped in expecting a firm refusal which didn't come, just a simple question. 'What will yer father say havin' a lodger shoved on'im without warnin'?'

'Oh him,' Alice said, meaning no disrespect, Fred Ruddick as easy as a pair of old shoes. 'Fred'll not turn a hair an Aa'll be glad o' yer company. He's i' fore shift this week an' next,' Suddenly conscious of Lottie's clean, tidy appearances and her own filthy disarray. 'Aa'll see an' get washed every night afore bed.' One final bid to remove all obstacles.

Lottie took note of Alice's dishevelled state with a feeling of horror, secretly appalled, but nothing soap and water wouldn't fix if she did accept the offer. Liberal use of both would be first priority, on the girl and the house, one of the worst hovels in the village. There were a fair number of them around, women with big families who lost heart and found it impossible to cope, usually there was quite a transformation as their daughters grew up and took a hand.

Alice sensed the wavering and knew when to press her advantage playing on a soft heart, sure Lottie had one. 'Aa get feared at nights when them drunks from the Trap come knockin' at me door. Hard up fer a woman when the' come after my kind.' Fully conscious of her limitations where men were concerned. 'Aa don't want somebody t'give me a babby.' Hand to mouth in absolute dismay as soon as the words left her lips.

'Aye Alice, keep the beggars at bay, they're only after one thing and that's not all it's cracked out t'be. Let them show their faces when Aa'm around and it's the chamber pot they'll be gettin' chucked over their stupid heads, that they will.' Alice chortled in appreciation quick to sense victory beaming satisfaction. 'This is fer the back door,' she said and produced an enormous key. 'If Fred happens t'be in, say Aa sent ya, he's not the one fer askin' a load o' questions. Pop the kettle on the grid an' have a rake i'the pantry. Aa'll not be far behind ya.'

Lottie took the proffered key and nodded understanding, too choked up to reply. Alice Ruddick in the role of Good Samaritan, so often derided in the village, she was ashamed now to have been among the tormentors on the odd occasion. Talk about heaping coals of fire on a body's head.

She got to her feet and bent to pick up the cumbersome load, only to be forestalled by one long, skinny arm stretched across the fence to lift it without any apparent effort, as strong as an ox as the saying goes. 'Too heavy fer a lass that's havin' a babby,' Alice said and set it down away from the smelly muck heap much to Lottie's relief.

'Thanks,' she mumbled, much too weary to deny her condition, little use anyway, but gazed at Alice Ruddick and knew somehow there was no condemnation. Hazel eyes met grey and held fast, a long searching look, no words needed. It was the beginning of a friendship destined to endure through many eventful years in circumstances neither of them could possibly foresee. Strange bedfellows, maybe, but each to fulfil a need for the other if in entirely different ways.

The significant moment ended with a breezy 'See ya later,' from Alice, first to break the silence, secretly elated to have a friend, someone to confide in and share her lonely hours. Lottie Hanson, often admired from afar and envied, such a bonny lass, was the sort of person Alice would have liked to be given any choice.

Lottie left her there, among the mixture of rotting vegetation and horse manure, pitchfork in hand and back to work with renewed will. A tuneless rendering of 'Onward Christian Soldiers' was heard until well downhill as a much happier young woman tramped along, rid of her immediate worry and the old bass bag, which contained all she now possessed, Ralph was sure to see nothing came her way from the family home. A stranger installed to make use of her mother's precious things, some of which should be hers, cut off without the proverbial penny as it were. Preston Workhouse was no longer a grim spectre on the horizon, the key to Fred Ruddick's house gripped firmly in her hand a definite life line, without the comfort of which she would surely be sunk. The Almighty answered prayers in some peculiar ways.

Alice attacked the pile of foul smelling dung with gusto and marvelled at such an unexpected stroke of good fortune. For once life seemed to be moving in her favour, an ill wind that blew nobody any good. 'Them beggars'll get nowt more out o'me,' she fervently vowed, village gossips waiting in vain for further news of Lottie's affairs and fully expecting this gawky lass to provide it. Alice imagined the expressions on many faces when they heard where Lottie was living, loyalty to a newly found friend firmly cemented as they moved towards an uncertain future, their paths to run parallel for longer than either of them could possibly know.

As for Lottie, her relaxed state of mind only lasted until she reached the foot of the hill and turned towards Saltersgate, impossible to avoid Cud Matthews' smallholding, passed without sight of him twice already that day but third time unlucky unfortunately. He was leaning across the five barred gate which led into his property, Annie's really, inherited from her father, an only child. It provided a bare living, there were two sons from the marriage but too young to do more than the simplest of chores and Cud himself was no grafter. Annie bore the brunt, the industrious member of the household, hers a most unenviable lot.

It was only the matter of seconds before Cud became alive to her approach and straightened up, down from the gate to deal with the situation in hand. 'Let'im start any shenanigans wi' me and he'll get more than 'ee wants t'hear,' she promised, already steeled for the ordeal ahead, that bright auburn head flung high as usual, the only sign of disturbance two flashes of crimson staining her high cheekbones. A set young face marred by a multi coloured bruise the soreness still there and one eye likely to turn black before long. Cud saw immediately that Miss High an' Mighty had been in the wars, his eyes wickedly alight, absorbing every inch of her body in a mixture of speculation and male appraisal.

'Have ye seen Jake lately, Lottie hinny?' Knowing fine well she hadn't 'Aa've never clapped eyes on the son of a bitch fer ages. But y'know how it is with'im, always after fresh fields to conquer, off wi' one an' on with another. Hard t'keep up wi.' A big smirk on his ugly face.

'Then why d'ya bother tryin'?' Not the reaction he anticipated. 'No, Aa haven't and when Aa do, Aa'll have nowt t'say to the blaggard. Aa hear Lily Collins give'im the push. Good fer her.' Lily, not prepared to wait for his affair with Lottie to run its course had sought and found pastures new, Jake the one to be dumped for a change, not to his liking as might be imagined.

With Lottie in this mood, a different lass to the one he met and tormented six months earlier, Cud was rather nonplussed but carried on with his jibes. 'He didn't fret long, he never does. Down by the river now, Aa reckon. He'll come back when'ees good an' ready.'

Lottie looked him straight in the eye and didn't turn a hair. The whole of Saltergate knew of Jake's on and off sojourn in the City Road area of Newcastle, seamy quarters with just the right sort of women. Disgusted to think she had known all that and still allowed herself to be led up the garden path. There was no accounting for such stupidity.

Cud tried different tactics. 'Ye cost me half a crown,' he said, hoping to be asked why but Lottie didn't bite and went into attack instead. 'If ye've got any half crowns t'chuck away, Aa reckon your Annie would be glad o'them,' she told him and wondered how Annie Flynn, that was, let herself be taken in by somebody of Cud's sort. The sad humour in this thought never crossed her mind, too busy trying to keep one step ahead in this battle of wits. A bet of some kind she gathered in which she was involved and Cud needed to be encouraged to spill the beans. Not a hope.

By this time he was fed up with it all, his mind as usual strayed to erotic thoughts centred upon this young lass, a mean soul eaten up with malice. But Lottie had already turned away prepared to move on, sick of the whole rotten business, fully resolved not to show any signs of haste just contempt, pride in every line of her retreating form as she left him seething.

'Little Goody Two Shoes,' he muttered sullenly. Good not an adjective that could be applied to Lottie Hanson any longer, whose pert nose he longed to rub in the mire but he gloated in the fact that Jake had done it for him. 'Run,' he bellowed after her, in total frustration. 'Y'canna get far enough. Aa bet me last ha'penny there's a bairn on the way an' that'll fettle ya.' Kicking the hard ground in uncontrollable fury he stubbed his toe, hopping around on the other foot in agony and mortification at his failure to ruffle her apparent indifference, completely unaware of how much effort this exercise in self control had taken. The oaths that escaped his slobbering mouth were quite unprintable.

The harsh sound of that strident voice and the filth spilled into the cold air throbbed in Lottie's ears when the door of Number 10 Lizzie Street closed behind her, sanctuary at last, glad to find herself alone in the house, Fred Ruddick nowhere to be seen, weary beyond words her spirits were at their lowest ebb.

Blessing indeed, this terraced dwelling was in the first street of the village, first or last depending upon approach. There was nobody around to witness her arrival but stepping out in daylight would be a different ball game, tongues soon in action and the village grapevine most effective. She vowed there and then never to venture forth among them if given any choice.

In less than six months, Lottie would pay a heavy price for Jake Snowdon's seduction, many hours of regret would pass between now and the birth of her child. A bairn to bring up in unenviable circumstances dreadful to contemplate, a heavy cross to bear for those moments of madness in Batey's field.

Full of utter despondency she absorbed the squalor of her surroundings, no further than the kitchen as yet and God knows what the rest of the house was like. This was to be her infant's birthplace unless some radical change in circumstances occurred in the meantime and not much hope in that direction. Suddenly she was possessed by an overwhelming sense of dejection, a leaden weight around a desolate heart, the fear of not being able to bond with a child conceived in such a hateful situation and sired by a man she wholly detested.

Defeated by the thought of all that was to come, the unhappy lass crawled into the confines of a battered armchair, minus most of its stuffing, and wept. She had a hollow feeling in the core of her being, caught in a trap from which there seemed no possible means of escape.

* ** *

On that very first evening of Lottie Hanson's stay in the Ruddick home, a tin bath was hauled in front of the kitchen fire, Fred dismissed to the local pub and Alice immersed in hot water to be thoroughly scrubbed with a flannel cloth and soap. The bed the two girls were to share was stripped and remade with sheets and covers found in an old tin trunk, lain there smelling of mothballs since Sally Ruddick's day, while her hapless daughter made do with a motley assortment of what could only be called rags. Now they were ready for the tub to be used as dusters or whatever other purpose they might happen to serve. Fred's bed got the same treatment, a big surprise when he crawled into it after work the following morning squeaky clean, the tin bath ready for him also, the whole pattern of his life about to change for the better. He accepted Lottie's introduction into the family circle without question, a kindly chap who deserved a brighter future, much encouraged by these early signs.

News of this incredible happening spread around the village in a flash, Janey Wilson was absolutely appalled when it came to her ears and stopped speaking to Ralph for weeks after, the situation did improve to some degree when a friendship blossomed between Margaret Hanson and herself, the former slowly adapting to life in those parts, vastly different from service as ladies' maid in an upper class establishment, ended just before her son Robert came into the world.

Lottie's name never crossed her brother's lips, a man who hated the very idea of the family being dragged through the mud. A sort of class system existed within the lower echelon, with some folk as always better managers of the little they had than others, for which they laid claim to higher status, thinking themselves a cut above the rest. The Hansons were in this category, a lot of pride at stake.

Fred Ruddick's topsy turvy life altered in drastic fashion, the domestic front no longer in Alice's incapable hands. He revelled in darned socks, clean shirts and decently cooked food, Lottie well versed in the art of making something out of nothing, taught by example from a very early age.

Fred's marriage to Sally Innes twenty years before united a couple from two vastly different religious persuasions, Roman Catholic and Salvation Army, the burning of incense and tambourine bashing hardly compatible. Producing a retarded child was seen by both families as an Act of God, each certain the Almighty was on their side, Alice was accepted into neither circle. Sally sought religion for her daughter and herself elsewhere and both attended the local Methodist chapel on a regular basis. Even after his wife's untimely death Fred saw no reason for change, although frequenting no place of worship himself he allowed Alice to carry on as usual despite repeated pressure from the Catholic priest to return to the Faith, solemn warnings about his Immortal Soul. 'Aa promised Sal,' he stubbornly insisted, more in awe of the dear departed than the hierarchy of the Holy Catholic Church.

Lottie attacked dirt with savage intensity wherever she found it, seemingly obsessed by a mania for constant use of soap and water, as if to cleanse herself of guilt in process, still absolutely riddled with it. Confined to the house by choice, she resisted Alice's earnest pleas to do otherwise. 'It'll be bad fer you an' the babby,' the anxious lass said times without number, up against a stubbornness to break down. Lottie did indulge in short meanders after dark, a stroll around the block, little chance of being seen with neighbours huddled close to blazing fires, winter already upon them, one of the few perks coal miners and their families enjoyed.

'Aa'll not have that lot gapin' at me,' she said in protest whenever tackled, her pinched, unhappy face a great source of anxiety to her benefactors, Fred worried about her but never interfered, full of sympathy for her plight and immensely grateful for the friendship bestowed upon a much loved daughter, Alice was sadly lacking female companionship since her mother's demise, her father well aware of what she sometimes suffered at the hands of ignorant people.

November came in with a succession of grey, cheerless days, doing nothing to lift Lottie out of the doldrums and Alice's irrepressible good humour could be rather wearing. The big lass, often accosted in the street and asked about her friend's condition, sly enquiries usually turned aside with 'Champion man, champion. Aa'll be sure t'tell'er y'asked,' tongue in cheek as she said it and jubilant at disappointed looks on curious faces.

Only the sincere concern of someone like Janey Wilson deserved the truth and she grieved when Alice confided in her, no mention made of Lottie in Tod's hearing, enough trouble expected from that particular quarter before very long. Rumour had at last reached Janey about Mary's involvement with the O'Neal lad and she waited fearfully for Tod to get wind of it. That it should not have become common knowledge sooner was nothing short of a miracle, Tommy's blackmailing was about to come to an end when the weight of both religions was brought to bear upon two young folk very much in love. A love which never stood a chance in prevailing circumstances.

Alice had the canny knack of gleaning information without giving any away and won the battle of one-upmanship hands down. 'Ye'll never guess what Aa heard the day,' her usual preliminary after visits to the local Co-op, a hot bed of gossip. Lottie was too dispirited to care, a bellyful of nosy females, hard to remember them as one time friends and neighbours.

'There's talk o'them fillin' in the Bottom Quarry pond,' Alice once informed her. 'The gaffer's on about bringin' men from Choppin'ton t'work at Polrigg. Me father says he's openin' up a new flat i' the pit. They'll be needin' houses. It'll take some rubble t'get t'the bottom o'that Choppington, another colliery further north, older and likely to run out, families forced to leave familiar ground for work elsewhere.'

The mere mention of this quarry reminded Lottie of a strong inclination to throw herself into the murky pond when she first knew of her pregnancy. One or two local lasses had taken this drastic way out over the years, Saltersgate awash with tears at their funerals. 'Rotten hypocrites, the lot o' them,' she thought in disgust. Less tittle tattle and a helping hand was worth more than floods of crocodile tears.

'Aa wouldn't fancy livin' on top o' that quarry, filled in or not,' Alice said at the time and wondered why Lottie gave a loud cackle of dry laughter usually devoid of humour nowadays. But a laugh of any sort was something to be thankful for, even empty sounding like this.

* * *

A couple of weeks later she arrived home from work, creating her usual trail of havoc, like a bull in a china shop. Not that china had any place in this humble abode. Sally Ruddick's few precious pieces didn't last long after her death, ending up in the pawn shop or broken by her ham fisted daughter. An odd assortment of crockery was all that remained, most of it chipped and badly discoloured, the chips irreplaceable but the ugly tannin removed with the use of salt and a great deal of elbow grease.

Down on her knees, Lottie raised herself awkwardly into a standing position and sharply berated the culprit. 'This place'll soon be back t'where

Aa started,' scrubbing bare boards no easy task for someone in her condition. 'If Aa grafted from now till Doomsday it wouldn't make any difference,' she groaned in despair, no amount of effort likely to change the poverty stricken atmosphere in a long neglected abode, everything past its best, well worn or just ill used, so unlike her former home. Nevertheless Fred and Alice wallowed in the changed circumstances, scrupulously clean whatever else the place lacked, nothing better to compare it with, more than contented with their present lot.

In a bid for independence, Lottie did manage to subscribe to the household budget by laundering for a family in Branton Village, of the same ilk as Mary Wilson's employers and just as finicky, the Ruddick's kitchen was often festooned with washing hung around to dry. Alice helped by toting bundles up and down the Mutton Road, a highway between the two villages, various explanations abounded regarding its name. A road towards which Lottie held strong aversion, the scene of her first encounter with Jake Snowdon five months earlier.

'Carry yer bundle, lass,' he proffered, seeming to appear from nowhere, a crafty manoeuvre planned to the very last detail after careful research into the girl's regular routine. 'No thanks,' she stammered, rather anxious not to seen in the company of this well known womaniser. 'Howway hinny,' he coaxed refusing to be snubbed, 'Aa'll not eat ya and Aa'll walk in front if it bothers ya,' said with a disarming smile, Jake at his most charming, trying his best not to appear as black as he was painted. He was assured of success when Lottie succumbed to this cajolery and didn't hurry away, the first step on the road to disaster as she now knew to her sorrow.

'Aa must o'been wrong i' me mind,' she agonised, still haunted by Jake's false image, chastising a susceptible young heart for its betrayal. Anger was soon replaced by terrible anguish, which she was prepared to wallow in when Alice barged across the room towards her. 'Mind that blessed bucket,' she snapped, her distraught manner completely lost upon a one track mind, almost bursting with what she had to say, unable to contain herself. 'Guess what Aa just heard,' she blurted out, impervious to obvious signs of irritation.

'Aa'm in no mood for your guessy games, Alice Ruddick,' Lottie blazed. 'Just look at the floor, Aa've been on me knees for varnigh on hour,' thoroughly disgruntled.

'And haven't Aa told y'many a time t'leave the donkey work me,' she was reminded, answering in a flash, 'Aye, an'have the place the wreck it was afore,' immediately contrite, no use taking frustration out on Alice, gormless may be but a canny lass. 'Go on,' she sighed in exasperation, 'Aa'm listenin,' and waited to be regaled with the latest bit of news.

'He's back,' came the triumphant disclosure, no need to ask who the he in question was, this unexpected announcement of Jake's return was sufficient to send a cold shiver right through Lottie's taut body, sick to her stomach and almost ready to collapse, Jake at a distance gave her much more peace of mind. Now the gossip would start up again aided and abetted by that loathsome, lying tongue, once plunged inside her own mouth, her soft lips curled in distaste at the very thought of it.

But Alice, riding high aboard a band wagon, was impossible to contain and failed to realise how these silly romantic notions built around Lottie and the father of her child might alter the Ruddick family's present existence. 'Ye'll be getting' in touch t'tell'im about the babby,' she prattled on, soon disillusioned, assailed by a barrage of heated words.

'That Aa'll not. D'ya fondly imagine he hasn't heard the glad tidings afore now, even the dogs are barkin' it.' A quick breath and the attack continued in full force. 'Yer dafter than Aa thought. Get this inta yer head once an'fer all, him an' me's finished – fer good!' almost past herself with rage. Such reasoning was beyond comprehension by someone who saw marriage as a be all and end all in any woman's life, a blissful state she herself could never hope to attain. How the word blissful fitted some of the marital couplings around her was hard to imagine.

With a feeling of having gone too far, Lottie tried to change the subject. 'Yer sharp the day,' she said but Alice merely grunted in response, obviously put out and didn't ruffle easily. 'The jobs that were left need daylight,' she sullenly explained but never one to huff for long brightened almost immediately. 'Aa fetched a few eggs,' anxious to be in the good books again and grabbed at a means to achieve it. The hand delved into her apron pocket emerged covered in a yellow gooey substance and with it a sheepish grin. 'They're broken,' she stated needlessly in a situation that spoke for itself.

A peal of raucous laughter echoed through the cluttered kitchen. 'Only somebody like you would carry eggs in an apron pocket,' Lottie chided in amusement. 'Get the thing off an' be canny, y'might t'save one or two.' With nothing much in the house eggs were a good stand by. The pantry was always like Mother Hubbard's cupboard just before Pay Friday, once a fortnight. 'Go on,' she urged, 'Or else the blessed things'll cook on ya.'

Alice did manage to rescue a couple and passed them over, bending to wash her sticky hands in the bucket that caused the earlier hullabaloo, hygiene not something she worried too much about. Fully restored to good humour she realised what Jake's dismissal from Lottie's world could mean to her. 'It's likely ye'll bidin' wi' Fred an' me then?' she ventured, a possibility which held enormous appeal.

'Mebbe,' Lottie answered, rubbing the sticky eggs with the floor cloth, rather dismayed at the thought of permanent residence in this poverty stricken abode but quite sufficient to catapult Alice into spontaneous action. Long, skinny arms thrown around her neck in a bearlike hug, a voice Lottie scarcely recognised as her own begging her to be careful. Her heart sank at the prospect of any child born in such a dump, this one branded as bastard from the very beginning. A sharp knock at the door jerked her troubled mind into sudden awareness.

'Keep them out,' she implored in instant panic and clutched at Alice's bony arm in forceful restraint, that young Miss doing her best to calm her. 'It'll just be them bairns playin' knocky nine doors,' she soothed, trying to pull free. 'Hardly anybody comes here an never t'the front door,' she soothed but Lottie was beyond control once more. 'Aa don't want t'see nobody, nobody, y'hear,' almost past herself.

'Aa'll sharp send the little beggars flyin,' Alice promised and hurriedly departed, these lively confrontations right up her street, no more than a child herself at times, even at nineteen years of age.

Soon came the mumble of voices but none of the juicy language Alice was prone to use on such occasions, despite a strong Methodist indoctrination. In front of her on the doorstep stood a woman whose strong resemblance to Lottie's mother was plain to be seen, except for a haughty demeanour, cold grey eyes and a hard, uncompromising mouth. Bessie, nee Finlay, had been a brown eyed woman of gentle manner and an air of warmth which drew people to her, none of this was apparent in her elder sister, their kinship confirmed with her first words. 'My niece is staying here, I believe,' straight to the point, the grand lady and no mistake. Alice barely had time to mumble 'Aye,' before being swept aside to allow the stranger into the house, never for one moment doubting her welcome, but soon to be disillusioned.

A rustle of taffeta petticoats accompanied her majestic sweep into the kitchen, where a tight lipped young woman awaited, the sight of her sufficient to arouse a determination in Lottie to be as awkward as possible. Family relationship didn't mean unconditional acceptance, there were too many old scores to settle. The disorderly room and her own dishevelled appearance were absorbed in one all encompassing glance, a haughty nose wrinkled in distaste.

'You know who I am, of course, Charlotte. Your mother's elder sister, Aunt Jessica,' moving closer but soon halted in her tracks by Lottie's cutting remarks. 'Why should Aa know any such thing? Y'weren't at me mother's funeral, none o' her kin showed their faces that day.' This long festering sore point overdue airing, an unexpected opportunity Bessie Hanson's daughter didn't intend to miss.

Quite taken aback by such outspokenness cold grey eyes flashed resentment, Jessica felt obliged to give some explanation for her absence. 'I happened to be in London at the time, Madam needed me to be in charge of household affairs with the master home on furlough.' An attempt to allay her niece's hostility and to stress her own importance.

Lottie refused to make it easy for her but failed to take Alice into consideration, who rushed to give the posh visitor a seat, first dusted down with the sleeve of a grubby blouse, choosing to ignore the baleful expression in her friend's eyes. 'Let the old bitch stew a bit,' was that young woman's spiteful reaction. 'Turnin' up after all this time an' lookin' fer the red carpet.' Mad as a hatter at Alice's servility.

Jessica took the proffered chair without a word of thanks and sat down, her back straight, mainly because of an uncomfortable laced corset but striking a regal pose to intimidate her sharp tongued niece. 'You must understand,' she began in further effort towards reconciliation, inwardly seething, accustomed to the utmost respect from such lesser beings.

'Understand what?' Lottie threw at her prepared to do battle on her mother's behalf, so many years without contact, to be ostracised by her own kin so hard to bear. 'Me father was never good enough fer the Finlays,' she hotly accused, straight to the core of the matter, Jessica quick to reply. 'My sister was always headstrong never able to accept advice. She did have other suitors.' Still irked by Bessie's popularity with the opposite sex when they were young. 'Perhaps she may have lived longer in different circumstances. Not that we had anything against your father's character – but –' The 'but' said everything.

Lottie glared at her and bristled strongly. This haughty creature was so unlike the mother she loved and lost too soon even if there was a strong resemblance. She wondered why her aunt came to seek her out after all this time, never seen face to face during the whole of her eighteen years, only pointed out to her at odd times on Branton High Street, she had been aware of her mother's sadness at the way things were.

The voice that broke into these reflections was full of impatience, in further attempt to breach Lottie's defences, Jessica unfortunate in her choice of words. 'I called on your brother, who wasn't available. His wife told me where to find you. Such a nice refined young woman.' She seemed surprised that this should be the case.

So much condescension in these begrudging words of praise but the mere fact of Margaret revealing her whereabouts made Lottie see red. 'Kind of'er t'be sure,' she said, her tone ripe with sarcasm and vowed to dig her toes in harder than ever. This uppitty aunt of hers got right under her skin.

But at this stage Jessica's tolerance took a swift nose dive. 'Enough of this nonsense,' she barked, sick of these preliminaries and anxious to get to the real purpose of her visit without further shilly shallying. 'I heard of your unfortunate situation and discussed the matter with my employer who is willing to offer you a position on her household staff, under my supervision, naturally.' Expecting a rush of gratitude, she was highly disappointed. 'Naturally!' Lottie mocked. 'Funny she should want t'bother'er head wi'the likes o'me when we've never set eyes on one another. She wouldn't know me from Adam.' Looking her aunt straight in the eyes, fully resolved not to betray her nervousness even if her knees had turned to jelly.

Jessica was coldly disapproving. 'Mrs Cranshawe is a LADY,' with due emphasis on this latter word, annoyed to hear her mistress spoken of in such fashion and furious to be getting nowhere fast with this fiery little vixen. 'Madam is accustomed to helping those in need. Besides she values my services very highly and you are recommended. After all you are my only sister's child.'

'Some sister you turned out t'be,' Lottie grunted scornfully, suspicious of altruistic motives ascribed to her so called betters, nothing for nothing to be sure. Although, to be truthful, the offer held more appeal than continued residence with the Ruddicks, despite their great kindness towards her.

The female member of that family stood by open mouthed, amazed at Lottie's attitude, unable to recognise it as another way of removing this dearest of friends out of her own sphere. 'Where would Aa be livin' if Aa did say Aa would come?' A glint in Jessica Finlay's eyes at this first sign of weakening, not before time.

'Rothwell House in Oakfields,' which brought two swift intakes of breath, it was recognised as a place where the real toffs lived, far above the Boyles and Lottie's employers, those for whom she laundered, Scobie by name. 'It's a lot t'think about,' she made very plain that no decision had yet been made, filled with an uneasiness she couldn't quite fathom, certain her autocratic relative wasn't to be trusted. If any nest was to be feathered it would definitely be her own, there had to be some ulterior motive.

'A simple yes or no is all I require,' Jessica's tone very abrupt, 'Well Charlotte?' she prompted, thin eyebrows lifted in enquiry. Lottie took a deep breath and asked the all important question. 'And Aa'm t'keep the babby when it comes?' On tenterhooks awaiting the reply.

'Of course you will keep the child but please refer to it as such. Madam deplores the rough speech in this area. You must rid yourself of coarse habits.' That stung and Lottie's tongue ran riot. 'Me speech might be rougher than yours but Aa am properly house trained an' know how t'use a knife an fork, me mother made sure o'such things. She did come from the same stable as yerself, don't ferget.' A final dig she was unable to resist but could live to regret.

Jessica stiffened, thin lips pursued in disapproval, flushed from below her scrawny neck upwards. This precocious little minx needed a tight rein, too much to say for herself by far. 'Control your quick tongue, my girl, employers don't take kindly to such impertinence,' she saw fit to warn. 'Now, if you have made your mind up at last I shall wait outside in the carriage until you have collected your belongings. Don't bring a load of rubbish, you will be supplied with suitable uniforms.' Lottie panicked at the swiftness of it all. No strange room would see her bedded down that night, tomorrow maybe if she didn't think better of it. 'Aa'll not be leavin' here at a minute's notice, so if it canna wait till the morra Aa'll not be comin.' One last bid for decision making before she surrendered herself completely into someone else's hands.

Jessica tutted loudly but didn't argue the point. 'Tomorrow then,' she acquiesced and just managed to keep her temper. 'I shall send Jackson with the pony trap at eight sharp. Be ready.' Furious at Lottie's behaviour, fully resolved to lick her niece into shape from the outset. 'See that you are neatly dressed and CLEAN,' was her parting shot as shot as she sailed out of the room, two wide eyed girls staring in amazement. A slammed door told them she had left the house.

Lottie giggled. 'Now what d'ya think o'that performance, Alice?' Well satisfied with her own role in the recent dramatic scene. 'Neatly dressed and

CLEAN,' she mimicked, 'And no wonder. If Aa look like you, the old bitch has a right t'be worried,' The accompanying mirth quite infectious. 'Ya didn't know Aa had such toffee nosed relations, did ya? Her an' Ralph's wife would make a fine pair.' Spiteful conjecture which suited Alice down to the ground, delighted to see Lottie's face alive with mischief, little realising how much trouble her headstrong friend had already stored up for herself.

Lottie, bordering on hysteria, prattled on. 'Well, she's in fer a shock. It's me Sunda' best Aa'll be wearin'. Aa'll show'er, as Aa will. All them airs an' graces.' The situation was suddenly made clear to Alice, a crestfallen look came over her homely face. A parting of the ways almost upon them, she was too kind hearted to dampen her companion's high spirits but terribly dismayed.

An ebullient mood which lasted until later that evening when tucked up in bed together for the last time, Lottie realised that soon there would be no Alice to cuddle into for comfort and a host of fears began to manifest themselves. Tormented by indecision she tossed on her pillows, a sad farewell already said to Fred Ruddick who would be on his way home from Polrigg when she left next morning, sorry to see her go for a number of reasons, not least among them the difference it would make in his own day to day existence, but ruefully accepting it was too good to last.

Sporadic shivers transferred themselves to Alice's bony frame. 'Ye'll be all right,' she soothed, 'Better fer the babby when it comes. Them sort'll see yer clothed an' fed, s'long as y'do yer turn.' Words of wisdom from a supposedly simple mind, the class system was never stronger. Murmurs of unrest at Polrigg grew louder every day, strike talk was constantly in the air but miners were not yet organised enough to muster sufficient clout to claim their dues. 'Mebbe ye'll meet some other chap that doesn't mind takin' on somebody else's bairn t'get a champion lass fer a wife,' Alice said, totally unprepared for the storm that broke around her ears when Lottie suddenly let fly, a wild look in widely dilated eyes. A torrent of words escaped her quivering lips. 'If any man lays a finger on me again, Aa'll swing fer the beggar.' A vehement threat torn from an anguished mind. Repeated over and again in deep distress as nervous hands plucked feverishly at the white Alhambra quilt, an inconsequential thought in the middle of it all that it wouldn't stay white for long. Ages before the spasm ended and she dissolved into bitter but silent tears.

Alice failed to understand the full extent of her friend's agony and could only try to give comfort, drawing Lottie down from her upright position under the bedclothes. The room was eventually bathed in a dark silence, the tears all gone but sleep elusive, the storm although fierce while it lasted had now abated but the memory of Jake's perfidy still lingered to torment a restless soul. A blessing if she never knew the truth of the part her dead father played in her destruction, her life ruined by a spiteful act of revenge. But there, in that darkened room, Lottie Hanson made the solemn vow never to forgive or forget, with a child as yet unborn a constant reminder this was certain to be no difficult task.

Daybreak was almost upon them when the unhappy girl dozed off, only to dream of herself in the Bottom Quarry pond, a hard struggle to get out, no hand outstretched to save her from drowning. Filled with an overwhelming desire to let the icy water take her into its bottomless depths she awoke gasping for breath bathed in sweat, the place beside her still warm to the touch but empty. Time to get up, goodbyes to be said before Alice left for work on the farm, never late. It was still dark outside but the early hours of the morning had come and the day must be faced whatever it might hold. A mistress yet unknown and well under the thumb of her mother's elder sister, who promised to be a real martinet. No telling what her usual lack of control may have brought upon her.

It was a very subdued and apprehensive young woman who hurried into her Sunday best after a hurried wash in very cold water. With fingers splayed across a rounded belly in utter dismay before she donned the outer garments, knowing in her heart the die was already cast and she had already become another helpless pawn of fate.

* * *

All in all it was a most eventful evening. Ralph Hanson was late home from Polrigg, his particular cavil blocked in by a fall of stone, not serious but bad enough to hold these men back while other day shift men rose to the surface in the rackety wooden cage. This meant that by some stroke of fate Jessica Finlay chose the right time for her visit to Maria Street, doubtful if her nephew would have allowed her access to his home. But Margaret, although aware of the rift between them, fell back on an inherent sense of good manners to invite Ralph's aunt into the house, glad of darkness and swirling fog to escape watchful eyes. Most folk were around their own firesides unless forced out of doors for one reason or another. One thing the miners didn't have to worry about was coal, unless on strike when the old pit heap took on a different shape by the digging of even more holes in search of the precious black ore, imprisonment likely if they were caught. A blind eye was often turned by its custodians, men employed by the gaffer for this unenviable task but sympathetic in most cases towards the miners, they would chase maybe but seldom catch.

Some time after Jessica Finlay left with the information she sought, Ralph arrived home chilled to the bone, hungry and much irritated by the delay. Completely on edge, Margaret waited until his ablutions were almost over, that same tin bath in which Lottie tried to wash away her shame full of filthy water and her husband ten shades lighter than before.

'What can that old battleaxe want wi' our Lottie?' he grunted when told. 'Years since Aa clapped eyes on'er. Didn't think sh'was on speakin'terms wi' this side o'the family.' He took it much calmer than his wife imagined, who felt herself relax and blue eyes cleared of the anxiety in them when the subject was broached. Little wonder she was somewhat afraid of Ralph's temper since that terrible set to with his sister, no mention made of her since, obviously a closed chapter.

'The old bitch would get an eyeful in Fred Ruddick's mucky hole. This place is a palace,' he gloated, seeming rather pleased his aunt had sight of his own spotless home, very proud of it, a pride badly dented by Lottie's come down in the world. For a Hanson to end up in such a pig sty was the last straw but no more than she deserved, he had total belief in Old Testament teachings, a revengeful God to be feared by all sinners and she had sinned. The legitimacy of his own son Robbie was not to be doubted, still seething from the unforgivable insinuation thrown at him in anger, not a forgiving man.

When he at last sat down to eat, Margaret dragged the tin bath towards the back door. Cold air swept in as she emptied it bucket by bucket down the outside drain, back breaking work for such a slight young woman but it was her job, no offer of help, a strict code of who did what in colliery villages. A man's labour was confined to the pit and his garden, mostly allotments, one a sort of antidote for the other. Not that Ralph didn't lend a hand on occasion but always in private, never willing to lose face among his fellows, he was hardly conscious of what she was doing this particular evening, his mind elsewhere.

As she worked, Margaret wondered if Ralph knew of Jake Snowdon's return to the village, the Co-op had been agog with the news earlier in the day. If he did, no word of it passed his lips, his hands seemingly washed of the whole distasteful affair.

'Aa'll be pushin'off t'the Tute after me dinner,' he told her, demolishing a big bowl of tapioca on top of a huge helping of leek pudding. Stodge followed by more stodge, guaranteed to stick to the ribs. 'What doesn't fatten'll help t'fill,' a well used saying thereabouts. Meat was not always on the menu, and only then the cheapest of cuts of offal ... a rabbit poached from John Coulter's fields was a welcome addition to the daily fare and well worth the risk of being caught.

Half an hour later Margaret watched her husband struggle into a well worn jacket. 'This blessed thing most o' shrunk,' he woefully declared, obliged to leave a couple of buttons loose for comfort, nothing to be done about the over short sleeves, it was a relic from pre-war days and truly outgrown, his wife sadly aware of the few clothes he possessed. The traditional navy serge suit was carefully sponged and pressed, then laid away for Sunday church going and special occasions, mostly funerals.

'Must you go out?' a wistful question from a woman who spent her days with only a small boy for company, Robbie Hanson now fast asleep in bed, his mother not looking forward to a lonely evening, she was not yet into gossip around neighbours' mat frames, although gradually coming to terms with local custom. Full acceptance of this stranger in their midst was impeded by her refined manner of speech, too much like the gaffers to inspire confidence in those with good reason to hate their guts. Her friendship with Janey Wilson was likely to be the 'open sesame' to eventual acceptance, she was much respected in the community.

'Sorry lass,' came in answer to the softly spoken enquiry. 'There's something needs settlin',' and Margaret realised Ralph knew of Jake's return to the village, confrontation was definitely on the cards. She worried lest that explosive temper showed itself again and it came to physical combat, the other man was an unknown quantity, all she knew of him came from hearsay.

'Trust that blaggard t'pick the Tute,' her husband grunted, obviously out of sorts, this abbreviation used for the meeting place miners frequented between shifts, young and old. A place of refuge from nagging tongues, and boisterous bairns, but mostly a forum for airing grievances, plenty of them. A long room, its space mainly absorbed by a full sized billiard table, donated in benevolence by Lord Somebody or Other and generally much in demand.

Once out of doors, Ralph Hanson crossed towards Theresa Street corner, the lamp post area deserted due to the foggy night. He took a right turn into Chapel Street to enter the Institute by a door at the rear, which opened upon a smoke filled room full of chattering men, in small groups along three sides of it, the fireside area occupied by retired miners, old men, huddled close around a blazing fire, needing the heat, not much flesh on work worn bones.

He gave a quick look around but no sign of Jake, 'Late fer'is own funeral,' Ralph thought in derision, knowing too well this unscupulous rogue was sure to make an entrance, it was all part of the game. He made a bee line towards the far end where men of his own cavil were in vociferous mood. 'Y'got it shifted then?' one of them said as he approached, meaning the stone. 'Aye,' Ralph answered, 'That's what made' is late but sooner than some.' Very obvious to whom he referred, there had been talk of the meeting with Jake earlier that day and curiosity was rife among his work mates.

The cues and billiard balls lay idle, there were more men present than usual, those who knew of the expected show down, not put off by the cold, foggy weather. A peculiar combination of pipe smoke and body odour permeated the air, hygiene definitely not regarded as first priority with a number of them, especially the veterans whose bladders didn't function properly and their proximity to the heat made matters worse. Jackie Phillips, Ralph's friend since boyhood days and co-worker, had been spouting forth volubly before Ralph's arrival upon the scene, the two men different as chalk from cheese, a strange friendship. One a regular church goer and the other more akin to the devil at times but good hearted and very loyal, fine for any man to have at his back. The war separated them for a while but they soon picked up where they left off, their relationship too firmly cemented by preceding years.

Beside this little group were men who worked another seam in the pit. 'Ye tell this lot what it's like in our flat, Ralph,' Jackie said, obviously needing support. 'Bad,' came the answer, 'Three deputations since Aa picked up again but the gaffer doesn't want t'know. It would mean leavin' a whole flat idle and that would hit the old beggar's pocket too much. Only one other option if ye've got the stomach fer it.'

Pandemonium reigned, moderates preached caution to hot heads, one voice above another, most men ready to take strike action before real disaster overtook them, water and gas deadly enemies of the underground worker.

His own problem took second place as Ralph's mind diverted to this very crucial issue, totally absorbed in it when an oily voice echoed from the other end of the room. 'Canny on lads or somebody's gonna have a heart attack. The prodigal's back, where's the fatted calf?' Jake Snowdon obviously in excellent form.

'What the hell – –' Jackie protested. 'Oh, it's ye,' his face darkening in anger when he saw who it was, 'That's all w'need,' with a desperate look in Ralph's direction, knowing too well the fiery temper that lay beneath a surface of apparent calm.

'Where've ye been hidin' yerself?' one man threw at Jake, just the right words to set the wheels in motion, his reply ripe with suggestion. 'Aa've been busy,' no mistaking the implication.

'Busy afore y'went an'all, if all w'hear is true,' came back at him in swift retort, coarse sniggers from all directions as the chatting ceased. Jake had his audience and began to play to the gallery.

'Y'shouldn't believe all y'hear or mebbe y'should,' he smirked, all eyes upon him as intended, Jackie close to Ralph saw his friend's knuckles whiten, a challenge issued by those boldly triumphant eyes and another careless tongue, unmindful of Ralph's presence hastened the proceedings, not entirely to Jake's liking who wanted it dragged out, savoured to the full.

'Howway lad. It's common gossip about ye an' Lottie Hanson. Did all right there, didn't ya,' A loud gasp at this forthright remark, the whole assembly intrigued by the situation, fast building up to something very interesting. Not so different from their womenfolk when it came to the crunch.

The sparks had to fly and encouraged by the sweet smell of victory Jake waited for Ralph's reaction, no point to the exercise if that Holy Joe's nose wasn't rubbed in the muck. He hadn't long to wait, his adversary already moving towards him. 'Take it easy,' Ralph's mind cautioned, possessed by an overwhelming urge to fasten his hands around that swarthy neck but face to face in the matter of seconds his voice was amazingly controlled, too much so, Jackie fretted sensitive to his long time marra's every mood.

'Afore this whole thing gets right out o'hand,' Ralph began benignly enough. 'Ye an' me had better step outside Jake Snowdon. W'don't need other folk hangin' onto every last word.' A proposal which didn't suit the other man's sadistic purpose.

'Oh aye,' he sneered, certain he held all the aces, too sure of himself to care about skating on thin ice. 'There's nowt than canna be settled here an'now.' Not prepared to give an inch.

Rage mounted in Ralph Hanson's taut body and made restraint impossible, his opponent spoiling for a fight and past caring what he said. 'What makes y'think Aa'm the only one that's had it off wi'your lass. Y'should o'stopped at home an'kept on eye on the flighty bitch, instead o'hoppin' off t'be one o'them glory boys,' he taunted and went too far, he never knew what hit him. In a split second the air became charged with electricity and his slackened jaw took the full impact of a punishing blow. A fierce uppercut that sent him hurtling into the space somebody had stepped back to clear and furious words echoed around his ears.

'Take that load o'filth back,' Ralph bellowed, 'Our Lottie was out of'er mind getting' mixed up wi' your sort but she isn't the whore yer makin'er out t'be.' His dander was right up, fists at the ready.

Murmurs of agreement reached Jake's tingling ears, a general feeling that Lottie had been the victim of an unscrupulous rogue. Excitement grew as he scrambled to his feet, loudly claiming a lucky punch. The bad blood between himself and the Hansons was about to reach an inevitable show down, years in coming.

He lunged forward and tried to take Ralph by surprise but a neat side step failed his attempt at a return blow and he staggered right off course to fall flat on his face, long legs astride his prone body, an avenging angel standing over him, the victor and everyone knew it.

'On yet feet, Snowdon, don't go t'sleep down there,' came among the guffaws, mostly from those who favoured Ralph, Jake's handful of cronies disgusted at his performance. 'Let yer deeds match yer mouth,' yelled at him in harsh derision when he made no move to get up again.

The two men were decidedly ill matched, although almost of an age, one badly out of condition with drink and loose living, the other fit enough for anything, Jake was downed for a third time when he rose and made a thrust in Ralph's direction, eager to regain the esteem of his work mates. He lay there, motionless, bleary eyes fixed on a ceiling which seemed to be going around in circles, sickened by the taste of his own blood, ignominious in defeat.

Jeering comments echoed through the smoke filled room and Jake's hatred for the Hansons spilled over. 'That's enough,' he ground out sullenly, a pretty picture with a tongue too big for his mouth and unsteady on his feet, filled with venom that knew no bounds.

'Aa'll grant ya this round but Aa'll bide me time,' he snarled, 'That sister o'yours'll be beggin' fer marriage after Aa've kept'er waitin fer a few months. Ye'll both be sorry fer this night's work.'

Ralph's fist lifted again ready to silence that loathsome tongue forever but thought better of it. 'Yet not worth hangin' for. It might be news t'ya but sh'has no intentions o'marrying ya. That was my idea when Aa came here but she's better off without ya. An'keep away from'er or ye'll not get off s'easy another time.' And with a final snort of contempt he turned to rejoin his own mates, Jackie Phillips jubilant patting his back in approval, Ralph was somewhat of a hero to this volatile little fellow.

Those left beside Jake moved away in disgust and past himself with rage he pushed his way out of the building, mouthing obscene oaths, furious at the scathing remarks and the ribald laughter that followed him.

'Damn Ralph Hanson an' the self righteous bastard that spawned 'im,' he spluttered, a battered face and deflated ego more than he could bear. Searching a befuddled mind for ways to get even, sure that Lottie Hanson carried his brat, an everlasting reminder of their brief acquaintance and he hoped the little perisher looked like him, that would settle the score with a vengeance.

The old bravado soon returned to bolster him up and chortling to himself he forged ahead through the ever thickening fog, heavy because of so many brightly burning fires that belched smoke through rows of chimneys. Lily Collins was out of the running, still sore at her desertion but there was always another wife to be found, willing to be bedded for the sheer hell of it, no strings attached. His body although aching was still alive with anticipation to be satisfied later that night with a bit of luck.

Totally immersed in such sensual thoughts, this over sexed lout disappeared into the darkness of a cold November night, home to tidy up and lick his wounds. As he so rightly claimed there was always another woman to satisfy his sexual needs, better to have kept to that sort than despoil the innocence of an eighteen year old lass, who had to live with the stigma of child bearing and unmarried in a village where she would never be allowed to forget, the bairn she carried the saddest part of the whole sorry tale and a constant reminder for the rest of her life.

* * *

Lottie was on tenterhooks well before eight o'clock the morning after her aunt's visit, very much on edge when a smart pony trap trundled into Lizzie Street and drew up at the front door at about ten minutes to nine, the driver full of apologies for being late. 'Aa stopped by Rawdon Station t'pick up a parcel fer'er Highness an' the train was overdue,' he said by way of explanation after a prolonged wolf whistle at Lottie's appearance, as smart as a carrot in her Sunday best, blushing furiously at this sound of appreciation.

The outfit, well pressed, was vastly different from the workaday skirt and jumper but not so warm, she missed the shawl that generally draped her slender shoulders, glad when she tried it on to find this other skirt roomy enough, a wee bit tight round the waist but still be able to conceal any give away signs. The matching jacket fitted quite nicely and flared at the bottom around her tummy and hips, an added advantage, the navy two piece was well worn but quite presentable. It was chilly without the shawl but pride had that stuffed away in the bundle which contained her few possessions, some things were left for Alice but it was doubtful if they would fit.

'Is this the lot?' a six foot giant with striking blue eyes inquired, an openly admiring expression on his rugged face. Not handsome in the strictest sense of the word but definitely good looking, with a nice friendly smile. 'She sayed not t'bring a load o'rubbish,' Lottie told him, basking in the admiration and didn't mind being whistled at by such a personable fellow. Not a laddie by any means but young enough, certainly that, a strange reaction for someone who had sworn off men for life, just a temporary lapse however.

'Sounds like'er,' which indicated this man had little regard for her aunt which endeared him all the more. 'Aa varnigh changed me mind, Aa thought y'weren'y comin,' she complained, her irritation all gone but no harm in confessing she had been rather miffed.

'Mebbe ye'll soon wish y'had,' handing her into the trap bundle and all. 'Shove this around ya,' a travelling rug held out towards her. 'Be off wi'ya, ye young varmints,' he ordered, shooing off several nosy children on their way to school. But a twinkle in those blue eyes suggested he was fond of bairns and the scolding didn't amount to much.

Curtains twitched in the downstairs window of Number Eight, probably more than one pair of eyes on the look out. She imagined heads close together after they left and tongues wagging for the rest of the day as they impatiently awaited Alice's return from work, smug in the sure knowledge that they wouldn't get a peep out of her loyal friend, too smart for them nowadays by far.

Alice had departed long before six o'clock. amid copious tears and a fond farewell. 'Aa'll miss ya,' she moaned, really upset, 'Ye'll not come back t'Saltersgate if y'can help it an' them fancy folk won't want me around there.' So very true, Lottie made no demur. 'Y'know Aa'll get t'see ya as soon as Aa can,' with no definite promise of where and when, her own eyes full of tears when they hugged for the last time. 'And thanks Alice.' She choked, 'T'Fred an'you fer taken me in, Aa'll never ferget.' One thing she could say in all sincerity. 'An' mind y'keep the place clean an'see that Fred gets his grub,' knowing even as she said it that Alice's fervent nod didn't mean a thing, life in the Ruddick household would soon return to the pre-Lottie period of utter confusion. Poor Fred.

Her travelling companion put her straight at ease. 'Me name is Jackson but Mattie t'me friends, so call me that.' She was gratified to be placed in this special category after such a brief acquaintance.

Mattie told her he hailed from Byker, near the far side of the big viaduct between it and Newcastle. Not that it meant much to someone who had never ventured outside a two mile radius of her native village. He 'lived in' in a flat above the stables and only went home on the odd occasion, the money he sent by post on a regular basis probably more important than the sight of him. 'Aa'm kept pretty busy one way or another,' he said, enough to make Lottie wonder what sort of establishment she was about to enter and if she would fit in, quite scary really.

Cud Matthews, long astir in the top field, stared unbelievingly as they trotted past, the look on his face a real treat. 'Nice mornin, Cud,' she shouted across, a saucy look on her bonny face, giving her Sunday bonnet a cheeky uplift for good measure. One in the eye for Jake Snowdon who would hear about this latest happening in no time at all, enormously chuffed that her escort was such a fine looking chap, hard to assess what age he actually was, but maybe in Ralph's group, she reckoned, her happiness evaporated somewhat at the thought of the rift between them, never like to be mended.

Jackson wondered at her swift change of mood but silently applauded the lass's spirit, well acquainted with the reputation of the rogue who seduced her and his connection with Cud Matthews, a right pair of miscreants. 'Better on this side than that,' he stated dryly, Saltersgate Mental Asylum wall to their left. A place which gave Lottie the creeps, even more frightening than Preston Workhouse, whose terrors had now faded somewhat. Memory began to loosen her tongue and she prattled on.

'The last time the buzzer went, warders were chasin' a young chap through the village in his linin's.' Blushing furiously at the mere mention of this item of male underwear. 'They got'im though.' A certain note of satisfaction in her voice.

'Aa reckon they did, at that. Where could'ee go. Mebbe just as far from that place as'ee could get.' He sighed in reflection. 'Aa once ran away t'sea but got no further than the Quayside afore Aa was fetched back. W'all feel like runnin' away at some time or other.' An undeniable fact.

'What's the Quayside like?' she asked, genuinely interested, somewhat taken aback by Jackson's sharp reply. 'No place fer a bonny young lass. Best bide where y'are, whatever,' he advised with a sympathetic look thus confirming knowledge of her condition, Aunt Jessica's tongue had obviously been busy since last night but just as well he knew the score, some of it at least.

'That's the way to Newcastle,' he informed her as they turned with the wall. 'The Town Moor's not far from here.' One fact she was aware of, reminded of Sunday after chapel walks to its nearest edge then back to Saltersgate via Branton Village, the perimeter of a narrow restricted world.

'New flats,' she was told as Mattie answered the unspoken question in her bright hazel eyes when they passed a dozen or more labourers well into a mornings work on a nearby building site. 'And a right rumpus there's been about them goin' up from folk over there!' pointing towards an avenue of three storied terraced houses, fine middle class homes. 'Lowerin' the tone o' the area, so they say. Bloody snobs!' he snorted and apologised for his language but sounded so irritated Lottie quickly changed the subject.

'He's a fine little chap,' she said in praise of the tiny pony who trotted along in sprightly fashion, his hot breath spiralling into the autumn air.

'He will be one o'these days when'ee learns who's boss an' stops pullin' at the reins,' came the dry retort, an underlying message on his words, a veiled warning perhaps that life in Rothwell House wouldn't be a bed of roses. Not that she expected such, Jessica Finlay had all the makings of a tyrant and off on the wrong foot to start with didn't help. She hadn't sufficient sense to keep her big mouth shut.

'D'ya like yer work?' she ventured to ask, in need of some sort of assurance, teasingly direct when he looked her in the eyes. 'Nowt wrong with it this mornin,' he acknowledged with a grin, no doubt as to his meaning, bonnier than ever in her confusion, he was delighted to see her blush but soon serious again.

'It's a fair enough livin'. Aa never did fancy the pits or shipyards and Aa'm not cut out t'be a farmer, feedin' animals just fer slaughter. A bit of a hypocrite when Aa tuck inta meat wi' the rest o'them but what other work is there? They tell me there's talk o' the men comin' out at Polrigg.'

Her beautiful eyes misted over. 'Me father was killed at the pit, the tubs ran off the line an' there was a fall o'stone,' Her voice flat, the memory still had the power to hurt, 'Poor lass,' he sympathised in silence. All that and more t'come, the situation in Rothwell House was rather fraught most of the time.

In the matter of minutes they entered a vastly different world, an area of elegant, detached mansions set among tall trees and trim lawns with no shortage of part time gardeners in the villages round about, keen to make an extra bob or two. Nothing here to offend the aesthetic eye and Lottie's less discerning eye was very much impressed by what they beheld. She was even more astounded when Jackson guided the lively pony through one of the wide gateways, fascinated by the grey stone pillars at either side, mounted by sculptured lions' heads, the name of the house carved into them, one word on each, an impressive sight.

Seconds later Jackson drew to a halt and handed her the reins. 'Aa' better shut the gates this time, afore that wife notices, sh'has eyes i' the back of 'er head,' he muttered, leaving her to gentle Tiger, anything less like a ferocious animal than the dapper little pony was hard to imagine. She was forced to wonder who 'she' or 'that wife' might be, not exactly fond descriptions.

But almost before she could say 'Jack Robinson' Mattie climbed aboard again and proceeded along the gravel drive, soon taking an offshoot to the servant's entrance, she had only the briefest glimpse of the front of the house. Her aunt came immediately upon the scene, impeccably attired in black from the neck downwards. 'Another old crow,' she decided, likening one aunt to another. Maude Elliott and Jessica Finlay cast from the same sort of mould, one more refined that the other she had to admit if begrudgingly, not inclined to say anything complimentary about either.

'Here w'are, lass,' Jackson said cheerfully as they pulled to a stop and jumped down to steady Tiger then lifted her to the ground in strong arms. 'Ye bide there an' Aa'll fetch yer bundle.' A kindly gesture which found no favour with Jessica Finlay.

'Charlotte can manage herself,' she snapped, 'Her sort aren't accustomed to being waited upon. You must have other work to do. Enough of the morning wasted already.' Dismissed with an imperious flick of the wrist, Jackson, poker faced, watched Lottie struggle to unload her bundle, too much of a stretch and an awkward performance.

'Unfeelin' old bitch,' he grunted, leading Tiger off to be unharnessed and rubbed down. 'That face would turn milk sour. What a welcome, God help'er,' snorting in disgust but careful not to be seen or heard. This canny young lass was already taken to his heart, a heart as big as the size of him.

‘Like a blessed prison warder,’ Lottie chuntered silently, rather intimidated by a big bunch of keys dangling from the beaded belt around her aunt’s trim waist. An air of refinement which her own mother must have had at one time was still there to some degree after years in a rougher environment, any change due to a keen desire not to be different from friends and neighbours. Like her sister-in-law in a way, who would have to learn, but she banished the thought, much too disturbing to allow such ideas to enter her head.

‘No time to dawdle,’ she was told and followed obediently as Jessica preceded her first into the lower regions of the house, hampered by the weight of her bundle, more awkward than actually heavy, dragging it behind her, a woeful little figure.

Jackson watched as they entered Rothwell House and repeated aloud what he muttered earlier, Tiger’s long ears pricking at the harsh tone of voice. ‘God help’er,’ he grieved, long enough in the service of this particular family to know what a hard task mistress the older woman could be. And the other one, that pampered creature who seldom frequented the downstairs area would surely take strong dislike to a lass whose natural beauty could not be denied, nor lessened by the wearing of shabby if tidy clothes. God help her indeed, Jackson sadly aware of his own inability to stand up against this formidable duo if they elected to show their true colours which wasn’t unlikely.

Seventy-five stairs later, each one counted, the last flight carpetless, linoleum covered instead, Lottie found herself in a tiny attic bedroom, its only light through a small window in the ceiling above her head, sloping of course, the roof of the house. The little she managed to glimpse of other parts, on her way up, spelt luxury in the fullest sense of the word, money certainly talked in this establishment.

A host of instructions flew from Jessica Finlay’s lips, almost in staccato. ‘Use the back stairs always, unless on duty in the rest of the house. Those are your uniforms.’ Pointing towards the trundle bed where several washed out garments lay across a multi-coloured patch work quilt. ‘And do be sparing with the candles, one will be allocated each week, get quickly into bed and don’t waste it, they do cost money.’ ‘Aye,’ Lottie thought, ‘all the way to a ha’penny apiece.’ Hard to stifle the giggle that rose to her lips and she mentally divided a candle into seven equal parts, each night expected to be a race against time, speculating how long the thing would take to burn itself out.

She envied her aunt’s stamina, so many stairs and no sign of exertion and herself gasping like a broken winded cuddy. The rasping tongue still rapped out orders and scarcely stopped to take a breath. ‘Change into the blue twill,’ she was told, ‘The last girl was about your size. The black dress and white aprons are for best, keep them in good condition, the little cap goes with them, wear the mop cap with the ordinary things. Come downstairs when you are ready, half the morning is over already and dozens of jobs are waiting to be done. Don’t dilly.’ Not an inviting prospect, straight into action and only just arrived.

An agitated mind wanted to shriek at her aunt to take her hook, sick twice that morning before she got here, whether from nerves or pregnancy impossible to tell, probably a bit of both. Her head buzzed alarmingly as Jessica Finlay still rabbited on in full flow. 'One thing you must remember, Charlotte,' she said at last with her hand raised to the iron door latch, there was no lock, anyone able to mooch around at will, no place to hide any personal bits and pieces. She waited to hear what was so important to remember and couldn't help feeling a chill as the words stuck in her ears. 'If you wish life to be pleasant in Rothwell House you must learn to obey without question, no slackness,' her aunt said and added sternly. 'There is no need to coddle yourself, birth is a natural process,' departing to the sound of rustling petticoats and jangling keys soon to be listened for continually and never discounted.

When the door finally closed behind her, Lottie flopped onto the bed and heard springs give under her weight, not certain whether to laugh or cry, with dozens of unanswered questions in a bewildered mind. No mention of wages, she was probably expected to work for a roof over her head and food in her belly. God knows she badly needed both with a bairn on the way. Were there other servants apart from Mattie Jackson and Aunt Jessica? But that is what the old stickler was in self glorified capacity, quite something in her own opinion. And when would she meet her new mistress? An alarming prospect which she wanted over and done with as soon as possible.

She shrugged these thoughts aside, likely to be answered soon enough, testing sagging springs by bouncing up and down with joint pressure of hands and buttocks. A lumpy mattress as expected but a tired body would soon find its own hollow, suddenly she was overwhelmed with nostalgia for her bed in Twenty Four Maria Street, even Alice Ruddick's a king pin compared to this, which actually spoke volumes.

A closer inspection of the room showed it was adequately furnished, no wardrobe just three hooks behind the door, a wash hand stand with the usual ewer and bowl, and a three drawer chest. The cane bottomed chair at the bedside had seen better days but there would be little time for sitting if Aunt Jessica ran true to form. Standard equipment for a servant's bedroom, no luxury in this part of the house, just bare essentials. Another essential was discovered when the back of one foot made contact with an enamel chamber pot, a clanging sound. Even Alice Ruddick's was china, albeit chipped in many places, what a laugh.

She struggled into one of the blue uniforms, chill damp air soon found warm flesh when she removed her outer clothing and folded it neatly away. The uniform was an ill fitting garment, intended for a much larger person, but a quick glance in a mirror confirmed that a swelling body would soon fill it out with a few tucks in the bodice. She pulled a long face at the thought of it, once so proud of her shapely young figure.

This traumatic day had more or less just begun and others like it had taken their toll, she was absolutely drained both mentally and physically, the entire situation assessed with great misgivings. One thing to be thankful for, a blessing indeed, there would be no sharing every hour both day and night with someone else. This tiny room would be a bolt hole at the end of each day if the going got rough, a strange unreal world far removed from Jake Snowdon and any further harassment he might have in mind, out of bounds for anyone of his description. He would be soon shown the door if ever he dared show his face, which was most unlikely.

A chill of apprehension chose that very moment to invade her body, nothing to do with the coldness of the room. Instinct warned her not to linger but she felt strangely reluctant to leave its sanctuary for whatever awaited downstairs, a grim faced aunt for certain and wondered if Jessica Finlay knew how to smile.

Courage came to her rescue, as usual, that straightening of a young back and enormous effort made to raise drooping spirits as she made her way to the kitchen area with no idea of just how difficult life would be in this upper class household, the reality beyond imagination. Her undoubtable mettle was guaranteed to be severely tested in the months ahead and the Hanson temper strained to the limit, a sense of control to be achieved painfully and little by little.

* * *

It was well into the afternoon before Lottie was summoned to 'the presence', a first sight of the woman whose whims and demands were to control her entire existence from then on. But the true situation in Rothwell House had been revealed to her hours earlier by Martha Connelly, a diminutive daily with a hunched back and a grudge against the world. A world which contained not only Jessica Finlay but the person who really ruled the roost, Felicity Cranshawe, mistress of the whole domain.

Martha travelled from South Branton each morning and toiled until late afternoon at a multitude of tasks, the last of them to prepare the evening meal before she departed for the home she shared with her mother, a senile old lady, left to God and good neighbours while her crippled daughter earned a meagre living for both of them.

Jessica Finlay wasn't full of the milk of human kindness, not the sort to give Martha leftovers to take home. There was plenty of such but she preferred to have food items collected by a local farmer for dog food or pig swill. Pork, sausages and other farm produce were provided in lieu. There were no fleas on Lottie's aunt, who managed to line her own pocket in a roundabout way, being in charge of the household purse in a residence where nothing was spared.

The two servants were quickly introduced when Lottie made her appearance and soon settled down to the many chores waiting to be done, gossip a main part of the exercise. Martha's opinion of her superiors was divulged without reservation, of Felicity Cranshawe she spoke most disparagingly. 'The Missis might look like an angel wi' that pink an' white complexion an' golden hair but she's a black hearted devil under all'er finery and as tricky as they come. Canna bear t'be anywhere near me 'cause Aa'm like this,' meaning her disability. Not content to let it rest there she carried on to down Lottie's aunt, very outspoken.

'Believe me, hinny, there's nowt t'pick atween them. Jessica's a regular slave driver, gets'er pound o'flesh and more. Pardon me fer sayin, so, seein' that she's kin.'

Lottie snorted in derision. 'Say what y'like, Aa've got no room fer'er. Y'get t'choose yer friends but relations just come wi'the package.' All the incentive Martha needed to carry on, first making sure the tyrant wasn't within earshot. Jessica just dished out a host of orders and left, her presence obviously required upstairs.

'Nobody i' their right mind would claim relationship wi' that sour faced bitch, if they could help it. An' don't be taken in cause sh'employs a cripple and a lass wi'a bairn on the way. We come cheap, your sort an'mine, no other choice. But there's method in'er madness, a canny few have come an' gone i' my time, couldn't stand Madam's tantrums.'

But Lottie, although in full agreement about her aunt, decided to withhold judgement on the mistress of the house. Warped in body, warped in mind maybe. She had made too many hasty conclusions of late and look where they got her.

Martha began to talk about Madam's absent husband. 'Just one year wed when the poor fella decides t'bide i'the army. Her old man would o'bought 'im out t'please'er. In afore the war an' didn't show face till a few months ago. Cold bitch, Aa reckon, but'ee fettled'er on his last leave. Cried'er eyes out when sh'knew about the babby an'drank'er way through bottles o' gin. I'm fed up wi'boilin' water fer hot baths. Once bairns get there they take some shiftin'.'

The look on Lottie's face said it all, 'Yer aunt didn't tell ya Her Highness was in the family way, Aa guess?'

'Y'guess right. The crafty old so an' so,' she wondered why all the secrecy.

'She's crafty all right, close mouthed when it's anythin t'do wi' the Missis. Mebbe sh'reckoned y'wouldn't come if y'knew there was gonna be two babbies i'the house.'

'Well w'both know if one has t'be neglected, which one it'll be.' No illusions on that score. 'What's HE like?' her curiosity aroused and Martha didn't have to ask who she meant.

'Upper crust but no title, that was a sore point, his father was a younger son. Madam would o' liked bein' called Lady Somethin' or Other. The master's all right, a proper gent, but Aa think his goose is cooked, wi'her ettlin' t'play the martyr when the babby comes, aided an' abetted by that aunt o'yours.' And encouraged by the sight of Lottie's eyes widened in amazement, carried on to fill her ears with even more knowledge, a captive audience.

Geoffrey Cranshawe began to emerge as a person, obviously unworthy of mention by Jessica Finlay, whom she figured as a man hater in any case. The nerve of a wizened old spinster to say birth was a natural process! What did she know about it, doubtful if any man ever looked at her twice. A lackey, that's all she was, her mistress's devoted slave.

'If Aa was him,' Martha told her, 'Aa'd get meself posted t'the back o'beyond and even that's not far enough away wi' the wife he's landed wi', poor beggar. Just about twenty when they were wed.'

Lottie chortled in amusement. Life would never be dull with Martha around, her liking for the little woman increased by the minute, so outrageous at times she couldn't believe it, her tongue in full throttle.

'There'll be no more babbies after this one,' she declared. 'Madam has no likin' fer that side o' married life, he'll have t'seek consolation in somebody else's bed,' and sounded so matter of fact, Lottie's Methodist morality rose in swift protest.

'Ee Martha, y'shouldn't talk like that,' feeling obliged to deliver some sort of reprimand, a timid rebuke which made no real impression.

'Why shouldn't Aa? That's what getting' wed is for. Ye ask Father Simmons.' Steeped in the infallibility of Catholic dogma.

'If Aa want t'ask anybody, it'll not be a blinkin' Catholic priest,' Lottie rapped out in reply, rather perturbed to discover Martha was in the opposite camp. The prejudice of generations about to raise its ugly head to destroy any hope of friendship between the two of them, and looked like succeeding until Martha's bird like face crinkled in amusement.

'Well that settles one thing, aa reckon. Aa'm Catholic an'you're Protestant an'there's no fear o'either of us changin'fer the other,' came the dry retort and Lottie's teeth showed up white and gleaming in her bright young face, their separate creeds disposed of as a bone of contention right from the start, the initial danger averted without disaster.

A couple of hours later when a lunch of cold ham, pease pudding and pickles was over and cleared away, Lottie skipped upstairs after Jessica Finlay, absolutely overawed by the sheer opulence of her surroundings, even more so by the elegant beauty of the young lady who was stretched out on a Regency style sofa, alongside a blazing coal fire, her pregnancy very obvious despite the cut of a gorgeous blue velvet creation specially designed to hide the fact, apparently without success.

'This is Charlotte, Madam,' Jessica announced and pressed her niece forward when long tapered fingers beckoned, ill humour displayed in a pair of cold blue eyes, enough to make the young servant squirm uneasily, Mattie Jackson's prediction was about to prove correct.

'What's the matter with'er?' she fretted, 'Aa haven't had a chance t'open me mouth and she's lookin'daggers at me,' impossible to her to understand the complexities of a shallow mind. Hers was beauty unadorned, natural, no expensive artifice needed to improve upon it, no velvet or lace to enhance what nature so generously endowed. In a mere servant at that, it was impossible for a vain, envious mind to accept with any sort of grace.

From these first moments their relationship was doomed, with years of unhappiness to follow. With no inkling of the malice the sight of her had unwittingly provoked, Lottie bobbed a tiny curtsy in accordance with instructions given on the way upstairs, greatly in awe of this fine lady.

'Charlotte!' Felicity scorned. 'Rather a grand name for such an unimportant little person,' Words deliberately chosen to inflict hurt and humiliation, intended to reduce the defenceless girl to nothing from the onset.

'It's the name Aa was given, Ma'am,' Lottie faltered, unconscious of a note of censure in her quiet tone, such treatment quite beyond comprehension.

Jessica hastened to retrieve a situation which threatened to get out of hand. 'If you think it is too fancy, Madam, she will be quite willing to change it,' and steely eyes dared her niece to contradict, Lottie was given no time to answer, Felicity Cranshawe's empty laughter already echoed around the overheated room.

'It is of no importance, I may decide to call her Hanson. How would that suit you, my girl?' Sensing a rebellious spirit and thought it might be amusing to discover how much she would suffer in silence.

'Anything you say, Madam,' her aunt's fawning manner enough to make Lottie cringe in her well worn shoes.

'Let the girl answer for herself,' Felicity snapped 'She does have a tongue in her stupid head, I suppose,' ready to pounce if the young servant stepped out of line.

Lottie bristled. What warped sense of satisfaction was there to be gained from such behaviour? But two could play her little game. 'Charlotte or Hanson, which ever suits ya, Ma'am,' she answered rather too meekly but kept an impassive face throughout, determined to give no cause for complaint, the damage already done.

Thus thwarted, Felicity started to whine. 'My back aches Finlay, you must rub it for me,' Jessica immediately at her side. 'Back to the kitchen, girl,' she ordered and fussed around her peevish employer as if her niece no longer existed.

From the safe distance of the first floor landing, Lottie muttered scornfully. 'A proper hot house plant that's what she is,' halting to take a deep gulp of air into tight lungs. Her light footsteps soon skimmed the rich Wilton carpet, no sound on its thick pile. She was convinced now that Martha Connelly was spot on in her assessment of this fine lady's character and ready to admit it. To this end and to get the whole sorry tale off her chest she stormed into the kitchen, hoping to find sympathetic ears.

* * *

Two pairs of eyes lifted in surprise when Lottie burst into the kitchen, still in high dudgeon, Martha and Mattie Jackson hobnobbing over a pot of tea, free to indulge with the housekeeper safely ensconced in the upper part of the house. A bucket of water and scrubbing brush lay idle on the floor, ready to be rushed into use when the dragon announced her imminent arrival upon the scene. Lottie's lighter footsteps were unlikely to be mistaken for those of her aunt and always the sound of those jingling keys to send out an early warning message.

'All right fer some,' the angry lass snapped, rather piqued to find them so comfortable and apparently unconcerned, a feeling which soon erupted into a spate of condemnation directed elsewhere. 'Y'were right, Martha, she is a bitch, soon showed'er claws sh'did. As fer that aunt o'mine she's nowt but a blinkin' lap dog.' Impervious to the amused expressions on the faces of her listeners, who had heard similar outbursts from other servants before they stormed out of the house, none inclined to stay under Jessica Finlay's harsh regime and Madam's unpredictable ways. The prettier they were the more threat she seemed to see in them, ridiculous really for someone with so much of everything to feel so insecure.

'D'ya know what sh'called me? An unimportant little person, that's what sh'sayed.' A fair imitation of Felicity's affected drawl. Mattie Jackson burst out laughing only to have her wrath turned on him instead. 'It's nowt t'laugh at. Just 'cause they're rollin' in money, they think th'can say what th'like,' she hotly reproved, those big luminous eyes fiercely alight.

'An' so they can,' came the dry remark. 'Simmer down. No sense getting' in a stew over somethin' y'canna make better of. Our sort have no rights, an'the sooner y'get that inta yer head the easier it'll be. Take a few lessons from Tiger,' he advised, the little pony nearly broken in. He downed his tea in one long gulp, a placid attitude which irritated Lottie even more, ready to retaliate when Martha chipped in to say her piece.

'Just a few hours i'the place an' yer up in arms already. Jackson's right, y'just have t'swallow it an'blow off steam when they're out o'the way. But judgin' by that red hair o'yours it'll take some doin'.' Thrusting an empty cup towards her. 'Pour yerself a cup o'tea. Go on —' she urged as Lottie hesitated. 'The old dragon's supposed t'do most o'the cooking since Milly Rutter left but ferby stirrin' a pot or two and findin' fault the rest is left t'me. Roast beef an' Yorkshire pudding the night. Aa pop the Yorkshire in afore Aa leave an'she dishes up. The pots shoved i' the scullery sink fer me i'the mornin'. That'll be one of your jobs from now on.' Rather pleased at the thought but not yet finished. 'Aa betcha she's upstairs rubbin'er ladyship's back. Spends most of'er time doin'that these days. Anybody would think sh'was the first wife t'have a bairn.'

'Aa wish somebody would rub my back,' Lottie moaned and eased her weary body into a chair, the changes in it unbelievable. 'Aa'm fair gaspin',' she admitted and reached for the teapot, thinking the while that roast beef and Yorkshire pudding would make a meal fit for a king. At least she would be well fed, good for her and the bairn she was carrying.

'Here lass, Aa'll rub yer back,' Jackson offered and ignored the lift to

Martha's thin eyebrows, who watched with undisguised interest as he began to massage Lottie's neck and shoulders, calloused hands amazingly gentle, which brought a deep sigh of contentment. The kitchen warm and cosy, an open fire at one end and hugs black stove at the other. No wet clothes here to emit that peculiar stench or a tin bath hogging the fireside area at awkward times.

Mattie's fingers soothed her into reflection, able to review the situation in which she found herself more calmly, rather worried about the bad beginning with her mistress, her treatment considered most unfair, and that fiery temper not in play until she left the room. Saddened by all she must bear for the sake of an unborn child.

Mattie's kindly ministrations came to a sudden halt, the big man enjoying this close contact far too much for comfort, he was a normal chap who usually avoided any sort of relationship with women. 'D'ya know who Mrs High an'Mighty is?' he asked to break the spell and brought Lottie swiftly back to earth.

'Aa haven't the foggiest,' was the answer, wondering at the significance of such a question. What did it matter to her?

'John Starrett, coal owner and gentleman farmer, he's her old man. Owns Belford and Studley as well as Polrigg, and most o'the land round about them. This is a moneyed house.' Amazed at the look of horror on a flushed face, her beautiful eyes widely dilated.

'Don't mention that penny pinchin' blackguard t'me,' she spat out furiously, 'No wonder she's the way sh'is with him fer a father. Me mother never got a penny piece when me father was killed at the pit. We'd of been out o'the house like a shot if Ralph an' me Uncle Billy hadn't been workin' there,' she blazed, hardly stopping for breath. 'Aa was expectin' me notice any day, by that time me Uncle had gone t'live with an aunt in South Shields, getting'too old fer the pit.' Truly incensed by this unwelcome bit of news. 'If anybody had mentioned it afore wild horses wouldn't of dragged me here. Aa wonder what else that old schemer's got up'er sleeve. Billy isn't me uncle really, Aa just call'im that,' the last bit added as an afterthought, as if it needed explanation.

Martha tutted sympathy, disturbed by the obvious strength of Lottie's feelings. 'Nowt Aa hope,' she said consolingly, 'But y'are here an'just have t'make the best of it. That's right, isn't it Mattie?' And turned to Jackson for support who sincerely wished he had kept his mouth shut, having unwittingly stirred up a hornets nest. But he decided to get the whole lot out of the way once and for all, no more unpleasant surprises.

'The old man coughed up fer this lot an' pays fer the upkeep. The house in London belongs t'the Cranshawes, in their family fer years. Left to His Nibs by his late father. But his uncle got the title, passed on t'his son.'

Two houses for one family immediately aroused Lottie's interest despite her disgruntlement and she listed carefully as Jackson carried on. 'D''ya fancy a trip t'the Capital,' he ventured to ask, 'Thet's where she'll be off to, come the turn' o the year.'

'Mebbe not this year,' Martha prompted but Jackson merely grunted and carried on.

'Her style might be a bit cramped but it's there the partyin' is an that's right up'er street. It'll take more than a bairn six months on the way t'stop'er. She has t'spend Christmas at Whitegates t'keep her father sweet. That's his country place near Stamform'am. Just wait till y'set eyes on that house.'

'That's three blessed houses,' Lottie shot out. 'And it's the men at his pits that provide the whole caboodle, slavin' their guts out.' Distressed enough without Jackson's mention of Christmas, the first without her mother. Not that she wished her mother in the middle of the mess she had created for herself.

'We bide here over Christmas, burst pipes an'all,' Mattie said, painting the whole picture. The more she knew the better she would handle it or so he hoped. Lottie was still somewhat of an unknown quantity, a red hot temper and moody with it at times. 'Last year Aa walked t'Byker through Jesmond Dene. Fed up wi'Jessica's moans and groans at bein' left behind. Like cuttin' an arm or leg off when she's separated from her upstairs. The folk at Whitegates canna stand the old besom and them other lasses had gone by then, so that meant only her an'me. Martha got packed off home when the chores were done.'

Questions hovered on Lottie's lips, especially about the departed servants. The cook's name rang no bell, probably from some other part outside the Saltersgate area, the same as Mattie Jackson. Why had he stayed so long? Maybe it was different for a man and he did have his bolt hole above the stables. Perhaps the gaffer was more his boss than Madam.

Only a few hours since nine o'clock that morning and it seemed a lifetime away, her next question was directed at Martha who had gone very quiet and seemed rather put out, the undercurrents in this house were coming to the surface thick and fast. 'Will you be here on Christmas Day?' she asked, surprised at the bitterness in Martha's voice when she answered.

'Aye, in the mornin' till the work's done, then Aa'm sent home. She could nicely have me mother here, Jackson would fetch'er i' the pony trap. Last year was a misery from beginnin' t'end. The gaffer's Christmas Box helped but not enough. Hardly any coal fer a fire an'not even a few bits an'pieces t'take home. Full an'plenty i' this house, Aa made it all, but sh'damn well made sure Aa didn't help meself t'anythin.' The decided impression given was she would have done so given the opportunity.

Lottie clucked in sympathy but had no chance to say anything before the sound of a door closing in the upper regions of the house sounded the alarm, Jessica on the warpath. The table was cleared in a jiffy and pots rushed into the scullery. 'Pray sh'doesn't see them,' Martha hissed. 'Get a brush i'yer hand an' start scrubbin'.' Mattie Jackson was already on his way to the stables.

The dreaded ogre soon made an appearance, her beady eyes everywhere at once and straight way in her niece's direction, the atmosphere thick with a tension neither of them understood, Madam was probably in one of her difficult moods but she had not long to wait for enlightenment. 'Stand up girl,' she barked and stood there grim faced as Lottie struggled to obey. Wet hands rubbed down her white apron, still dressed as her aunt considered suitable for the visit upstairs. Without warning a vengeful hand whipped across Lottie's face, forceful enough to knock the astonished lass off balance.

'You will learn to keep a civil tongue in your head. Do I make myself clear?' came the stern command sharp eyes ablaze, completely out of control.

Nothing was clear but her niece did manage to mumble in the affirmative, absolutely stunned by this latest development. 'Mrs Cranshawe is your benefactor and you will treat her as such. Some girls in your position end up in the Workhouse.' She obviously relished the sound of this reference on her tongue.

Martha no longer feigned work but sat back on her heels and pulled a comical face. Lottie found it hard to stifle a giggle and tried to keep a tight rein on her temper, not far from hysterics with a face so savagely treated and limbs atremble.

'Now hurry up with this floor and you, girl, change into a hessian apron. The one you are wearing will need to be rubbed through. Stop feeling sorry for yourself, just think of Madam who bears up so well in her delicate condition.' Her parting shot as she stalked out of the room, its two remaining occupants absolutely flabbergasted at the extent of her rage, the venom lashed out towards her defenceless niece.

Lottie stood there struggling for composure, impossible now to stem the volume of tears with two members of her family who felt justified in the use of physical abuse. She was forced to admit Ralph did receive some provocation but this present act of aggression for some unknown fault had no excuse, unforgivable absolutely unforgivable.

Martha, speechless for a change, deemed it useless to urge the lass to rebellion, it would serve no purpose. Now with the floodgates fully open a young treble voice echoed through the room, vehement in anger, word after word in quick succession. 'If that old biddy lifts a finger t'me again, Aa'll bounce'er right across that floor, old wife or not. She had no right, no right at all,' and ran to Martha for comfort, down on her knees, the tiny woman clutched around the waist, now standing up.

'There now,' a soothing voice coaxed. That hard shell Martha cultivated in self defence no longer apparent as work worn hands stroked Lottie's bright head of hair in such unbelievable tenderness. 'Have a good cry, hinny. It'll mend nowt but ye'll feel better fer it.' Greatly relieved when the girl's taut body relaxed and the tears ran in much softer fashion. 'Ye'll need all yer spirit t'bide i' this house wi' them two blossoms. A stony road y'have t'travel.' Nothing but truth. Martha knew Lottie would pay for her mistake, there was no pity for misfits like herself or those who broke the rules of recognised behaviour as she had done.

'Let me get a flannel t'that face,' she said brusquely, 'Ye'll be a rare sight the morra if Aa don't put somethin' on it pretty sharp. No need t'let them crow, just make as if nowt happened,' she said as Lottie hesitated. 'W'can do with a bit o'bonny young life around here and ye've got Mattie an'me t'give ya a helpin' hand.' A wide grin accompanied her following words, grey eyes twinkling. 'There's some vinegar i' that cupboard over there, the bottom shelf. 'That'll take the swellin' down. Better on fish an'chips Aa'll grant ya but that face o'yours has more need of it. Go on, fetch it.'

Heartened by Martha's concern, Lottie did as ordered, the little daily immensely touched to see slim young shoulders lift in firm resolution. 'Ye'll be fine after this. Mebbe it'll sting a bit.' And carefully dabbed the ugly weals caused by vicious fingers, hiding her own feelings in a burst of irritation. 'Stand still or ye'll get poked i' the eye wi' this flannel.'

Before she left for the day, Martha made it her business to acquaint Mattie Jackson with all that happened, eloquent in praise of Lottie's resilience. 'That lass's got guts,' she said admiringly. 'After what that wife did to'er, sharp pulled 'erself together.' Reminded of young shoulders lifted in adversity.

'Aye, an' w'both know she'll need all'er guts an' mebbe not s'easy when'er time gets nearer,' Jackson added, surprised at the strength of his own feelings, greatly concerned about someone so recently met, taken aback that Martha seemed to share them, she was never known to take to anyone so quickly as this.

Just as well the future remains a closed book, its pages turned one by one, the hope alive in every heart that sufficient to the day would be the grace thereof. Nobody was more in need of grace than this eighteen year old girl, chosen by fate as one of its hapless victims, paying the price for her father's unfortunate encounter with Jake Snowdon all those years ago. In trying to spare another lass the filth of a lewd tongue he had subjected his own daughter to something even more destructive with dire consequences.

* * *

In the weeks following Lottie's introduction to Rothwell House and its inhabitants, Martha Connelly and Mattie Jackson soon became all that stood between this newly found friend and utter despair. Jessica Finlay seemed to be engaged in some senseless vendetta and never missed a single opportunity to take her niece to task, however trivial the offence. 'Nit pickin' and sheer bloody mindedness,' according to Martha, amazed at the enormous restraint applied by such a naturally rebellious nature. Always practical, the little daily's remedy was simple. 'Pour yerself a cup o'tea,' she would say, gallons of her magic brew downed as they entered the pre-Christmas period and the situation developed into something even worse.

'Don't let the old bitch get t'ya,' Jackson continually encouraged, worried sick at the way she appeared to be wilting before their very eyes, hard pushed to determine which of the two women was the greatest offender. Jessica's constant harping on her niece's slipshod methods, absolutely impervious to the wounded look on Lottie's face when she laid the blame at

Bessie Hanson's door, or Madam, forever making derogatory remarks about the young servant's lowly background, secure in the knowledge that to answer back wasn't an option if Lottie wished to keep her job, blackmail of the worst kind and clear indication of this fancy young woman's shallow mind.

Jessica usually got the brunt of Martha's spleen. 'Sh'must think we're a couple o'pack horses,' she groused, whenever Jessica pushed and prodded unreasonably, but she was never brave enough to take the housekeeper on. The work load imposed upon them was often too much for two pairs of hands, although Lottie's addition to the household staff did make a difference, prepared to stick in and do more than her share, despite the obvious impediment of the changes in her pregnant young body.

Mattie Jackson, a veritable tower of strength, made sure coal was brought in, most of it carried indoors when Jessica was incarcerated with her employer. There were numerous fires around the big house, fuel no problem to a colliery owner's daughter, this help was much appreciated by a crippled woman and a young lass almost six months into her time. The treatment of Felicity and herself was vastly different, coddling not in the reckoning where Lottie was concerned, never supposed to tire.

Shopping expeditions occupied a great deal of this good fellow's day. He stood by the carriage in the vicinity of various emporiums for hours on end, while Felicity spent her devoted father's money with careless abandon. No expense was spared on presents for friends and relatives, her servants never even considered. They were left to John Starrett's generosity when the festive season arrived to use largesse in gratitude for another year of faithful service, something his selfish daughter didn't deem at all necessary.

As the dark month of December moved on, the household chores mounted considerably, Jessica was no help at all except in doling out orders and regular inspections. Most of her time was occupied with her peevish mistress whose claims for attention were ridiculously demanding. To such a spoilt young madam carrying a child was a confounded nuisance, an upset in her lifestyle she strongly resented. She had not a maternal bone in her pampered body, cosseted every inch of the road towards motherhood by a woman who almost grovelled at her dainty feet.

One afternoon, Jackson entered the upstairs sanctum to receive orders for the following morning, a trip to Whitegates decided upon to fetch holly and fir trees for Christmas decoration, there being an abundance of both in the grounds of John Starrett's country home. 'Take the large carriage,' Felicity told him, 'If the forecasts are to be believed the roads may be blocked at any time. Set off early and don't dawdle, you should be back before nightfall. And do be careful with the new upholstery,' she added sharply, 'Take some old covers. I don't want pine needles sticking all over it.' All this and more until Jackson was ruffled out of his usual calm.

'Aa've had a bellyful o'that wife,' he muttered sullenly on returning to the kitchen. Madam's whining voice still echoed in his ears. 'One o'these days

Aa'll be askin'er if sh'thinks it's a bit laddie she's talkin' to.' Terribly rattled by Felicity's deprecating manner.

'Just blowin' off steam,' Martha whispered sotto voce, Lottie was secretly relieved not to be on the receiving end of that sarcastic tongue. She was in a mind to acknowledge for once at least, that ruffled feathers were far less important than being well fed and in her position the very necessary security of a roof above her head.

Felicity Cranshawe said nothing about taking a passenger along with him and, had she known, would have definitely denied Lottie the pleasure but the next morning there she was perched beside Jackson in the greyness of a cold winter's day, revelling in a glorious sense of freedom, ashamed to remember the cold water she threw on the idea when first it was mooted.

'Ye're out of yer mind,' she had derided, very low in spirits when Jackson suggested it, 'Y'know fine what me aunt's like,' was her doleful comment. 'She's sure t'put the dampner on anythin' o'the sort where Aa'm concerned. And there's always her up them stairs.'

Jackson lost patience with such a negative attitude. 'That's right, look on the black side. Leave Jessica t'me. If Aa can fix her the Missis'll be no problem.' Blue eyes twinkled as he went on to say. 'But if yer not keen on the idea –' and left it at that, hoping for some fiery denial of such a possibility.

'Not keen' Lottie choked in response, absolutely devoid of any feeling except bitterness. 'Aa'd run all the way there an' back t'get away from them two fer a bit. They're killin'me by inches.' Her fingers spread across a protruding body in significant gesture. 'This is all that's keepin' me here,' Jackson was all the more determined to succeed by fair means or foul.

The rest of that day dragged out interminably, Lottie was totally pessimistic and took no heed of Jackson's assurances that everything would work out fine. Felicity had taken herself off mid afternoon on a round of social visits. Jackson was let off the hook when she was invited to stay for dinner at one place of call and welcomed the proposal that the family coachman would bring her home. Martha was long gone when she at last returned early in excellent humour, a mood which transferred itself to her devoted housekeeper and opened the door for negotiations on Lottie's behalf when the slightly tipsy mistress of Rothwell House was put to bed.

'Beggin' yer pardon, Ma'am,' he began, having an opportune moment, just the right amount of respect in that Geordie intonated voice. 'Mebbe y'haven't noticed, bein's'busy all the time,' Jessica's attention immediately aroused. 'Yes, Yes,' she tutted, her thin eyebrows raised in enquiry always short on patience. 'If you have something to say get on with it man,' and expected him to continue without delay.

But Mattie Jackson had no intention of being rushed into making a wrong move and approached the subject very carefully indeed, well aware Jessica Finlay was nobody's fool. 'Aa reckon we'll be havin' that lass i'bed afore'er time,' he mentioned casually with a nod in Lottie's direction, seated at the other end of the room hanging on every word. Her heart pounded at an alarming rate, looking exactly as she felt, a washed out rag. 'Aa know yer ettlin on'er workin' till she's varnigh due. Aa hope nowt untoward happens.' Jessica's speculating glance a great incentive to carry on.

Lottie held her breath, astounded at such tactics and also noticed that her aunt seemed to be weighing the situation very carefully, a significant 'Oh?' as the words sank in. 'She is lookin' a bit peeky,' he pointed out becoming more confident by the minute. 'The only fresh air she gets is after dark, a turn round the garden, and the night air's no good t'anybody in her condition.'

'So?' Jessica snapped, obliged to concede the girl did appear a bit under the weather and considered the inconvenience of an early confinement. She had expected her niece to work almost to the last minute and be straight into harness again after the shortest lying in period possible, with someone so young there should be no problem.

Jackson recognised signs of irritation and immediately got to the point, no sense in dragging it out. 'Aa'm off t'Whitegates come mornin''. How about me takin'er along fer the ride? No fresher air than that, Aa reckon. It might help'er t'go the full stretch.'

Lottie almost gasped at his audacity still convinced of an unfavourable reaction. 'All very well,' the housekeeper said, 'But who will do her day's work?' Exactly what he expected to hear and was fully prepared knowing how Jessica's calculating mind worked.

'The work's no problem,' he stated with confidence, encouraged by the sweet smell of success. 'Three of us t'get stuck in afore w'go an' we'll be back afore dark. Madam's off fer the day t'the Wisharts.' Another fact ascertained and guaranteed to weigh the balance in his favour. No peevish mistress to contend with, somewhat of a blessing although Jessica would be the last to admit.

'All right,' came the reluctant concession, after the briefest of pauses. 'Charlotte may accompany you but don't make a meal of it. Neither of you is employed for jaunts into the countryside.' Typical of the woman but Jackson had won and gloated inwardly, careful not to show it.

'Remember now,' she ordered. 'Do what is required of you and don't linger. They will give you lunch, the horses need to be fed and rested a while but not too long. When do you intend to set off?'

'Nine or thereabouts Ma'am, three hours should be long enough t'get through the main chores, nowt'll be neglected.' Giving the impression of a man dedicated to his work, Jessica nodding approval.

'See that you wrap up well,' she told Lottie whose beautiful eyes were aglow lighting up her whole countenance, so like her mother as a girl that Jessica softened for a moment but was soon back into character. 'It would be most inconvenient if you end up coughing and sneezing all over the house.'

More than satisfied with his artful manipulation Jackson turned to Lottie tongue in check. 'Say thanks t'yer aunt fer'er kindness,' he prompted and winked behind the housekeeper's back. The woman preened under this blatant cajolery as her niece managed to member the appropriate words. 'Silly old bitch,' her mind scorned. 'Not s'smart as sh'thinks.' Full of admiration for Jackson's clever strategy.

With victory his to savour the conqueror willed the old besom to depart, which she did at last after a host of instructions for the next day. 'Aa thowt she'd never go,' Lottie breathed in relief when the door finally closed behind their slave driver's back, on tenterhooks the whole time in case her aunt reconsidered. 'We did it, lass, we bloomin' well did it!' Mattie enthused, absolutely cock a hoop but Lottie stoutly refused the credit. 'You did it, Mattie, all by yerself,' she insisted amid a bear like hug, which knocked him momentarily off balance, totally unaware of this in her excitement immediately full of plans, with the off chance of seeing Alice if she was working in one of the fields on Fencer's on Fencer's Hill, probably no other opportunity this side of Christmas. Her friend would be sure to like the warm 'hug ma tight' knitted out of odd balls of wool unearthed by Martha from a stairfoot cupboard, one for her also and now busy with socks for Mattie Jackson. 'It's been there since pussy was a cat,' the little hunchback said when she queried the taking of it. 'Just wait till Martha hears the news,' she exulted, reminded of the tiny hunchback who already knew of Jackson's intentions but remained gloomily sceptical.

Mattie Jackson allowed himself to be carried along on this tide of youthful exuberance, immensely gratified by such enthusiasm, the exercise truly worthwhile and so nice to witness such a wonderful transformation. It was half an hour and another cup of cocoa before he managed to bundle her off to bed and made tracks for the stable.

'Aa'll not sleep a wink,' she concluded, beyond caring, ready to tackle that long climb to the top of the house, which became more arduous every night, all the puffing and panting lost in elation when she sank down on her bed, something to look forward to at last.

Jackson watched her go and stood for a moment or two in deep reflection, surprised at his own keen anticipation of the next day's outing. 'Damn it all, Aa'm actin'like some daft young laddie,' he admitted rather sheepishly as he crossed the stable yard, the house locked up behind him. This trip into the countryside was no new experience, the road to Whitegates travelled many times over the years, on errands for Felicity Cranshawe to her well heeled father.

The growing feeling he had for Lottie was most disturbing, he was totally obsessed by a bonny elfin face and two gorgeous hazel eyes, not to mention that crown of glorious auburn hair which he longed to see loose around her slender shoulders. Long dormant desires awoke within him, the urge to hold the softness of a woman's body in his arms. The hug Lottie gave him, so spontaneous, stirred a need for more of the same and not from just any woman. One very special eighteen year old had stolen his heart, a girl who grew bigger every day with another fellow's bastard bairn.

This giant of a man had no problem visualising mother and child as his own, a possibility not beyond reach. The few precious hours away from the house could provide an opportunity to test the ground, marriage definitely in mind. A very pleasing prospect to take to his bed in the flat above the coach house, already thought of as a family home.

* * *

True to her prediction, Lottie did spend a sleepless night, tossing and turning on her lumpy mattress, a swollen body made it very difficult to find a comfortable resting place. She heard every stroke of the Asylum clock, on the hour and the half hour, glad when it struck five and she was able to grope her way downstairs for early morning chores. In the kitchen, both fire and stove were burning brightly, thanks to the hero of the night before and a welcome cup of tea awaited her, just the pick me up needed mentally and physically, tiredness and eager anticipation a strange mixture.

Almost on the dot of six, Martha arrived, chilled to the marrow after a long, lonely walk from South Branton, badly lit roads to contend with and some with no light at all. If she was nervous the little woman never admitted the fact, it was something that had to be done regardless of any misgivings for her own safety.

'There's a rabbit off!' she exclaimed in amazement when regaled with Lottie's glad tidings, a vocabulary full of quaint Geordie-isms. 'Jessica's not given t'acts o'kindness, so don't get carried away,' she warned between puffs on icy fingers, standing with her back to the big black stove to find a measure of warmth before she started her working day.

'Trust you t'spoil it,' Lottie burst out angrily still highly excited and tried hard to pull herself together, afraid she might be doomed to disappointment, reluctant to contemplate Martha could be right, her aunt quite capable of dashing hopes out of sheer badness.

'Take it easy,' Jackson soothed, 'Ye'll be fit fer nowt if y'carry on like this.' Martha's bird like head nodding agreement.

'Aye,' she said, 'Who's t'say the old biddy won't change'er mind after she's slept on it.' Actually putting the possibility into words but she quickly changed her tune at the crestfallen look on the girl's face, tears not far away. 'But mebbe not,' she hastened to add, 'Even she has t'act like she's human sometime. Howway,' she bustled, outdoor clothing speedily divested and swinging into action. 'Whose turn is it fer them blessed fires?' meaning the upstairs drawing room and Madam's private lounge, instantly rewarded by a beaming smile, Lottie's spirits soon uplifted.

'Mine,' the eager lass readily accepted. 'Have yer cup o'tea.' Exchanging a significant look with Mattie Jackson, both of them were well used to Martha's swift changes of mood, now prepared to dig in and do her share of the mountain of chores which awaited them.

Less than an hour later, Jessica Finlay came upon the scene, there to keep a strict eye on operations until Felicity awoke and needed her ministrations. 'I will just have toast, this morning,' she said and seated herself at one end of the kitchen table, ready to be waited upon, no sign of going back on her word, much to Lottie's relief. Martha muttered under her breath as she reached for the toasting fork, while a happy young lass busied herself, setting out her aunt's special bone china cup, saucer and plate which made the bold statement of her superior rating in the order of things thereabouts.

Lottie hummed a little ditty as she scuttled around, happy as a sand boy and the sound of it warmed the hearts of her two friends, down in the dumps so often it had almost become a way of life. Her misery was so easily transferred to those obliged to watch her wallow in it, day after day.

At eight forty-five there was no holding her. Dressed ready to travel, she stood near the basement window, willing Jackson's long legs to come down the outside stairway.

'Yer like a hen on a hot griddle,' Martha sighed in exasperation as the impatient girl went from one foot to the other, all of a twitter, greatly relieved when the legs did appear, their owner ready for the road, the stable chores all done. Coach and horses were awaiting them in the yard. 'Will ye sit inside or ride up top wi'me?' Jackson questioned, it was soon very apparent what the answer was, Lottie seated aloft beside him in full view of everyone when the elegant conveyance trundled out of the stable yard. Martha's face still registered the disapproval already expressed in words. 'No place fer a lass in your condition. What if y'topple over.' This possibility was greeted with carefree, infectious laughter and Jackson joined in, proud to be in the company of such a bonny young lass.

'Stop yer fussin'. Aa'll see sh'comes t'no harm,' he said and a somewhat mollified Martha stepped back from the coach just as Jessica Finlay appeared to see them off the premises, the coach moving as Martha mumbled, 'If that old bitch smiled 'er face would crack.' Lottie was hard pushed to stifle a giggle, glad to be on their way, still afraid her irascible relative might cry halt to the outing, even at the eleventh hour.

They soon turned out of the gates, Jackson had opened them earlier and in a fit of defiance didn't stop to close them. 'She'll blame the milkman,' he chortled and Lottie fully appreciated this little act of mischief. The dull December morning was made brighter by a radiant face, alive with pleasure and looking even younger than her eighteen years.

'Them two seem easier t'handle than Tiger used t'be,' she remarked, reminded of the little pony's spirited antics on her previous journey along this same route, although in the opposite direction.

'Aye,' Jackson conceded, 'These beauties are well trained Aa'll grant ya, cost a pretty penny the pair o'them but the laddo's better then'ee was a few weeks ago, like somebody else Aa could mention, learnin' fast to do what'ee's told.'

She giggled in amusement, his meaning well taken and thought how smart he looked in the livery Madam insisted he wore and said so. 'Like a blessed tailor's dummy,' grunted self consciously but secretly gratified, prepared to read more into her admiration than intended. Lottie regarded him as a sort of father figure, always there to back her up if possible, a buffer against her aunt's harsh treatment. Her young heart warmed towards him but nowhere near the dreams Jackson nurtured, absolutely smitten.

Just a few months on the right side of thirty, the Cranshawes' coachman had never 'mucked around' with women, as he chose to put it, wary after a teenage involvement which ended rather badly. 'Ye'll take some catchin', lad,' Martha often chaffed, fully convinced he was a confirmed bachelor who would never be inveigled into matrimony.

Rightly or wrongly, Jackson laid all blame at Snowdon's door so, at last well underway, he decided to take the plunge and made a tentative approach. 'Have y'ever thought that gettin' wed might solve yer problem, Lottie. Many a bloke would give'is right arm t'get a fine lass like yerself, even if means givin' a bairn his name.' He was afraid to be more explicit which happened to be a big mistake, totally unprepared for the storm that broke around his ears, the vehemence of her reply took him completely by surprise.

Bright, hazel eyes glittered angrily and heated words tore from tightened lips. 'Getting' wed's the last thing Aa would think of, that's fer sure.' A hard, inflexible attitude he found most disturbing. 'Aa'm off men fer the rest o'my life,' she vowed and proceeded to dash his hopes. 'Aa've had me fill o'the beggars, one way an'another, so don't talk t'me about marriage.'

Absolutely deflated he couldn't keep the aggrieved note out of his voice annoyed at such defamation of the whole male sex in general. 'Aa'm a man,' he countered rather bitterly, 'or mebbe y'haven't noticed.'

'Aye,' she agreed wholeheartedly, 'An' a fine specimen at that, but yer more than that t'me. Martha, Alice Ruddick an'yerself are me friends, the only ones Aa've got,' she told him serious faced. 'There'll be no weddin' ring fer me. Anyway,' she added woefully, 'Who would want Jake Snowdon's leavin's. God help me bairn if it looks like 'im.' Unable to keep the distaste out of her voice.

Jackson missed his cue, the time for him to declare his intentions. 'Aa'll have ya Lottie,' all he needed to say and there may be have been some hope, the words on the tip of his tongue, much too reticent to extol his own virtues, the opportunity was lost as he lapsed into sullen silence.

Embarrassment forced Lottie to prattle on about nothing in particular, marriage a subject she preferred not to discuss, diverted at the same time into scanning the surrounding fields for sight of Alice Ruddick, whose working day was well into operation, more than three hours of it already gone.

Suddenly her excitement knew no bounds, 'There sh'is, there sh'is. Stop the coach, Mattie.' Overjoyed to see that familiar scarecrow figure beyond the hedge, in a field to their right, a tousled head quickly uplifted at the sound of Lottie's voice.

'Canny on, lass' Jackson pleaded and pulled at the reins but Lottie was already scrambling down, her condition forgotton in the sheer exhilaration of seeing Alice again, a pleasure shared, that homely face wreathed in smiles as they held hands through a break of sorts among branches bereft of leaves.

'My, w'are comin' on i' the world, ridin' i' that fancy contraption, just like royalty, how've y'been anyway?' All in one breath. 'Champion,' Lottie lied, unwilling to burden Alice with her woes. 'Aa've missed ya,' she confessed, her hands gripped even harder at this heartfelt admission.

A lot of catching up to do, Alice straight on to the next question. 'Well, what's it t'be? News or scandal?'

Lottie's eyes sparkled with mischief. 'News of course, Aa've provided most o'scandal lately,' which brought laughing retort from her companion's lips.

'Ye were only a nine days wonder. They've got their claws inta somebody else now. Not that the nosy devils don't fish fer information but they get short change out o'me. Anyway Aa canna tell them what Aa don't know.' A wee hint of reproach which Lottie chose to ignore.

The idea of Saltersgate gossips trying to worm news of her out of Alice made her chuckle with satisaction but she was obliged to listen as the lass gabbled on. 'Meggie Briggs is just about ready fer bed with'er sixth an', Seppy swears it's the lodger's. God help'er if it ends up wi'Bob Storey's big conk, no mistakin' that.' This menage à trois was well known in the village, hard to tell which of the other five were sired by her husband, a strange situation which seemed to work most of the time, the husband a bit of an ass. A spontaneous burst of laughter reached Jackson at his place in the roadway, quite piqued to be excluded and not introduced to Alice, still sore at Lottie's rejection of men in general, inclined to take it much too personally.

Oblivious to his presence, Alice went on to acquaint Lottie with news of rather disconcerting nature. 'Aa reckon the strike's on at last. The men are at the end of their rope. It's all that water, they're feared o'real serious floodin' i' the Low Main.'

'Is it that bad?' Lottie queried anxiously. These were her folk, but she was now completely out of touch in a house where talk of strike action was taboo. 'What d'ya think? Me father comes in soakin, after every shift, Aa'm hard pushed t'get the things dried afore the next'un. He's past workin i' such conditions with the chest he's got.' No need to tell Lottie about filthy pit clothes which stank to high heaven as they dried out. 'When's it likely t'start?' A passing thought for Ralph's well being was soon dismissed, still very much at odds with her puritanical brother, the rift between them widened with every day that passed.

'There's a meetin' i' the chapel vestry the night,' Alice said 'Fred'll be at the pit but there'll be plenty t'say aye when it's put t'the vote.' Followed by a burst of fierce hatred. 'Somebody wants t'string that John Starrett from the nearest lamp post,' she snapped and looked as if she might easily relish the job herself.

Lottie felt sick, so ashamed of her connection with such a tyrant, surprised this bit of news hadn't reached the village as yet but it was the wrong time to indulge in confidences when feelings ran so high. She was spared further thought on the matter by the sound of Jackson's impatient voice. 'Howway lass, break it up. It's a canny way t'Stamfordham an' w'don't have all day,' very grouchy, jealous of the obvious rapport between these two girls.

'Stamford'am, eh?' Alice yelled back at him and got a non committal grunt in reply. 'Men,' she snorted as he turned to the coach, her bushy eyebrows raised in derision.

Lottie sniggered but soon became serious again. 'How'll Aa get t'know if yer all right?' she queried, 'Aa'm shut away from everybody these days,' exactly how she wanted it to be, still concerned but brightened somewhat when she remembered Alice's gift and ran to fetch it from the coach. 'Fer me?' the gawky lass breathed in astonishment. 'Aa've never had a present since me mother died, except an orange an' apple at Christmas.' Clumsy fingers struggled with the wrapping, overwhelmed when she unveiled the knitted garment. 'It's champion,' she enthused and immediately tried it on, struggling out of a well worn man's jacket to do so. 'Aa'll wear it t'bed an' all. It's chilly in that back bedroom.' Hours of work, sometimes by candlelight, were well rewarded by the pleasure on that open face. An extra candle was often slipped to Lottie by Mattie Jackson, no asking where they came from.

'Dinna fret about me,' Alice said, 'Ye'll hear soon enough if the strike's on. Aa could nicely land on yer doorstep fer a crust o'bread.' Vivid pictures came to mind of Jessica Finlay's face if such a thing should happen. 'And ye'll get it,' she rashly promised, 'even if Aa have t'pinch it from under me aunt's long nose.'

There was a spontaneous hug from Alice before she clambered aboard the coach, all pleasure taken from this eagerly anticipated trip by the disquieting news. Sensitive to her every mood, Jackson gave a deep sigh. 'All right, what's eatin'ya,' he questioned, full of sympathy when he heard the reason for her despondency. 'No use frettin'. Once the men make up their minds nowt'll stop them, right or wrong.'

'Right, of course,' she barked at him, prepared to do battle if he uttered one detrimental word against her own kind. But suddenly it was all too much for her she started to tremble, heavy sobs racked her swollen body. 'Aa hate them,' she cried through chattering teeth, 'My God, how Aa hate the whole damned lot, o'them.' No stemming the tears or the angry words which sprang from a blistering tongue, freely let loose. 'What d'any o'them care fer the likes o'us, just a host o'lackies t'wipe their backsides or near enough. One o'these days they'll get their come uppence, see if they don't.' Hazel eyes ablaze with hatred for her suppressors, Jessica Finlay high on the list, somebody who considered herself almost on par with her superiors, a typical working class snob.

Mattie felt quite helpless but decided tears would do the lass no harm, kept bottled up for weeks through one crisis after another, this was just the straw that broke the camel's back. Eleven years older than Lottie, Jackson held no illusions, an ordinary fellow well acquainted with the many drawbacks of being lower class, he was wise enough to swim with the tide rather than drown in the depths of despair. His kindly heart ached at the sight of her distress, such intensity of feeling liable to tear her apart. His hopes that this drive into the countryside might restore jaded spirits were completely dashed and he fervently wished the meeting with Alice Ruddick had never taken place with those strong reminders of the life she left behind her.

But the fates were not kindly disposed towards either of them, or so it seemed, any hopes he may have harboured already gone, there were many more difficult days ahead and a lot of tears to be shed, given the circumstances and individuals concerned. Lottie would be the most vulnerable of them all.

A strong sense of gloom rode along with the moving vehicle and its occupants, that earlier feeling of expectancy was no longer there to spur him on and, for the moment and quite out of character, Jackson was unable to arouse that dogged determination which usually stood him in good stead. It all weighed so heavily upon him, Lottie's personal woes and her rejection too heavy a load to carry. And, angry with himself for indulging in such negative emotions, he cracked the whip into the air to urge the horses on, suddenly anxious to have the whole day over and done with, so great his disappointment in the way it had all come apart.

* * *

The outing to Whitegates might have been termed a disaster from beginning to end, although the end had yet to come but didn't token too well considering the overall mood. The black stallions were in fine fettle and enjoyed the freedom of country roads, curbed from time to time by a competent driver. Jackson made every effort to draw Lottie into conversation only to be answered in curt monosyllables, he gave up after a while, thoroughly disgusted with her behaviour. A spanking was what she needed and a good one but he remembered the hands lifted against her of late and cancelled the thought.

Lottie caught her first glimpse of the big country house as it basked in an isolated spell of winter sunshine. Usually it was screened from roadside view by a thick belt of trees, which were still there of course but mostly minus their foliage. Set amid these trees and undulating park land, John Starrett's country home bore all the signs of gracious living and made Rothwell House pale in comparison as Jackson ventured to comment, but was just grunted at for his pains. Lottie didn't want to find anything to praise or take delight in, although her eyes told her otherwise.

The visitors were made welcome in the servants' quarters, its occupants glad of diversion, plenty of menials in this establishment. 'Enough t'run Buckin'ham Palace,' she complained, thinking of all the work in Rothwell House and only three of them to do it, further irritated when given a guided tour of the magnificent mansion, impressed despite herself but with little real pleasure for someone determined not to enjoy the experience.

A portrait of Felicity, specially commissioned, graced the wall above the marble mantelpiece in the drawing room on the first floor, her mistress's beauty skilfully enhanced by the artist's obvious expertise. The coldness of those striking blue eyes was discreetly softened by someone who knew what was expected of him by wealthy clients. To paint what they wanted to see not what he actually saw. Lottie murmured the expected words of admiration but unfavourably compared the luxury surrounding her with the lot of Saltergate mining folk who seldom had more than two pennies to rub against one another. Men and women who slaved to provide such opulence for this one affluent gentleman.

When they returned to the kitchen, she politely refused offers of food from a rosy cheeked cook. 'Aa couldn't eat a bite,' she said, the thought of even one mouthful of John Starrett's food absolutely abhorrent. Foolish reasoning when Rothwell House existed upon this man's generosity towards his only child, denied nothing that money could buy. It was the gaffer's food Lottie ate day after day and thoroughly enjoyed it.

This lack of appetite caused no concern, wrongly attributed to her condition, significant looks were exchanged between female employees, unaware of these silly qualms. Jackson ignored her childish behaviour and tucked in with obvious relish. 'Suit yerself,' he muttered, none too pleased at a day turned sour through no fault of his own. 'Better belly burst than good food waste,' he quoted deliberately and turned away from the reproach in her expressive eyes to eat his fill without compunction.

They left Whitegates well before three in deference to Jessica Finlay's instructions. 'All Aa need is t'get on the wrong side o'that miserable bitch and it'll make the day complete,' he mumbled, fully convinced Lottie was 'cuttin'er nose off t'spite 'er face' possessed by a strong inclination to take her to task.

The homeward journey proved to be another silent affair and both parties heaved a sigh of relief when the top of Fencers' Hill came into view, Quarry Cottages to their left when they turned downhill. Lottie speculated whether Maude Elliott was hidden behind her venetian blind watching all comings and goings, it was almost too dark to see, they would just make it before it really settled in. She cursed whatever fate burdened her with two wicked witches as close relatives, she was not kindly disposed towards either of them, which was hardly surprising.

The last of the day's quarry carts trundled through the gate at their right, weary men and tired horses soon to seek a well earned rest, some workmen with long walks in front of them.

Mattie Jackson tightened rein to negotiate a wide bend in the road, a tricky business due to the steep gradient and was flagged down within yards of Coulter's farmhouse by one of the hinds who flung his arms aloft in great excitement. Jackson saw red. 'Out o'the way y'stupid gowk,' he yelled in exasperation, furious at having to swerve onto the grass verge to avoid collision. 'Ye must be barmy standin' i' the way o'gallopin' horses. Thank yer lucky stars Aa know what Aa'm doin',' he railed and loudly berated the gormless chap, not in the least perturbed by the danger he was in.

'The strike's off,' the man shouted, as if this explained everything. Lottie's heart missed a beat then righted itself, her good humour miraculously restored and she took a quick look round for sight of Alice. She wished the whole day might begin again, spoilt by her foolishness, words of apology on the edge of her tongue.

But this ecstatic feeling was very short lived. 'Y'needn't waste time lookin'fer Alice Ruddick,' their informant hastened to say, full of his own importance. 'She's long off home, 'er father and a chap called Jackie Phillips got killed down the pit the day. The water came floodin' in and loosened the props.' Lottie gaped at him in disbelief but a scream rose to her throat, only to stay there, struck dumb by the horror of it all. Poor harmless Fred, a true friend when she needed one most, her bewildered mind, was anxious to reject what it could scarcely take in. Not true, she told herself and stared with frantic eyes, from one man to the other in search of denial, nothing but pity on their solemn faces. Then fear took hold, paralysing fear, as another terrifying possibility besieged a numbed mind. 'Me brother,' she choked and clung to Jackson's arm in desperation, her eyes wide with horror.

'Jackie Phillips is yer brother then?' the farm worker questioned, even more drama in the situation than he thought, enjoying being part of it all in a morbid sort of way. He had been an interested spectator of her meeting with Alice earlier that day, very impressed by the liveried coachman and the handsome conveyance with its cargo of greenery.

'No, no,' Lottie shot out frantically. 'Me brother was i'the same flat,' and stared as the man shook his head, 'Just the two'o' them,' he said, Mattie Jackson gruff in reply. 'An' that's too many,' the big man grunted and felt Lottie's body sag in relief. For the moment Ralph's safety was of most importance, thankful he was unharmed.

Jackson drew her unresistingly into the comforting circle of one arm and controlled the restless horses with the other, as if these dumb beasts knew something was amiss. Lottie wept, broken hearted, her ravaged face pressed into his uniform jacket. 'They'll have t'see t'that water now,' she spluttered between sobs. 'How long afore things get better fer the likes of us? How many more bairns'll lose their fathers?' Now reminded of Lizzie Phillips left with three children, in a worse predicament than poor Alice, who at least had a job and only herself to worry about but no relatives to stand by her in time of trouble. None of Fred or Sally Ruddick's family cared whether the lass lived or died. The Catholics were guaranteed to make every effort to have their lost sheep accepted back into the faith, even after death, expecting his insurance money to pay the necessary dues.

A barbed tongue heaped curses upon the Starretts, father and daughter. Lottie raged against those at whose feet she laid blame until the storm abated and she lay across Mattie Jackson, absolutely exhausted by the strength of such gut tearing emotions.

'She's in a sorry state,' their companion of the past ten minutes or so said, prepared to keep up the chatter. Mattie willed him to depart, 'Howway me beauties,' he coaxed and turned full attention upon the horses, the disturbed animals scraping the ground in agitation. The gawky youth was dismissed effectively with his next words, 'Howway lads, there's nowt fer us here. Let's off home.' In normal circumstances Lottie may have questioned the word home in connection with Rothwell House, Felicity Cranshawe's establishment only regarded as a port in a storm. Not so Mattie Jackson, who fell back on the trite saying 'home is where the heart is.' So wrapped up in the lass held close to his body that it had become a strange sort of paradise since she came to live under its roof. He reckoned deep friendship might be a good enough basis for marriage, hope was not abandoned that it could develop into something stronger. After all she had leant on him in her grief, losing sight of the fact that nobody else was there.

He felt the full weight of Lottie's prone body against him, grateful for these precious moments of physical contact. Jake Snowdon well out of the running was a definite boost to his prospects. Just a matter of choosing the right time to make another more positive approach well into self delusion.

As if to hasten this wonderful possibility, Jackson spurred the horses on, ashamed to find his own spirits amazingly high in the face of this recent tragedy. But, as Alice Ruddick reasoned a few weeks previously, it was an ill wind that blew nobody any good, her hopes dashed by Lottie's departure and now she had something worse to cope with. Mattie Jackson, usually so practical and down to earth, was only chasing rainbows where Lottie was concerned, in this hour of stress he acted as a stand in for John Hanson, her dead father, nothing more.

* * *

The voice came from behind, sharp as any whiplash, one Lottie come to recognise only too well. 'What are you doing, girl?' it rapped out, no jingling keys or rustle of petticoats, a deliberate ploy to catch her on the hop. The crafty old besom had the keys clasped tightly in her hand, as for the underwear, goodness knows what.

'Nothin' Aunt Jessica, nothin,' she stammered, not the best choice of words as soon discovered. 'You aren't paid to do nothing,' the older woman stressed. 'Listening outside the drawing room door I expect. If I thought we were – –' The implication very easy to assume. 'No, no, Aa wasn't,' and struggled to make plausible explanation. 'Aa, Aa saw some dust on the bannister. Aa know how particular y'are,' Thankful for the duster clutched tightly in her fingers, which her aunt didn't miss, those beady eyes narrowed into speculative slits.

'If I imagined for one moment you were telling lies, I would take my hand across your impudent face,' she threatened, only half convinced. Hot blood rushed to Lottie's temples and her mind shrieked in protest, no way would that even happen again without retaliation. 'If she lifts a finger t'me,' she fumed, 'Aa'll chuck'er down them blessed stairs, the miserable old bitch.' The indignity of that former vicious blow never to be forgotten.

Jessica ran an exploratory finger along the highly polished surface while Lottie held her breath. 'Hum,' she snorted, 'I suggest you get on with it and make a better job than that indolent creature downstairs.' Martha was supposed to have done that particular chore earlier in the day. 'I shall speak to her,' the housekeeper promised and Lottie imagined Martha's reaction, furious to be accused of slackness and because of her.

Jessica finally took her leave and Lottie crept closer to the drawing room door, fully conscious of the risk involved but willing to take a chance, soon all ears at the sound of her own name on Madam's oily tongue. 'Charlotte, that's the name she was given. These peasants do have illusions of grandeur. You have no idea how the girl reacted when I suggested it was most unsuitable for a mere servant. Quite uppity, I can tell you.'

A husky voice soon made reply, easily recognised as that of Angela Lawrence, 'Felicity darling,' she drawled in sympathy, 'The Ladies' Aid to Unmarried Mothers doesn't expect you to actually house one of the stupid girls. What will you do when the child arrives? Have it adopted, I suppose?'

Lottie stifled a gasp and moved to hold on to the stair rail to steady herself but had to hear Madam's answer and moved back to the door. 'Oh no,' Felicity said, highly amused, 'Finlay did promise the girl she could keep the child and I must stay on the right side of dear Jessica, such a treasure and absolutely devoted.'

Furious at herself for listening she stood there, glued to the spot almost. 'What sort of girl is she?' someone else asked, not a voice she had heard before, probably some newcomer to Madam's circle, ever changing. Not long before Felicity's answer came and revealed the full extent of the woman's malice.

'Just the usual working class type,' she disparaged. 'No breeding whatsoever and not much intelligence. I suppose one might say she is pretty, in a common sort of way.' A few raised eyebrows at such an uncalled for description of a young servant, which unfortunately Lottie didn't see and classed the women all alike. She cringed to hear herself spoken of in such derogatory fashion but the hateful voice still rabbited on. 'Would you like to meet Charlotte?' Madam inquired, definitely the last straw. A peep show for these fancy women, the mean streak in Felicity only too apparent to her hapless underdog.

A creaking door, one never oiled despite frequent requests from Jessica Finlay, sent out its warning, Lottie was soon in full flight down the wide stairway immune to her aunt's protests when they passed in the hall and the distressed girl made a bee line for the kitchen. No sooner was she through the door than Martha went into attack.

'Well, me lass, what's this Aa hear about not dustin' the bannisters. Y'know fine well Aa did them this mornin' afore'er ladyship was up an' about. Just been given what for by that old besom.'

'Save it,' Lottie snapped. 'If ye've got a bone t'pick wi' me just chew on it a bit longer. And if me aunt wants t'know where Aa am say owt y'have a mind.' She grabbed her grey woollen shawl from the coat rack as she bolted, Martha left dumb with astonishment, Lottie's behaviour was beyond comprehension.

'Well Aa never,' she breathed at last. 'Aa'll do just that, hinny, just t'see the look on the old biddy's face,' and chuckled at the delightful prospect, her irritation already forgotten. She knew Lottie's flight would only take her as far as the stables to pour whatever it was into Mattie Jackson's sympathetic ears.

He got the whole story, told in great agitation by the highly strung lass and listened as always until the stormy outburst came to an end. 'Lottie, hinny,' he sighed in exasperation, 'That fiery temper'll be the death of ya one o'these days. The sooner y'cultivate a thick skin the better. Learn t'play them fancy wives at their own game. Y'should o'waited an' gone upstairs when sh'sent fer ya, instead o'stirrin up trouble fer yerself.'

'Not likely,' came the vehement retort, 'Fat chance o'me lettin' them look at me as if Aa'd just crawled out o'the woodwork,' her bright eyes full of fire and scarlet faced.

Jackson blew his stack. 'Shut up an' let me finish,' he barked at her, unusually angry. 'Y'come here t'wind off and when Aa give y'advice y'chuck it back i'me face.'

She calmed down. 'All right, Aa promise not t'say another word. Cross me heart an hope t'die.' And made the appropriate gesture.

Her confidante carried on, slightly mollified. 'Let them have their bit o'sport. When they've finished, they'll dip their hands inta them beaded bags an' give ya a copper or two.' His blue eyes hardened. 'Money is what y'need i'this world, it can buy anythin'. That's what old Starrett did fer his daughter. The Cranshawes have the real breedin' and the open sesame t'all the big nobs' mansions but the gaffer's got the brass an' he pulls the strings.'

Lottie stared at him, wide eyed, rather disturbed by these theories but had to admit Jackson's philosophies made sense. She gave a loud sniff, wiped her tear filled eyes when she was told and waited for what came next. 'Now ye've got t'eat humble pie,' Mattie warned. With no idea how to explain her behaviour, what sort of tale to concoct, there was little comfort to be taken from the following words. 'Y'can be sure Martha made a meal of it. Aa reckon y'owe'er one fer the dustin' business, anyway,' he quipped and gave a roguish grin at her woebegone expression.

Jessica Finlay was quite sceptical when Lottie used her pregnancy as an excuse but had to acknowledge that women in that condition often did peculiar things, Madam a prime example. There were no unfortunate repercussions, whatever explanations were given, Felicity was too busy playing Lady Bountiful to dwell upon Lottie's non appearance. The lass breathed again, another hurdle crossed.

An uneasy truce settled upon the big house and its occupants, guaranteed to carry them right up to the festive season with no real upsets, a few trifling incidents as might be expected but that was all. A miracle indeed with so many different temperaments gathered together under the one roof, all the necessary ingredients for constant upheaval.

Thus with tension lessened to some degree, Lottie began to fret about Alice Ruddick. No man to work at the colliery no house, it was as simple as that, the golden rule in every colliery village, no exceptions made. So, on December 21st Alice's worst fears were realised, a recently appointed pit deputy, newly wed, got the keys for Number Ten Lizzie Street and wasted no time moving in, sentiment a luxury the working classes seldom could afford. There was no animosity on Alice's part, the situation understood and accepted without any fuss. Curious neighbours watched as the girl's bits and pieces were turfed into the lane, in the hope that something of use might come their way, they were not unfeeling, just practical. Where Alice was going none of it mattered, the most surprising outcome of the whole affair was enough to set tongues wagging for days on end.

Alice arrived at the servants' entrance of Rothwell House barely an hour before her new employer departed for Whitegates in her father's fashionable carriage, coach and driver placed at her disposal which saved Jackson the journey there and back in one day. Both events brought equal pleasure below stairs, apart from Jessica Finlay who resented being left behind. John Starrett was absolutely immovable on this particular point, her fellow servants were inclined to gloat at her obvious chagrin. They would rather she had gone with Madam, of course, but it did mean only one pain in the neck instead of two.

Lottie's moans and groans about her friend's sorry plight got Martha really worked up, although sympathetic. 'She'll never get by on'er own an' who'll take'er in,' had become a perpetual dirge. 'Aa bet most o'them tripped back fer the ham tea,' Lottie raged 'Aa should o'gone t'that funeral,' she said, conscience stricken, too cowardly to make a spectacle of herself with half the world and his brother in attendance.

'It was a grand affair,' Martha told her, quite impressed by Fred's last appearance on earth, in a fine coffin with brass handles, six of his work mates as underbearers. 'She must o'kept up her father's insurance,' one fact Lottie could confirm, the few coppers had been paid out of her own purse on several occasions.

Postumously restored into the faith he chose to abandon in life, Fred was laid to rest in the Catholic cemetery, separated by a couple of miles from his beloved Sally, who occupied a lonely grave in South Branton churchyard. Alice was like putty in the hands of her papist relatives who took complete charge and disowned her again when the funeral was over. Both Fred and Jackie Phillips, Ralph's friend, were played to their graves in different locations by the village band.

'Why don't y' tackle yer aunt?' Martha suggested out of the blue. 'Sh'might easily take Alice on if sh'comes cheap. There used t'be two livin' in maids afore you came. A roof over the lass's head if nowt else and all found.' Lottie's mind was soon alive to this splendid possibility, with more animation shown than for quite some time.

'D'ya think sh'will?' Afraid to be too optimistic, Martha was very impatient in reply. 'Take the bull by the horns and ask'er but be sure she's in a good fettle,' she cautioned. 'Aa know Jessica isn't the easiest t'deal with but sh'does have an eye fer the main chance and Alice could be one answer to'er prayers when it comes t'your confinement.' The waiting seemed endless, patience never one of Lottie's strong points, but Alice's whole future depended on her, she had to make the effort and did so, eventually, really up tight.

Jessica appeared to give the request serious consideration. 'A good worker, you say. I wasn't too impressed by what I saw of her,' and Lottie's heart hit rock bottom. 'Alice is used t'hard graft. She had just come in from workin' at the farm. Mr Coulter'll be sorry t'lose'er but she needs a livin' in place.' Fingers crossed as she awaited further reaction.

'I shall speak to Madam,' Jessica said, which meant it was as good as settled, Felicity was not into the hiring of servants and plain, gawky Alice was not likely to arouse any anagonistic feelings. Lottie was suddenly anxious that the big lass might jib at working for the pit gaffer's daughter, a fear totally unfounded. She was only capable of dealing with one problem at a time, finding a place to live was the one that existed at the moment. If Felicity Cranshawe was a means of solving it all to the good, nothing else mattered, pit gaffer's daughter or not.

The former farm girl settled in without any bother and her instalment in Rothwell House relieved Lottie of one big anxiety. Someone in the attic bedroom next to her own gave a deep sense of assurance. What if her child chose to arrive during the night, a knock on the wall was all it would take to get help. On that very first day, Alice stared in awe at the gaily decorated Christmas tree on the first floor landing and others in various parts of the house. Completely enthralled by dozens of brightly coloured baubles and glittering strands of tinsel, even more so by the mountain of food under preparation below stairs. 'Is some o'that fer us?' she questioned hopefully, inclined to regard Rothwell House as a wonderful Aladdin's cave, a feeling she never lost as the years rolled by and so much occurred in a troubled household.

'If yer lucky,' Martha grunted, unable to share the newcomer's childlike enthusiasm, her own plans so uncertain. She laughed shortly when Lottie muttered 'Aye they feed us all right, just like their dogs an'horses. They'd shoot us an'all when we're no more use if it wasn't against the law.' Down in the dumps at the time, as erratic in mood as the weather itself.

Mattie Jackson stood the atmosphere as long as he could then approached Jessica on Martha's behalf, willing to risk a dressing down if there was no chance of improving the situation otherwise. The upshot being that Mrs Connelly and Martha were invited to spend Christmas Day at Rothwell House, there being no higher authority around to consult for any decision.

'The old faggot most o'got out o'the right side o'the bed fer once,' was Martha's rejoinder, never one to accept charity with a good grace. She never knew of Jackson's intervention, just another good deed to be ticked against the kindly chap's name. Martha's misery evaporated, sufficient reward in itself.

Early Christmas morning the old lady arrived at the servant's entrance dressed in faded finery, smelling strongly of moth balls. A black frock, beaded cape and bonnet, none of them worn for years and miles too big for a shrunken frame. She beamed widely at everyone, including Jessica Finlay, who managed the vestige of a smile. Martha's mother was delighted to be there, a real treat for a usually housebound woman.

Mattie Jackson joined the Connellys in worship at St Aloysius, en route from South Branton, 'Aa'didn' know y' were Catholic,' Lottie muttered as if he had suddenly become a leper. 'Aa'm nowt,' he said, 'Aa' just went cause o'the day it was. Aa didn't see anybody wi'horns and a long tail,' sarcasm which brought a rosy flush to her cheeks, relieved nevertheless that Jackson owed no allegiance to the Church of Rome. She remembered her father's voice strong in conviction. 'Yer Protestant lass, an' don't ferget it.' Less heartache if she had taken heed and avoided Jake Snowdon like the plague. Alice did use persuasive powers to make her attend chapel with her, to no avail, the first time she had ever missed in her life, taken as a babe in arms.

Christmas over, Madam came back from her duty visit to Whitegates, where she had been bored to distraction and mostly on the wagon, just sly drinking out of her father's sight, a few bottles of gin tucked away in her luggage, which she was careful to remove before a maid servant unpacked. Her presence created enough extra work to keep them all fully occupied over the New Year, the usual moans and groans, a plaintive chorus led by Martha, in excellent voice.

Parties and more parties at home and elsewhere, pregnancy was not allowed to be a deterrent, followed immediately by preparations for the visit to London, still on the agenda as Jackson predicted. Saltersgate mining community toasted the year nineteen hundred and four with whatever came to hand, home brewed rhubarb and elderberry wine both quite potent, ginger cordial for non alcoholic drinkers but some of the hard stuff which they could ill afford. Idle shifts galore afterwards and no work, no wages, which only made matters worse, if that indeed were possible. But everyone knew that penny pinching would carry on throughout the year ahead, the gaffers called for wage cuts and longer hours, blind to the poverty all around them. The rich gave large donations to whatever church they frequented, so certain these vastly different ways of life were as God intended them to be, doing The Almighty a grave injustice.

* * *

'What does sh'want t'go s'far wi'both her an'me the way w'ar,' Lottie said for the umpteenth time, 'An, why just me an' me aunt going' with'er?' The visit to London looming like a dark cloud on the immediate horizon.

'That's what Aa'd like t'know,' Mattie Jackson grunted, angry at his own exclusion from Madam's entourage. 'She should know Aa'll be needed all the more wi'two o'them gettin' on i' their time.' The thought of Lottie being miles away was hard to accept. 'Aa'll be stuck down there wi'nobody but them two an that's as good as nowt,' she moaned in misery, neither Jessica Finlay nor her mistress likely to be any comfort to a homesick exile, who hadn't even set foot in Newcastle on Tyne, barely four miles distant. Martha and Alice were sympathetic no doubt, but found it all a bit much with both Lottie and Jackson in the depths of despair most of the time.

Martha now 'lived in', the change in circumstances came just after New Year when Edith Connelly died in her sleep, a merciful release for both the mother and her crippled daughter. The tiny hunchback took her demise for the blessing it was and made no great display of grief, she was now installed in another of the attic bedrooms, Alice and Lottie close neighbours. A companionable trio, with one candle doing the work of three for short relaxed sessions before they finally retired for the night, their own special domain with no unwelcome intruders.

'Ye'll be back afore the end o' March,' Martha prophesied in an effort to cheer the pregnant lass up, 'Madam's due about then an'the old man wants 'er here when the bairn comes. Got his mind set on a grandson.'

'And he'll get one,' Lottie snorted. Fully convinced that the gaffer's sort got everything they wanted. 'Aa hope it keeps fine fer the rotten old devil,' she muttered, never easy to lift out of the doldrums, almost a permanent state. She had not clapped eyes on John Starrett since she came to work there and didn't care if she never did, totally antagonistic towards the pit gaffer. Alice Ruddick wallowed in the comparative luxury of her present way of life, far removed from Number Ten Lizzie Street in all aspects, no hang ups whatsoever. Her favourite pastime was to visit Saltersgate and lord it over less fortunate acquaintances, too simple minded to recognise the dangerous game she played, folk in the village were possessed of long memories.

'Gossip about me an' my affairs, Alice Ruddick and Aa'll scratch yer eyes out,' Lottie threatened whenever Alice left the house but she did the lass grave injustice, she was empty headed maybe yet essentially loyal and much aggrieved at her friend's lack of trust, devoted to her as much as ever.

News always poured unsolicited from a garrulous tongue when the gormless lass returned, no need to question, with something special to divulge on one occasion, all agog. 'They've started t'lay foundations on the old quarry, everybody i' the place is after one o'the houses, yer two aunts among them.' Meaning Ethel and Lizzie Ann, the youngest pair.

'It hasn't had time t'settle proper, not s'long since they filled it in,' Lottie said 'Let's hope they get one an' the whole caboodle collapses. Serves them right.' Still no room for any of her kin folk. She was right about the quarry but safety was never a first consideration among the bosses, expediency won every time. Rubbish and rubble had been carted there for weeks to fill in the big crater, not so deep as they originally assessed. There was a larger area of solid ground outside the filled in area, which could be avoided by making it into gardens with a top layer of decent soil.

One evening just after darkness descended upon them Jackson made his appearance, obviously upset about something but reluctant to divulge the reason somehow. Lottie, at the kitchen table wading through a pile of ironing and growing hotter by the minute looked up and waited for him to speak.

'There's a chap outside wants t'see ya lass.' No name was given but his grim expression was a right give away. She tottered forward and leant against the table, weak at the knees. 'Tell 'im t'hop it,' she managed to choke out while Martha prised the hot iron out of her clenched hand. No need to mention Jake Snowdon by name, only too evident who the unwelcome visitor happened to be. 'Back t'the sink,' Martha ordered Alice who hovered around full of curiosity and the sharpness of her tone sent the lass scuttling across the room in swift obedience.

'All right, ye bide where y'are an' Aa'll sort 'im out, a bloody nerve showin' his ugly mug around here,' Mattie raged, no stomach for what he had to do. 'Mind, Aa don't reckon he's the sort t'be put off.' One fact Lottie already knew to her sorrow, Jake's persistence and her own ignorance a recipe for disaster, the final consquences soon to be faced but for him to come to Rothwell House was a right imposition. Martha heaped curses on men in general, excluding Mattie Jackson of course, while Alice, romantic to the core edged her way forward again and began to ramble on in her usual naïve fashion. 'He's come t'fetch ya, Lottie. Finds he canna live without you an' his bairn.' Soon to be rudely disillusioned, Lottie was not in the mood for such downright rubbish.

'Hold yer tongue,' she blazed, 'Talkin' like a ha'penny book,' and fiery words tumbled from her lips without restraint. 'What makes y'think Aa'm ready t'fall inta that blaggard's arms the way he treated me. Pride's mebbe all Aa've got left an' that's had a bashin', but Aa'm hangin' on t'some of it.' Her temper came to the rescue this time as she tried to pull herself together.

Jackson came back grimmer than ever, just as she expected, Jake's stubborness a foregone conclusion. 'Short o'shovin his teeth down the back of 'is neck there's nowt Aa can do,' and felt somehow he had failed her.

'Right then,' came the prompt reply. 'Leave 'im t' me, Aa'll sharp put paid t'that blinkin' knave, see if Aa don't.' No longer a quivering jelly, there was renewed purpose in every line of an ungainly body as she waddled towards the basement door, her back straight as ever, ready to act on her own behalf, a formidable sight.

Martha shouted encouragement in a shrill voice, 'Tell 'im where t'get off hinny,' then immediately turned on Alice barely recovered from Lottie's earlier tirade. 'Stop that blubberin', nowt in that thick head but water,' the simple girl reduced to copious tears by the whole distressful business.

Jackson longed to lay rough hands on Jake but Lottie's whole manner indicated she could handle Old Nick herself in her present frame of mind, no physical violence called for. His hatred for this renowned lecher spilled over, a fellow who by his rotten behaviour made Lottie wary of other men, with a total aversion to the entire male sex in the natural way of things. Beneath the subdued amber light of the coach house, she braved herself for the ordeal, determined to betray no sign of tumult in a racing heart. 'Five minutes,' she rapped out. 'More than y'deserve,' and freezed him with contempt.

'Aa've been thinkin',' Jake drawled and looked at her with insolent eyes, so sure of his fatal charm. 'Ye've got nowt t'think with, yer brains are somewhere else,' and raked down his body significantly, pleased to see his swarthy face redden, knowing she had touched a nerve. This belated contact was instigated by the local Catholic priest, very concerned when any child was fathered by one of his flock in or out of matrimony. He was anxious that the coming child should be born into the Catholic faith. Marriage was insisted upon even at this belated time, something which had no part in the nefarious scheme conjured up all those months ago.

Lottie's mouth twisted in derision. 'Ye should o'done yer thinkin' long afore now, mebbe saved the whole o'Saltersgate pointing the finger o'scorn. Aa've survived that, the rest should be a piece o'cake.' And steeled herself against any impact this brash philanderer might have on a treacherous young heart.

'It's my bairn y'are carryin',' he snarled in surly resentment, thoroughly disconcerted by this inflexible attitude, hard to imagine what he expected after months of neglect. 'Aa've got me rights,' he muttered. 'Father Reilly says,' the words barely out of his mouth before Lottie rushed into further attack, truly incensed that this spineless oaf needed a spur to do what a should have been his duty. 'Ye tell that Holy Moses t'mind his own business. This bairn'll be fetched up Protestant with or without a father,' she spat at him and turned the screw deliberately. 'Ye weren't the only lad t'cast eyes i' my direction, Jake Snowdon.' A swift intake of breath as the implication sank in. Hot colour rose from a thickened neck into an incredulous face, Lottie was amazed at her audacity. 'Mebbe what ye took somebody else had afore ya, ever think o'that?' A downright lie, of course, this obnoxious creature was the first to lay hands on her.

Jake's mind reeled beneath the impact, astounded to learn this girl was prepared to sacrifice her reputation to be rid of him but experienced enough to know he was her first lover and threw out the challenge. 'That's a lie, a bloody lie!' purple with rage, maddened by the cleverness of her rejection, a real blow to an inflated ago. To be cast aside by an inexperienced eighteen year old lass, infinitely more appealing since last they met, memories of that meeting came vividly to mind.

Lottie's glorious hazel eyes blazed with triumph. 'Mebbe it is an'mebbe it isn't,' she taunted, 'Nobody knows but me. This is one bairn that'll escape yer papist net, thank God,' and thrust his outstretched hand aside, glorying in the look on his irate face.

Jake glared, his devilish eyes dangerously alight, infuriated by such apparent indifference, Ralph Hanson's telling blows were mild punishment compared to his sister's withering contempt. Now Lottie had placed herself out of reach he wanted her again, that old, familiar urge strong in his loins, ready to plead his case with all the charm he could muster. In desperation he found his tongue, an elusive something fast slipping out of his grasp. 'Remember Batey's field, it could be like that again in a soft feather bed with a ring on yer finger but better next time. Aa promise ya.' A proposal he never meant to make to any woman. 'Batey's field!' Lottie hissed. 'That was a nightmare. An animal that's what y'were Jake Snowdon. It meant nowt t'me. Somethin' y'took that Aa wasn't willin' t'give. God help any lass that takes ya on. But one thing sure it winna be me.' She stopped to take a breath only to begin again in much quieter tone. 'Aye hinny, Aa'll sharp ferget but ye'll not. Every time y'see me bairn ye'll be wonderin' if it's yours. Let's hope it takes after me t'keep y'guessin.'

The final thrust, the biter bitten, it was Jake's turn to flee with scornful laughter wrapped around his ears. He obeyed a compelling urge to put distance between himself and a desirable young woman who wanted none of him, stripped his ego bare. Lottie's triumph was complete.

When the gate latch dropped into place, not a moment too soon, she sank to the cobbled ground her courage wilted, shattered by yet another emotional experience. Mattie Jackson, worried when she failed to return to the house, found her some time later. 'Howway lass, it's cold down there, ye'll catch yer death,' he coaxed and bent to lift her to her feet. 'Just say the word an' Aa'll run after'im. A punch i' the nose is what'ees askin' fer.' A quick look at her to see if Jake had resorted to violence, enough provocation he guessed, if the sound of raised voices counted for anything.

She pushed his helping hand aside and scrambled awkwardly into a standing position, suddenly averse to any man's touch, even Mattie Jackson's a dear friend. 'No need fer that, Mattie,' she said, 'Aa reckon Aa punched 'im hard enough, where it hurt the most.' The hardness of her voice echoed through the frosty air. 'Jake Snowdon'l not bother me again, Aa've seen t'that'. Utter satisfaction in every word as she spun around to berate Alice and Martha, brought out of doors by overwhelming curiosity. 'Stop gawpin', the pair o'ya. Aa guess y'heard some o'what Aa sayed but a lot of it wasn't true, no matter what the gossips get from a fella that's had 'is marchin' orders.' Wondering what Jake's version of their meeting would be, poured into a young priest's ears at the next confessional. A man of the cloth who probably pitied any lass who fell foul of his sort. Not too surprised that his plan had backfired and all the Hail Marys in the world wouldn't save such a rogue's Immortal Soul.

'Yer priceless,' Jackson marvelled, amazed at such resilience. 'Aa canna keep up wi' ya,' he tutted, rather taken aback at the look in her eyes, as hard as flint, and most disturbing. 'Aa'm priceless all right an' that's what Aa intend t'be from now on t'any man. Nobody'll get the chance t'bring me down again, ever.' A sobering thought for the fellow beside her, who adored her almost to distraction.

Three days later, Felicity Cranshawe and two of her female staff, with Mattie Jackson in attendance, rode into Newcastle, there to board a south bound train, Lottie quite inconsolable, huddled close to him on the driver's seat. It had been more of an effort than ever to climb up high, even with a helping hand. Not much to be seen of her except a chalk white face and two expressive eyes, full of mute appeal. Muffled almost to the eyeballs in warm, outdoor clothing, still shivering with cold but mostly apprehension, preferable to being closeted inside the carriage, with the two women she had grown to hate, her companions for goodness knows how long a time.

'Be sure t'look after yerself,' Jackson ordered brusquely as they proceeded through busy town streets. 'There'll be no chance t'say anythin' when w'reach the station, Aa'll have t'see t'the baggage.' There was a ton of it aboard, Madam never travelled light.

With the big portico already in sight as they rounded St John's in Grainger Street, Lottie's heart plunged even further into the depths. 'See that y'write as soon as y'get there,' Jackson urged, disturbed by the pallor of her face and the nervous way she plucked at the sleeve of his rough textured jacket.

An hour later, still haunted by this pitiful sight, he rode alone through the bustling Haymarket almost by instinct, his mind elsewhere, then along the Town Moor edge towards Branton Village, the mood in Rothwell House more than he could stand when he got there, both Martha and Alice down in the dumps, quite enough without the place awash with tears, the younger woman's bladder close to her eyes as Martha chose to express, a well used Geordieism where Alice was concerned.

In a railway carriage for the very first time, Lottie tried to contain her own tears as the distance widened, terribly disconsolate despite assurances they would be home before the end of March, cutting it rather fine. Madam was such a creature of whim, no telling what might happen, perhaps any ploy to keep them in London, her own comings and goings so dependent upon an unpredictable woman whose word was law, the Capital City their ultimate destination and the length of her stay impossible to determine. Not the most comforting of thoughts to take on such a long journey, which might well have been to the other side of the world.

* * *

The gloom surrounding the lower echelon in Rothwell House took some time to lift, although Alice's tears dried up almost immediately, always copious but never known to last long. Little wonder Martha heaved a deep sigh of relief when Jackson entered the kitchen, early one morning, a common buff envelope waved aloft and a huge grin spread right across his face, something nobody had seen for the past ten days. Lottie's first letter since she left for London and never had anything been more welcome.

'Not afore time,' Martha grunted, 'Aa was beginnin' t'think that scowl was on yer face fer good.' After which pointed reference to his atrocious behaviour she sat down, ready to be regaled with news of their absent friend.

Alice could hardly contain herself. 'Go on, what does sh'have t'say?' Impatient as ever, Jackson all thumbs in his effort to oblige. 'Just hold yer horses an' Aa'll tell ya,' wishing he could creep off somewhere to digest Lottie's letter but there was no chance of that. Neither woman could read nor write and such a move was bound to arouse suspicion in any case, his feelings towards Lottie kept strictly private or so he imagined.

A quick scan of the scribbled lines then he started to read aloud, any personal references to be skipped over, long sentences in childish handwriting, a dearth of capitals and little punctuation, the lass was far from literate. Full of the southward journey, Madam sick most of the way and Jessica Finlay clucking like a mother hen. 'But not over me,' she complained, 'Aa just had t'get on wi' the fetchin' an' carryin'.'

'Aa bet sh' had,' Martha commiserated, well able to picture the scene in that first class railway carriage and Lottie on the receiving end of Madam's ill humour as usual. 'It'll be a good thing when sh'gets back t'them that care about' er,' she said, Alice nodding her head off in agreement. 'Never mind them two,' she pleaded, anxious to hear the rest.

'Sh'says here,' Jackson continued 'there's a big park near the house called Kensin'ton Gardens and a monument put up by the old queen in memory of er husband. Lottie reckoned it must o'cost a bob or two.' His brow wrinkled into deep furrows. 'Funny Aa remember nowt about a park,' Martha was quick to add that mention of a public house might be different, but not in any seriousness, Jackson was no real drinker.

'Parks are fer women t'sit in wi'bairns in prams,' he insisted, Alice quick off the mark in reproval. 'Of all the cheek, Mattie Jackson. Who is it that sits on his backside while Aa muck the stables out?' Just good natured banter and no offence taken. Alice revelled in these dirty jobs and loved the horses, the farm a great miss, she was not so happy at the kitchen sink but the rest suited her fine, security she had never known before.

Jackson made a great show of folding the letter to put it away, unread, sufficient to provoke Martha into prompt reaction against Alice for the diversion. 'There's somebody around here getting too big fer their boots. Shut up,' she was told, the words accompanied by a sharp flick across the ear, only possible because the big lass was sitting at the kitchen table where she tucked into her fourth slice of bread and jam, the bread freshly baked. 'That belly o'yours is a bottomless pit.' Martha snorted and pulled the whole lot out of reach, truly convinced Alice's main purpose in life was to make up for past deprivation. She munched away as Jackson gave them the gist of Lottie's letter, secretly upset there was nothing for his eyes alone, just generalities. 'One page o'nowt,' he muttered when it came to an end, so much less than he needed to hear, a remark greeted with deliberate sarcasm. 'Who was it that sayed just a line would be enough?' Martha put in drily, words he had so often quoted over the past few days. 'Have a heart man. We all know what Jessica's like, the poor lass'll be glad t'crawl inta bed at night. Her nose'll be kept t'the grindstone and that's a fact.' The sad truth but the wrong thing to say to a lovelorn fellow, immediately concerned lest his beloved was overworked in her condition. Inclined to forget the resilience of youth and Lottie's undeniable guts, sure to stand her in good stead when pressure was brought to bear.

Lottie bloomed while Madam wilted, Felicity's delicate features were puffed and distorted, more than vanity would endure, her young servant's life made a misery, impossible to please however hard the girl tried. Her aunt's tyranny was another cross to bear.

In the seclusion of his stable refuge, Jackson read the double page of writing once again, bitterly disappointed at the lack of personal touch. 'Aa miss ya Mattie,' would have been a great joy but wasn't there, just treated on par with Martha and Alice, nobody special. 'Y' should o'married me,' came the plaintive cry to four silent walls and forgot he had never really asked, heard only by a tiny pony and two black stallions, all bewildered by their keeper's noisy anguish.

One item of news previously skipped brought a faint glimmer of amusement into Jackson's melancholy eyes. 'The master isn't back yet an' me aunt harps on about it, says it's all his fault and its time 'ee was. Aa reckon sh'doesn't like'im very much, which means Aa will when Aa get t'see 'im.' A throaty chuckle despite his despondency, he had a great respect for Geoffrey Cranshawe, considered too good for the gaffer's spoilt daughter, a real gent. Nothing much to come home to even if his wife was in the family way. There was something radically wrong with that marriage, had been right from the beginning.

'The Askews aren't s'bad fer southerners,' Lottie condescended to say. 'Not that Aa'd see the wife i'me way when it comes t'hard graft.' Full of north country conceit when it entered the sphere of working ability. Jackson had drunk many a pint of ale in Charlie Askew's company over the years but held some reservations regarding Fanny, his well proportioned wife, who definitely ruled the roost. A good cook he had to admit, many a gastronomical delight eaten at the huge kitchen table. The Askews had no room for Felicity. 'Not a patch on the old Missis,' Fanny declared, 'She was a proper lady,' Madam was relegated to a much lower place in the order of things.

Two weeks passed before the next letter arrived and, to crown all Jackson was away from the house when it did come, the whole of the past fortnight spent waylaying the postman before he reached the front entrance. This particular morning he was out on an errand for John Starrett, to one of his three collieries, all within close distance.

'Now w'might get some peace,' Martha tutted, as he tore open the usual buff envelope with an eagerness he failed to conceal. 'She's been cryin',' he growled, quick to notice smudges on the single sheet of paper, torn from a cheap exercise book. 'What has that damned pair been up t'now?' blame immediately placed where it surely belonged. 'Get on with it lad,' Martha prodded, 'Read what the lass has t'say this time,' busy as she spoke but no sign of urgency, Jessica Finlay's absence was a real boon, relieved from the housekeeper's constant interference.

'No business bidin' down there, the lass should be among'er own sort when she has the bairn.'

'So, they're stoppin'in London?' Martha was disappointed but not unduly surprised despite her former optimism about an early return. Mattie's reaction was sufficient to cause raised eyebrows and immediate speculation, a long held suspicion now confirmed.

'Aye, they're bidin',' Jackson said. 'It says here Madam's not fit t'travel. The daft bitch shouldn't o'gone i'the first place, takin' that canny lass s'far from home.' An impassioned speech, with no sympathy to spare for his sick employer, who was really out of sorts and advised not to risk the long journey. His customary guard came down and Martha laid a consoling hand on his broad shoulder as he slumped across the table, resisting an impulse to stroke his bowed head. 'Yer fond o'that lass, Mattie,' she stated in a quiet voice and saw his whole body stiffen in alarm, too late to cover his foolish indiscretion, 'An' what if Aa am?' he shot back defensively, suddenly erect in his chair, unwilling to display any further sign of weakness.

'All right t'be fond lad, w'all are,' she deemed fit to advise but added a word of caution. 'As long as it's no more than that. Lottie likes ya well enough, the same as me an' Alice, mebbe a bit more but not as ye want it t'be.' Painfully blunt but better he knew the full score. 'Nobody realises that more than me but nowt can alter what Aa feel about her,' he said in despair, the sight of a grown man almost reduced to tears was sufficient to arouse Martha's deepest sympathy. She made no further comment and an awkward silence descended upon them, rudely interrupted when Alice barged into the room, mercifully too late to learn of Jackson's obsession with her dearest friend.

'Not one word, mind ya,' he hissed under his breath, 'That lass canna keep'er own watter,' fully resolved there would be no further revelations, an intimate confidence between Martha and himself who covered up in a burst of aggression. 'D'ye have t'come inta my kitchen stinkin'o'horse muck?' she rapped at the intruder, whose general appearance left much to be desired.

'A champion smell,' Alice defended, quite unperturbed at this reference to her personal hygiene. 'Can Aa take Tiger out on the road fer a bit, it's a grand day.' A request greeted with an exaggerated sigh, their male companion master of himself once more. 'Aa'll be up the creek without a paddle if Jessica finds out but aye, y'can take'im. Mind that trap, it's not the sturdiest o'vehicles.' The words were barely uttered before she was out of the room, no time given for second thoughts.

'That'll keep her off the subject o'Lottie fer a bit. Give ya a chance t'sort yerself out. She'll have hitched up already, knows what a soft touch y'are. Aa sometimes wish Aa was more like the lass, nowt bother's 'er fer long. Mebbe she's better off than them wi'all their senses,' Jackson was rather doubtful. 'One way o'lookin at, Aa suppose, but there's more t'Alice than most folk think and one thing sure, sh'has a way wi'horses. Sh'makes my job a damned sight easier, when them two aren't around.' One fact Martha didn't care to dispute. Tiger was already harnessed to put between the shafts, always amenable nowadays. With no time lost the gawky lass was soon on her way, closely watched by those she left behind. Both of them braved cold

February air to see her off the premises. Martha shivered in her thin shoes amazed at Alice's toughness, not even a shawl to protect those brawny shoulders.

Jackson chuckled as she left the yard still laughing when they went indoors. 'Aa could well imagine that lass drivin' a chariot inta battle and God help the enemy, the sight of her enough t'scare the livin' daylight out o'them?' A vivid picture of a twentieth century Boadicea setting her foes to right. Jackson was a well read man but a comparison which passed right over Martha's head, disinclined towards any romantic nonsense as she called it. Her main concern was the menus for that particular day, John Starrett's orders given before he left that morning. In residence quite often while Felicity was away, he was not likely to take kindly to the lengthened stay in Harrow Square.

Ever practical, Martha grunted in disapproval, 'Aa hope that flighty madam remembers there's veg t'prepare,' and set about her own chores with a will. Jackson took himself off to read Lottie's letter a second time, disinclined to indulge in further conversation, Alice's timely arrival had been a godsend. Too much said already his soul laid bare, and none too sure of Martha's discretion, quite wrong as it happened, she was talkative no doubt but she knew when to keep her mouth shut. In this case to open it unwisely could only do untold harm, discretion was the better part of valour.

* * *

Saltersgate was to be Alice's final destination, unable to resist the opportunity to show off in the village, to drive through it with smart little Tiger in the pony trap right up her street. It was a definite bid to make folk sit up and take notice but not the wisest thing to do.

First into Branton, labelled village but rather more than that, a place which seemed to grow in small ways with every day that passed. Highly elated by this special treat, she drove by the many and varied shops beside the Great North Road, an area very much alive on this chilly but fine Monday morning, well astir after the recognised day of rest and church going. The former was rather a fallacy although such harmless pastimes as knitting and sewing were definitely out of order.

New buildings had already sprung up on the green belt between it and Saltersgate, many changes and more to come, the big, imposing mental hospital surrounded on all sides by an assortment of dwelling places and shops in Saltersgate, Ashrigg and Branton, the exclusive Oakfields set apart from the rest in the spendour born out of affluence.

The happy wanderer soon emerged from this general hubbub and carried on in a northerly direction, cow pasture with odd fields under the plough to left and right. Urban tentacles had not reached out this far as yet. Hedgerows still bore evidence of the last fall of snow, the roadway clear with some remains of heavy drifts still to be seen here and there but they gradually disappeared little by little when the sun chose to shine for brief spells. A mile or so of such terrain before she got to the western boundary of Branton Park, well known in racing circles for its fine course.

A number of Saltersgate men enjoyed the thrill of the turf and attended whenever there was a meeting, idle shifts to indulge in this addictive pleasure. Money was gambled away, although badly needed for better purpose, by those ever hopeful of that big win to solve some of their monetary problems but generally they only managed to create more.

Alice took off to the left into land totally given over to farming of all kinds, the only signs of occupation were stone built houses and the necessary barns and outbuildings. Most of it was grazing land but not too far away to the right was a winding wheel and the mountain of slag from Polrigg Colliery, ugly blots on an otherwise pleasant landscape. Mostly tenant farmers with John Starrett as landlord, only a small part of his extensive acreage of land, he was a very prosperous man.

Alice sang as she rode alongside these fields, tuneless maybe but full expression of the wonderful sense of freedom which was hers for a while. Alone except for the tiny pony, his mane flung into the air as happy as the girl herself. Nobody here to call her daft Alice and dish out the treatment endured since early childhood. Alice's sort was always fair game for the ignorant, made to feel less than nothing by a community at large.

She kept to ruts made by other vehicles, great care taken to avoid pot holes as she moved closer to Saltersgate by these back roads. Her careless rapture was soon to be destroyed when she entered the village, to reap what she had recently sown and she could not have picked a worse day. The mere sight of her in Felicity Cranshawe's elegant contraption was sufficient to ignite a very short fuse. The streets were thronged, Monday the day when active poss sticks created a drum like accompaniment to the usual routine, these familiar implements were strangely silent. Both men and women congregated in small groups, the clamour of angry voices all around. Women, as usual, the least inhibited as they screeched frustration, the deeper tones of menfolk adding to the general uproar, something sadly amiss.

Alice sensed the hostile atmosphere and was scared to death but carried on bravely, despite the malicious murmurs from all sides as she attempted to manoeuvre the light conveyance through those who deliberately blocked her passage, absolutely terrified when one screaming virago broke loose to hurl abuse, egged on by her cronies. Lizzie Phillips, recently widowed and in vicious mood, out for blood, two bewildered youngsters clinging to her long black skirt. Less than three months since Jackie died in the same accident that took Alice's father. A bereaved woman, considerably soured by the experience and almost at the end of her tether.

'The nerve of ya,' she yelled at the hapless lass and leant against the trap, liable to upset its precarious balance, her obvious aim. 'Ye comin' among us in that fancy rig. Workin' fer the gaffer's daughter, when it was them that killed my Jackie and yer own father,' she raged, Tiger becoming increasingly restless between the shafts.

'Hold on there,' Alice pleaded, 'The poor beast's terrified.' But it fell on deaf ears, the woman was too far gone, no stopping this demented creature.

'How does that fat bastard think we manage. Locked them out, that's what'ee's done cause they wouldn't take a cut in wages.' A different voice, that of a woman who suckled a child at her breast, no longer an infant but better than another plate to fill. Not that the bairn got much nourishment from a mother drastically underfed. The action was a comfort of sorts that was all.

Alice soon got the message, the gaffer was at the root of it and she worked for his daughter, something even she understood, as simple as that. 'Aa just graft fer me bread an'butter the same as anybody else,' she argued defensively, greeted with a snort of derision. 'Butter sh' says, drippin'fer us an'little o'that afore long if that hard bastard doesn't give in,' was thrown at her. Not one friendly face, everyone tight lipped with uncompromising looks which boded ill for a helpless quarry.

Totally unhinged, Lizzie Phillips kept up the impetus. 'Done all right fer yerselves, ye an' Lottie Hanson, but she hasn't the gall t'come among decent folk.' Alice tensed with fear, afraid of bodily harm to herself and the pony. The canny little fellow didn't deserve such harsh treatment, her main anxiety.

Lizzie, high as a kite, was right into her stride. 'Howway lasses, let's pull the daft bitch out o'trap,' she shouted, totally deranged. 'Sh'canna ride wi'the hounds an'run wi'the hare.' A cruel notion which held enormous appeal, the whole assembly in ugly mood. Lizzie was determined someone should pay for Jackie's death and her own sorrow. Albeit a fellow sufferer, absolutely beyond the bounds of reason.

Savage fingers clawed at Alice's clothing but she clung tenaciously to the reins, strong emotions fanned into flame by her untimely arrival at their midst. No longer one of their own, a gaffer's lass which made her a pariah and deserved to be treated as such.

But salvation came from a most unlikely source as a neatly dressed woman pushed her way through the anagonistic crowd, a child in her arms. 'Enough, enough I say,' the words from a refined tongue, alien among so many Geordie voices. Their language crude but ignored by the intruder, who used one arm to pull Lizzie away from the trap, bellowing in protest. 'Ye mind yer own affairs, y'aren't one o'us. Y'canna even talk proper.' Amusing if less serious.

Trembling beneath such animosity, Margaret Hanson ordered Alice to steady the pony and moved towards the frightened beast's head to gentle him with soft, reassuring words. Tiger gave a whinny of gratitude in return, glad to be under some sort of control once more.

Silence hung in the air, full of menace, ready to erupt into further uproar when the woman recovered from their initial surprise, Lizzie was first to find her tongue, wild with rage. 'What d'ye know about life i' these parts, Alice Ruddick's gone over t'the gaffers, the same as yer sister-in-law. Th'both deserve what's comin t'them. And ye'better keep yer nose out of it,' she threatened, only to be rounded upon, Margaret's tone no longer subdued. 'Foolish talk. My husband is locked out of Polrigg too but this poor girl isn't responsible for that,' she insisted, Lizzie straight into retaliation. 'She's a traitor, a bloody traitor, and w'know what t'do wi'them i' these parts.' An echo of agreement from many throats.

Margaret kept them talking and the resentment soon diverted herself, giving Alice an opportunity to recover somewhat. She held onto Tiger's reins, still afraid of the outcome but slightly more in control of the situation, her champion still at his head. Ralph Hanson's wife carried on forcefully, not to be silenced before she had her say. 'This is just a flash in the pan. We all work for John Starrett and our men will be back again very soon, they can't hold out.' Only to be shouted down. 'Not till they get the promise o'more money out o'the greedy bugger.' Many voices raised in agreement on this vital issue, not prepared to listen to any sort of reason. But Margaret persisted. 'We can't win these battles, our children's hunger won't let us,' and heaved a sigh of relief when the women moved aside. For the moment at least she held the advantage and intended to use it, some already ashamed of their behaviour. Not Lizzie Phillips, still in aggressive frame of mind. 'All right fer you, Mrs High an'Mighty. Your man wasn't killed at the pit, leavin, ya wi'three bairns. The oldest's just nine an'he's at the pit heap scrattin'fer coal. Just ye wait till somethin' happens t'wipe the smarmy look off yer face.'

'Hold that sharp tongue o'yours, Lizzie,' another voice rapped out. A staunch Catholic who crossed herself to ward off disaster, very superstitious, no desire to take further part in the whole nasty business.

Much braver than she felt, Margaret looked her main opponent straight in the eyes, dreadfully disturbed by the pure malice mirrored there. 'I grieve for your loss. Jackie was a friend of my husband from boyhood and he speaks well of him. We all live with fear when our men work underground but I would never wish misfortune such as yours on any other person.'

'Aye, Aa reckon that t'be the truth,' came from the rear and Janey Wilson pushed herself forward, too late to witness the whole affair but never slow on the uptake. 'Go on hinny, ye'll have no more bother, send Alice Ruddick on'er way.' Full of admiration for Margaret's courageous stand, a formidable ally and the women all knew it.

Margaret gave tremulous thanks and hastened Alice along our of harm's way. A very upset lass, eager for the safety of Rothwell House, where Jackson would be at his wits end about her prolonged absence and Martha on her high horse, the vegetables still to be prepared for the evening meal. She left Margaret without a single word of gratitude not even a backward glance as the way ahead miraculously cleared at Janey's insistence. Some women were very contrite but others rather resentful of the southerner's interference in village affairs.

Janey took a reluctant Lizzie Phillips indoors, in a dreadful state still ranting on. Two distressed bairns followed in her wake, such strange behaviour was difficult for them to comprehend, there had been too much disturbance in their young lives of late. There was tea and a little chat before they returned to a house so cheerless without Jackie's lively presence. Still a roof over their heads because his father worked at the pit, often the worse for drink. The widowed lass was obliged to barricade herself and the young ones in at night to avoid abuse and sexual advances. Things the demented woman chose not to disclose, any roof was better than none at all. Margaret and her neighbour exchanged brief nods

Before they parted company, the pallor of the younger woman's face was of equal concern to Janey, who realised nevertheless that Alice Ruddick's deliverer would prefer to lick her wounds in private, the sort of person she was and she had certainly weighed her up correctly.

Once indoors the air of composure vanished and she fell to the floor sobbing bitterly, with every reason to the doubt the wisdom of her recent actions, a champion for someone she barely knew. But, a fellow human in distress was enough justification for her soft heart, a troubled mind harder to convince. The fragile relationship between herself and Saltersgate female population was on a knife's edge and maybe damaged beyond repair. And how would Ralph react?

Her husband heard the whole sorry tale from Janey later that day, with a strict warning from his neighbour to say nowt. 'Let the lass speak fer'erself if sh'feels the need,' she advised, a confession Margaret didn't deem necessary, different should he make first approach. Somehow pleased by his wife's ability to get stuck in on an occasion such as this, Ralph left well alone, anxious for Margaret to find her own level in village life, somewhat reassured by this latest episode which proved her capable of doing just that. It would only take time and patience.

A much subdued young lass drove back to Rothwell House, immediately on the sharp end of Martha's tongue but soon halted by the sight of her dishevelled appearance and absolutely aghast when the sorry tale was told. 'A lot o'savages, that's what they are. Ye bide away from the village from now on me lass' she ordered brusquely, Alice was amazed at such unusual concern.

'Frightened,' Mattie Jackson declared, 'All scared out o' the wits. Bad enough t'manage with a pay packet goin' inta the house never mind nowt at all. Fear makes ya do funny things at times.'

The logic of which went right over their heads as might be expected. Alice sniffed louder than ever while Martha grunted her disapproval and unconsciously touched a sore spot with her next words. 'Lottie's mebbe best where sh'is wi'such goins on,' she said, Jackson quick to disagree. 'She'd be far better off here with us,' he claimed, still not able to come to terms with the thought of Lottie's prolonged absence. 'And ye,' he barked at Alice in frustration, 'Y' knew there was a lock out, y'must o'been barmy showin'yer face in Saltersgate. It'll be a long time afore y'get that rig on the road again. Thank yer lucky stars there's just a scratch or two Aa can touch up. An'tidy yerself up, yer a right mess.'

She did look appalling, hardly a hair in place, that sandy mane torn from its pins by vindictive fingers, bruises on arms and face and ripped clothing to vouch for the truth of her story. Only in one respect did she stray from it, no mention of Margaret, Janey Wilson fixed as the heroine in Alice's mind, which simply retained what she wanted to believe, all else deliberately blotted from memory.

The pitiful saga was repeated time and again over the oncoming weeks, much embellished in her inimitable style but Margaret still received no credit for her part in the rescue. She was dreadfully afraid Lottie would hear of it and disapprove of any contact with her brother's wife. A grave injustice in a determination to keep on good terms with her dearest friend, never to learn of her sister-in-law's heroic stand.

The lock out came to an end in the matter of days, sooner even then Margaret expected, any attempt at rebellion guaranteed to suffer the same fate. Saltersgate miners went back to work cap in hand, tails between their legs, conditions no better and wages reduced. Empty bellies won the day for the gaffer, guaranteed to do so for years to come, this sojourn in a wilderness of poverty and despair fated to be long and very arduous.

* * *

Lottie lay flat on her back, strangely fascinated by an assortment of weird shapes which cavorted in a macabre sort of dance on the low ceiling above her head. She soon realised a flickering candle played its nightly charade with furniture and other objects around the tiny room, her own bedroom at the top of the Cranshawe's House in Harrow Square, just a stone's throw from Kensington Gardens.

Once recognised for what they were, the shapes ceased to cause alarm and she sank deeper into the feather mattress, secure in the familiarity of her surroundings. A semi conscious state penetrated by a low murmur of voices, one vaguely disturbing, but an addled mind refused to give faces to them and she submerged into a thick blanket of fog. Now there was no searing pain to tear her body apart and she felt weightless almost, so different from an agony endured for hours on end, such torture as never known before.

Lottie's cold fingers groped tentatively across the patchwork quilt in search of human contact, a hand to hold, any hand would do, plagued by a persistent niggle that something was wrong, terribly wrong. 'There now, ducky,' somebody whispered close to ear and her searching fingers felt the welcome touch of warm flesh. 'Rest easy,' she heard the voice day, 'All over and done with, nothing left for you to worry about.'

Worry about what, she fretted, and struggled hard to put a name to the voice. Why couldn't she remember? Yet somehow she was possessed of a strong desire for this forgetfulness to last forever, strangely reluctant to emerge into reality, discover what the mist was hiding from her. Then suddenly a name, Fanny, of course, Fanny Askew, her Cockney accent unmistakable. A bustling little woman who talked a lot but never failed to be kind, a thought which engendered a warm feeling of safety. But safe from whom or what she couldn't imagine.

'Poor young thing,' her comforter said in a hushed tone, 'No sense in tellin' her now, better wait till mornin', nothin' seems so bad in the light of day. Heaven knows I wouldn't want to be the one to break the news.' A sentiment swiftly refuted. 'Nonsense, Charlotte must be told at once, then she can put the whole business behind her, we all can.' That other voice now recognised and devoid of anything except pure irritation. Aunt Jessica, the person she hated most in the world, she and her mistress, both on a par in cruelty towards her.

A bewildered mind tried to grasp at elusive thoughts, something she couldn't recollect but felt she must and was afraid to make the effort, her young face uplifted in silent but eloquent appeal, Jessica Finlay impervious to the distress in her niece's haunted eyes. 'Your child is dead, Charlotte, stillborn. All for the best I believe.' A shattering revelation delivered in a cold, emotionless manner, no softening of the blow.

Fanny Askew gasped in horror as Lottie's mouth opened wide to shriek denial but no sound came, incredulous eyes turned from one woman to the other, unable to accept the enormity of what she had just been told. Why should her baby be born dead? A healthy lass with never a day's illness in her life apart from the usual childhood complaints. There had to be some mistake.

Fanny made no attempt to mince words, red with indignation. 'There was no need for that,' she said in heightened tone, 'Bad enough without blurtin' it out in such a way,' and did her best to console the stricken girl. 'Cry love, let the grief come, let it all out,' she coaxed, immune to Jessica Finlay's tut of impatience and blocked the housekeeper's way when she moved purposefully towards the bed.

'Move aside, Fanny, I shall deal with this,' she snapped, completely taken aback at the little woman's reaction. 'Not a chance. I wouldn't leave you t'look after a wounded animal, let alone a broken hearted girl,' and finished with a snort of disgust and a final condemnation, 'You've done more than enough harm for one night.' Not at all intimidated by Jessica Finlay's baleful glare she ignored the heartless woman from then on to turn full attention upon the wretched lass, who thrashed around the bed in sheer agony of mind, absolutely distraught. The sound of a latch as it fell into place told her the disgruntled female had left the room.

'I haven't heard the last of this little lot,' she accepted ruefully, sure of the wrath to come but totally unperturbed, she was more valuable to the household than madam's lap dog any day of the week, Lottie was her main concern. Much relieved when the writhing ceased and tears began to flow. 'That's it mi love, let it go, Fanny's here. The old bitch has gone and good riddance,' she soothed, motherly arms wrapped around a heaving body, greatly disturbed by the bereaved girl's anguish.

Much later, in the privacy of their own bedroom, Fanny confided in Charlie, still up tight at Jessica Finlay's outrageous behaviour. 'It wasn't sufficient t'tell her in that way, she had t'come back half an hour later with the little dead body. Just like a skinned rabbit it was.' Agitated even in retrospect.

Charlie swore out loud and attached a few strong adjectives to Jessica Finlay's name, no fan of hers in the first place, able to add further information to what his wife already knew. 'I was sent to tell Doctor Clements to come in the mornin'. The old biddy had a busy day all told, Madam delivered in the afternoon and Lottie a few hours later, midwife t'both. I didn't think she would know how, her being a spinster,' he said, amazed at the sequence of events and Jessica's important role in the whole affair.

Fanny eased her ampled proportions under the bedclothes. 'Be what she may, Charlie, she must have had a fine old time with all the goin's on. But not t'send for the doctor, what was she thinkin' of? No chance of savin' the little boy, he never drew breath,' she said with a heartfelt sigh.

'She said there was nobody t'send for the doctor with both of us out of the house and she couldn't leave herself.'

'Fair set I was for goin' to Bookham for your mother's birthday but wild horses wouldn't have dragged me if I knew what would happen.' Fanny was most contrite.

Charlie made sympathetic noises and assured her nobody could have known. 'One early and the other late,' he remarked and slid into into bed beside her but not before he carefully wound the solid silver watch presented to him by Colonel Mark Cranshawe for loyal service to the family. 'Three o'clock,' he muttered as he performed this nightly ritual with due ceremony. 'And up again at six. A lot t'do tomorrow and Jessica in a foul temper, no doubt. The woman doesn't like to be crossed. It's a funny business altogether,' he stated reflectively, 'Considerin' the way Madam was held all along. Like a dyin' duck most of the time. I would have staked my last penny on her havin'a stillborn infant. Lottie was always fit as a fiddle except for the way the pair of them went at her.' A chuckle of amusement at some thought or other, foolishly expressed. 'Y'don't think the old girl made a switch?' Rather astounded at his wife's explosive reaction.

'I most certainly do not,' she said and clapped a silencing hand across his wide open mouth, gagging a little at the unexpectedness of it all. Fanny's feelings were given voice in no uncertain manner. 'If you have any sense in that bald head of yours, you'll keep such wicked notions to yourself or we'll both be out on our ears. You must be mad, Charles Askew,' His baptismal name only used when annoyed with him for some reason as she definitely was now.

'A joke, Fanny, a joke,' he spluttered when she removed her hand, genuinely upset by his wife's concern. 'A poor sort of joke,' she said in rebuke, 'which could land us in a lot of trouble if you don't keep your mouth shut. Anyway, if one had to be taken it was the right one, God forgive me for sayin so. What chance had she of bringin' it up proper and her not wed. For the best, Charlie, for the best,' she declared and settled down for a few hours sleep, leaving an exhausted lass alone in her attic room, the reality to be faced again in the light of day.

Fanny took her breakfast on a tray just after seven, nicely set out, and said almost the same to Lottie, who was unwilling to accept the food or the homily.

How could that wizened body in the wicker basket be her child when she felt nothing but revulsion at the sight it it? Never a tear when Charlie took it away to be buried in unconsecrated ground nearby. A boy, who might have been named after her father, John Matthew perhaps because of Mattie Jackson's constant support. None of her flesh and blood, she disclaimed, obliged to turn away from the naked pity in Fanny Askew's eyes.

The Cockney servant took great pains to point the danger of voicing such sentiments in her aunt's hearing, certain to make matters worse, one fact that even overwhelming grief had to accept, Jessica Finlay's attitude was easy to imagine, more detested now than ever before.

When she reviewed the past twenty four hours, she found it hard to believe so much had happened, a sequence of events to alter her entire existence, to bear a child and lose it so tragically. Cruelly denied the joy of motherhood as she would be of love in marriage, she felt resentful and very bitter, left with a permanent scar on an aching heart.

* * *

It had all begun the previous morning with an awkward struggle out of bed yet filled with sense of well being not experienced for quite some time, which only lasted until the Askews departed for Victoria Station, from which moment on everything changed in such drastic fashion.

'It's me time, Aa think, Aunt Jessica,' she faltered, troubled with an aching back and another unmistakable sign, terribly embarrassed when water trickled down her legs, soaking her woollen stockings and dripped onto the linoleum covered floor. 'Aa'll sharp mop it up,' she hastened to say, Jessica Finlay none too pleased at this premature development. 'All right, get on with it,' she grunted, ill humour most apparent. 'Then go to your room. How many pains have you had and at what intervals?' Double dutch to the bewildered lass, who stared at her in amazement, her aunt immediately derisive. 'Good heavens girl, did my sister tell you nothing? It would behove you to find out when you get yourself into such a predicament. You can't have had any real pain or you would know.' This from a confirmed spinster, whose knowledge came from the books she had read since her mistress became pregnant.

As if to prove her wrong, Lottie suddenly doubled up under a savage attack which tore ruthlessly through her body and made her gasp for breath. 'Your first, obviously,' Jessica said and waited impassively until the agonising spasm took its heavy toll. 'You will be some time yet but no fuss and no noise, Madam is unwell this morning and must be my main consideration. Put on a clean night dress and get into bed. See that you protect the mattress with a rubber sheet. There are newspapers under the sink, take them with you.' The orders were delivered in quick succession, no sympathy towards the apprehensive girl who barely knew what to expect, what she had experienced not very pleasant and just the beginning, the purpose of the newspaper an absolute mystery.

The pain subsided but mute appeal crept into Lottie's luminous eyes. 'What shall Aa do wi'the cloth?' she said after mopping up with some effort, the wet rag clenched in her fist. 'What do you think?' came the sarcastic retort, 'Rinse it out of course and hang in outside to freshen. I should have thought that was obvious.' Unable to contain her impatience, Lottie's early labour was a decided inconvenience.

'Why didn't you say something before Fanny left? Now I must do everything myself,' soon reminded that Fanny hadn't been off for ages, which didn't go down at all well, Lottie's plea to stay downstairs was given curt denial, even her aunt's company being preferable to being left alone at the top of the house. She longed to be in Rothwell House her friends close at hand, not just this heartless creature to depend upon.

'Do as you are told,' Jessica barked, not to be thwarted, in no mood for insubordination. 'Remember you brought this upon yourself,' was the cruel retort as Lottie began the long haul to her attic room, forced to stop several times for breath, weighed down by the bundle of newspaper, carried at her aunt's insistence.

It was the start of a lonely day, punctuated at ever decreasing intervals of fearsome attacks of pain, sure her whole body would be torn apart in the process. If this was childbirth, no wonder Alice Greenhaugh was old before her time, convinced that her husband should be shot for cruelty.

Jessica made an appearance at eleven thirty and watched as Lottie forced down a few mouthfuls of clear soup, barely a word spoken, no reassurance, nothing, the usual offhand behaviour she had come to expect. After which the housekeeper looked in from time to time until the ordeal reached its final stages, somewhere towards evening.

By some strange quirk of fate, Lottie's labour ran almost parallel with that of her mistress, a baby girl born to Felicity at four in the afternoon, a few hours before Lottie's stillborn son arrived, which meant he never drew a single breath, no lusty cry to announce his coming into the world, straight from his mother's womb into the cold arms of death. A cruel blow after nine months of waiting and she knew now that despite the circumstances of his conception she would have loved her son.

Lost in these soul destroying thoughts, Lottie buried her face deep into the soft pillows, already drenched with tears and offered up a prayer for its tiny soul, flesh of her flesh, useless to deny that fact any longer, prepared to accept it as a punishment for her sins, harsh though it might be.

Then suddenly she had a flash of memory, the missing piece of a jigsaw slotted into place, the echo of a baby's cry loud in her ears before she sank into oblivion, worn out after hours of sheer agony.

With a heart fit to burst and unaware of the implication she tried to recapture the joy of that moment, exhausted but content because her child was born at last. This feeling was soon replaced by one of cold realisation as the dreadful truth penetrated her numbed senses and she flinched from it, asking herself why Jessica Finlay insisted the child was stillborn when she recalled that wonderful sound of a new life coming into being.

Some time elapsed before a shocked mind recovered enough to reason properly, soon very much alert and absolutely appalled at what this latest development signified. Her aunt's attitude shrieked of guilt and deception, so angry when she asked after Madam and her child, natural enough one would have thought. Strange to threaten the madhouse if accusations were made when none were intended. She had had no idea of what might be involved until this very moment, it was almost too dreadful to contemplate.

If her suspicions were true, the infant who lay in the well appointed nursery on the first floor had no right to be there, its origins much more humble. But protest and accusation were futile, it was Aunt Jessica's word against hers, supported by Madam, the whole weight of the system stacked against her.

The distraught young lass cried out in anguish to a God who did not seem to care and almost drowned in despair. Her aunt had surely travelled down the road to damnation and wondered if Felicity Cranshawe knew of the duplicity. How much more was she expected to bear? Jake's betrayal which began it all, Ralph's rejection and now this incredible situation, the real truth never likely to be divulged, to go through the rest of her life plagued with doubt. No hope of any redress for someone in such a lowly position in life.

But the idea of turning away from the child she believed to be hers never entered Lottie's head, life without contact of some sort was too painful to visualise. What a load to carry with her through the years, the class barrier erected high between them, no end to the torment. An agonising sound tore from her lips, like the cry of an animal caught in a snare which held her fast and tightened ever more securely around her.

Informed by John Starrett of the ill starred circumstances, Rothwell House servants grieved for Lottie's loss but wetted the new Cranshawe baby's head in excellent sherry provided by her proud grandfather. They eagerly awaited the return of their friend and the infant, rather less overjoyed at the thought of Madam and Jessica Finlay due to intrude upon them at the same time. Both Martha and Mattie Jackson believed that things had turned out for the best although sad at heart for what Lottie must be going through and so far from home. Alice was the only one to wallow in disappointment, her simple mind unable to accept this dreadful stroke of misfortune. Not that her grief, noisily expressed as usual and quite genuine, was expected to last for any length of time. When Lottie returned to the fold the joy at seeing her again would outweigh all other considerations, and they all hoped it would be soon, Mattie Jackson most of all.

The big fellow sent a letter of condolence, the only one she received, Martha and Alice were illiterate and who else was there to care. News of it, naturally, reached Saltersgate, Margaret's tears were shed in private, Ralph silent on the matter as might be expected whatever his thoughts and feelings. Janey Wilson grieved for the lass but life under her own roof was unbearable with Tod's reaction to Mary's love affair, secret no longer. The pit belt did not come into action, mainly because of Janey's firm stand for once in her married life, not able to go along with her husband's obvious intention, Tommy was deprived of money and satisfaction. Mary, of course, was broken hearted, the relationship brought to an end by strong disapproval on both sides, the big guns used to great effect.

Mattie's letter and a further epistle got no answer as Lottie struggled to achieve a sense of normality, too sick at heart to indulge in ordinary chit chat and dreadfully afraid Jackson might read between the lines if she wrote in any other vein. Certain in her own mind that even this closest of friends must never know of her suspicion, a defensive wall to erect before they met again, a mammoth task for someone in a perpetual state of torment and indecision.

Bloody but unbowed, the poor lass emerged from her ordeal, a great deal of effort was required to keep calm when she wanted to hurl accusations right, left and centre. 'She's getting' over it,' Fanny said, 'Praise the Lord.' But Charlie, much more perceptive, noticed the look in Lottie's hazel eyes, in which the innocence of youth had been replaced by an indefinable something the kindly man did not understand, not just grief. He remembered the strange conversation with Fanny, her outrage quite justified but deliberated again, nevertheless, then dismissed the thoughts as absolute nonsense, much safer in this assumption.

On the long journey north, several weeks later, given a tiny bundle to hold, Lottie tended to the infant's needs along almost three hundred miles of railway track. Madam occupied the whole of Jessica Finlay's attention as usual, neither woman remotely interested in the child but quick to berate the young nurse when it cried. Not that Lottie minded, already fiercely protective towards her precious charge, fully convinced the tiny girl baby was her own child.

Many tedious hours lay between them and their final destination, where Mattie Jackson awaited with transport and Lottie braced herself to meet his keen, blue eyes without a blink. Her other friends also when she arrived home and basked in the admiration showered upon the baby, aglow with pride of achievement, certain that one day truth would prevail, which the odds stacked against her made such a remote possibility. 'Aa'll love'er t'death,' she vowed, the sight of that tiny body held so close and the adoration in those beautiful hazel eyes almost too much for Mattie Jackson to bear, nothing there for anyone else, his own hopes dashed.

Lottie's devoted swain sighed in resignation. 'An' Aa was daft enough t'think sh'might turn t'me,' he grieved, forced to accept the hopelessness of his own cause. 'That bairn's all she wants, anybody would imagine it was hers the way sh'hangs onta it,' he said to Martha, an expression of sympathy in those dull grey eyes. 'Aa'll make some tea,' she mumbled, sick at heart for Lottie's loss but fully convinced the girl was young enough to bounce back again. 'She'll give'erself wholeheartedly t'this other one,' she told herself, certain that caring for Felicity Cranshawe's child would be Lottie's salvation, an ironic truth.

Those below stairs were able to relax once their peevish mistress was fed and settled down to rest after her long journey. John Starrett unavoidably detained at one of his collieries was not expected until later. 'Restin',' Martha snorted, 'Aa know who has the most right t'be worn out,' alarmed at the sight of Lottie's pinched white face. 'Not her or that other selfish bitch fer sure. She wants'er grub taken to'er room. That's a job fer you,' she barked at Alice, totally absorbed in Lottie and the new baby. Everything back to square one in Rothwell House, the peace shattered and God knows what might lie ahead.

To Alice Ruddick a 'babby was a babby,' whoever owned it and she continued to drool over the latest addition to the household, whose true identity none of them were ever to know or even suspect. A child who would be brought up as one of the ruling classes. Blessing indeed if she inherited none of her mother's shallow nature, as Martha often remarked. Lottie's concern came from another direction altogether. 'Aa'll do me best t'make sure nowt o'Jake Snowdon comes out in'er,' she silently vowed. 'Sh'canna be like her upstairs when it was me that birthed'er.' Immense satisfaction in this bitter sweet conviction.

Felicity back in residence brought the usual upsets in the daily lives of her servants, soon it was very evident that motherhood had not mellowed this demanding creature, both tyrants in excellent form. The status quo, with all its drawbacks was again in operation, no difference except for the welcome diversion of a tiny infant in their midst, despite the extra work her presence created. Lottie devoted all the time she could spare to the child's welfare, a nanny was already installed but didn't look as if she would last long, a definite clash of personalities with Jessica Finlay. To Lottie, everything she did was a labour of love, no task considered too great. A mother's love which has no equal, as she truly believed herself to be. They named her child Victoria.

* * *

Harrowing memories of those months in Harrow Square and the final outcome were destined to remain in Lottie Hanson's mind for the rest of her life. How could it be otherwise, when the situation meant daily contact with a child she might never be able to claim as her own, yet too heartbreaking to imagine the alternative of total separation from someone so much part of herself and always would be

The morning after Victoria's birth, Doctor Clements duly arrived but made no comment about his exclusion from the two confinements. Nor did he show any adverse reaction when Jessica Finlay intimated her mistress would not be able to suckle the infant, an attitude quite common among upper class females who itched to resume the lifestyle severely curtailed by pregnancy, breast feeding regarded as a distasteful, restrictive practice.

With a bedside manner left behind two floors below in Felicity Cranshawe's luxurious surroundings, he made short work of his stay with her young servant maid. 'Give it to this girl to wet nurse,' was his suggestion on the matter of nourishing the new baby. 'Working class women are like brood mares, they have to be,' he added tersely, rather put out by the struggle to an attic bedroom and totally insensitive to this lesser mortal's feelings, who suffered some delusion about her child not being stillborn, he had no time for such nonsense. A great exaggeration by Jessica Finlay, when Lottie only exclaimed once in her grief that it couldn't be true, but forced to accept the fact when a wizened body was thrust into her line of vision, then taken away to be buried in unconsecrated ground by Charlie Askew.

The doctor's examination of the distressed nineteen year old was very perfunctory indeed, a mere going through the motions, the girl's mistress his main concern, whose wealthy father would pay his enormous bill without question. 'Keep her in bed the usual lying in period,' said of Lottie, 'Less maybe in her case. The infant can be brought to her for feeding.' Her future role was duly allocated and no longer his concern.

Victoria was a beautiful baby, who took after nobody in particular, although bright blue eyes and downy golden hair were, naturally, attributed to Felicity. 'Lots of young'uns have them first go off,' Martha insisted with a loud grunt and protested just as strongly when John Starrett claimed that his granddaughter did possess some family features. 'The bairn's like'erself an' nobody else,' she stated most emphatically, Lottie was only too relieved that hazel eyes and auburn hair were not in evidence, no resemblance to Jake Snowdon or herself, thank God.

'Lottie's far too much tied up wi' that bairn,' Mattie Jackson often bemoaned, forced to take a back seat and eaten up with jealousy at the love she bestowed upon Victoria, not realising how hard it was not to confide in him as always. 'It's natural man,' Martha assured him. 'What wi' hers taken the way it was, there's love goin' spare an'the bairn might as well have it. God knows that so called mother o'hers doesn't know she's on the face o'the earth, the novelty sharp wore off. On the hard cart if it wasn't fer us and the old man. He thinks the sun shines out of'er backside.' Crudely expressed as always and somewhat begrudging in the gaffer's praise, totally prejudiced against her upper class masters.

John Starrett may have preferred a grandson but soon fell under the spell of a girl baby's undoubted charms. 'Next time,' he said to Felicity but missed the look of pure disgust on his daughter's face, who had no repeat performance in mind. Sex, in or out of the marital bed was an obnoxious thought, made perfectly clear to her husband when he returned from overseas duty shortly after the birth.

A dreadful scene took place, after which Geoffrey stormed out of the house in fury to take up residence at his club, paying regular visits to his daughter whilst still in England, his estranged wife seldom around, out usually on some of her jaunts, making up for lost time. A sad end to this young man's effort towards reconciliation, deluded into thinking parenthood would draw them closer together, a real family at last. An utter fiasco.

Just emerged from Victoria's nursery, he entered his wife's sitting room on the same floor and pressed fervent lips against smooth white flesh, in gratitude for such an adorable infant. 'She is absolutely delightful, darling,' he enthused, past grievances laid aside, with no idea how disconcerted Felicity was at his unexpected arrival upon the scene, barely enough time to pop two violet cashous into her mouth to eliminate the sickly odour of gin, quite willing to bask in undeserved adoration.

Geoffrey's wife had a growing drink problem, a taste for the colourless liquid acquired when she swallowed so much of it in vain attempts to terminate an unwanted pregnancy. Afterwards it was a means of coping with boredom, she became almost totally dependent upon the boost it gave her, which she grew to need more and more, its adverse effects inreasingly difficult to conceal. She was somewhat tipsy at the present time, having drunk an incredible amount since early morning and now well into afternoon.

She suffered his caresses without protest, her mouth carefully averted and for one brief moment wished she might have been different. Geoffrey was unbelievably handsome, the ladies in her immediate circle envied his masculinity, the majority of them with wealthy drips for husbands. An envy which appealed to this shallow woman's vanity, the image of an ideal marriage had to be sustained, made easier by Geoffrey's army career and now appeared even more solid with the birth of a child. If Lottie's suspicion could ever be substantiated, this was the biggest mockery of all.

As she submittted to her husband's ardent advances, Felicity decided such inclinations needed to be curbed before they got out of hand, smugly confident of her ability to deal with the situation, ready to go into a well rehearsed act, plaintively murmuring she was much too delicate for child bearing.

Geoffrey scarcely heard, eager lips pressed tiny kisses across his wife's expensively perfumed neck. He had had no intimate contact in just over nine months and Felicity was a beautiful woman. Quite enchanted by the scent and feel of her, his mouth moved slowly downwards to rest in the inviting hollow between firm young breasts, rising provocatively above the soft frill of a low cut gown, Felicity never reluctant to flaunt her assets. A heady experience for a love starved soldier, who felt a throbbing pulse and drew the wrong conclusion. This time would be different, separation all to the good if he had returned to the arms of a warmly responsive wife.

But somehow in the back of a bemused mind her words registered, their meaning not fully digested. 'Then we must be careful, darling,' he breathed huskily and became even more adventurous, certain of reciprocal ardour from a once frigid woman, who recognised the danger signals and pulled away, fully resolved not to let him go further. Geoffrey was meant to see her as some ethereal being, much too fragile for base human desire. 'You don't understand,' she said in petulant voice, her well thought out scenario not going according to plan.

'I might have known,' Geoffrey scorned and drew back in disgust, the meaning suddenly all too clear. 'South Africa, a brief furlough and now this. Becoming pregnant was never on the agenda was it? You were always a cold fish. It isn't pleasant to think of rape in connection with one's own wife. Damn it woman, if you have such an aversion to normal sex between husband and wife, why did you marry? I have never made excessive demands upon you.' His laughter self derisive, 'Fool I was to imagine things might have changed. You surely don't expect me to behave like a celibate monk?'

'Why should I care how many women you have if it means leaving me alone? The whole business is sordid, absolutely sordid!' her voice shrill in defiance, nostrils flaring and a mouth twisted into ugly lines. 'I have given you a child, what more do you want?'

'A wife,' he snapped. 'A loving woman who doesn't make me feel like some sort of animal whenever I come near her.' The look on his face changing to utter disbelief when a loud hiccough spring from her pouting lips and those blue eyes widened in dismay,

'You are drunk!' he gasped, 'My God woman. To add to the rest of your sins you've hit the bottle. How long has this been going on?'

'Nothing has been going on, as you so nicely put it,' she slurred, the picture of injured innocence, which didn't exactly fit. 'I may take a little now and again for medicinal purposes.' But her control had already begun to slip and she bristled strongly, annoyed at his accusing attitude, unused to being held for judgement. How dare he criticise her actions? He wasn't the one to carry a child for nine long months with all that terrifying agony at the end of it, drunk and full of self pity.

The potent gin and overheated room combined to take effect and she flopped into a chair, watching through half closed eyes as her husband made thorough search throughout the suite eventually to face her once again, three empty and one full bottle of gin in his hands. 'Medicinal purposes?' he mocked and threw them into the big marble fireplace, where they shattered into many pieces, liquid splashing in all directions. The sound of breaking glass reached the outside landing, where Jessica Finlay hovered anxiously, never far away.

One of Geoffrey's freed hands tugged at the bell rope. 'I don't have to guess who keeps you supplied. Shall we have a word with dear Jessica?' There was mutual dislike between this man and his wife's devoted servant, who wasn't long in coming and took the scene in at once. The broken bottles, her master's grim face and Madam sprawled in unladylike fashion across a large upholstered chair, this latter a sight she had seen many times of late.

'What do you know of this?' Geoffrey snarled at her, straight into attack. 'Of what, sir?' she answered and infuriated him by such feigned ignorance, Geoffrey's rage wrapped itself around her ears. 'The gin, damn you woman, you know very well what I mean.' Apparently unruffled, she replied with scarcely veiled insolence. 'Oh yes, the broken glass. Shall I get Charlotte to clear it up, sir?' Her master was quick to retaliate. 'No, you will not, there are questions to be answered, truthfully may I hope?' His voice ripe with sarcasm. 'How long have you been supplying your mistress with gin or must I enquire in other directions?' Meaning the Askews, of course, who probably knew more than this conspiratorial pair imagined.

The housekeeper shrank from such direct approach but gave no outward sign of any discomfiture, never a flicker on her impassive face, staring in amazement when Felicity leapt from the chair and went for her husband with clawing fingers. 'Don't answer him,' she shrieked, thwarted by two strong hands firmly clasped around her wrists in relentless grip, Geoffrey tight lipped and very angry. 'Be quiet,' he hissed, 'we don't want all our dirty linen washed in public. But Jessica isn't public is she, not a thing she doesn't already know, I guess, with myself as villain of the piece, naturally,' his finely chiselled mouth curled in derision.

Jessica rushed verbally to Madam's defence, appalled to see her beloved mistress treated in such fashion, 'Madam only takes small amounts of gin each day, on doctor's orders. It was a very difficult pregnancy, sir.' Her tone suggesting where the blame for this lay, the entire concept of sex and the marital bed totally abhorrent to a spinster mind.

'Three empty bottles and one full, all hidden away,' Geoffrey scorned, 'surely not in such a well ordered household.' Jessica was immensely proud of her organising ability. His speech was miraculously controlled by this time but had a distinct edge to it.

'Some of Charlotte's work has been neglected lately. The girl is rather occupied with your daughter, sir,' still retaining her composure but inwardly perturbed, a side to Madam's husband never seen before.

'Ah yes – she feeds Victoria, doesn't she? I always assumed that to be a mother's privilege but some women aren't meant to be mothers or wives.' Here he stopped, suddenly sick of the whole sordid business. 'You may go,' he barked, 'have this mess cleared away after I leave.' And thus abruptly dismissed, he watched Jessica Finlay glide out of the room, having gone as far as she dared and anxious to escape further interrogation. Her true feelings carefully masked but she was full of hatred towards the man who handled her mistress so disrespectfully.

Geoffrey soon released Felicity with a savage thrust from both hands, sickened by the feel of her flesh. 'She lies well for you,' he taunted, 'but to no purpose. The sight of you in such condition is all the confirmation I need. No one off occurrence I would assume,' and with a shrug of indifference carried on, 'drink yourself stupid, if you must, but harm one hair of my daughter's head or disgrace the family name and I'll twist that useless neck. Make no mistake about it.' An idle threat maybe, but if ever a man had cause this one certainly did. The loathing in his eyes loosened Felicity's tongue and she let fly, screaming abuse, the worst of her venom held back until he strode out of the room, Geoffrey rather afraid of actual physical violence towards her in his present mood. 'What makes you so special? My father's money bought my way into your damned aristocratic family and don't you forget it. One word from me and he'll cut off your allowance, then see how far an officer's pay will go. It won't even pay your bloody mess bills.' Beside herself with rage but not too far gone to realise none of this must reach her father's ears. A man who believed in the sanctity of marriage or, at least, of presenting the right image to the world at large. Mabel Starrett and her daughter were made from the same frigid mould, the gaffer's own marriage had been an empty, loveless one. Not that any hint of scandal touched his name and warned Felicity the same applied to her. 'If you or your husband every stray be discreet or I wash my hands of you,' and John Starrett did hold the purse strings.

Felicity staggered across the room towards a huge Chinese vase, removed some decorative peacock feathers and produced another bottle of gin, one Geoffrey had missed. She found a glass and poured herself a stiff drink, still furious at his high handed behaviour, chuckling at her own cleverness.

Less than half an hour later she had downed sufficient to make her really maudlin and wallowed in self pity, all blame laid at Geoffrey's door and mouthing oaths no lady should ever have known. Obscene ravings and full throated laughter were clearly heard in the nursery, on the same floor, where Lottie listened in astonishment, a hungry little mouth nuzzled into a full breast. What happened between man and wife was none of her business but this fancy piece was much coarser than some of the worst randies in Saltersgate's cobbled lanes.

When Jessica Finlay entered the nursery with a face like thunder she kept a still tongue, her aunt never batting an eyelid at what was going on, seemingly immune to the obscenities on madam's gin loosened tongue. Then suddenly there was silence, Felicity obviously knocked senseless and, despite her aunt's usual reluctance towards any menial task, Lottie was not ordered to clear up the mess in the other room. This Jessica Finlay would see to herself while Madam slept it off, the less others knew of her mistress's indiscretions the better.

But Lottie had heard enough, soon aware when her master stormed out of the house, the sound of a violently slammed door. 'He'll bide away if he's got any sense,' she decided, quite impressed by her first encounter with Madam's soldier husband, so gentle with her charge and very civil. 'Kind,' she told herself. A look of absolute awe on his undeniably handsome face when a tiny hand wrapped around his little finger, certain there were tears in those dark eyes.

'That wife doesn't deserve what she's got, t'be sure,' cruelly deprived of her own rights where this beloved child was concerned. A lost soul in a nightmare situation and so far from home, very much alone. Victoria represented all she had in the world and would grow up to call another woman by the name of mother or its equivalent, whatever title the impostor chose to adopt. And Felicity Cramshawe was an impostor in the worst possible way.

* * *

Victoria toddled happily through her early childhood, only denied affection by the woman known to her as 'Mama' who flitted through her life at odd intervals and provided no sense of security, this came to her from other sources, Grandpa and Lottie, both very dear to the little one's heart. 'Papa' lots of fun when around and she was kept reminded of him constantly by Lottie, who strangely enough didn't find it difficult to accept Geoffrey as the father figure in Victoria's life.

The child's fifth birthday present came from Peshawar, in India, Captain Cranshawe being away from the United Kingdom more often than not, mainly by choice. Distance between Felicity and himself was essential to keep up the pretence of 'happy families', which meant that John Starrett took over full control of the little one's life.

The gift, a gorgeous sari in a small size, arrived at Harrow Square, delivered by a young subaltern home on furlough, who returned to the Frontier declaring the captain had a dashed beautiful wife, completely captivated by big blue eyes and shining blonde hair, Felicity was very flirtatious, reasonably sober at the time. Geoffrey merely smiled and said nothing to disillusion the impressionable youngster, although his marriage was over, only legal ties remained. He had an army career to hide behind where his father-in-law was concerned, who needed to be kept sweet for obvious reasons.

Soon after Felicity's return from London with Victoria a tiny infant, the pit gaffer and his daughter's servant met on the stairs, John very much aware of the attractive young woman, had never really been conscious of her presence in the past. Drawn now by beautiful hazel eyes and bright auburn hair he stopped to ask her name and saw how nervous she seemed to be, he was a charming man when he chose and prepared to put her at ease.

'Charlotte, sir,' she answered quickly, rather embarrassed by such attention, and fully expected some cutting reference to the name being too grand for a humble servant. Suddenly she was reminded to bend the knee, as instilled into her by Jessica Finlay, due deference to her betters an absolute must.

'After a Queen eh? See that you take good care of my granddaughter, a little queen if ever there was one, rightly named,' he said, gazing down at her from his near six feet in height, a spendid figure of a man, still quite handsome, although well past middle age.

'Yes, Aa will sir. All the time,' she managed to stammer self consciously, an answer given in great sincerity, the tending of Victoria her main purpose in life.

He patted her head and smiled benevolently, then continued on his way, an hour late for a meeting with Studley miners, some of those damned Trade Unionists. Let the beggars wait, their constant harping was enough to plague a saint, give in to their latest request for more pay and coal would be priced off the market, never off his back with future demands. Poor, undereducated miners were no match for this hard headed businessman but the learning process had already begun.

All Lottie could think of as she watched him go was that 'one o'them' had spoken to her as a human being, strange indeed it should be the pit gaffer, a man she was brought up to detest. Neither master nor servant could possibly know this was the beginning of a love hate relationship between coal owner and collier's daughter, destined to colour their parallel existence for many years ahead, Victoria the precious bond to unite them in friendship, their different stations in life so often a dividing factor.

This special birthday was celebrated in the customary over the top fashion, two white cotton handkerchiefs patiently crocheted around the edges seeming rather insignificant among so many expensive gifts but the fact that Victoria brought one to her and said 'Lottie blow,' plus a big hug as a thank you, made her day. The impostor her daughter called Mama, was conspicuous by her absence, a source of great annoyance to John Starrett, absolutely appalled at Felicity's lack of interest in her child. Victoria was the apple of this wealthy man's eye.

The previous summer, earnest discussion had taken place between the colliery owner and his son-in-law, likely to bring big changes to Rothwell House. Geoffrey, home on extended leave spent most of it at Whitegates with Victoria, with one flying visit from Felicity. So brief, John Starrett couldn't fail to recognise the rift in their marriage and dealt them the usual spiel, no scandal being attached to the family name, then thankfully left it alone. There was little he could do except dangle the purse strings over their heads in threatening manner, fully aware he wouldn't withdraw financial support but the possibility continued to be a most effective weapon.

The old house was at its beautiful best in lovely June weather, sharp contrast to the stuffy, oppressive atmosphere in Saltersgate's cobbled lanes. Earth closets stank to high heaven and women sweltered over the same fires that warmed them in winter, still a necessity for day to day living. Blankets and other bed covers festooned washing lines throughout the village, an opportunity too good to miss, better to make the most of good weather while it lasted.

'Another year and Victoria will need some schooling,' John Starrett stated at the time, in swift departure from mining topics, both careful to avoid discussing Felicity, a real bone of contention between them. 'She can't be allowed to run wild forever,' the gaffer said of his granddaughter expecting and receiving no contradictions from her father, who was seldom around in any case.

He looked every inch the country squire, dressed smartly as always, this day in a cream linen jacket, well pressed brown trousers and a wide Panama hat, plus an immaculate cream shirt and a plain coloured tie. Casual wear for him but still more formal than his companion, out of uniform in very laid back attire, not exactly to John Starrett's approval.

The change of topic was very welcome, the younger man was quite sympathetic towards miners in their struggle for an eight hour day, with no progress at all so far. He was reminded of a little jingle heard on the streets of Newcastle, passing through. 'Eight hours for work, eight hours to play, eight hours for sleep and eight shillings a day.' Reasonable enough one might have thought but the gaffer didn't agree, Geoffrey's outlook broadened somewhat by his years in the army, where blood ran the same colour from officers and men alike in conflict.

John Starrett didn't wait for comment on his proposal. 'A governess is what she needs, someone to get rid of the rough edges. Charlotte is a splendid lass and really devoted but my granddaughter will be heir to this some day and more besides,' he said with justifiable pride and a sweeping gesture to encompass his magnificent acres, a wonderful heritage.

'I shall be glad to leave everything to you, sir,' Geoffrey admitted, in the hope that the other man would pick up the tab, money was always a problem. Felicity was certainly right about mess bills playing havoc with a chap's resources on that damned frontier, something she had mentioned often enough, the dependency upon her father he truly deplored but was obliged to accept.

The sound of Victoria's laughter brought fond smiles to the faces of both devotees, who turned to watch her at play, Lottie in close attendance as usual. Geoffrey's young male eyes, very discerning, were quick to absorb the young servant girl's natural beauty, feasting upon it until John Starrett broke the spell. These moments of awareness were to be remembered quite vividly in years to come.

'I shall make some enquiries,' the colliery owner stated, seeing no need for further deliberation, plans for Victoria's future already in the pipeline. Geoffrey knew only too well that the matter would have been gone into very carefully. He wondered how much his father-in-law knew of Felicity's drinking habit, realising she kept well out of her father's orbit and with a man always willing to believe the best of her the pretence was working, for the time being at least.

The wheels were well in motion for a start to Victoria's education long before Geoffrey left for India again, John Starrett never one to allow the grass to grow under his feet. 'Somebody capable enough to teach the three R's should be sufficient at this stage,' he had informed Harold Peabody, vicar of the country parish and grateful recipient of many fine donations. Such generosity from a man who haggled interminably over an extra copper or two for his colliery workmen. 'A clergyman's daughter, perhaps. One with the necessary graces to pass on to her young charge. Only for a few years,' he added, asking for help in this direction. 'Victoria is already enrolled in one of the finest boarding schools in England, Switzerland later to finish off.'

Lottie listened to news of the gaffer's plans in great dismay, the gap about to widen between herself and the light of her life. 'She'd better be good to'er,' she passionately declared during the course of conversation below stairs, her guard allowed to slip for one dangerous moment, a quizzical expression on Mattie Jackson's homely face. 'If sh' beats 'er once a day an' twice on Sundays it has nowt t'do wi'you hinny. Anybody would think sh'was yours the way y'carry on,' he grunted and Lottie's face whitened, alarm bells ringing, saved by Alice Ruddick, who butted in without thought. 'Y'make a fool o'yerself wi' that lassie. High time y'got back among yer own kind an' found a lad. More than five years since ye've even spoken t'one Aa reckon.' The simple truth but a foolish observation as she soon discovered, Lottie blazed forth in indignation.

'Aa've had me fill o'men Alice Ruddick. There's more t'life than lyin' on yer back an' lettin' them have their way wi' ya. Aa'll go t'Saltersgate when Aa'm ready not afore. Aa'm surprised y'showed yer face there again after the way Lizzie Phillips an' that lot treated ya.' Wanting to lash out against all and sundry.

Alice's face crumpled in distress, saved from further harassment by Jessica Finlay's timely intervention, her presence completely forgotten, seated in morose silence at the kitchen table as she did so often those days. There or closeted in her own rooms, abandoned by Felicity who abhorred old age, time well and truly taking toll on Lottie's aunt. 'We'll have no more of that disgusting talk in this house,' she said with a touch of her former asperity, seldom seen as she sank into a pit of despondency, her beloved mistress usually in London without her. But she had been home in Rothwell House for the past few days to keep her father sweet. 'Has Madam sent for me, I thought I heard her bell?'

'Y'did,' Martha took great delight in telling her, 'Lottie went upstairs. She has t'take Madam's elevenses from now on.' Great emphasis laid on the 'she'.

Jessica's thin lips quivered but she kept her dignity, aware of the enormous satisfaction in Martha's tone. 'Oh, I see,' she acknowledged 'Madam is so considerate of me and tries to save my legs as much as possible. It is a long climb to her suite.' Upset no doubt but pathetically pleased to have Felicity under the same roof as herself for a while at least.

'Considerate my foot,' Martha scorned when the older woman crept back to her own quarters to brood in solitude, waiting for a summons from her idol, never likely to arrive. Now written off after years of faithful service, there was not an ounce of sentiment in Felicity's shallow nature.

'Poor old bitch,' Alice burst forth in a wave of compassion and soon found herself on the sharp edge of Martha's tongue, any show of sympathy towards the arch enemy totally out of order.

'Poor old nothin,' she rapped out, 'For the first time in'er life that miserable old so an' so's getting' a taste of 'er own medicine. Keep yer pity fer them that deserve it. Jessica's not one o' them.'

For some strange reason, on this occasion Lottie agreed with Alice and began to fret about her aunt's future, cause to wonder why she should even care. 'They'll not turn'er out, will they Mattie?' she questioned, ignoring the withering look from across the room, Jackson very blunt. 'Y'never can tell wi'these fancy folk. Alright s'long as y'serve yer turn. But it'll be Preston fer'er if they do. Sh'could have some money saved up but mebbe not enough.' He had more faith in John Starrett than his selfish daughter but there was no predicting which way either would jump when it came to the crunch.

The mere mention of Preston brought back memories of her own horror at such a prospect. 'Not there, surely. Sh'hardly eats sufficient t'bait a mouse trap and she's doin'less than nothin' anyway. We could manage the lot an'never feel the difference.' Shot down immediately for such an outrageous suggestion, Martha very hostile. 'Speak for yerself, Lottie Hanson. Ye've got a short mem'ry me lass.'

'Aa've forgotten nothin',' Lottie told her and wondered what Martha would say if she knew the whole story, beginning to wish she had never opened her mouth.

'Sh'asked yer mother for Christmas once,' Alice found the courage to remind their diminutive friend. 'Count me in, Lottie.' Anxious to be on good terms again after their earlier fracas.

'And a fat lot o'good that'll do'er,' Martha snorted. 'The only thing yer good at is muckin'out stables an' the like,' she barked and silenced Alice but not Mattie Jackson. 'What Alice does i' the stables lets me help wi'the donkey work around the house. Anyway y'should think hard. There but for the grace o' God,' he quoted significantly.

'The Bible now, is it?' certain that all words of wisdom came from the holy book. 'Aa reckon the good Lord washed 'is hands o'Jessica ages ago,' she ended in scorn then clammed up, her feelings well and truly aired. But they knew Martha of yore, if and when the occasion arose she would heave to and do her share but not without protest, a tiny body but a lengthy tongue in recompense or so it might appear, the power of which the downstairs occupants in Rothwell House had all felt at one time or another, only silent when it came to her superiors, wise enough to know on which side her bread was buttered and when to keep a still tongue.

* * *

Two days later Mattie Jackson was detailed to take the large open carriage to Newcastle Central to pick up the new governess, a one man reception committee, returning after a while with his passenger, suitably impressed.

'There Aa was, expectin' a right old battle axe, instead o'which she's just a slip of a lass, mebbe scared t'death at comin'among us northern savages.'

The 'slip of a lass' as Jackson described Marianne Spalding, did look far less than her twenty nine years, a pleasant, obviously well bred young woman with no airs and graces and a direct, friendly manner which met with full approval in the servants' quarters. All except Lottie, quite put out by such a favourable reaction on so short an acquaintance, polite, of course, when introduced, but stubbornly determined to reserve judgement, there was much more at stake for her than any of them could possibly realise. 'Ladylike but not taffy nosed,' Martha declared when Jessica Finlay whisked the newcomer off to meet the mistress of the house, only to be back within minutes, red eyed and alone, apparently dismissed with a snub, on the receiving end of so many during this lightning visit. Fecility was not at all pleased to be dragged away from London, in Rothwell House at her father's insistence to greet the child's governess, what any real mother would have wished to do without being forced into it.

'Well, me lass?' Martha taunted, still niggled by Lottie's recent show of sympathy towards Jessica Finlay. 'Is this one good enough fer yer precious bairn,' barely finished before an explosive barrage of words whipped across her ears, Lottie's temper given full release. 'One of these days that tongue o'yours'll get y'hanged. Sh'seems all right but some folk aren't ready t'make snap judgements,' she hotly accused, rather piqued at Jackson's obvious interest in this latest addition to the household staff and she firmly refused to take part in any further discussion.' A kind face she assured herself, 'An' Aa bet there's plenty o'brains i' that tidy head. The bairn'll soon know more than me,' heavyhearted at the thought of her own limited knowledge. Keep them ignorant, that's what the gaffers want, she heard her father say many times, John Hanson was sure education was the answer and looked forward to the day when teaching lasted beyond thirteen. More than pit work would then be available for the lads and other choices for the opposite sex apart from domestic service. But he was never destined to see it come to pass.

Marianne wasted no time, Victoria's lessons began the following day and, quick to sense Lottie's reserve towards herself, and the affinity with her young pupil, she set out to make ally instead of enemy. The girl's obvious interest in elementary class work urged her to take a shot in the dark, willing to risk a snub for her pains.

'What I am teaching Victoria is very basic, Lottie, a waste of time for someone of your advanced years,' and encouraged by a giggle of amusement carried on, 'Maybe you would like to pick up where you left off?' Candid grey eyes raised in enquiry, an illuminated face was all the answer she required.

'Oh Miss,' escaped her companion's trembling lips, absolutely bowled over by this amazing proposal, not sure whether to laugh or cry, enormous effort needed to take it all in and pull herself together. 'I gather you are interested?' Marianne said, the answer in a flash, 'D'ya think Aa could?' Here was someone eager to learn, a challenge to any teacher worth her salt. 'There will be time in the evenings when we can talk and read together,' Marianne said, her hands suddenly clasped in fervour.

'That's what Aa want, more than anything i'the world.'

Not exactly true, Victoria claimed as her own child held priority over all. 'Aa want t'learn. Aa hate knowin' s'little,' came from the depths of her heart, a mother's heart, willing to grasp at any straw to lessen the gap between Victoria and herself which was now beginning to widen.

'That's settled then,' Marianne said brusquely, suddenly conscious of a little girl's interest in their conversation, a bright child, this fact had soon been established, quite certain Lottie had great potential also and she was quite excited at the task in front of her, bringing knowledge into both minds. Inclined towards pessimism by recent setbacks in her young life, Lottie was soon back to reality, already thinking Madam was certain to put some obstacle in the way, Jessica Finlay not even a consideration nowawdays, in a world of her own most of the time. 'What will Madam say?' she queried, her voice very flat.

Marianne seemed to have no worries on that score and said so. 'Madam doesn't have to know. If we both perform our duties satisfactorily, she can have no reason for objection,' Lottie was sorely tempted to say their mistress didn't have to have a reason for anything, but Marianne, only a day in Rothwell House, with help from Martha had soon assessed the situation, already critical of the woman's lack of interest in her daughter's future.

The two women began to make plans, the first session that evening after supper an arrangement which didn't go down too well in certain directions. 'What d'ya want t'be like them fer?' Martha protested, right up in arms at the idea of further education, angry to think Lottie wanted to adopt the ways of their masters, secure in her present relationships and dreadfully afraid of change. 'There's nowt the matter wi'how y'are,' she went on to proclaim with strong endorsement from Alice. 'The more y'get like them, the less ye'll want t'do wi' us,' the simple lass wilted, not easy to console, despite firm assurances that friends were friends whatever happened.

Mattie Jackson was the only one to offer any encouragement. 'Let the lass get all the learnin' sh'can,' he countered, his hopes of matrimony long since abandoned. Marianne could teach Lottie a lot in other ways too, he reckoned, quite taken with the young gentlewoman, who held superior status in the household but was going to fit in nicely, Lottie her latest conquest and that in less than a day, full of admiration.

Victoria's governess was expected to take her meals 'en famille' which, after Madam's early departure, usually meant only her charge and herself, with John Starrett on the odd occasion when business matters kept him in town, spending as much time in Rothwell House as possible, Victoria the magnet that drew him there. The house in Harrow Square did not find itself covered in dust sheets very often, Felicity was a regular visitor, always unaccompanied for obvious reasons. Not that her exploits remained secret, letters from the Askews were most revealing.

Lottie always waited at table, another of the tasks inherited from her aunt who, according to Martha, was 'away wi'the fairies' and wandered the house aimlessly, what had become the woman's sole purpose in life now removed from her sphere, totally abandoned by her heartless employer. Early in the relationship of teacher and pupil, Lottie deemed it wiser to make a clean breast of her disastrous affair with Jake Snowdon, rather she told the shameful story than anyone else, fully resolved to get this painful revelation out of the way, before another phase began. 'Put it all behind you,' her new mentor advised 'you don't have any feelings in that direction, I hope.' Lottie's reply very spontaneous. 'Nothin' except a whole lot o'disgust at him and me. That rogue's not worth a single thought. Hoppin' mad at meself fer bein' taken in, a blessed idiot. It's just a bad dream.'

Marianne found it hard to believe this beautiful young woman required no tuition in two of life's main experiences, unlike herself a twenty nine year old spinster, with no first hand knowledge of sex or childbirth. Yet, somehow, Lottie still managed to retain a distinct air of innocence. 'Don't worry,' she emphasised, 'There will be someone else, someday. You are very young and with your looks – Well, you aren't a plain Jane like myself.'

'Oh Miss, y'aren't plain,' something akin to worship shone in Lottie's bright hazel eyes, already captivated by the true feminine graces of this newly acquired friend. She did not disclaim men in general as before, the scars from her seduction had begun to heal, she was now willing to accept the possibility of another man in her life. Rather touched by such obvious hero worship Marianne smiled and went on to give a bit of good advice. 'See that your heart doesn't rule your head a second time,' she said, already conscious of the impulsive streak in Lottie's nature. 'That Aa won't,' shot back at her in all sincerity. 'Anyway you'll be around t'see Aa mind me P's and Q's,' her companion, quick to appreciate this sharp wit, laughed in response, intensely moved by the beauty in an animated face, of which its owner seemed totally unconscious. The prospect of wonderful new dreams shone out of the girl's glorious eyes, illuminated by the heady thought of close companionship with someone of real intelligence, so eager was she to broaden her own mind. Only Jessica Finlay's infamous behaviour remained a secret, too dangerous to share with anyone.

Suddenly those same eyes clouded and did not go unnoticed. Something was troubling her, Marianne grieved, wondering if she would ever reach the depths of Lottie's mind. Such an open face, so easy to read most times, but a veil had come over it, hiding what? This she never discovered even in the closeness of friendship which was to grow between them. Besides, Lottie imagined Marianne might think it too far fetched, better to keep the suspicion where it had always been, locked away in her own mind, in the fervent hope that one day all might be revealed, a hope inclined to fade somewhat as time rolled by.

* * *

'Well Charlotte, have you lost your tongue? I am offering you your aunt's position as housekeeper. What do you say to that?' John Starrett awaited a reaction which didn't come immediately, Lottie much too taken aback at this amazing proposal but she sensed the gaffer's impatience and managed to stammer out a reply. 'Yes sir, thank you sir, if you really think I can do it.' Shaking in her shoes but she realised this man expected a favourable answer, not used to being denied his own way.

'Dammit girl, you are doing it now. Do you fondly imagine I haven't assessed the situation over the past two years, the smooth running of this house is entirely due to your efforts. Of course the rest of them do their share,' he said in anticipation of what she opened her mouth to say. 'You are the mainstay and now I intend to make it official. Here, take this,' A gold sovereign was thrust towards her which she had to accept, everything seemingly cut and dried. 'Get yourself some suitable clothing as befits your new position,' he ordered brusquely, 'No more of those shapeless garments, something smart but definitely not black.' His discerning male eye was very conscious of the good figure that even an ill fitting maid of all work's uniform failed to disguise, even more so of Lottie's spectacular colouring, those bright auburn locks neatly braided, just showing at the front of her cap, and the sheer impact of stunning hazel eyes, a delightful combination. He did not entertain thoughts of any dalliance but a man would have to be dead not to notice her attributes and John Starrett, although getting on in years, was very much alive.

'You don't have to be scared of anything at all. You will be responsible to me and nobody else,' he was quick to assure her. 'I meant to organise this some time ago but never got down to it.' Rising to his feet behind the leather topped desk in the study window, the interview over. 'Now that is settled I can take myself off to Polrigg. Someone has to put the fear of death into those damned Union officials and my colliery manager is useless, they run rings around him. He'll be out of a job by the end of this week.' Ill chosen words, reminding her yet again of the enormous gulf between them, the hated colliery owner and a miner's daughter. John Starrett was inclined to forget her connection with those he derided so much, more so since an air of refinement had grown around her, due to Marianne's influence. He tended to undermine the feelings she ought to have towards him, his sort and hers natural enemies, from two vastly different backgrounds. Their mutual love for Victoria was the only common denominator.

Thinking of backgrounds brought to mind some upsetting news from Saltersgate that very morning, Alice the prophet of doom as usual. Who else? 'Janey Wilson's got consum'tion,' she said, 'riddled with it so they tell me. Folk reckon sh'hasn't long t'live. A shame, she's a canny little body.' Nothing good to say about Tod. 'Aa've got no room fer that man o'hers nor their Tommy. They say –' Prepared to continue in full flow but halted in her tracks by the expression on Lottie's face, one she recognised only too well and knew when to hold her tongue.

Lottie had to agree with these sentiments, it was Mary Wilson and Janey herself she felt sorry for, well acquainted with the family situation. Mary still slaved after the Boyle family in Branton Village and now had more to do at home. She had no inclination to take up with anyone else since her break with Paddy O'Neal, seen recently on Branton High Street, and unhappiness was written all over the poor girl's face. Rumour had it that Tommy shopped his sister, a greedy lad with no scruples, so it might well be true, amazed it hadn't reached Tod's ears before it did. But it meant nothing to her brother if she chose to be a spinster, except for being someone to pick up where his sick mother was forced to leave off, self seeking to the core. There had to be some way Lottie could help if Tod's stiff necked pride allowed him to accept. Before John Starrett made to leave his study, she plucked up courage to intercede on her aunt's behalf, his reply was immediate and quite unexpected. 'Finlay deserves some consideration for years of devoted service. Never my cup of tea but not yours either, I guess – –' not waiting for agreement or otherwise. 'It would be preferable if she moved to the top of the house,' and proposed Lottie and the former housekeeper should change quarters. This was not very practical with the number of stairs involved but she rightly gathered he would go this far and no further, thus refraining from comment.

'Shall I inform your aunt?' he asked as she began to open the door, an offer refused in over polite fashion, rather galled to be dependent upon him, a man who doled out charity so offhandedly, the gold sovereign still clutched tightly in the palm of her hand, tangible evidence of such benevolence, she had a strong impulse to throw it back in his face but easily suppressed it, she had much better control of her feelings than of yore.

How Jessica Finlay would take this astounding proposition was anyone's guess and she found herself wishing she had been less foolhardy and allowed the gaffer to do his own dirty work, she was rather apprehensive but needlessly so, as soon discovered. Her aunt was willing to remain in Rothwell House under any condition, prepared to accept anything except total separation from her beloved mistress. What might happen to Jessica was of no concern to such an uncaring person, usually too befuddled to think clearly in any case and so seldom there.

'You have come a long way in seven years,' her aunt said with a derisive curl of the lips. 'Entirely due to my guidance, of course. But I don't expect you to know the meaning of gratitude,' and really believed this preposterous statement to be the truth. Remembering this same accusation from Aunt Maude, all those years ago, the fact stung.

'I do know the meaning, Aunt Jessica,' she answered with a definite bite to the words, 'but don't see how it fits in your case. Anything you may have done was to suit your own purpose or Madam's and it's surprising how far some people will go in such situations.' Hoping to arouse a spark of feeling or at least a betraying flush. Shades of the old Jessica came straight to the fore, very sarcastic.

'I doubt if you have what it takes to assume such responsibility, your attitude towards authority has always left much to be desired. Don't let this go to your head,' she thought it necessary to warn, not yet finished. 'You seem to have ingratiated yourself with the master,' meaning John Starrett. 'But even the best of men can be taken in by a pretty face.' A back handed compliment if ever there was one. 'You will require my keys,' already unfastening the familiar beaded belt from around her waist. Lottie cringed at the sight of it, a much hated symbol of overbearing authority. 'Just the keys,' she insisted, unwilling to lay hands on this offensive article, which represented more than seven years of oppression along with jingling keys and the rustle of taffeta.

'As you wish,' Jessica said with a knowing smirk. 'Remember where your loyalty lies. Madam needs someone she can trust implicitly, discretion is always required in certain matters.' This was the closest she came to any mention of Felicity's addiction, now an alcoholic and beyond redemption.

Lottie had one of the attics converted into a small sitting room to the accompaniment of very vocal opposition from Martha and Alice, loud in protest, the idea of the old dragon as a neighbour not to their liking. They grumbled even more as winter progressed, the carrying of coal was a big problem, Mattie Jackson was not always available. It was seemingly impossible to educate Alice in a 'head saving legs' exercise, heavy buckets of coal and ashes were too much for Martha's diminutive form. 'We've always had t'freeze up there, why can't she?' a constant complaint and it had to be explained that an old woman wouldn't sit around all day without a fire. Lottie's temper was tested to its limit on many occasions and enormous patience was required when the atmosphere became rather heated.

Her aunt's occupation of these attic rooms created other problems. At first she came downstairs for meals and sat a while but gradually appeared less and less until not at all. Toilet facilities were naturally a problem, there was some incontinence to deal with eventually, which Martha washed her hands of completely, a chore given to Alice who had no hang ups in that respect, never squeamish about any of the dirtier jobs, nothing for a lass who once worked on the land.

In the spring of the following year, the elderly woman took to her bed with a heavy dose of bronchitis and soon started to go downhill, at which stage Lottie decided the main burden should rest upon herself, immensely touched when, despite their grumbles, the others rallied round. 'Just fer your sake,' Martha stressed. 'The old bitch could lie there an'rot if Aa thought ye'd let'er.' She was no hypocrite where Jessica Finlay was concerned.

When Marianne asked if there was anything she could do, Lottie simply asked her to spend more time with Victoria. 'An imposition I know but she mustn't feel deserted and I won't have much spare time.' The little girl was her main worry as always and there was no telling how long her aunt would hang on, always strong willed which often helped, not that she thought so in this case, Madam's cruel abandonment had done a great deal of harm, with never a visit to Jessica's bedside when she deigned to spend a few days in

Rothwell House, which wasn't very often. Perhaps she had no heart left to do battle with death which so often won in these unenlightened days. Jessica Finlay wasn't long for this world and would go out of it completely unmourned, sad indeed but true.

* * *

So it was barely a year after her promotion to housekeeper, Lottie kept vigil at her aunt's bedside and wondered why she of all people should be there at all and if Jessica Finlay recognised her presence. The change in this young woman was unbelievable, a different person altogether, Marianne the teacher no doubt and deserving of much credit but she was a very apt pupil. Ironic to think that the bed now occupied by a dying woman, closely related but apart in almost every other way, once sheltered her own weary body and witnessed oceans of tears, reduced to them so often by cruel treatment.

In almost eight years under this roof not a single word of affection ever escaped Jessica Finlay's thin lips, most times pursed in disapproval. It was hard to imagine this emaciated being as the insufferable martinet who turned an eighteen year old girl's existence into a veritable nightmare, Jessica Finlay was totally undeserving of any consideration bestowed upon her.

Lottie's thoughts inevitably turned to Harrow Square, the happenings there indelibly printed on her mind, in all of which Jessica Finlay had played a very important role. She saw great significance in the fact of never being asked to accompany her mistress since, the Askews were still in residence but other staff were coming and going with monotonous regularity, Fanny most uneasy about this state of affairs. 'We'll be murdered in our beds that's what,' she insisted, not keen on so much casual labour and she slept with a rolling pin on the bedside table. But none of them stayed for any length of time, ruffled feathers often to be smoothed, Madam constantly under the influence of drink and totally unpredictable in her behaviour.

Lottie kept in touch, a task taken over from Mattie Jackson, mainly to improve her writing and grammar but not forgetful of Fanny's kindness in those far off days, she and her husband thought fondly of as she watched a clear blue sky through the attic window. London would be in very festive mood on this particular day, the coronation of George the Fifth in Westminster Abbey, and royalist to the core her two friends would be in the midst of it. Of all the days her aunt could have chosen to die, had it been her choice, this was an auspicious occasion to be boasted of in heaven. Not that the wicked old besom should enter those pearly gates with so much on her conscience, stoking the fires in Hades would be more like real justice.

Except for the laboured breathing of the tiny figure on the bed, Rothwell House lay silent, they were too far away to hear if anything was going on outside, as well it might be. Martha and Alice did offer to keep her company but Lottie realised the attraction of Saltersgate's celebrations, no second bidding was needed to dispatch them in childlike anticipation to the scene of action, a highlight in their mostly dull existence. The past was long since gone and forgotten by Alice, perfectly willing to let bygones be bygones.

Early that morning, Jackson drove Marianne and Victoria to Whitegates where John Starrett had financed celebrations for his household staff and estate workers. He had a different attitude towards the mining community, the men had the day off but without pay. Some concession, Lottie scorned, a definite minus point for the gaffer in their up and down relationship.

Felicity had taken herself off to London to be in thick of it, having spent two or three days in Rothwell House and created havoc, with no visit to the bedside of her faithful retainer. Parties and balls with more drink than she could handle would be the order of each day, often put to bed by Fanny Askew, carried there by Charlie, his wife's ministrations being deliberately rough, secure in the knowledge her mistress would remember nothing the following day, it would be well into afternoon before she actually surfaced, when the usual pattern began all over again. The Askews were wholly contemptuous of Madam's dissipated way of life.

Everyone was so intent upon their various pursuits that no thought was given to Geoffrey Cranshawe, now on his way north to be reunited with his seven year old daughter after an absence of almost two years. He wasted no time when the ship docked to return to his depot at Aldershot, he made no attempt to visit his estranged wife, their marriage stripped of all pretence. To see Victoria was this man's only goal.

Jessica Finlay stirred, the first sign of movement for quite a time. Lottie's heart tightened, thinking surely her aunt must speak before going to meet her Maker, a soul relieved of its dreadful burden. She leant towards her, there was what seemed a tiny flicker of recognition in those sunken eyes as colourless lips struggled to form a word. A name would suffice. Victoria. Enough to confirm that long harboured suspicion, an end to speculation if nothing more, some satisfaction for a tortured mind.

The effort proved too much for Jessica Finlay's failing strength, just that faintest whisper of what might have been 'Sorry' and she slipped away, any secret she possessed gone with her, Lottie's disappointment was almost physical pain. She recoiled from closure of the dead woman's eyes, fervently wishing someone else was there to perform the necessary rites, her whole instinct to flee the tiny room and its lifeless occupant.

It took tremendous willpower to go in search of linen from an airing cupboard on the second floor landing and badly shattered nerves shrieked in protest when the imperative sound of the front door bell echoed through the big house. Lottie pulled herself together and sped towards the ground floor vestibule, two doors to unlock, the second opened with unnecessary force and she fell straight into the arms of an army officer, ready to pull the bell a second time.

Geoffrey Cranshawe used this hand and the other to steady an obviously overwrought young woman and the sweet smell of lavender filled his nostrils, he was incredibly disturbed by the feel of a soft female body, a pleasure long denied and soon taken from him as Lottie tore herself free in utter confusion.

'Oh sir', she breathed in dismay, recognising who it was. 'What must you think of me?' very flushed and most disconcerted. Geoffrey's eyes revealed exactly what he thought, openly admiring. Scarcely able to believe this was the same young woman who drew his attention three years previously at Whitegates, that lovely June day. The voice was so different also, just the slightest intonation of the Northumbrian, not so easy to wholly eradicate. 'I think you are a sight for any man's eyes,' he gallantly quipped but really meant it, she was lovelier than ever. 'I haven't had a pretty young woman throw herself at me for ages,' he went on to say in teasing fashion, anxious to put her at ease and pleased when a tremulous smile crossed her tear stained face.

Lottie felt obliged to explain her actions. 'It was most remiss of me, sir, you must forgive me. My aunt has just died and I am alone in the house,' she told him in distress, the image of Madam's husband never forgotten since their first meeting in London, seven years before, choked then at his pride in Victoria.

'Where is everyone?' becoming matter of fact to save her further embarrassment. 'I landed at Tilbury early this morning and came north after first reporting to my base,' he said and watched her visibly relax, apparently relieved to be on a safer ground.

'It is nice to have you home again, sir, a long time away. Miss Victoria often talks about you. She is at Whitegates with her governess, Jackson drove them there this morning. Martha and Alice are in Saltersgate for the celebrations.'

'The Coronation, of course, I had quite forgotten, although there was plenty of activity in London this morning, not easy getting to the railway station. My wife is there, I suppose?' His tone altering when he mentioned Felicity.

'Yes indeed, sir,' and wondered why he didn't call at Harrow Square to discover for himself. Then she suddenly realised they had got no further than the vestibule, his luggage still out of doors. 'Goodness me, we had better step inside,' and made to pick up his one valise. 'I'll take that,' he insisted, 'I am badly in need of exercise after so much travelling. My other bags are being sent on, my batman is seeing to them.'

He picked up the case with no apparent effort and stepped across the threshold into the house, Lottie moving aside to allow him entry, rather touched to see her make hurried repairs to a tear stained face with a lace handkerchief produced from her uniform pocket. 'Where will you put me?' he asked and Lottie struggled for a sense of normality, undeniably shaken by this man's presence.

'The bed in one of the guest rooms is always kept aired, sir, unless you would prefer Madam's suite?' Pleased to hear him say the guest room would be fine, not to know how nauseated he felt at the thought of Felicity's cloying presence, her perfume obviously lingered in the air, very much aware of that fresh smell of lavender which now tanalised his nostrils. He pulled himself together. 'When I have deposited this bag we must attend to your aunt,' well acquainted with the rites attached to death and the need for them to be dealt with without delay.

Lottie stared after his retreating back in amazement and shortly afterwards they entered the attic room, it was not long before Jessica Finlay's body was prepared in readiness for her coffin, master and servant at opposite sides of a bed pulled away from the wall, Geoffrey with his sleeves rolled up was an unfamiliar sight. Intensely aware of one another, they were drawn together by ministrations to a woman they both detested in life. An odd situation in all ways and one she would have deplored, the intimacy of it especially. Lottie was full of tears for the important knowledge locked away in the dead woman's mind, her reaction completely misunderstood.

'I never imagined anyone would shed tears for old Finlay,' Geoffrey said, his dark eyes softened in sympathy for this warm hearted young woman, who smiled at him in gratitude, greatly overcome. How could she explain to this man of all men the tears were not for her aunt but for lost hope? The truth would shock him to the core, when it could rob him of the daughter he loved so much, her gain but his loss and she had no desire to give him hurt. She was surprised at the amount of respect he inspired in her, loving respect, and chided herself for such foolishness. A case of heart ruling head as Marianne warned against, just someone there when she badly needed the support of another human being that was all, but she was honest enough to admit the enormity of such self delusion, so very much attracted to this man, and prayed for strength to cry halt before it was too late.

* * *

Fate took a hand, as it so often does, and threw two young people together for the next few hours, who definitely shouldn't have been, it being unwise to foster any sort of attraction between them. Suddenly reminded of her duties as housekeeper, Lottie hastily gathered scattered wits as Geoffrey and herself left the attic bedroom. 'There is food in the kitchen, sir,' she said, anxious now to get on more solid footing, 'You must be hungry. Settle yourself in the small dining room and I'll serve you a meal as soon as possible.' But Geoffrey had no intention of doing any such thing and said so most emphatically, 'Not on your life. Sit there in solitary splendour,' he scorned, 'I shall come down to the kitchen when I have washed and changed out of uniform.' He was still in it apart from his jacket, left behind when he accompanied Lottie to the dead woman's bedside. 'But sir, it isn't proper, you must realise that as well as I do,' she protested, somewhat feebly, and mentally chastised herself for a sudden lift to her spirits. This breathtaking handome man wanted to spend more time with her but, however flattering this might be, no good could come from ignoring the rules. Nobody knew better than she did that one step in the wrong direction and disaster was certain to follow. Geoffrey smiled at her confusion and gently remonstrated. 'Lottie, you and I have just prepared a dead body for burial, which wasn't in the order of things either. So, right or wrong, whichever, the kitchen it shall be,' already on his way to the room he had been allocated. 'Yes, sir,' she murmured lamely and watched him go, then continued downstairs, warmed by an inner glow. Her name sounded so different on his lips, Charlotte evoked so many painful memories, especially that first meeting with his wife, and she reminded herself he did have a wife, the most significant of barriers, stiffening in purpose against such forbidden desire being allowed possession of both mind and heart.

Geoffrey insisted she joined him and the cold fare provided went down very well with lots of conversation, some laughter despite the dead body lying upstairs, partially due to good wine, she was coaxed into accepting one glass although under protest. 'It isn't every day a new king is crowned,' he said in excuse, persuasive enough to dismiss Methodist doctrine instilled since childhood. It was impossible not to be captivated by Geoffrey Cranshawe's natural charm, he made her feel so utterly feminine, and his male hormones were very active indeed after such long denial, this attractive young woman was a pure delight. Victoria was a main topic, Geoffrey drank in tales of her childhood, so much he had missed, Lottie was more than willing to expand upon the little girl's doings. Time seemed to fly on wings but soon her unease at the situation began to reassert itself, afraid that Martha and Alice might burst in upon them. So much in tune he immediately sensed her worry and spared the embarrassment of asking him to leave, 'It's getting late,' he said, 'if the pony trap is available I could drive myself to Whitegates in the morning and would like an early start.' Quick to observe an almost imperceptible sigh of relief, endearing himself even more by this eagerness to see Victoria.

'Of course,' she replied, 'Alice will harness Tiger for you, he will enjoy the run,' and tried not to make too much of the fact that his big hand enveloped hers a shade longer than necessary when they said goodnight. The memory of his touch still lingered long after he left. 'Fool,' she derided, 'will you never learn?' Fully convinced an unruly heart was about to let her down a second time. Martha and Alice were late in arriving home, flushed with ale and very talkative, neither woman surprised to hear of Jessica's demise and not in the least concerned. 'Aa'll not pretend t'be sorry,' Martha said in her usual forthright manner, 'Yer aunt was an old bitch right t'the end, dyin' doesn't give'er wings and a halo. How y'put up with it these past few months beats me.'

'How did y'manage on yer own?' Alice asked, who got to thinking about the laying out of a dead body, a morbid interest in death and its associations. 'Fine,' she was told, no more than that, the secret of Geoffrey Cranshawe's assistance hugged close to Lottie's heart, the knowledge most unwise to share 'The bairn'll be over the moon,' Martha did say when told of the young master's homecoming. 'One of Nature's gentlemen,' she called him, mellowed by ale and a whole day of pleasure. 'Ye'll have t'see t'the funeral arrangement bein'er next o'kin,' her mind already geared towards the catering for it, to Martha's way of thinking yet another celebration, strange maybe but true.

'I shall do that tomorrow,' Lottie agreed, 'I wonder if Aunt Jessica had insurance?' she speculated in the fervent hope this contingency was covered, loathe to use her own savings for such purpose. Martha was a mine of information as usual. 'There's a box under'er bed sh'kept locked. Sh'watched every move when Aa was cleanin'. God knows what sh'has stuffed away i' the blessed thing,' wanting her curiosity satisfied as might be expected, a feeling fully reciprocated as Lottie's heart turned somersault. A box under the bed could only mean safe keeping for articles of value to its owner, private papers, money perhaps and, most wished for of all, some belated confession of guilt to be revealed only after death.

'Probably nothing of importance, except an insurance policy I hope,' she said, trying to be offhand but her heart was thumping and she ignored the looks of disappointment when she refused assistance. If the box held any secrets they were for her eyes alone until she decided what measures to take. That longed for moment maybe was at hand but it was one she had almost come to dread. So many strong relationships formed over the years, the pit gaffer and now Geoffrey Cranshawe for whom revelation would be a great catastrophe.

The long summer day was at an end when Lottie lit a candle to re enter the room of death, where apprehension sent a cold shiver through her tense body. Senseless to fear the dead but those painful years of her aunt's turbulent reign had left their mark, the sight of that inert figure, although shrouded, made her knees tremble as she began to grope for the all important container. At first it appeared Martha might be mistaken, until trembling fingers made contact with cold metal and she pulled the receptacle towards her by a leather strap, almost frantic in her haste. Where was the key? Finally it was discovered in an ornament, a small china vase labelled 'A Present from Whitley Bay', too common for Aunt Jessica's taste one would imagine but maybe of sentimental value, not that such feelings figured much in her aunt's nature.

She moved ewer and bowl from the wash hand stand and laid the box on its marble surface, praying for guidance as its contents revealed themselves. Family photographs, her mother as a girl, grandparents she had never known, marriage lines, birth certificates, she was astonished to discover her aunt was only sixty years of age. Paraphernalia of all description and tucked among it an insurance policy, one big problem solved at least. She was absolutely flabbergasted when she came across a canvas bag that clinked as it moved, gasping at the contents, sovereigns, many of them glittering wickedly in the dim light, an amazing sight totally unexpected.

But a sealed envelope bearing her own name in copperplate handwriting was of most concern, fumbling nervously as she began to open it, praying hard for the long awaited confirmation it might contain.

'Dear Charlotte' was the heading, indeed a mockery when no love existed between them, so very conscious of her aunt's voice as she started to read, that well remembered tone and never more brutal than when it announced the stillbirth of her child. A lie that should have choked her there and then.

'You are my closest living relative,' Jessica wrote, Ralph was obviously not in the reckoning, the money hers to do with as she wished with strict orders not to waste it, authority there to the very end, orders regarding funeral arrangements most explicit, only Mattie Jackson and Lottie herself to attend. 'I wish to be buried in Branton Cemetery beside my parents. When you read this letter I shall be making full atonement for my sins and pray the Lord will be merciful.'

'God might forgive the scheming old witch but I never shall,' Lottie spat out in rage, reeling from yet another shattering blow. No hope left, no other avenue open to her, the finality was almost too much to bear, far worse than any physical abuse she had suffered. She might have known Jessica would do nothing to betray her fickle employer, Victoria's rightful parentage was never to be disclosed. 'I don't want her damned tainted money,' she shot out minutes later, throwing the gold sovereigns across the kitchen table to the accompaniment of oohs and ahs from her companions, open mouthed in disbelief. 'There could be varnigh a hundred o'them,' Martha gasped, taking it upon herself to count the hoard, quite illiterate but not where money was concerned, each coin piled up and counted, almost in reverence. 'Just think what y'can do with it. Y'deserve every penny, sh'took that much an'more out o'yer hide in eight years,' never one to soften her words.

Lottie was struggling hard for control. 'I shan't spend a penny of it on myself,' she vowed. 'Some day there might be a real need of it somewhere or other and that's where it will go with a smack in the eye for the miserable old bitch. Damn her rotten soul to hell.' Such a spate of vindictiveness that even Martha stared in amazement, Alice was absolutely dumbfounded, the former strangely enough ready to voice firm disapproval of the outburst.

'That's a bit over the top, isn't it,' such vehemence from Lottie was beyond comprehension, a limit to what folk should say at these times, retribution in the hands of the Lord.

But the look Lottie gave her forbade further comment and Alice, whose interest in the golden treasure trove had soon evaporated, began to rave about the day's happenings elsewhere and Martha soon joined in, both eloquent about the village children's dressed up displays, red, white and blue everywhere. Costumes made out of old sheets, dyed and sewn by mothers, grandmothers, anyone good with a needle got together to make it a real parade of national colours. The bairns danced, marched, sang patriotic songs and tucked in to the food provided, the ingredients given by local tradesmen and shopkeepers, womenfolk slaving over hot ovens for hours on end. Alice was agog with it all, even more talkative than usual, Martha hardly able to have her say at times. 'Lizzie Phillips sayed her two youngest had been practisin' fer weeks. Jimmy's ready fer the pit come October an' Selina's varnigh eleven,' came out in a rush from Lottie's simple friend's mouth, any former grievances no more than a vague memory on either side. There was a rumour that a decent, middle aged widower with no bairns was setting his cap for Lizzie. Lottie listened as the comical pair got everything off their chests, herself an outsider completely alienated from Saltersgate folk, once by victimisation but now further apart than ever, education the real divider and that by choice. She had no regrets about the hard struggle it was to learn, most of the rough edges had been rubbed off in the process, all done to keep herself closer to Victoria, who always came first.

The Coronation celebrations were over, resources stretched to the limit for one day of glorious carnival, a bright oasis in a desert of gloom, the memory of it feasted upon until the next excuse for festivity chanced their way. Jessica Finlay's funeral was already high on Martha's agenda, not yet informed of the terms of her will. The sparks were sure to fly and Lottie wasn't ready for that yet, the following day would be soon enough.

After a decent interval she took her leave, too tired physically and mentally to pay full attention to their chatter, Victoria was due home again soon, and she was desperate for sight of the child she could never claim. Suddenly she was reminded that Geoffrey was making the journey to Whitegates come morning and Alice hadn't been told, six o'clock would be soon enough, no doubt, to give the order. He would leave immediately after breakfast, anxious to see his daughter, an irony really, amazed at herself for wishing he was the child's father, better than the rogue who sired her. She remembered that encounter under the coach house lantern and the words flung at Jake Snowdon then. 'Aa hope sh'looks like me an' keeps y'guessin'.' But she thanked the Lord that Victoria resembled neither mother nor father, a great blessing indeed, no sign of Jake mirrored in the face of her beautiful child.

'She's not the same lass,' Martha lamented over a cup of cocoa, after they saw the last of her for the night. 'It's all that book learnin'. Mattie Jackson can think what'ee likes but sh'was a bonny sight happier the way sh'was afore. Now she's neither one thing or t'other.' An apt description of an unenviable situation, Lottie was on the dividing line between two separate worlds, no real part of either. An empty sort of No-Man's-Land and a very lonely place to be.

As she had done so often in the past, Lottie cried herself to sleep but her dreams were not the troubled sort she expected after so much trauma, invaded instead by fantasies wrapped around a handsome soldier. So far beyond her reach and, recollecting the following morning, she wondered yet again why she was always so self destructive and drawn towards forbidden fruit.

* * *

All hell was let loose on the morning of Jessica Finlay's funeral, the kitchen in constant uproar as Martha alternated between sulking and bouts of ranting and raving. This was the case ever since she discovered Alice and herself were denied the peculiar pleasure of attending the late housekeeper's last appearance upon earth, resentment expressed continually in excellent voice.

'We're all part o' the same fam'ly,' she insisted, ready to claim a connection strongly refuted while Lottie's aunt was alive. 'Carrin'er spite t'the grave,' one angry complaint, Jackson tired of hearing the same old story, only to be regaled even further. 'How would ye feel if y'were left out?' was the plaintive cry, totally obsessed with the whole ridiculous business and impossible to shut her up for any length of time.

'Aa'm not exactly overjoyed about goin' but Lottie can do with a bit o'support,' he patiently explained, not that it did any good, nothing would, but he fervently hoped the great hullabaloo would cease when the funeral was over. The final curtain had come to Jessica Finlay's stormy reign, not sorry in the least it had at last come to an end, even her continued presence in the house, without any real status, had been heavy going for all of them, especially Lottie.

But Martha held strong opinions on what befitted such occasions, proper respect meant being in evidence at the grave side, even if the late lamented had been no particular friend beforehand, which was surely the truth in this instance. Nothing to do with it, she declared, quite serious in this assumption, a strange view but widely held in this hypocritical age.

Mattie put up with Martha's behaviour just as they had always done, the odd reproof now and again until, absolutely fed to the teeth, he rounded on her in no uncertain fashion, she having gone rather a bit too far. 'Hold yer tongue wife. An'ye stop noddin'yer head off at evrythin' sh'says, Alice Ruddick. A right pair t'be sure, makin' such a carry on when y'hated 'er guts. Mebbe she's getting 'er own back fer the past twelve months.' In reference to Martha's callous attitude on a number of occasions.

'Whose side are ye on, Mattie Jackson? Y'know the dance sh'led us all fer years.' Stretched to the full height of her four feet nothing, bursting with righteous indignation.

'All the more reason fer bidin' away, Martha. The wife's dead an' gone, let'er rest,' sighing in sheer exasperation.

'A fat lot o'restin' she'll do wi' all that's on'er conscience,' she snapped at him, in process of chopping mint to go with the fine leg of lamb, John Starrett's requested menu for dinner that evening, he was a great one for indulgence in the good things in life, food high on the agenda.

Alice gave a loud sniff to express her displeasure and retreated to the stables, her usual bolt hole, miffed maybe but never known to keep it up for any length of time, Martha and herself usually voice and echo, as Jackson labelled them, an apt description.

A pair of real comedians, he thought and chuckled to himself. If it were Jessica's intention to hit back, this definitely had the required effect, funerals were very high on their list of social occasions. A nice piece of gammon was boiled for lunch, the customary pease pudding to go with it, tradition had been followed in this one respect at least.

Shortly after the latest contretemps, Lottie's appearance was greeted in stony silence, loud grunts and banging of kitchen utensils more eloquent than words. Jackson's raised eyebrows said it all and Lottie acknowledged the warning with an imperceptible nod and came to the conclusion a bit of psychology was required, setting out to make use of it.

'Time to make tracks, Mattie,' she stated, easing her fingers into black cotton gloves. 'The hearse will be here shortly. The gaffer said it was quite in order to pull up at the front entrance to save them coming down the basement stairs, three flights was more than enough to deal with.'

She stood in front of the kitchen mirror and gave a wee tilt to her leghorn straw hat, the feverish chopping had ceased, a bird like head raised in interest. 'The master isn't attending because of Aunt Jessica's wishes but she would have been over the moon with the flowers sent from Whitegates this morning.'

'Aye, especially with that black edged card that says who they're from,' he stated drily and went on to comment on Madam's unconcern, not a single bloom. 'After all yer aunt did fer'er,' The full, horrific extent of that known only to Lottie herself. The only floral tributes apart from John Starrett's were some from her and a bunch out of Rothwell House garden from the rest of them, Martha's doing. Jackson had been dragged in to write the card but drew the line at 'from her friends in Rothwell House' and merely added their names, like it or otherwise, definitely the latter, considered most inadequate.

They heard the sound of hooves as the hearse arrived and Lottie, followed by Mattie Jackson made towards the inner stairs, aware of a sudden commotion as Martha downed tools and hastened out of doors, not to be deprived of seeing the gaffer's flowers and the cortege leaving the house.

'Trust Martha,' Lottie laughed, 'Nothing to say she couldn't see Aunt Jessica off the premises,' Jackson joined in the merriment. 'Guess what's fer lunch,' he chortled, laughing even louder at the prompt reply. 'Ham and pease pudding,' Lottie chanted, well and truly versed in the workings of their diminutive friend's mind. Alice was already alerted, no doubt, to tag on out of doors, just as curious.

The journey to South Branton was in John Starrett's carriage, driven from Whitegates that morning, his own coachman at the reins, this offer had been made when funeral matters were discussed, travelling down a few days earlier to help Lottie. 'Jackson can be a passenger and travel in style,' he said, 'I believe that fellow Humble in Woodbine Road does an excellent job. Tell him you are in my service.' He knew about the insurance policy and the gold sovereigns, and was determined Lottie would be left with as much as possible at the end of it all.

She was quick to remark upon Mattie's appearance when they settled in the coach, resplendent in navy suit and bowler hat, the former sponged and pressed by Martha amid a spate of grumbles. Not at all confortable thus arrayed he merely grunted and prised a stiff white collar away from his Adam's apple. 'Aa reckoned Aa had t'make some effort wi' ye dressed t'the nines,' said with an approving look, 'Black suits ya,' a colour never worn nowadays, too reminiscent of her cantankerous old aunts, she was only dressed in it now according to custom. It was too warm for a coat but a plain dress in light weight material suited the purpose, a useful addition to her limited wardrobe and striking just the right note for the occasion. As Mattie warned, plenty of folk would be around to see her on such a day, hardly a comforting thought.

Jessica Finlay's former role sat well on her niece's shoulders, such a post never dreamed of, now on the same level as Marianne, who continued to give further education to her star pupil. Victoria's lessons were going well also, a bright young thing, which gave Lottie immense satisfaction. Although pleased with her own prowess she remained firmly convinced that ladies were definitely born not made.

'That's more like it,' John Starrett said when, the gold sovereign spent, she paraded before him in a grey, uniform dress with its white collar, that one and similar worn ever since, the gaffer gratified to be proved right about a good figure, formerly well concealed. A young woman who seemed to grow prettier every day, a decided improvement in speech and deportment.

Felicity made no objection when Lottie was promoted to housekeeper, she was seldom around in any case but too much indebted to her father to oppose his decisions. Her addiction began to show, camouflage became ever more difficult as dissipation set in, but John Starrett chose to bury his head in the sand, obviously afraid of what he might discover.

'Better the devil sh'knows,' Martha said at the time. 'She'll not want any nosy newcomer around t'see'er goin's on. It isn't everybody that keeps their mouth shut,' quite right in this assumption. The animosity remained but Felicity needed Lottie's discretion and cried truce, both women prepared to stay within the bounds of their respective positions. An uneasy truce, no doubt, but reasonably successful for the time being at least.

Mattie Jackson watched Lottie's face change colour as they neared the churchyard gates, a slow drive dictated by custom which seemed an eternity. 'Funeral Private' printed in the obituary column of the local newspaper was no deterrent to Saltersgate folk, a fair number assembled, one gaunt figure towering above the rest.

'Aunt Ethel,' she breathed in dismay. One down, two to go was the sorry thought and on the look out for her other aunts she soon saw Lizzie Ann darting hither and thither for place of vantage, like a sharp nosed ferret. But there was no sign of Maude Elliott, for which blessing she sighed in relief, her composure soon shattered when Jinny Roberts peered brazenly into the coach, obviously her aunt's deputy, ready to carry every last detail to those eagerly waiting ears, her bosom friend evidently unable to attend.

With her arm held in reassuring grip, Mattie Jackson handed her down, the hostility of those in attendance strongly felt as she passed by to follow the coffin. She was soon aware of whispering tongues, the first opportunity to sharpen them on her since that memorable Friday afternoon so long ago. Given so much time the whole affair might have died a death, other reputations had been torn to shreds in the interim period, but they were resurrected now because this young woman chose to hob nob with the gaffer's family and seemed to have grown like them. There was no sign of the lass born and bred among them. Working class bigotry was equally as strong as that of their upper class masters, whom they hated so much.

Lottie's heart sank even further as the slow moving cortege passed into the confines of the actual graveyard and a loud, well remembered voice boomed its malice through soft summer air. 'It's the fine lady w'are these days, Cud. Look at that head tossed s'high. Not even a glance. Aa can think of a time sh'was a lot more friendly. The anniversary's just about comin'up.' Jake, fully prepared to exact vengeance for that scornful rejection underneath the coach house lantern, now, more than willing to shame her in public, with no respect for the solemn occasion.

'Steady lass, steady,' Jackson whispered, 'Make on y'haven't heard,' aware of a fierce trembling in her slender body, and filled with a strong urge to push his big fist into the other man's sneering face. But his words had the required effect, Lottie met Jake's bold stare with coldly indifferent eyes, who truly disconcerted was first to turn away. He might have known, this lass was made of sterner stuff than any women he ever had dealings with.

The opportunity slipped away, as uninvited mourners, in twos and threes formed an effective barrier and Jake made no attempt to follow, sullen, in what he recognised as another defeat, more shaken than he cared to admit by the glint of sunshine on that bright auburn hair beneath Lottie's stylish hat, a dark mind filled with a strange mixture of spite and regret.

Cud Matthews shuffled uneasily in his hobnailed boots, rather disturbed by the place chosen for another vengeful action, 'Howway man,' he urged, 'There's more t'do than hang around here all day. Give it a miss, that lass has stepped far beyond yer reach,' his companion totally disinclined to take any notice.

Once outside the churchyard gates, Jake spat his rage into a nearby gutter and began to mutter threats of further retribution. 'There'll be another time,' he spluttered, kicking the hard ground. 'One o' these days Aa'll fix that little madam good an' proper. It doesn't matter a monkey's cuss how long Aa have t'wait.' Wholly incensed by his failure to break Lottie's spirit. 'There should o'been a bairn,' he grunted in disgust and strode off in the direction of Branton. A bairn that looked like him, his evil mind ran on, a hard time livin' that down, cursing the fact that the child was stillborn. 'Tryin' t'make on nowt happened between us,' he said aloud, unconscious of curious glances from passers by.

Cud kept his distance. 'It's all very well fer him,' he smarted, 'He just needs t'go t'Confession, Aa'm Church o' England.' Amusing from someone who never crossed St Mary's doorstep, constantly informed by Annie the place would fall down if ever he did. Not that the sarcasm registered.

Strangely enough Cud was really put out, truly convinced his sins would weigh heavier with the Almighty without weekly absolution. That and the fact that his feeelings had undergone an enormous change at the sight of Lottie altered beyond belief, eight years older and much more the lady. It was one thing to take down a collier's daughter but the pit gaffer wielded a lot of authority in those parts and owned the land leased to Cud as a smallholding. It would be disastrous to get on the wrong side of his landlord, he could see his livelihood going up in smoke. Thus thinking he slouched after Jake who still wallowed in malice and frustration.

Out of yet another painful experience came the sure knowledge, as Lottie reflected later, that nothing was forgotten, animosity still rankled in Jake's warped mind, but she was loathe to acknowledge some debt to Jessica Finlay after all. If Victoria was her child as she had every reason to believe, conceived during that much regretted union in Batey's Field, she was well out of her real father's reach, a consoling thought. 'You are better with the father you know,' she said to the absent Victoria, no credit attached to Felicity, supposed to be a mother but who accepted nothing that came with the role. Geoffrey is so different, she mused, and straightaway pulled herself up short. No right to use this man's Christian name, yet she still repeated it over and again, music to her ears. She was in love, deeply in love, for the very first time, old enough to recognise the difference, but at once berated herself for such foolish thoughts. All the polish in the world would never make her Geoffrey Cranshawe's equal. Besides there was Felicity and marriage, not easy to dismiss, but neither was the image of Geoffrey and the dreams she constantly wove around him. Already she was in too deep, much too deep for any peace of mind.

* * *

When the man in question took the journey to Whitegates the morning after Jessica Finlay's death, the slow ride helped to clear his head, in a state of turmoil after the happenings of the previous evening. He had hardly slept a wink, absolutely bowled over by the wife's young housekeeper, according to the rules strictly out of bounds, he was left with a strong feeling of something more to life than hitherto experienced. A delightfully feminine woman who made him feel like a man again and so lovely. There had been one or two brief dalliances over the years but not recently, he had no real desire for that sort of thing. But what else did he envisage, could possibly contemplate, his life an absolute mess at present and no hope of ever being anything else.

The funeral over, Lottie eagerly awaited the return of Rothwell House's absentees, Geoffrey's handsome face ever before her eyes, the memory of that fine, manly body and those dark, exciting eyes following her every move around the attic room made her pulse race alarmingly.

The tingling sensation if they happened to touch, not always by accident, both with an urgent need for closer physical contact. Love didn't come in this swift, uncontrollable fashion, she told herself, a foolish notion not to be encouraged, that long ago indiscretion painfully resurrected at her aunt's funeral.

An hour or two had elapsed since the ham and pease pudding lunch, complete with salad and a varied assortment of home made pickles, pronounced delicious by the gaffer when Lottie returned to the small dining room to clear the table. She tried to rid her mind of such vain imaginings, a hopeless exercise, and prodded Martha and Alice into action, almost to the point of rebellion, Martha still up tight began to wax vocal, 'Anybody would think there's no tomorra,' she loudly protested and, with Lottie out of earshot, actually made unfavourable comparison with Jessica Finlay, 'Bossiness must run i' the that blinkin' fam'ly,' which said everything about their friend's behaviour. No head on confrontation, just Martha like ways of expressing her feelings and, once again, kitchen utensils were in for some very rough handling.

Amid all this there was little reference to the funeral and the two servants eagerly anticipated Alice's next visit to Saltersgate, there to pick up what both Lottie and Mattie Jackson chose to keep from them. Jake Snowdon's part in it was likely to be swallowed with the utmost relish when it reached Martha's ears, probably embellished beyond belief. One thing certain, Martha would immediately find a swift change of target for the sharp edge of her waspish tongue, not that Lottie wanted Jake Snowdon to be the topic of any sort of conversation in the big house.

The telephone rang at four that afternoon, its imperative summons from the front hallway, with a quick dash up the inner stairs to answer it Lottie took the call, Jackson out and neither Martha nor Alice capable of dealing with this latest innovation. 'Who wants them new fangled things, anyway,' a constant cry and its ring ignored when they were alone in the house. Sometimes John Starrett was at the other end and got really hot under the collar if nobody answered it. The phone had been installed for business purposes and also to keep in touch with Whitegates and Harrow Square, the situation in the latter deteriorating with every passing day, with Felicity becoming an absolute wreck.

Quite out of breath, Lottie grabbed the receiver from the wall and held it to her ear, even more flustered when Geoffrey Cranshawe's deep tone echoed across the wire and she listened in a bemused fashion to what he had to say, it was wonderful just to hear the thrilling sound of his voice, all aglow from head to toe.

She quickly pulled herself together, pleased no curious eyes were upon her and answered a question which only just registered. 'No trouble to hold dinner, sir,' she assured him, 'The joint is in the oven but Martha won't start other preparations for an hour at least.' Giggling rather self consciously at what he asked next. 'No I won't tell you what we are having, it will be a surprise,' amazed at her own effrontery but completely reassured when a chuckle came in reply. 'Yes, later, perhaps,' she said to the next question, blushing furiously. Then there was silence, neither of them hung up. A meaningful second or two with the feel of soft lips caressing her ear, an insane idea of closeness with so much distance between, indeed mutual, two young people in absolute harmony of heart and mind. With the disengaged tone came an incredible sense of loss.

It was a different person who tripped back to the kitchen, there to inform Martha dinner would be an hour later than usual, the absentees home to share it, a change of mood very obvious but they assumed Victoria's return to the fold to be the reason for it. 'And before you say anything we might have a cup of tea. I reckon we've earned it,' just the right recipe to restore good humour, Mattie Jackson spot on as usual, at the mention of his favourite brew.

'Shout that lass in from the stables,' came the brusque order, 'An' when sh'comes,' Martha continued, 'Tell'er she's supposed t'be kitchen maid i' this place,' But there was no need to seek Alice out, she was quick on Jackson's heels, straight on the end of a withering tongue.

'There y'are,' Martha barked. 'Get them mucky hands washed an' a clean apron on, there's extra veg t'peel fer dinner. When ye've had yer tea, fetch a cabbage from the kitchen garden. Yer like a blinkin' scarecrow. John Coulter must o'had a job keepin' the birds away after y'left.' Never particular what came out of her mouth, especially to Alice and young Grace Jennings, a Saltersgate lassie hired to help out, six to twelve every weekday. Grace was not so thick skinned as Alice and Lottie was often obliged to adopt the role of peacemaker where the newcomer was concerned.

'It'll be champion havin' that bairn back i' the house again. This place isn't the same without'er,' Jackson remarked, a sentiment Lottie fully endorsed, his criticism of her slavish devotion not so evident nowadays.

'Miss Spaldin's a miss an'all, isn't sha, Mattie?' Martha said, instantly rewarded by a flush of embarrassment on his homely face. 'Aye, she's a miss an' all, as y'say,' he answered rather sheepishly and seemed to be exercising enormous self control.

Lottie's eyebrows knitted in amazement at this starting innuendo, hard to believe such a sly inference but little things came to mind and her long time friend looked like a man on the spot. 'Of course Marianne is a miss,' she put in hastily. Nothing worse than having one's soul laid bare and very much aware of Jackson's discomfort she began to steer the conversation into safer channels. Martha neded to be diverted but how? The funeral, of course, any mention of that would definitely claim her attention.

The subterfuge worked. 'Ethel and Lizzie Ann were at the churchyard this morning,' she said quite casually and soon held the floor, Alice rushed to fetch a cabbage, back in a couple of shakes almost, and brought a bowl of potatoes to the table, determined not to miss out but intent on keeping Martha sweet at the same time. The relieved expression on Jackson's face showed he was glad to be let off the hook, knowing explanations would have to be made but fortunately in private, Lottie's clever intervention face saving to say the least.

She told them just enough to keep them happy without mentioning Jake Snowdon, an episode she wanted to forget, so sure that one day the whole nasty business could blow up in her face, Jake was not the one to let sleeping dogs lie and she shuddered at the idea of all the whispering behind her back when Alice picked that tasty morsel up in Saltersgate. Not for the first time did she think of saying goodbye to Rothwell House and indeed the whole area, seeking employment elsewhere, but knew she never would, drawn as a moth to the flame where Victoria was concerned and now Geoffrey, courting even more trouble if she allowed herself to dwell upon him, well aware of her own vulnerability.

Her eyes feasted upon his tall, handsome figure as he stepped out of the coach and turned to lift Victoria down, Mattie was already on hand to help Marianne, a strange look between them. A momentary glance soon forgotten when Geoffrey smiled and said, 'Hello Lottie, your peace is shattered I'm afraid.' Immensely touched by the way Victoria greeted her, so much genuine affection between his daughter and this lovely woman. Lottie found it hard to look him in the eyes but managed with enormous effort. 'Nice to have you all home, sir.' Nice, such an inadequate word to cover how she really felt. An impossible situation already in the making, a married man who believed he had fathered the child she still hoped to claim some day, now a very remote possibility with Jessica dead and gone. Tormented enough without the added burden of a love that could never be fulfilled.

* * *

'Aa might o'guessed them sharp eyes would miss nowt,' Jackson grunted ruefully, Marianne and himself were seated in Lottie's private quarters, about to put their mutual friend in the picture, the situation rather forced upon them by Martha's untoward remarks earlier in the day. A knock at the door after dinner that evening found them both standing there when she opened it, not at all surprised. Mattie somewhat ill at ease but Marianne calm and dignified as always.

'You might,' Lottie laughed, rather enjoying his obvious discomfort, 'Martha seldom misses a trick,' amazed indeed that she herself hadn't seen signs of the growing attraction between them and said so when they settled down with a cup of tea.

'Much too occupied with your aunt,' Marianne sympathised. 'And keeping the situation on a low key. Martha certainly didn't make it too easy for you.'

'It's over now,' was the abrupt reply and her mentor realised she didn't want to talk about it. That same shadow came over her face, witnessed on several occasions and couldn't be figured out, always a sense that it was something else, a something which went so much deeper.

'Thank goodness fer that,' Mattie said with a great big sigh, 'Aa wouldn't o'thought she had time t'bother about Marianne an'me, especially over these past few days, what wi'the Coronation an' all.' Lottie laughed. 'Martha slots everything into its place, the other things were over, now it's your turn. So – tell me everything,' she ordered, 'I've been hearing wedding bells since four this afternoon,' and saw Marianne's face flush to a bright rosy red. There were lots of things she wanted to know about this unexpected alliance but decided to be practical. 'What plans have you made?' enormously touched by the happiness which surrounded them, two people very close to her heart, finding it hard not to be envious but so delighted, apart from one or two misgivings, dismissed for the moment, they could wait. Jackson tried to slow the pace. 'Hold yer horses, hinny. Give us time t'get used t'other folk knowin'. W'hadn't reckoned on that s'soon,' he said rather ruefully but Marianne was quite prepared to answer Lottie's question.

'No definite plans,' she freely admitted, 'A lot depends upon you,' and received an encouraging reply without hesitation, Lottie quick to respond. 'Anything, you know that, you just have to ask.'

'Wait will y'hear what it is,' Mattie suggested drily, knowing how often this dearest of friends acted on impulse. Truth to tell he felt rather guilty to think he once entertained marriage with Lottie, thankful indeed she was never aware of his foolish dreams, the full extent of such wisely kept from Martha, with no more confidences, she fondly imagined she nipped the lot in the bud with straight talking, no idea how long he agonised, the five years it took to accept the fact that she only regarded him as an older brother or father figure, Ralph and herself completely estranged and John Hanson's tragic demise at a very young age.

But Marianne's impatience soon showed and he felt obliged to take the bull by the horns. 'W'both want t'bide here but only if w'can make some sort o'home t'gether,' ending in a embarrassed rush. 'Aa'm not willin' t'bide where Aa am now wi' me wife i' the big house.'

Lottie laughed. 'What you mean is, you want to set up house above the stables. And why not indeed? There are three good sized rooms. Mattie only uses one apart from the kitchen. It could be made into a little palace if we all get stuck in.' The look in Marianne's grey eyes spoke volumes, a huge beam from Jackson an added bonus, Lottie hugged by both in turn. Quite a demonstration from a usually sedate young lady who burst forth in delight. 'We knew you would see it our way,' absolutely ecstatic. 'W'hoped,' Jackson prompted. 'An' Lottie's just the first hurdle, the powers that be might have somethin' diff'rent t'say. Raised eyebrows at us getting' wed at all, a lady body an'her boss's coachman,' One of Lottie's misgivings was thus voiced, a more than likely possibility but one she was determined to overcome.

'Such absolute nonsense,' came in swift retort, Marianne was quite indignant. 'Should there be any objection along those lines we can seek positions elsewhere as a married couple,' hand to mouth in dismay. 'Goodness me, I sound like a nagging wife already,' a tiny giggle accomopanying this. She was not a beautiful woman in the strict sense of the word but happiness radiated from her and showed in a lovely smile and a pair of sparkling eyes. It was Marianne Spalding's moment, happiness she never dreamt of ever being hers.

Jackson's love for this gentle woman illuminated his rugged countenance and a wide grin greeted this show of spirit in someone generally very contained. 'Aa like me women wi' a bit o'somethin' in them,' he chaffed. 'It makes life a lot more interestin.'

'And just how many women have you known, Mattie Jackson?' Marianne questioned, pretending to be sorely affronted at the very idea, soon laughing as he began to count the fingers on both hands. Long conversations had made Jackson's entire life an open book, nothing being withheld apart from the obsession he once held for Lottie, better neither woman should ever know of it. A very wise decision.

Lottie smiled at their obvious rapport and all about vanished at the sight of so much deep affection, a tiny pang of jealousy was soon stifled. 'I'll speak to the Master,' she promised, intending it to be Geoffrey Cranshawe, any excuse to be near him, aware of the likely consequences but bewitched enough to dice with danger.

The following day she sought him out to plead her friends' case, totally unconscious of the spell she cast upon him. He remembered the warmth of that slender body in his arms, an auburn head just below his chin, no effort needed to imagine her elfin face uplifted to receive his kiss. Soft, appealing lips responsive to a hungry mouth and he was starving for closer contact with this enchanting creature, it was difficult for him to stay within those bounds which correct behaviour imposed upon him, little knowing how strongly his feelings were reciprocated.

'Perhaps a word in my father-in-law's ear,' he suggested, 'But I don't envisage any objections,' instantly rewarded by eloquent eyes smiling her gratitude, radiant enough to make his heart lose a beat, utterly fascinated by the graceful movement of a slim form as she walked away. It was a while before he recovered sufficiently to telephone John Starrett at Whitegates with the startling news.

'Good God,' the gaffer exclaimed, 'Jackson and Miss Spalding, whatever next.' But after the initial impact he only made one stipulation. 'Let them make their home above the stables, by all means, but Charlotte must sleep in the room next to Victoria. We can't have the child with a whole landing to herself. A pity her parents aren't around more often.' He found it easier to deliver these words of censure across the wire and Geoffrey found it hard to keep back a reminder that his absences were obligatory, unlike Felicity who preferred the company of a bottle of gin to that of her own daughter. The child scarcely knew her mother in the flesh, just a beautiful lady on numerous studio portraits scattered around the house at John Starrett's insistence. Wedding preparations were right up Martha's street, the cake was soon made and stored away to be iced, great plans afoot for the rest, she was absolutely in her element. 'Keep her in check,' Marianne pleaded as the whole affair began to reach alarming proportions, far distant from the small reception Jackson and herself wanted. But nothing short of direct orders were any use and these Lottie was loath to give, just words of restraint now and again and she hoped for the best. She was busy herself with Marianne's dress and her own, a labour of love for the teaching bestowed upon her over the past few years.

The simple but attractive garment fell from the bride to be's tiny waist to slim ankles in soft folds, dozens of tiny pin tucks in the bodice, neck and long sleeves trimmed with an edging of fine ecru lace, surprisingly donated by the gaffer. 'Picked it up in France years ago,' he said, 'no use lying in a drawer,' once again in favour for such a kind gesture. It matched the colour Marianne had chosen, brown strangely enough but it suited her and could be worn afterwards, always a consideration in their station in life, one occasion finery a luxury they usually couldn't afford. Lottie was sorely tempted to produce some of Jessica Finlay's money but shrank from giving offence.

Alice being Alice expected a white veil and orange blossom, ever the romantic. 'Too old for that,' she was told but Marianne did promise to wear a sprig of the traditional white flower in the wide brim of her cream straw hat, a posy of tea roses to complete the picture, with all of which the simple lass had to be satisfied, head in the clouds as usual.

Out of courtesy, Madam was duly informed of the arrangements but showed no interest whatsoever and declined to come again until Christmas, not even then if she could wriggle out of it, which was doubtful. Whitegates was a confounded bore and presented difficulties because of her addiction to the bottle but John Starrett threatened to cut the purse strings and really meant it if she didn't comply, a drastic measure which was long overdue.

The Reverend Spalding expressed his regrets, too infirm to travel to Northumberland, or so he said in a letter which arrived at the same time as china and other articles to be bequeathed on marriage by Marianne's late mother, he was an austere man whose whole existence centred around his church in Sussex. An order for a small amount of money was enclosed, with no further communication until a few years later with news of his death and mention of a legacy to follow when his affairs were settled, an end to a non existent father and daughter relationship.

Jackson's family sent a tiny gift but also refused the invitation, introduced to Marianne but completely out of their depth where she was concerned, her superior breeding made them uneasy. 'Sorry Matthew,' she said in deep concern, 'I am not what they wanted for you,' quite upset by rejection from both sides. 'Don't fret lass,' he soothed. 'Yer what Aa want an' that's all that counts. The real break came years ago. If y'don't mind me sendin'a bob or two, now and again, they'll be more than satisfied.' In which prediction he was quite correct, money always a deciding factor. Lottie said she was sorry but made no further comment, family relationships were the very devil, she being still estranged from Ralph after almost eight long years, a situation stoically accepted, any real bitterness gone, just a deep sadness that it should have to be so and reconciliation seemingly impossible.

'Forget your worries,' Marianne said one day as they worked alongside in the flat, making Lottie's eyes lift in enquiry. 'Matthew and I have more in common than most people imagine,' having always been aware of her friend's unspoken concern.

Those beautiful hazel eyes did not turn away in embarrassment, Lottie's look was totally guileless, unwilling to deny the truth, Marianne deserving of no less. 'I realise that now but must admit I did have serious doubts, perhaps not how you might imagine. There is one big danger, Mattie does have lots of pride and could be hurt if you set out to change him too much. Some of you is certain to rub off on him and better it should be that way. But I still can't believe I had no idea what was happening right in front of my eyes.'

'It surprised me too, when I realised how I felt about him and discovered the feeling to be mutual. Besides, I always imagined Matthew to be smitten with you.'

'Me?' Lottie gasped, genuinely taken aback, 'Mattie would be horrified to know you entertained such thoughts. He has always been like a father or an elder brother, I don't have either unfortunately.' Ralph's existence was sadly dismissed. Marianne chuckled, a delightful sound. 'He won't ever know. Perhaps years from now when we are old and grey I shall unburden myself but not yet. You are much too attractive for any woman's peace of mind and it might put ideas into his head. If you still have misgivings forget them, I love him dearly and, as you once said to me,' and here she dimpled in mischief, 'you are around to watch my P's and Q's. Remember?' At which point they fell into one another's arms and wept tears of joy, both quite overcome,. There until a voice boomed at them from the doorway.

'It's a weddin' we're supposed t'be getting' ready for, not a wake,' the man under discussion protested, only to be told that women always cried at weddings, it was their privilege. Lottie was first to recover, after which followed repartee of similar nature, but she soon excused herself on some flimsy pretext to allow them a little privacy, hard to come by with so many comings and goings.

* * *

To everyone's surprise and, perhaps, to make up for Felicity's lack of interest in the proceedings, John Starrett graciously accepted an invitation to the wedding and, as he did for Jessica Finlay's funeral, offered the services of coach and coachman for the day, an open carriage this time with white covers on the seats and the traditional rosettes on the horses' necks. The black stallions replaced the other pair when they arrived from Whitegates, Jackson was very touched and proud as punch at this magnificent gesture. Lottie once again warming to the man she ought to hate.

Victoria, greatly excited over the whole affair was even more so when she knew her beloved grandfather would be there, it was the first celebration of its kind the child had attended, awaiting the big day in enormous impatience and seemed to be everywhere at once. She was under Martha's feet in the kitchen, so called helping in the flat and Geoffrey almost driven mad with dozens of awkward questions, on home posting for a while with a few days leave.

'There is only one bed in the coach house,' she stated one day, out of the blue. 'Will Marianne and Jackson both have to sleep in it?' Her father's face was impassive as he searched for a suitable reply. 'Married people do sleep together darling,' he managed at last and hoped this particular line of questioning would end there, but Victoria was apparently not satisfied with the answer.

'Mama and yourself don't sleep in the same bed and you are married people,' she persisted in all innocence. 'How can we?' came out rather abruptly. 'Mama is often in London and your Papa is a soldier.' An explanation which appeared to suffice for the moment, dreading the day when the questions became harder to answer truthfully, with a well above average mind to contend with as Victoria grew older.

Jackson's dilemma concerning a 'best man' was solved by the gaffer in his usual high handed manner. 'Ask my son-in-law,' he suggested. 'He is cooling his heels at present, until another overseas posting comes along, I suppose,' sounding disgruntled at the thought of it. 'I would do it myself, dammit, if I were his age. It isn't as if half the world and his brother will be there.' An unexpected attitude from such a man but John Starrett never ceased to surprise Lottie, her fluctuation of emotions becoming increasingly difficult to handle.

So it was, blushingly beautiful, she emerged from church into the bright sunshine of an August afternoon, her hand on Geoffrey Cranshawe's arm, entranced by the intimacy of these precious moments. Fate seemed determined to throw them together and she struggled valiantly not to betray her feelings towards him. It wasn't South Branton church but she, somehow, expected to hear Jake Snowdon's sarcastic voice echo from some shadowy corner but nothing happened and there were few onlookers, Saltersgate folk seemed to have missed out on this quiet wedding, it was a weekday after all. Alice and Grace had, obviously, taken her warnings to heart not to broadcast it around the village. Nothing must mar the perfection of this special occasion, Geoffrey so much part of it, a time to savour when the dreams ended as end they must eventually.

Only an inbred sense of propriety kept Geoffrey Cranshawe's eyes away from her, just a surreptitious glance now and again to absorb the beauty she personified. Those lovely elfin features enhanced, as always by the shining glory of her hair, arranged in a chignon, a much softer style than usual and crowned by a becoming straw hat, perfect match for the cornflower blue of her dress. She sensed his admiration and gloried in it, allowing herself to dream, those natural imaginings of a woman in love, as if this man and herself were the ones the parson made man and wife.

Marianne looked lovely too, smilingly so, Jackson's wide beam something to behold, the love in their eyes so plain to be seen, a love they had no need to hide. She was happy for them, these two wonderful friends, a happiness tinged with envy, due to the hopelessness of her own situation.

For some unknown reason Martha, who usually spoke well of the young master, saw fit to accuse him of condescension in Lottie's hearing at the small reception in the newly furnished flat. 'Tryin' t'make believe 'ees one o'us,' she muttered spitefully, her tongue loosened by rather too much ale, and Lottie's joy departed, cruelly dismissed by a few ill chosen words far from the truth. Geoffrey was genuinely happy to be there, especially in Lottie and Victoria's company. Once again Lottie found it difficult to draw a straight line between the classes, her loyalties stretched to the limit.

When the toasts were proposed and the speeches over, John Starrett excused himself, explaining why when Lottie saw him off the premises. 'A call from Belsford before I left for the church,' he said. 'Trouble of some sort my manager can't deal with. I got rid of Perkins and may have to do the same again.' Forgetful of her mining connections he began to rail against pit workers in general. 'I don't know what the damned men want, my employees are among the best paid in the country.' The truth, no doubt, but God help the rest if Polrigg wages were the yardstick to measure them by.

Disgusted at herself once again for not speaking out, his listener took his hat from the hall stand, her expressive face fortunately turned away, glad of these few seconds to recover. 'Your hat, sir,' she said, handing it to him. 'Will you be home for dinner?' asked as she did so. 'No, I shall go to my club. Martha won't be in a fit state to cook another meal today, I am sure something light will suffice. Have a word with my son-in-law. And you will be upstairs near Victoria tonight, the child may need a woman for some reason or other.' Such consideration was usually guaranteed to soften her heart towards him but failed to do so, her ruffled feathers refused to be smoothed on this occasion.

She followed him downstairs and watched the pony trap leave the yard, Tiger between the shafts, harnessed by Whitegate's coachman. The gaffer raised his hand and smiled, a gesture she found impossible to acknowledge, unable to reconcile herself to the two sides of his nature, thinking that love for Victoria should make him sympathetic towards the needs of poorer children. Correct mode of speech and manners taught by Marianne seemed treachery somehow, a betrayal of her own roots, her present life a cushy number in comparison, which filled her with shame. All pleasure in Geoffrey's company was destroyed, she convinced herself the gaffer and his son-in-law were cast from the same mould, very cool in manner when he came forward to greet her return to the festivities. 'Anything will do,' he replied, in answer to John Starrett's suggestion, rather disturbed by a change in attitude towards him, the barriers well and truly erected, his dark eyes full of mute enquiry, Lottie's only defence was to turn aside. Not long after he took his leave, Victoria with him, quite vociferous in protest, most reluctant to depart.

'Good riddance,' Martha triumphed. 'Now w'can really have a knees up,' none too comfortable in the company of her betters. Lottie bristled at such outspoken rudeness, ashamed to have banished Geoffrey, realising how much he had wanted to stay and deliberately made him feel like a fish out of water. She shouldn't have allowed herself to be influenced, Martha did everything by gut reaction at the time and no regrets afterwards.

There were only a handful of guests, the coachman and his wife from Whitegates, a young woman from the local book shop with whom Marianne had cultivated a relationship of sorts and who played the piano in a fashion. Enough to satisfy Martha and Alice, Grace Jennings too, brought in to help with the serving and washing up. The kindest to be said of Alice was unusual tidiness at the actual ceremony, now an incongruous sight in her normal state of disarray. Dancing with Martha, fly away hair released from restraining hair pins and the whole effect made even worse by over fussy apparel, not to be dissuaded in the purchase of what she considered the very thing for a wedding. Martha was little better, dressed in clothes which emphasised her deformity but neither woman was conscious of any shortcomings, enjoying it all to the full.

Marianne soon drew Lottie aside and said Jackson and herself had a train to catch, the coachman at their disposal, he and his wife quite willing to make a move, back to Whitegates straight from South Branton station. 'Thank you for everything,' Marianne murmured with a big hug for her friend. 'Rubbish,' came in return, an emotional moment, even more so when Jackson bent from his greater height to kiss her on the cheek. 'Ye've always been a grand lass,' he said huskily, about to close the door on an eventful chapter of his life, in which she had figured to a large extent, now holding his wife's hand to take them both into a new era.

'The place will be spick and span when you see it again,' was the promise as she watched them go, a very forlorn young woman, trying not to begrudge them their happiness, something which always seemed to be far from her own reach.

Cullercoats, on the Northumbrian coast, twelve miles distant, was to be their destination, a three day honeymoon, leave of absence and two guineas as a wedding present from the gaffer, they were relieved not to spend these first days of marriage under watchful eyes, spared the embarrassment of Martha's outspokenness, dreadfully near the bone at times with her crude remarks.

With Victoria eventually settled for the night, Lottie crept into the room next door, very conscious of her beloved Geoffrey at the other side. How she longed to go to him, the impulse resisted only by enormous willpower. She knew the act of love between them would be so different, far removed from Jake Snowdon's cruel seduction, well aware of the feelings this other man could arouse within her, on fire with longing to he held close in his arms, united at last body and soul.

'Thou shalt not covet' flashed through a tormented mind, as it battled with the urge for fulfilment of a love too sinful to encourage. He belonged to another woman, if only in the legal sense, Felicity's image was vivid enough to haunt her waking hours and disturb her dreams. The same sort of struggle was taking place in the next room, Geoffrey hard with need, painfully alive to the proximity of the woman he loved but fully determined not to take advantage as so many others of his acquaintance did, servant girls considered easy game and bastard offspring no unusual result from these liaisons, such inconveniences dealt with through the power of money, children of these unions abandoned without a single qualm, to be cared for by someone else.

Weary of long overseas assignments he still considered the sanity of putting another stretch of land and ocean between them, but thought of Victoria, wilfully neglected by her own mother which forced him to apply for home postings and likely to get them, he tried to banish Lottie from his mind, impossible to do so throughout a long, sleepless night, knowing how responsive she would be, the physical side of marriage rewarding as surely intended between man and wife. But he did have a wife already, although totally unworthy of the name.

Within the sound of the Great North Sea, a newly married couple consummated their marriage without reservation, perfectly attuned, Mattie Jackson gentle and considerate of his beloved Marianne, who had never been with any other man but responded unstintingly, pain for a brief while then ecstasy, lost in the joy of real fulfilment. Something Lottie Hanson was fully convinced would never be hers.

* * *

The harmful comments made at Jackson's wedding were soon forgotten by the person who delivered them, the young master back in favour, Martha never unduly concerned about any hurt she inflicted, no lasting pangs of conscience, her entire existence geared towards self preservation and expediency. Not so surprising with the hand that fate had dealt her, disability and all.

Geoffrey's promotion to Major and a staff position at Aldershot brought various reactions as might be expected. 'Mayja Cranshawe sounds real posh,' Alice breathed in awe when she heard the news, quite uppity when there were buttons to polish and Jackson wasn't available, 'Aa bet'ees the smartest chap there,' she exulted if called upon to deputise, a real labour of love, and watched in pride when he left the house to attend some function or other, no more thrilled than Lottie at the sight of his tall upright figure. A hopeless love, maybe, but dreams never seek permission to invade the mind and she indulged in them more often than was good for her, constantly warning herself it was impossible for a moth to flutter around a bright light without being burnt, a warning difficult to take on board.

Geoffrey accepted the rules laid down, prepared to suffer for precious moments of togetherness, even with others around them, often Victoria who saw no significance in fond looks nor the odd touch of hands, all most unwise but painfully exciting.

All roads led to Oakfields, London seldom saw him, except for odd visits to the War Office, even fewer to Harrow Square, to check the situation. Loyalty to their master was the sole reason for the Askews putting up with his wife's drunken behaviour, telephone numbers left in case of emergency. That, of course and the security of employment they had for years as old retainers. Not so old really, they had been quite young when they entered the Cranshawe's service, minor servants then in a grand house full of them.

John Starrett, reluctant to deal with Felicity himself tried to pass the buck. 'You ought to take a firmer hand,' he told Geoffrey, 'Victoria seldom sees her mother. Thank God for Charlotte. A laughable situation if it weren't so damned serious.'

'Felicity has always had too much of her own way. You can't expect her to change now,' Geoffrey answered, his turn for censure of another man's weakness in dealings with her. He was astounded at himself for speaking out, his father-in-law's face most expressive.

But there was real happiness for others as the newlyweds settled down to married bliss, Jackson's old quarters a real home from the outset. 'If only Matthew and I had met sooner,' Marianne grieved to Lottie one day. 'No matter how long we may have together I begrudge those wasted years.'

Lottie felt inclined to cry out that half a loaf was better than none and seemed so dispirited that Marianne came down from the clouds to take stock. 'Why don't you have a break?' she suggested, absolutely astounded when her friend flew off the handle. 'A break?' Lottie scorned, 'and what do you imagine would happen around here if I took myself off,' she snapped, Marianne's eyes wide with astonishment. How could she explain that to leave Rothwell House would be such a wrench with Geoffrey liable to appear unexpectedly on many occasions nowadays. She was afraid his orders might suddenly change and take him out of her sphere altogether, loath to admit this could be the only solution to their problem.

Mid October brought strike action to all three of the gaffer's collieries, unrest countrywide also. Furious at the men's demand for an extra penny an hour, John Starrett behaved as if they were asking for the moon. He installed himself in Rothwell House for the duration going around with a face like thunder most of the time, only Victoria able to woo him out of these black moods. 'Those dreadful men are upsetting Grandpa,' she pouted on one occasion and Lottie's raw nerves made her want to shriek in protest, tell this little madam that those she derided were her own kind, some with the same blood in their veins. Sad to think that class awareness had already begun to take its hold.

The strike didn't last long, it was the wrong time to be without adequate food and clothing, heat was not such a problem, the old pit heap soon into different shape with deeper digging, the very real chance of prison if caught. Deprivation sent them back to work but not before a few ugly incidents occurred, Rothwell House was a target, a heavy stone sent hurtling through the main dining room window, the gaffer absolutely incensed. 'Jail is where they should be, that would cool their ardour,' he ranted on. 'And that is where they'll go if they are caught.'

The identity of the perpetrators was never discovered much to Lottie's relief, although she did have her suspicion, Archie Beresford and Tommy Wilson had been seen earlier that day, probably on reconnaissance, an easy climb over the wall under darkness then off like a shot. With a head start, young legs and a knowledge of the area, they were soon back to the village by all the short cuts. If they were the culprits no harm would come to them through any words of hers, Tommy, Janey's son and Archie Beresford a young married man with three bairns.

Lottie fumed inwardly at Tommy's indulgence in such capers with his mother still clinging to life by a thread. Another parcel would not go amiss, the earlier ones obviously welcomed, delivered by the usual messenger, Alice sworn to secrecy, Martha was not in on this devious piece of work. Lottie had no qualms of conscience in giving John Starrett's food to a dying friend, able to convince herself he owed the Wilsons and their kind much more than that, their relationship going through a period of severe strain, the way things were.

Police constables patrolled the grounds and immediate area during hours of darkness. 'Clutterin' the place up,' according to Martha, who really enjoyed seeing new faces and supplied these guardians of the law with numerous cups of tea, telling them to make their own during the night, the back door left on the latch. This was much appreciated by the men, who kept careful look out for their sergeant, often liable to pay surprise visits. The actual job was one they didn't relish and hoped they never had to take anyone in, working class the same as themselves and badly put upon. They sincerely hoped nobody would be foolish enough to stick their necks out and be apprehended, in which case duty must be done.

* * *

The strike was on its last legs, resistance at a very low ebb when Robert Hanson came to seek Lottie out and arrived just as the street lamps were lit, straight into the arms of a vigilant copper. Not that the lad was trying to avoid anyone, his protests loud enough to waken the dead. 'Let me be, y'daft buggar,' he swore. 'Aa was doin' nowt, nowt at all,' struggling hard to break loose.

Drawn out of doors by the noise, Martha appeared upon the scene. 'Y'can put that one back, he's not old enough t'be one o'yer hardened criminals. Fetch'im in,' she ordered, leading the way down the basement steps into her warm kitchen, Robert only too willing to follow. The smell of food made immediate impact upon his nostrils and sent a warning of hope to an empty stomach, a perpetually empty one in a growing lad.

'Sit yerself on that chair an' tell me what it's all about,' she coaxed, the young bobby obviously ill at ease. 'It's me job,' he tried to explain. 'That little shaver's as strong as an ox,' groaning as he nursed a sore ankle.

'Hardly a shaver yet, Aa reckon. Hop it,' she said in abrupt dismissal, which the red faced policeman did without further ado. 'Now, young fella me lad, what are y'after?' quite taken a aback when he asked to see Lottie. 'She's me aunt,' he claimed, Alice now there open mouthed as usual, jumping to it as Martha rapped out orders. 'Stir yerself an' give the bairn a slice o'that loaf, t'be goin', on wi', plenty o'jam.' Very curious and eager to know the ins and outs of this present situation. It was certain one slice wouldn't suffice, Robert's striking blue eyes instantly alight at the prospect.

But, despite questioning and the sop to his stomach, the lad stuck to his guns and insisted on speaking to his aunt who, when summoned, lost no time in coming. It was the first time she had set eyes on her nephew since he was two, now ten years old by her reckoning and those blue eyes so like Victoria's, obviously from the same genes, a shock of bright auburn hair but cut very short, to minimise the possibility of nits she rightly supposed. She wondered if Ralph ever looked at his son and remembered her as a child.

'You're me aunt,' he accepted without further question, he too struck by the family resemblance. 'Aa've fetched a letter from me mother,' and rummaged in his pocket to extract it from the usual paraphernalia. So Margaret had sent him, Lottie thought in amazement, something vital for her to defy Ralph by making contact with the family outcast. 'Bring your bread and jam, Robert. Come with me,' she ordered brusquely, fully resolved any further business would be conducted in private, Martha and Alice all agog as might be expected.

She steered the youngster towards her own sitting room, ushered him in and closed the door, Martha was not above eavesdropping given the opportunity. He looked so clean and tidy, someone had obviously gone to great trouble to make him presentable despite the shabbiness of his clothes, everything neatly patched except for feet shod in boots well beyond repair. Hers were not the only eyes occupied in keen scrutiny, Robert Hanson enormously intrigued by first sight of this ladylike aunt whose name was seldom mentioned unless in derogatory fashion.

'Ye talk the same as me mother,' he blurted out, obviously disconcerted, the letter still in his hand, now held out towards her. 'Aa'm t'wait fer an answer an' me father hasn't t'know Aa've been here,' well rehearsed in his errand. Lottie told him to sit down by the fire before she opened it, absolutely stunned as the words sank in. Not prefixed with 'Dear Lottie' which would have been sheer hypocrisy she thought. Not to know Margaret had never condemned her just kept silent, perhaps the same thing, who can judge in such matters, unless closely involved.

'I am having a baby,' her sister-in-law wrote. 'My last two were born too soon and didn't live,' striking right to the core of Lottie's heart, so painful the association. 'It is doubtful whether I shall carry this one full time.' Not hard to imagine how difficult this was to write. 'We both want the child but Ralph would never ask for help, so I must risk his anger should he ever find out I went against his wishes. Robert understands, a deceit which I deplore but I am a desperate woman. I shall not hold it against you if you choose to ignore my letter.' Ignore it, Lottie thought, sore at heart, tousling Robert's hair affectionately who strange to say did not shrug her off, as might be expected. How could she turn her back on such a plea, moved to tears by the silent appeal in the blue eyes raised to hers. A lad old beyond his years who loved his mother enough to go against a strong minded father.

'Go back to the kitchen, Robert. Martha will give you a proper meal while I answer your mother's letter. I expect you are hungry, boys your age always are.' Given an eager nod of the head, the slice of bread and jam had been welcome indeed but just left him wanting more. God knows what he had eaten recently, she grieved, more ashamed than ever to be in this house of plenty.

'Howway son,' Martha said when told to feed him. 'Aa'll sharp fill that hungry belly. What d'ya say t'roast beef an'Yorkshire puddin's. Aa'll pop a few in the patty tins, the oven's hot. Aa guessed y'might be t'feed so Aa shoved a few taties on.'

Robert' blue eyes were like saucers. 'Y'aren't kiddin' Aa hope,' beaming when Martha pushed a piece of prime sirloin under his nose, done to a turn. 'Smell that,' she said and laughed at the ecstatic look on his young face. 'It's real,' she told him gleefully. Grown ups often caught the sharp end of the little woman's tongue but bairns were different and this one wasn't bothered about her deformity, she was an angel in shining wings to a hungry, ten year old boy.

Alone in her quarters, Lottie shed some bitter tears. Money was the obvious answer to Margaret's problem, coping with Ralph was his wife's affair if he ever found out. No doubt she had learnt how to deal with him over the years and knew what to keep to herself and ways to do it, this certainly one of those times.

She walked into the bedroom and took a box out of a drawer in her dressing table, hidden under neatly folded underclothes. Two bedrooms for her use since Marianne and Jackson tied the knot, most nights she slept upstairs close to Victoria but forced herself to move downstairs when Geoffrey was at home and John Starrett retreated to Whitegates, no fear of her beloved but dreadfully afraid of giving in to her own strong emotions. With the gaffer in residence the upstairs room had to be used, no other option. The box contained a number of sovereigns, none of it Jessica Finlay's money, that nest egg was safely deposited in a local bank, a measure recommended by Marianne when approached on the matter. She placed one of the coins in an envelope, a fair sum of money and would have sent more but it would be probably too difficult to explain such sudden wealth. The accompanying note was short and to the point. 'This might help,' but no signature lest it should fall into the wrong hands. Almost half an hour and a great deal of soul searching later, she returned to the kitchen where Robert was downing the last few mouthfuls of a huge helping of trifle, more convinced than ever Martha was an angel in disguise. 'Taken yer time haven't ya?' the angel grunted. 'His Lordship came in a few minutes ago,' her voice full of reproach. 'No need to panic,' Lottie soothed. 'He always has a glass of sherry and reads the evening paper, Victoria is in the coach house with Marianne,' smiling at Robert, his dish almost scraped clean.

'Aa've never seen a bairn shift s'much at once,' Martha chuckled in admiration, patting him on the head. 'Time to go, Robert,' Lottie declared somewhat abruptly to hide her feelings, stirred to the very depths of her being. If her nephew was so hungry, his pregnant mother could be past danger level, fervently hoping help was not too late.

'Aa'm ready, Aunt Lottie,' came with a blissful sigh, reluctant to leave such an earthly paradise where food was so plentiful. Tomarrow he would be hungry again with no guardian angel to satisfy his needs. 'Yer bonny,' he burst out as she fastened his well worn jacket, tucking the envelope into one of the pockets. 'So are you,' she grinned. 'It must run in the family,' amazed yet again by the similarity of two pairs of blue eyes, one pair smiling up at her with extreme fondness in them.

But soon those others of the same brilliant colour were staring straight at Robert in absolute amazement, Victoria now came upon this little scene and was definitely curious, never so close to the sight of poverty in her sheltered young life. 'Hello boy. Your jacket and trousers are both patched, why doesn't someone buy you new ones?' Spoken in all innocence but with an arrogance Lottie deplored. 'He needs some boots too,' she insisted and sensing the poor lad's discomfort, his aunt was very short to reply. 'His parents don't have money to buy new clothes, Miss Victoria, nor is he lucky enough to be blessed with a wealthy grandfather.' Astounded when the impetuous girl rushed straight into action, shouting back from the foot of the inside stairs. 'I shall talk to my grandad. He will buy the poor boy a pair of boots, I know he will,' off like a shot into the upper reaches of the house.

'Ye'd better get the laddie out o'here afore the balloon goes up,' Martha said and Lottie tried to propel Robert towards the outside door, none too sure of the gaffer's reaction should he find her nephew on his premises and given food into the bargain.

But circumstances were against her, John Starrett allowed himself to be dragged downstairs, unable to make head nor tail of Victoria's babbling. 'There he is, grandad,' she said, pointing at Robert, the bewildered laddie shaking in his well worn boots at the sight of the elderly gentleman's bewhiskered face, quick to sense an air of authority.

'Ah – and who have we here?' the question directed at Lottie who did not flinch from John Starrett's brusque enquiry, quite prepared to tell the truth. 'My nephew, Robert Hanson, sir. He brought a note from his mother,' and carried on in pure defiance, got it all out ready to face the music. 'He was hungry and I ordered Martha to feed him, his father is on strike and they don't have sufficient to eat. He is welcome to my share.' Amazed at her own effrontery, a strong note of censure in her voice. 'And whose fault is that. The work is there if the lazy devils want it.' Rather disconcerted by the youngster's appearance and the look of apprehension in a pair of blue eyes amazingly similar to those of his own granddaughter.

With a protective arm around Robert's thin shoulders, Lottie stood her ground. 'Not his fault, surely, women and children are usually the sufferers in any situation where their menfolk are involved.' Drawn up to every inch of her height, her declaration was nothing but truth, however unpalatable it might be to this affluent man.

A man who suddenly threw back his head and laughed, a deep throated chortle of sheer amusement. 'Don't tell me you are one of those confounded suffragettes. Women do have their place in the scheme of things but God help us if we allow them to rule the roost. May the day never come. Here boy,' he said his hand in and out of his waistcoat pocket but quickly forestalled. 'Not money, sir, that wouldn't be wise,' very definite in her refusal. 'A meal is something else altogether, once eaten nothing can be done about it. My brother is a proud man, stubborn too.' Conscious even as she spoke of a blow to that pride, tucked away in his son's pocket, an instinctive glance in that direction, John Starrett quick to guess the lad's mission.

Master and servant regarded one another quite seriously, Martha and Alice absolutely dumbfounded at the scene taking place and Lottie's part in it. The two antagonists were on opposite sides of the fence but both very much aware of the affinity they shared, a silver coin soon back in the gaffer's pocket. The scared laddie didn't waste any time in scarpering at Lottie's quiet command, completely ignorant of the elderly gentleman's identity, just as well for his peace of mind.

Victoria tugged at her grandfather's coat tail. 'The boy didn't want new boots, Grandad?' her blue eyes very quizzical, the situation quite beyond her. 'Not from me, child,' he said rather ruefully. 'Your grandfather is the wicked giant at the top of the beanstalk,' reminded of the fairy tale read to her the previous evening before bed, half expecting some jocular denial of this description from Lottie but none came, a direct look met the blandest of expressions. 'Who owned the goose that laid the golden egg,' on the tip of her tongue but decided she had ventured far enough to make her feelings known.

'Dinner is almost ready to be served, sir.' A remark which sent Martha running to the big stove. Lottie returned to household matters still troubled by Margaret's obvious plight and even more disturbed at the comparison between Robert's lot and that of Victoria, two first cousins.

'Thank you,' he answered, stiffly polite, so anxious for this young woman's approval and angry with himself for feeling that way. 'Victoria can eat with me.' Lottie was quick to point out that she had done so earlier with Marianne and Jackson. 'Then she can keep me company,' was the terse reply. 'She doesn't think I am a black hearted devil,' muttered as they left the room, quite out of sorts. Neither John Starrett nor his young housekeeper could possibly envisage his growing dependence upon her as the years rolled by, the one person whose steadfast loyalty would stand the test of time but never at the cost of blind obedience. Respect, of course, although a natural rebel, a trait he admired in her. Their alliance was most uneasy on many occasions but utterly dependable when the chips were down, as his daughter's condition was sure to bring them, often badly in need of a friend, this particular one destined to be a humble collier's daughter.

Running all the way along dimly lit roads, Robert Hanson soon reached home. 'Where's me Da?' his first question when he crossed the doorstep. 'At a Union Meeting,' his mother told him. 'Did you see your aunt?' anxiety written all over a thin, pallid face. 'Aye,' he answered triumphantly, 'and Aa got this,' handing the all important envelope over. 'A big plate o'dinner wi'meat an' all. Puddin' after that an' Aa'm fit t'bust.' Margaret's pleasure showed on her face at Lottie's kindness, relieved that the little in the pantry could be shared between Ralph and herself when he came home, Robert discreetly out of the way by then, probably upstairs in bed.

She gasped audibly when she saw the gold coin, as did the young messenger. 'That's a lot o' money isn't it? She's bonny an' all an' talks proper like you,' suddenly drawn close in his mother's arms. 'Kind too,' she acknowledged, 'You musn't say anything to your father. We'll take that washing back to Branton Village tomorrow and buy something in a shop where nobody knows us, to change this into florins and smaller amounts. Then we'll be able to buy milk, more of it, from Bob Batey. And you aren't to tell your father, ever. Promise me.'

Not really understanding the reason for such secrecy, Robert made the vow and kept it, staying long enough in Margaret's arms to feel the stirring of new life in her frail body. 'Is that the babby?' he whispered in awe, his copper head bent low to listen.

'That's the baby,' his mother corrected, overcome by the poignancy of this precious moment, one Hanson waiting for another to be born, knowing she must be selfish and feed herself if the child were to survive. 'Thank you, Lottie,' she mouthed above her son's head, quite certain that given different circumstances the two of them could have been good friends and accepted the fact that her sister-in-law could have turned Robert away, who to blame her if she had, cruelly ostracised by a brother for whom this generosity, God willing, would bring him another child.

* * *

The early years of King George V's reign continued to be uneasy ones in the coal fields, the poor seemed to become poorer and the wealthy more affluent than ever. There were jobs, plenty of them, in industry, on large estates and elsewhere but all menial and badly paid, those who were employed by titled gentry considering themselves better than miners and their kind and more inclined towards subservience in a time when the difference between the classes was very clearly defined.

Then came the equaliser as Europe erupted into warfare and Kaiser Wilhelm's armies invaded Belgium and France, Great Britain inevitably drawn into conflict to help its allies.

Death, never particular as to the rank or status of its victims, did its damndest and dreadful carnage began, young men flocked to the colours in their thousands from all walks of life. Rothwell House affected as every household in the land, one way or another, 1915 was well through when Marianne Jackson dropped her bombshell, Lottie staring at her in utter disbelief. 'You must be out of your mind,' she said, her voise an octave higher than usual. 'That sort of work is definitely not in your line. Alice and Grace, perhaps, who are both accustomed to hard graft. But you don't even do the heavier work in your own flat.' Prepared to hit below the belt to get the message home. Marianne was quick in her own defence. 'Only because you all think I need to be wrapped in cotton wool. It was not so bad until Victoria went to boarding school,' she argued, regretting these last words as soon as they left her lips, a very touchy subject where Lottie was concerned, almost six months now without sight of her beloved child.

'And whose fault was it? They have the children and anyone can look after them after that,' which in Felicity's case wasn't the whole truth. Lottie was possessed of an inherent working class distaste for the boarding school system, absolute cruelty to banish a youngster from the bosom of its family for weeks on end. In Victoria's case she was, naturally, thinking of herself and the big gap created in her life.

Marianne gave a deep sigh in sheer exasperation. 'I do agree it was partly myself to blame, saying I had taken her as far as I could and boarding school was the next step, talked about when I first came here as governess.' The umpteenth time of making this same explanation. 'You do have a bee in your bonnet about Victoria,' she went on to say, 'but with Madam installed here permanently, she is better out of the way.' A statement of fact impossible to refute and Lottie was too dispirited even to try, the whole set up an absolute disaster in every way. 'This war is getting us all down, nothing is the same. Mattie slaves his guts out in that blessed shipyard, then comes home to more work,' she bemoaned, so down in the mouth Marianne didn't know what to say, her brows puckered in a frown at Lottie's use of slang, still the teacher, but true to her word she had not tried to change Jackson, although some of her had rubbed off on him as expected.

'Don't exaggerate,' she remonstrated, thinking of her husband now, 'Mathew does work hard at Swan Hunter's but the rest of you make sure there is little or nothing for him to do when he gets home, apart from driving Mr Starrett on occasion. I am the lady around here and I am bored, decidedly bored. And don't tell me to knit socks for soldiers, I can't knit.'

Marianne did expect some opposition to her proposed hospital work but not such downright disapproval, Lottie was worse than her husband who eventually gave in when he saw how determined she was. 'Please yerself lass but see that yer shifts fit in wi'mine. Aa need y'here when Aa'm off.' Well aware a strong will existed beneath that gentle exterior, one lesson he had learnt from more than three years of marriage.

Telepathic as usual, Lottie asked the inevitable question. 'What did Mattie say? I presume you have told him about this hair brained scheme?' Marianne's answering tone was very impatient. 'Yes, I have told him and he said the same as yourself, initially. He insists that Nursing Auxiliary is just a fancy name for maid of all work but gave in nevertheless.' A look of pure satisfaction on her flushed face.

'And so it is,' Lottie rather piqued at Jackson for not laying the law down in this particular matter. 'Just wait until you fall foul of a starchy ward sister and then you'll know what cuddy's kicked ya.' A deliberate Geordieism meant to irritate, annoyed at her friend's persistence, because her own war effort amounted to nothing. Much against her will she was completely tied to

Rothwell House to keep a watchful eye on Felicity, that position made very clear when hostilities first began.

'Dammit girl, you are needed here,' John Starrett bellowed forth, really uptight. 'I have plenty on my plate keeping three collieries going with only old men and green youngsters to get the coal out.' Mine workers having joined up in their thousands, thoughout the industry. 'They should have been forced to stay in their jobs with coal so essential to the war effort,' he blustered. 'If I see any more posters of Kitchener pointing that finger I'll – – -' his intention left unexpressed. There was sense in what he said but this man's main irritation stemmed from a very different source.

John Starrett's pride had received a knock out blow when forced to accept Felicity's total addiction to alcohol, an absolute wreck. Nothing could be done, certain now she would never kick the habit. The depraved creature alternated between fits of maudlin self pity and uncontollable rages, often in drunken stupors for days on end, the times when peace reigned for a while, as a ravaged system sought oblivion. Not easy to manage when she emerged from them, always in aggressive mood and yelling for gin, shouting obscenities at whoever came near, usually the long suffering Lottie, who had unwillingly become her jailer.

It was just under six months since John Starrett's daugher was dragged screaming from the house in Harrow Square at the Askews' request, this London establishment seconded to the army as an officers' club, Fanny and Charlie still in control with a lot of assistance. Fanny threw herself into the cooking side of it with enormous gusto, an outlet for undoubtable culinary expertise. Periodical letters always made Lottie more disgruntled than ever, not that she begrudged these friends their new lifestyle but considered responsibility for a drunken female to be a waste of time and youthful energy, better used elsewhere with a country at war.

A private sanatorium had been suggested, Felicity was too far gone for treatment to work but would be better in the care of professionals, an option the gaffer refused to consider. A terrible onus was laid upon a pair of young shoulders, Lottie now twenty nine but age had not taken any toll as in so many cases, certainly more educated and refined and an even more attractive woman.

'Do what you must,' the gaffer said at the outset. 'Keep that poison away from her as much as possible,' her heart aching for his distress, only to plummet into the depths when he carried on to inform her Victoria would be going to boarding school, not to be subjected to such sordidness at her age. He was totally unaware of the blow he delivered, Lottie's senses reeling under the impact. Realising no amount of persuasion would change Marianne's mind, she retired to her own quarters, there to read a letter from Geoffrey Cranshawe, its contents digested for the umpteenth time since eight o'clock that morning. 'You will write,' he pleaded on parting, in a brief moment together away from watchful eyes, his contingent one of the first to go to the Front. No fond embrace, a mere touch of the fingers and an eloquent look, revealing his innermost feelings, a dynamic force denied fulfilment and this might easily be a last farewell. Folk were well past that 'over by Christmas' bravado, every sign of it being a long haul, the kind of warfare even seasoned troops had never experienced, a rude awakening for raw recruited men.

The letters arrived at irregular intervals, distinctive envelopes with the mark of the censor, Lottie always first to reach the front vestibule. It was much too awkward to explain why the young master should write to the family housekeeper, a secret hugged close to her loving heart. She wondered how long the letters would continue to come as she added this latest of them to several others aside in a dressing table drawer, always kept locked.

John Starrett had no idea what her ministrations to his daughter entailed, amazingly cunning when awake, the craving upon her and she was desperate enough to enlist the aid of anyone to procure her own particular poison. Tradesmen were warned not to supply it, unless the order came from Lottie, under threat of losing a valued customer. Less scrupulous ones obliged for a price but Felicity's legacy from her mother soon dwindled away and this avenue then closed.

Martha and Alice were both promised dire consequences if they acted as go betweens, the former quite outspoken as usual. 'Let the stupid bitch dig'er own grave, then we'll all get some peace,' she snorted in disgust, on high doh about the extra work Madam's presence created, goaded into heated reply when severely reprimanded. 'Aa thought ye of all folk would be glad t'see the back of'er an' that's the only way it's gonna happen,' she grunted, amazed at Lottie's reaction.

'When did I ever say I wanted her dead, Martha Connelly? Don't you dare utter such wicked nonsense.' A touch of conscience perhaps for the fantasies she wove around Madam's husband, adultery of the mind and most disturbing to an innate sense of morality.

In the winter of 1915, death did come to Rothwell House and affected Alice Ruddick most of all. One of the fine black stallions caught a chill and died within two days, followed shortly afterwards by his stable companion. 'A broken heart,' the disconsolate lass wailed, until Martha's logic cried halt to these noisy outpourings. 'All the canny lads getting' killed an' ye carry on about a pair o' horses. Cannon fodder anyway if the army got hold o' them.' No sensitivity but it worked, Alice's devotion was heaped upon Tiger, who thrived on extra spoiling and didn't seem to fret after his former friends. 'I shan't replace them,' John Starrett declared, 'With Jackson out of the house for hours on end, the pony trap is easier for me to handle.' A note of complaint in his gruff voice. He was still sore at Mattie's refusal to be put on the colliery pay roll and continue with his usual job. 'Aa wouldn't feel right, sir,' said in a tone which left no room for argument, the gaffer secretly admiring of his principles. 'Suit yourself,' he grunted at the time and informed Alice that Tiger was her sole responsibility from then on, the big lass cock-a-hoop, full of her own importance.

'There will be few carriages by the end of this war,' Marianne predicted, Alice tutting disbelievngly and told her not to be daft. 'How would w'manage without horses?' thinking the whole idea absolutely ridiculous. Martha was much more down to earth as usual. 'There'll be none o' the poor beasts left if them blinkin' Huns have their own way.' So many horses already slaughtered on the battlefield, alongside the men they served so faithfully, both expendable.

'Nowt'll be the same after this lot,' Jackson declared. 'Some folk'll make their pile an' others lose everythin'. But the gaffer's a survivor, if ever there was one, and Aa'm ready t'hitch my wagon t'his star. Aa'll learn how t'drive one o'them new contraptions or bust,' he vowed, obviously quite determined. The age of the motor car was just in its infancy.

* * *

War intruded into every aspect of human life, Saltersgate no different in this respect. Soldiers were billeted in St Joseph's and other local buildings, Catholic and Protestant children attending the Board School on a part time basis, mornings or afternoons, still separated by creed where teaching was involved, the sense of what was important vastly different in both cases.

Young men parted from sweethearts and wives often sought temporary consolation elsewhere, the probability of a short existence uppermost in all minds, many anxious to cram the whole of life's experiences into that brief training spell before they embarked for France, many of them never to return.

Some of these temporary alliances ended in disaster, as might be expected, gossips galore from Saltersgate through the usual channel. Lottie took little heed of the tittle tattle as Madam's condition deteriorated rapidly, one crisis after another, upheaval constantly invading the kitchen quarters, young Grace Jennings, more often than not, on the sharp end of Martha's tongue.

'All right,' Lottie snapped, walking straight into the midst of one stormy session, in no mood for it after a trying morning with Felicity, screaming blue murder until her keeper was forced to produce a bottle of gin, hidden away in a cupboard on the second floor landing. 'Use your own discretion,' John Starrett told her but she scarcely knew whether it was preferable to have his daughter ranting and raving for the beastly stuff or the same performance under the influence. The blissful peace of drunken stupors was always the deciding factor.

'Well?' she demanded, Grace wailing and Martha's loud indignation the last straw. Quite taken aback when it was the weeping girl who choked out a spate of words between sobs. 'Me father'll kill me when'ee finds out. Aa'm sure t'get the pit belt across me backside.' There was more than one man of Tod Wilson's sort in the village.

The truth suddenly dawned, this was no ordinary domestic disturbance and Lottie's irritation slipped away, banished by the spectre of another young lass in the same frightening position.

'All right Grace,' she soothed. 'It isn't the end of the world. Who is the man, will he take responsibility?' The answer came on a strangled note. 'He canna Miss. He's wed already,' her tearful brown eyes lowered in shame. 'More fool ye,' Martha shot at her, 'Them soldiers are just waitin'fer your sort,' silenced by a withering look. 'That's enough, Martha,' Lottie rebuked, 'If your memory is short mine isn't,' and the significance of her words went home as intended. 'Now Grace,' she said briskly, 'your parents must be told, your mother first, she will handle your father. Pop a shawl around your shoulders and go at once. Should he turn nasty and refuse to have you in the house, come back here, I shall arrange something.' Her hands clasped in fervour of gratitude, Grace was overwhelmed to receive such unexpected understanding.

'Oh Miss,' she breathed in relief, a tear stained face alight with hope. 'Y'don't know what a load ye've taken off me mind,' rubbing her eyes with a dry apron. 'I do know,' Lottie admitted ruefully, a look of puzzlement on the girl's face, obviously unaware of that long ago transgression. Not for long if her recollection of Frank Jennings was right, a coarse, foul mouthed fellow, thoughts cast aside to concentrate on tackling John Starrett, not the sort of task she relished but must be done if Grace were to be given refuge.

Shortly after the young lass scuttled off, she bearded the lion in his den. 'Well girl,' he queried from the magnificent leather topped desk, always pleased to see her, her constant behaviour quite refreshing in a rapidly changing life, part of his ruins around him. 'Trouble with my daughter?' he anticipated, a worried expression on his handsome face, obvious signs of age since Felicity's return to Rothwell House.

'No sir,' she quickly reassured him. 'Someone else's daughter this time, I'm afraid,' realising he must have heard those terrible ravings, the silence spoke for itself. 'It is rather a delicate matter, sir,' she faltered, soon aware of steady grey eyes twinkling in amusement. 'We must have discussed many delicate matters over the years, Charlotte. What could be so difficult to broach?' The whole sorry tale tumbled from her lips in sheer embarrassment, only to hear a deep sigh when she finished. 'One of those damned soldiers, I suppose,' he rapped out in disgust. 'Do you wish me to have a word with the man's commanding officer?'

'It wouldn't serve any purpose, sir, the man is already married. Grace's father is her problem and could turn her out on the street when he finds out, after a good belting I should imagine.'

'Do I know him?' he asked and went into reflection when she mentioned the name Jennings. 'Frank Jennings,' she said and waited for a reaction. 'The name does ring a bell but there are so many comings and goings these days, I am inclined to lose track.' He looked her straight in the eyes. 'You want the girl to stay here, is that it?' Never slow on the uptake and Lottie easy to read on most occasions. 'Another lame duck?' he said with raised eyebrows, well acquainted with her many kindnesses.

'Most of us are lame ducks at some time or other. Grace will need all the support she can get. Nobody knows that better than myself.'

The gaffer's eyebrows lifted even further at this obvious implication, her unfortunate situation forgotten after so many years, sad at this distressing reminder, impossible to connect this beautiful woman with that gauche eighteen year old girl. 'Do whatever you consider necessary,' he said, anxious not to cause her any more embarrassment. 'Household matters are your affair, more so this sort of predicament.'

Lottie stammered her thanks and turned to go, her hand already on the highly polished door knob when he spoke again. 'Your brother will be coming home from France before long, perhaps on his way. The government in its infinite wisdom,' he said sarcastically, 'has at last decided that experienced mine workers should be exempt from army service. As if the damned idiots weren't told that in the beginning. I made my feelings plain enough in high places,' he finished testily.

'Thank you, sir.' What else could she say, wondering how Ralph would feel, never one to have things decided for him, although even he must have had a belly full of the trenches by now and regard the pit a better option.

He shrugged the thanks off abruptly. 'Don't thank me. All I did was submit a list of serving men who are good colliers and your brother does come into that category. A nice ladylike wife he has too. She came to Polrigg one day while I was there to seek a job for her son.'

'Robert?' tore from her lips in horror, suddenly reminded of that bright auburn head and striking blue eyes, wondering if the gaffer would put two and two together and remember they once met. 'But he is just a laddie,' she protested strongly.

'Old enough, Charlotte, another few years and they'll put a gun in his hand and I won't be able to save him from the trenches. My pit is better than that, surely,' he answered drily.

A debatable point, she thought en route to the kitchen, some might consider it better to die for their country than endure a life of back breaking toil in Polrigg's dark caverns. They had no real idea of conditions in trenches, where generals continued to wage modern warfare with ancient methods. Most returning soldiers minimised the horror of it and assumed an air of false bravado, unwilling to lay extra burden on their loved ones. But women sensed the difference in men who went out with such faith in their cause and were never the same again. At least for the dead the horror was over.

But she did rejoice inwardly at Ralph's return to his family of three, increased by one when the gold sovereign kept Margaret from starvation and produced a fine, healthy child, a girl. News of the birth was brought to her by Alice, who recognised for Lottie, at least, the animosity had ended. Strangely enough she made no mention of the episode when Margaret came to her rescue, a closed book. 'Your Ralph's wife's had a babby,' was how it was put, Lottie was surprised when told the child was to be named Elizabeth after her paternal grandmother, Bessie Hanson's baptismal name but she ended up being called Liz by those closest to her.

A much chastened Grace returned returned within the hour, a pitiful bundle in her hand. 'Me mother says its best Aa should bide here if it's all right,' she sobbed in Lottie's comforting arms. 'In a state when Aa told'er, scared t'tell me father. He was at work but she'll keep in touch when he's in day shift.' Advised by a sorrowful mother not to risk a beating in her condition, although not very far on.

'The little attic between Martha and Alice will be yours. Now sit down and have your tea, take your things up at bedtime,' no second bidding required and tea soon became the most important thing in Grace's young life, three times around the loaf and she cheered up considerably much to Martha's disgust, who was given a stern warning to keep off the girl's back.

Geoffrey's continued absence was penance indeed, Lottie was obsessed by fear for her beloved's safety and every morning, if Felicity's state permitted, she walked Branton Road to read the casualty list on the council notice board and almost read the print off the form until she passed the letter 'C'. Other names hit her between the eyes, men and boys known from childhood, Patrick O'Neal there on one sad occasion, Mary Wilson's one time sweetheart, a widow now if they had been allowed to marry. Polly Flanagan, Catholic and therefore acceptable, caught him on the rebound and two children soon followed, Mary's present feelings were hard to visualise.

Lottie reckoned a few years of happiness in the interim period would be worth the tragedy at the end of it, even with children to rear alone, instead of the empty spinsterhood, Mary's chosen lot. A sobering thought to see her own situation as somewhat comparable should Geoffrey fail to survive, a love affair which only existed in two lonely hearts.

She prayed he might be spared, which in her darkest hours scarcely seemed possible, if machine gun fire didn't get them, wallowing wounded in Flanders mud so often did. And why should the good Lord seek her out for preferential treatment when men in their thousands were slaughtered every day? Someone who had never crossed the chapel door steps in years, the last time in any place of worship at Jackson's wedding. That glorious, never to be forgotten day when she walked out into the sunshine on her loved one's arm and went on to mar the rest with senseless behaviour, lost moments regretted even more in retrospect.

These were times when folk either became Godless, their faith in the Almighty absolutely destroyed, or clung to the faith of their fathers to carry them through, blame for this dreadful carnage still being apportioned decades later. A war to end wars they claimed but no longer believed it to be true supposition, their illusions had vanished along with so many other things. How could the world ever be the same again?

* * *

Martha stirred her strong disapproval into a bowl which contained butter and sugar, in process of making a chocolate cake, one of the gaffer's favourites, her sharp tongue unleashed as usual. 'Just another o'them chaps that's surprised t'find 'ees a father, in six months from the deed bein'done. Aa've never heard o' so many bairns born afore their due time. It beats me how the lads get taken in, this war's makin' some stronge bedfellas Aa tell ya. Just wait till it's over an' they see their handsome soldiers out o'uniform, burglars an' all sorts among them, Aa bet. If th'come back that is.' A loud cackle at her own caustic wit, something to sharpen it on when Grace Jennings announced her coming marriage to a nineteen year old recruit, stationed at Branton Park, the green not out of the unwitting youngster's eyes.

'Aa'll be goin' back home, Miss,' she told Lottie, flushed to the roots of mousy brown hair, 'Me mother needs help i'the house an' me da says its all right cause Aa'll be respectable again.' Another glaring example of the hypocrisy peculiar to those times. Martha's reaction a snort of derision and little wonder.

'Have you been honest about the baby?' Lottie's immediate question, downcast eyes and shuffling feet answer enough, Martha's mocking assessment spot on and more to issue forth when Grace departed with her goods and chattels. The girl's condition apparent to everyone, except the gullible lad she tricked into marriage.

'Frank Jennin's has nowt t'learn,' Martha went on to say, 'Not likely t'turn 'is back on an army allowance goin' inta the house. Alice says Meggie Jennin's is far from well, so the lass'll be around t'step inta'er mother's shoes an' see t'the rogue's creature comforts. Th'say somebody else satisfies them.' An implication not to be ignored, Martha's bird like head shook from side to side in disapproval, a tiny mouth primmed, small in size, maybe, but opened too wide on many occasions.

'Just gossip,' Lottie remonstrated, to give Martha free reign most unwise, the little woman's insatiable appetite for juicy morsels best not encouraged, but well aware Grace's father was associated with Polly Bennett, still on the same old game.

'Meggie's got a lump here,' Alice spluttered, her mouth full as usual, one hand laid across a flat bosom. 'There's nowt can be done fer'er,' she announced in matter of fact manner, totally unconscious of the ramifications for Grace and the rest of her family, all younger than the lass herself, soon to become both wife and mother, possibly widow with so many fighting men being lost on barbed wired battlefields in foreign lands.

Weighed down by so many problems, another Christmas almost upon them, it seemed as if her whole world was steeped in doom and gloom, Victoria was due home in a little over four weeks, something to look forward to, if Felicity's presence didn't hang over them like the sword of Damocles. 'How shall I keep Madam's condition away from her,' she moaned to Martha, an answer soon forthcoming.

'That drunken bitch should be locked up fer good,' she suggested, not for the first time as might be expected, 'Mebbe the old man'll see the light if it's a toss up atween her an'the lassie,' Lottie's constant prayer, never given voice. With Whitegates there for holiday periods, the two of them under the same roof at once had not been a problem, but the gaffer's country house was now taken over by the Army as a convalescent home for wounded officers. John Starrett was a permanent resident in Rothwell House for the duration, Lottie and himself occupying rooms at either side of Madam's first floor suite, where to put Victoria was quite a dilemma. 'Keep them well apart,' the gaffer ordered, ' They must meet, of course, but choose your times and as few as possible. Explain the situation somehow.' The onus was placed firmly on Lottie's overburdened shoulders. To tell an eleven year old the woman she knew as mother was a hopeless drunk, was out of the question, illness and supposed attacks of pain the obvious answer.

Victoria was given a room at the far end of the second floor landing, hoping that the long corridors and a flight of stairs would put enough distance between them, not ideal but no other solution than the one already thought of, should explanations be required. Laughing mirthlessly at such deliberate subterfuge, Felicity's door was always to be kept locked, at a loss what to do when she banged on it to be let out.

Lottie personally supervised all arrangements for the awaited homecoming, an entire household as well as the Jacksons full of eager anticpation, none of them able to envisage the big changes boarding school life had brought about, truly amazed when a very self possessed young girl returned to the fold. After a short spell of homesickness Victoria lapped the whole business up, shades of Lottie in a back that straightened against adversity and came to be admired for it, soon very popular indeed and a champion of the underdog.

'Aa couldn't believe me eyes,' Alice confessed, when delegated to collect her young mistress from South Branton Station, transferred from a main line train to a local one, to save her the busy Central and the sights she might see, as wounded soldiers were brought home to be cared for.

'There was Aa,' the big lass expounded, 'just standin' aside Tiger on the lead up the station, when this fine lassie comes up an'says "You are Alice, aren't you?" Makin' believe sh'wasn' sure it was me. Sh'stood by Tiger an'all until Aa saw t'the baggage.' Absolutely carried away and allowed the stage for a short while until Martha decided to cry halt. 'Aye, all right. We've all seen'er,' Victoria upstairs getting settled in.

It was well over a year since anyone, apart from Lottie had set eyes on their young mistress, several vacations spent at Whitegates, the last time with a foreign friend in tow, French and kept at school because of the war. One brief afternoon for Lottie, driven there and back by her employer, after making sure Madam was out for the count, frustrated at the shortness of this precious contact.

Now, with Victoria under the same roof, she kept her feelings under control but swelled with pride whenever she looked at this enormously attractuve young girl, signs of the beautiful woman she would be in years ahead. 'She is my daughter, I know she is,' her mind insisted. No resemblance except those striking blue eyes which reminded her of Ralph's son, hair still like spun gold, both features attributed to Felicity by John Starrett. His pride in the youngster was rather sad to see, realising his daughter had left him with very little joy in her, a hopeless wreck.

Numerous questions, of course, and a constant struggle to keep one step ahead. 'Why can't I see Mama now? Why is her door always locked? Why does she never come down to meals?' It was nerve racking to lie so blatantly with two keen eyes looking straight into hers and she felt like a barrel organ churning out the same old tune with her replies.

When obvious signs of strain began to show, John Starrett tried to bolster Lottie's flagging spirits. 'Just three more weeks, Charlotte. Victoria shall only pay short visits in future. We do have relatives and friends.'

She wanted to shriek at him to send Felicity into care but stayed within the bounds of her position as usual, unwilling to presume upon their special relationship to force the issue, very touched by the gaffer's growing dependence upon her loyalty and forbearance towards a woman she had every reason to hate. Victoria's visits to her mother's room were made in those quieter times when an exhausted woman scarcely knew who she was, Lottie always in attendance and conscious of being watched under half closed eyelids, imagining Madam played some sort of cat and mouse game, a feeling impossible to dismiss.

'We're sittin' on a keg o'gunpowder,' Martha claimed, constantly raving about the burden laid upon Lottie's slender shoulders. 'It's all right fer him,' meaning the gaffer. 'He gets away from it, even if it's just t'them pits o'his. Let's hope nowt blows up wi' Miss Victoria around t'see it. Its only'er father's money that keeps the drunken bitch here anyway. If it was ye or me we'd sharp be over the wall.' Referring to Saltersgate Asylum and a fact not to be denied. Strange to say, Ralph Hanson did accept the opportunity to return to the pit but others didn't, in Saltersgate and elsewhere. An ardent Trade Union supporter he forecast trouble when the war ended, if the men stayed cool that long, only patriotism held them back. With her services requested by John Coulter, a contemporary of the gaffer, Alice Ruddick returned to farm work on a part time basis. 'It's me war work,' she gloated, feeling quite important, and was really needed when very young men and older counterparts were called to arms. So much of Europe's young blood was already spilt, generals persisting in the waging of modern warfare with ancient weapons, costly blunders repeated time and again.

The wheels of Rothwell House were kept in motion with Martha's invaluable support, Alice at odd times as hours at the farm grew longer, with help from Jackson and Marianne whenever they could, Marianne's health was a cause for concern but she herself never complained. The household laundry was sent out, Mary Wilson glad of the extra money and eternally grateful to Lottie for making her mother's last days a lot easier, Janey dead and buried and Tod a much subdued man without his mainstay, an old man at fifty due to long, arduous shifts down the pit and a despondency which tore at his guts, his daughter and himself like two strangers under the same roof, a rift nothing was ever likely to mend.

Lottie grew even more despondent than ever when an aircraft factory began to operate on ground near the Town Moor's edge and knew that many of her school mates found employment in this new kind of work, very hush hush. Not that any of them were conscious of the whole picture, a number of different sections and, in any case to them it only meant more money going into the family kitty, never there for long. 'I should be doing something like that,' she bemoaned, her whole life centred around Rothwell House and, mainly, its wretched mistress.

Having a youngster in the house made more sense of Martha's feverish operations for the so called festive season, rather a misnomer considering the times. No shortages there, John Starrett's affluent position saw to that. Alice Ruddick could hardly wait for that special morning when a gift from her would be handed to Victoria, a tiny black spaniel, the runt of a litter born to Jessie at the farm. Rather dubious consent had been given by John Starrett after consultation with Lottie.

'I hope you realise what it involves,' he warned, 'Victoria goes back to school in the New Year, something else for you to look after,' a wry smile on his whiskered face. Lottie was quick to reply. 'With help from Alice when she is around,' she countered. No real solution, farm work occupied most of the big girl's time. But Victoria could be denied no pleasure Lottie was able to give and this was within her power.

'Another rod fer that back o'yours,' Martha stated with a grunt.' 'Just wait till the blessed animal wants out i' the middle o'the night.'

'With the master next door to Madam, I can sleep downstairs until it settles in,' she was told, an end to any further opposition. 'Besides, a dog's bark will be extra protection.' As much to convince herself as anyone else. She would make sure Felicity slept through the nights, even if it did mean resorting to the bottle. No qualms of conscience, Victoria's welfare came first and foremost as always, Madam just a huge bugbear, which her own regard for John Starrett forced her to put up with. God knows how long it would last, her mistress was still a young woman and physically strong despite mental dissipation. She could live for years, Lottie's young life being eaten up with hers, a hopeless victim of circumstance.

* * *

Two days after Christmas, the pup duly installed, Lottie had cause to remember Martha's words, awakened from sleep by its plaintive whines, not to be ignored. 'Hurry up, Hamlet' she urged, rather crossly, letting the little creature out and watching as a chubby body waddled across the cobbled yard into the bushes, soon lost in the inky darkness. She stood at the top of the basement stairs, where she had let the dog go, and shivered awaiting his return.

His chosen name proved to be a great source of amusement, Victoria recently introduced to The Prince of Denmark at school. 'It's different,' she said to Martha's disapproving grunt. 'No self respectin' beast should be given a name like that,' the little woman argued, not acquainted with the Bard of Avon, as might be expected, her schooling minimal. Alice defended the choice, saying it was Miss Victoria's dog and up to her what the animal was called. Straight into Martha's black book but, for once, absolutely unconcerned.

Hamlet showed no inclination to return, wallowing in freedom and wonderful new smells, deaf to Lottie's calls as she longed for the warmth of her soft, feather bed. The loud crunch of heavy footsteps on the gravel path made her stiffen with fear as a tall figure moved across the cobbles towards her, open mouthed ready to scream, in the hope Jackson would hear. A different feeling altogether when a familiar voice rang in her ears and blood rushed to her head. 'Steady my darling, steady,' it soothed, sending shivers of joy up and down her spine, melting into the strong arms that wrapped themselves around a trembling body.

'My love, my love, my dearest love,' she breathed in ecstasy and repeated Geoffrey's name over and over, as in those foolish dreams through long, agonising months of waiting, hoping and fearing. But this was no dream just glorious reality, almost too much to take in. 'You didn't tell me you were coming,' she stammered. No mention of leave in his last letter. Soon silenced by an eager mouth which searched to find instant response, hanging on for dear life. Nothing between them except an army greatcoat and thin night attire, even that too much, his buttons dug into soft flesh, the discomfort ignored. Her blue cashmere shawl in a heap around their feet as they clung together in the throes of perfect bliss. A loving woman's ardent greeting for her warrior home at last from the war.

For a while time stood still and nothing else mattered, no past or future, just the here and now in this first act of unfettered physical contact between them, an expression of the deep love they had for one another, the rest of the world forgotten as if it didn't exist.

A tiny bark from Hamlet brought Lottie down from the clouds in sudden realisation. 'Oh sir,' she muttered in confusion, words spoken against Geoffrey's lips, struggling a little to extricate herself from his arms, only to hear and feel chuckles of amusement as he deliberately deepened the kiss. Impossible to think clearly when his mouth proceeded to seek other targets, soft cheeks and areas of exposed flesh, no will to say him nay just total surrender, mutual desire expressed, paradise long denied them.

Soon, Lottie had to surface for air. Every nerve in her body tingled, barely enough strength to pull away from him. 'We musn't, we musn't,' she stammered, so wrong to be in this man's arms when he belonged to someone else, a someone whose sorry state he soon must face. Her heart ached at the thought of how he would feel.

'I must,' he told her masterfully and refused to let go, 'Who do you imagine has kept me sane all these months, my darling?' He choked on the words and held her even closer. 'Not Felicity I assure you,' knowing where her thoughts lay, well able to read his beloved's mind, his own bitterly repudiating the woman who bore his name. 'You have filled my thoughts, dreaming of moments like this. Now we can share the reality. You, you, my love,' he vowed, his voice thick with emotion. 'We seem to be fated to meet on doorsteps, my darling Lottie. No homecoming could be more perfect than this.'

They clung together in sheer desperation, kiss for kiss, passionate hungry kisses which took them along the road of no return. No holding back, a soft, womanly body merged into Geoffrey's lean frame, the promise of absolute surrender should he so desire. And he did desire, with every fibre of his being.

But sanity returned and his hold slackened. 'You are right, my darling, of course we musn't. It is just that I need you so much.' Finding it almost impossible to be strong, courage sustained through months of horror in the trenches but almost destroyed by the hopelessness of their situation.

Lottie's tender heart ached for his distress. Here was a man at the end of his tether, it was up to her to find enough strength for both of them. So easy to lose themselves in these moments of madness. She bent to pick up her shawl. 'Perhaps we should go inside,' she murmured flatly, the warmth of his body already missed. Dog and shawl ended up in Lottie's arms together, the tiny pup licking her cheek in pure affection. His bark may have saved them from serious indiscretion, not knowing whether to be thankful or not. Once inside the warm kitchen, one of the gas lights soon glowed, a taper lit from the big stove, happed up for the night. Lottie made a valiant effort to pull herself together, shocked beyond measure when she beheld her loved one, a gaunt stranger who had been right to the gates of hell. The horror of the present conflict was brought painfully home at the sight of him, his dark hair streaked with grey, haunted eyes sunk deep into his face. A regular soldier in such a dreadful state showing just how bad it really must be.

'You will want something to eat,' she faltered, suddenly conscious of her state of undress with no idea of how appealing she looked to a battle worn, love starved man, whose eyes absorbed every inch of her, an image to take back with him when he returned to the Front. So vastly different from the woman who wore his ring. Lottie would not cheat in marriage, the feel of her in his arms, so responsive, told him that, made him feel a man again after years of self denial. No dalliance of any sort since Jessica Finlay's death and so intense his need, afraid to touch her again, strong sexual urges eager for release. 'Sit down Lottie. Forget about food, we must talk,' soul weary and very despondent.

'What is there to say? No real solution to our problems, so let them be, talking won't do any good,' Lottie demurred, turning to give the stove a poke, in a vain effort to restore a sense of normality to the whole situation. 'Put that damned thing down,' Geoffrey spat out angrily, on a very short fuse. 'If there is one thing this bloody war should have taught us is to grab all the happiness one can. I will not spend the rest of my life tied to someone I can't bear to look at. I want you, darling, however long or short it may be, no guarantee anything will last.' The fences came down. 'But you can have me, my darling,' All resolution thrown to the wind, no sense of shame at this bold declaration. She adored Geoffrey to distraction, why shouldn't she surrender herself to him.

He stared at her, sorely tempted but adamant. 'No, damn you, I won't drag you through the mud. If we are going to be together it will be open and above board.' Trying to ignore a sense within telling him John Starrett would do anything to keep his daughter's farce of a marriage intact and the older man had plenty of what usually mattered most, money. He was willing to do this for her, with all that it meant. 'Victoria,' she cried helplessly, 'You would lose her Geoffrey, we both would,' For one dangerous moment she thought of making a full confession but the words stuck in her throat. No proof. Too big a price to pay. Her beloved child must not be hurt.

'Victoria adores you, Felicity has no interest in her,' he persisted, very obvious the matter had not been thought through, his feelings much too raw. Too many complications if they did as he proposed and anything happened to him. God forbid. Her daughter would have no-one except John Starrett, whose track record for rearing a child was rather doubtful, Felicity a prime example of being over indulged.

'Don't pressure me, Geoffrey,' she pleaded, aware of her own weakness with him so close, longing to be in his arms again and let the inevitable occur. But they were at an impasse, the moment maybe gone forever. For a while Geoffrey hesitated then decided to compromise. 'Don't worry, I shan't, not now. I am much too tired to try to breach your defences. It is two days since I left the Front, they said go and I went, damned quick, before they found some reason to keep me there. Experienced officers are in short supply, young lieutenants are being killed off like flies, my senior rank seems to have been worth something in that direction, so far. My short leaves have all been spent in France, behind the lines. My usual room I suppose?' His weariness bordering on complete exhaustion.

'No, sir. The second floor would be better next to Victoria but that bed isn't aired I'm afraid.' His arrival so unexpected, so wonderfully unexpected, the taste of it still on her lips. Geoffrey raised his eyebrows at the deliberate use of 'sir' and laughed shortly without humour. 'My darling,' he said, 'you don't have the faintest idea how we live out there, sometimes lucky to have anywhere to crash down. I am an officer, so pity those other poor devils, just faces to me I'm afraid, they change so often. Doesn't do to get too close to anyone. Did at first but they are all gone.' Sadness plucked at Lottie's heart strings as he picked Hamlet from the floor. 'This little tyke is better off than any of us, the bunks I hole into are still warm from some Hun who left in a hurry, leaving his fleas behind.' Normally he wouldn't have talked like this, but the flood gates were open. He gave a weak grin at the look on Lottie's face. 'Don't worry, little one, I was duly deloused when I came ashore and Fanny Askew prepared a bath stinking with disinfectant then gave me a decent meal. Perhaps you can still smell the damned stuff on me, she was most liberal with that and the food. Just tell me where to kip down and I'll manage.'

Lottie preceded him upstairs, finger to her lips as they traversed the first landing, the Askews had obviously kept their own counsel and he didn't know the score. 'No need to worry,' John Starrett always said when decisions were to be made, knowing Geoffrey had the right to control his wife's destiny and could have countermanded her father's wishes. Pure deceit from a man determined to have his own way and her husband's ultimate reaction difficult to assess. He wasn't going to be too pleased at his son-in-law's reappearance upon the scene but Victoria would be overjoyed.

'Good night, my dearest,' he whispered against her soft cheek before she left him at the bedroom door, his mouth lingering for a moment on her lips, too dangerous to go inside the room. So much more he might have said to her, unburdening himself of a dreadful weight of fear that time was running out and convinced his luck must change. Mad to let her go when consummation of their love would act like a balm to mind and soul in the dark days ahead, full of foreboding at the prospect of going back to France, a feeling impossible to drive away.

Lottie crawled into bed with a groan, Hamlet comfortably ensconced at her feet, just over an hour before Alice would be up for her early morning shift. Too late for sleep as she soon discovered, so she dressed and settled herself in a chair with the comfort of a cup of tea. Hamlet stretched out on the bed. Uncertainty, hopelessness and desire all combined to give her little peace. Not so Geoffrey who flopped out as soon as his head hit the pillow, plain tuckered out. He fell asleep with the well remembered scent of lavender in his nostrils, always connected with that first awareness of Lottie as a woman, more than half a decade ago, unaware that this was the bed she often slept in and that lavender lingered.

Martha came down at six, the open fire was lit, Alice off to the farm. 'The Major arrived during the early hours of the morning,' Lottie told her but kept her tell tale eyes averted, Martha needed so little to catch on and in this case would be sheer disaster. How she endured the remainder of that leave she never knew, glad for Victoria's demands upon his time. 'My God,' he gasped in horror later in the day when faced at last with what Felicity had become, unable to avoid a duty visit, his wife in a worse state than men in the trenches with a real excuse for taking refuge in the bottle. Drinking themselves stupid almost to deal with mud, machine guns and barbed wire. 'Is this the woman I must stay tied to for the rest of my life?' He threw at John Starrett in disgust, dark eyes full of reproach. The two men exchanged bitter words. 'She is long past helping,' Geoffrey stormed. 'Felicity should have been taken into care long ago but you refused to accept the situation. Have you no consideration for those obliged to look after her?' Thinking of all Lottie must have borne for so long a time.

'My daughter will stay in this house as long as I am alive,' the gaffer roared at him, painfully aware the decision was not his to make, rather disturbed by the contempt in Geoffrey's eyes, their roles reversed. Money no longer the bargaining power, daily contact with death and destruction beyond belief, the changing factor in Geoffrey Cranshawe's life. 'And after that?' he questioned scornfully. Only one option as far as he was concerned and prepared to stand his ground. 'She does have a husband and daughter. Victoria won't always be a child.' Senseless reasoning which made Geoffrey see red. 'And you would condemn your granddaughter to a life of that,' he scorned. 'Your daughter refused to be a normal wife to me,' determined to get everything out in the open. The emphasis on your daughter Felicity thus proclaimed once and for all, his voice dripping ice as he continued relentlessly. 'She turned me out of her bed and the servants mothered Victoria from birth, especially Lottie, who even fed her as an infant, sheer cruelty after losing her own baby. Such selfish behaviour hardly qualifies her for any consideration from husband or daughter.'

Absolute deadlock or so it seemed and God knows how it may have ended but for the timely intervention of a phone call from Polrigg, which took the gaffer out of the house for a while, allowing tempers to cool somewhat, and fate to take a hand as it so often does.

* * *

After the customary celebrations of the festive season, indulged in with a sort of frantic desperation, January 1916 seemed gloomier than usual. almost the whole of Europe at war and much further afield. With resources stretched beyond the limit, Saltersgate echoed to the same after-celebration complaints, food rationing an added inconvenience but really just more of the same for folk who spent their whole existence 'makin' do', items in short supply were only to be found 'under the counter' and there for those with money to buy, miners not among them. Towards the end of March the dreaded telegram arrived, placed first into Lottie's trembling fingers, who rushed immediately to John Starrett. He swiftly tore it open and read the heartbreaking contents out loud, 'believed killed' held out little hope of survival and merely prolonged the agony, final confirmation of death to follow shortly after.

Whether Geoffrey Cranshawe's fear was the natural feeling of a man who survived many battles, or some very real premonitions, was impossible to ascertain. He left Rothwell House fully convinced his days were numbered, an expression in those dark eyes which struck right to the depths of Lottie's heart. 'Take care, sir,' she managed to choke out, wanting so badly to feel the warmth of his precious body close to hers, recapturing those wonderful moments in the stable yard, to wonder yet again why they held back from total fulfilment of their love. So many eyes upon them when he departed, that mere touch of the fingers, Geoffrey's icy cold, his strong foreboding somehow transferred in this briefest of contact, now confirmed as their final parting.

'Aa reckon we've seen the last o'the Major,' Martha's gloomy forecast, Lottie's ashen face attributed to the intitial shock, nothing more, from which she would soon recover, death no stranger to anyone in those terrible times.

Instead, they saw a desolate young woman, her world shattered into many pieces, only able to give way to grief in the seclusion of her own rooms, through long sleepless nights.

It was Alice who wallowed in tears but, soon after could be heard whistling 'It's a long way to Tipperary' governed by a simple philosophy towards both life and death, immensely irritating to someone whose feelings were much more affected and it took enormous willpower to keep them under control.

John Starrett's mind was impossible to read but Lottie tried hard not to believe that being in sole control of Geoffrey's wife and daughter superseded any feeling of regret. Too late in Felicity's case, she had been sent to a private sanatorium at her husband's insistence before he left for France, her father's protests silenced in face of a happening which altered the whole situation.

Weeks later, after Geoffrey was presumed dead, Lottie confided in Marianne, only up to a point however, some aspects were never to be revealed. 'I can't understand how the key was in the door, I always checked,' she puzzled aloud and her confidante understood how Lottie blamed herself for, what turned out to be a blessing in disguise. 'Maybe I willed something of the sort to happen, subconsciously I mean, so Madam had to be sent away.'

'Nonsense,' came in swift reply and put the whole disastrous affair down to Victoria's natural curiosity, nearer the truth than she imagined. 'Besides, it only hastened a long overdue decision, without the Major on the scene Mr Starrett may have tried to gloss it over, his presence in the house providential.' 'No child should be subjected to the evil of a warped mind,' Lottie insisted, 'Oh, I realise Madam was completely deranged, God knows what she said to Victoria before I appeared on the scene, I didn't ask. But that heavy candlestick could have descended at any minute.' Her eyes closed to shut out the memory of Felicity's murderous expression. She hesitated, then began again. 'What you don't know, Marianne, is that Madam was stark naked, not a stitch of clothing on her body. A fine sight I must say.' Forced to recollect how beautiful Felicity used to be and what she had become. Marianne looked horrified as might be expected. 'I almost have it in my heart to feel sorry for the woman, to end up so lacking in human dignity.' She was thrown off balance by an immediate burst of anger. 'Save your pity for someone who deserves it,' Lottie snapped, resentful of her friend's tolerance, never likely to forget Victoria's screams and rushing upstairs to get there only seconds before Geoffrey and his father-in-law, both from different parts of the house. By this time she had placed herself between the frightened girl and an impending blow. 'She is mine, I tell you, they are both mine,' Felicity shrieked at her, dull blue eyes full of stark hatred, and in that moment Lottie knew Victoria was indeed her child, Madam party to Jessica Finlay's deception.

The blow never found a target, Geoffrey forcibly restrained his wife's descending hand, in no mood to be gentle. The gaffer reached for a bed cover to wrap around his daughter's writhing body, Lottie's last sight as she hurried Victoria out of the room at her beloved's terse command. 'Take her to Marianne,' he shouted after her, words almost drowned by the obscenities which fell from Madam's slobbering lips. 'Say no more than you must to anyone,' reached her ears on the landing, an unnecessary warning. Geoffrey was obviously still engaged in a struggle to contain a violent virago, the words followed by a hard slap and John Starrett's voice loud in protest. Then Felicity's screeching changed into that wailing sound Lottie had been listening to for months gone. Marianne gasped at the intensity of Lottie's disturbed emotions, a beautiful face which told of many sleepless nights, astonished at what she chose to disclose. Her concern was confided to Mattie Jackson after supper that same evening, in the privacy of the own flat. 'Lottie is wound up so tight, Matthew, something has to snap sooner or later,' and found her husband in full agreement, both firmly convinced Madam's departure should have eased the pressure on this dear friend. Mattie was more certain than ever that such a tempestuous young woman was never right for him.

'Aye,' he murmured, 'Aa can see the state she's in but mebbe yer lookin' i' the wrong direction fer what ails the lass.' A quizzical expression came over Marianne's face, aged very little apart from a few tell tale wrinkles, put there by the pain and suffering she encountered every day. She was still involved in hospital work despite all the misgivings, not a great deal of stamina but plenty of determination.

'What do you mean, Matthew?' she said, definitely puzzled and rather irked to think she may have been excluded from some confidence given to her husband. Able to read her like a book and often intrigued by the workings of the female mind, he decided to string her along a little. 'Yer barkin' up the wrong tree if y'think the business wi' Miss Victoria's all she has on'er mind. Somethin' else happened that fair took the wind out of'er sails.'

Marianne began to think aloud, hoping to chance upon the answer he was making her sweat to discover. 'Her cousin Jimmy Thompson was killed recently and others she knew in her younger days. Lottie takes it all to heart.' Not a flicker to prove she was right. 'You know better than anyone what sort of person she is.' But no reaction, Jackson's face impassive except for a tiny quirk around the mouth, unaccustomed to such curiosity in this beloved wife of his. 'Try a bit nearer home,' he suggested at last and waited for the penny to drop.

Her fine brows puckered than she gasped, unbelievingly. 'Not the Major, surely?' obviously appalled at the very idea, Jackson's answering tone was rather sharp, 'And why not? He was a fine, upstandin' fella.' Marianne was quick to reply. 'But she wouldn't be so foolish,' she said in amazement, possessed of an inherent sense of propriety, prevented from further comment by the force of her husband's anger.

'Don't let that mind o' yours run away wi'ya. Aa'm not sayin' there was owt o'that sort atween them but the feelin' was there, and it was mutual,' he added, 'Y'can take my word fer that. Look what'ee had fer a wife and there's no denyin' Lottie Hanson is a bonny lass, as good inside as out.'

'I can't believe she would allow herself to become involved after—' Here she broke off, flushed to the roots of her light brown hair. 'You know what I mean, Matthew – – not after Jake Snowdon.' The first time this name had ever been spoken between them. 'Nor would sha, not that way.' Long forgotten feelings were rekindled by this unfortunate reference to Lottie's seducer. 'Anyway, the two chaps couldn't be more different. One a downright rogue that took advantage of an innocent lass and the other – ' His gruff voice tailed off, deeply disturbed, painfully reminded of their own wedding and the role Geoffrey Cranshawe played in it, the shining happiness on Lottie's face, when his suspicion first took root. A flicker of jealousy flashed through Marianne's eyes, soon dismissed, knowing there was nothing to fear from Jackson's high regard for Lottie or their friend's sisterly devotion. Matthew must never discover how she envied the time before she came into their lives. That first sense of revulsion at the idea of some sort of liaison faded into insignificance as deep concern for a dear one's agony of mind and heart took its place. 'What can we do, Matthew?' she asked almost pleadingly, so anxious to ease the pain.

'Nowt,' he said abruptly, 'and don't go oozin' sympathy or she's sure t'cotton on. Lottie's got plenty up aloft. You helped t'put it there wi'all y' learnt 'er.' 'Taught,' Marianne found herself about to correct, but was wise enough to leave well alone. 'Just supposing the Major does happen to come back, some miracle happens, what then?' she sighed, really disturbed by this astounding twist to Lottie's story. 'Then they'll have their problems' he stated, solemn faced. 'Wi' Madam the way sh'is, he's stuck with'er that's what the law says. Might be better if'ee is gone, poor chap. There's hundreds o'bodies they never find. This damned rotten war,' he spat out furiously. So grateful for their five wonderful years of marriage, Marianne sought the comfort of loving arms. Jackson held his wife's slender body close. 'Not a pickin on'er,' he often said, but this gentle woman was his whole world and he still found it incredulous to be accepted as her husband. 'Sorrow an' trouble seem t'haunt the poor lass, Marianne,' he choked, reminded of a young back straightened, so often, against adversity, fully convinced she would rise above it all, with more courage than the rest of them put together. 'W'just have t'stand by an'offer the hand o'friendship when sh'asks fer it.' A poor substitute for love as Jackson knew himself from past experience. The difference between that and what he once felt for Lottie had been soon recognised when Marianne came into his life. But he also knew the grieving lass well enough to realise that when she gave her love to someone it would be forever and, if that someone were to be the Major it would be such a terrible waste. Not that she stood alone in her anguish as a senseless conflict dragged on and on, without an end in sight.

* * *

Lottie Hanson needed courage, as did so many in those dark days when, during the rest of that year new offensives took place, young men went 'over the top' in their thousands, many of them to inevitable death. Names of the fallen appeared on notice boards, and in the press, right across the far flung

British Empire, the western world drained of a whole generation of its youth on the battlefields of France and Belgium.

Saltersgate licked its wounds along with the rest and spoke constantly of places across The Channel, hitherto unknown, now part of daily life, to be remembered for years to come by those whose loved ones made the supreme sacrifice and now rested on foreign soil. A feeling of gloom surrounded all, nothing to brighten Lottie's existence apart from Victoria's periodic visits once again to Rothwell House, no more worries about the unpredictable behaviour of an alcoholic woman. A great load was lifted from the young housekeeper's shoulders.

For some considerable time Victoria made no reference to that former traumatic experience, was never encouraged to talk about it, a wise decision not hard to determine. Martha Connelly's inquisitive nature took great umbrage at being excluded from all knowledge of what actually occurred and, sensing some carefully hidden secret, was most frustrated. She had almost given up expecting to be put in the picture when Victoria emerged from the trauma and started to revel in its dramatic content, herself in the main role of course, and she had not far to seek for eager ears.

Lottie, safely closeted with John Starrett in his study for the day's orders could not have possibly foreseen what happened in her absence from the kitchen as Martha grasped the opportunity to pump the youngster for all she was worth, not that much encouragement was needed, Victoria was more than willing to expand.

'Mama was quite mad,' she said in youthful candour, 'standing in front of the mirror with nothing on, turning this way and that, making funny giggling noises.' And proceeded to demonstrate exactly how it was, Martha's tiny, birdlike face was a study, her curiosity being satisfied at last and right from the horse's mouth. 'Ages before she saw me,' Victoria said, immediately Martha asked how she got into a room always kept locked.

'Easily,' was the proud boast, 'I knew where Lottie kept the key and decided to visit Mama.' Even Martha was amazed at this forthright explanation with no sign of contrition for such foolish behaviour.

Now in full flow, she carried on, Martha all ears. 'I was rather afraid when Mama saw me. She began to shout and lifted that heavy candlestick.' Remembered fear dilated her bright blue eyes. 'I screamed blue murder,' she confessed, accepting the milk and biscuits offered as further inducement by her avid listener, anxious to hear the full story. It could only get more interesting. 'It wasn't me she called horrible names and threw accusations at, it was Lottie. She hated her I think.' Enough provocation for Alice, silent until now, to instantly explode, very uneasy at the turn things were taking. 'Yer mother had no right callin' Lottie, the way sh'had t'run after'er backside all them years,' she stoutly defended and refused to be intimidated by Martha's glowering expression.

'I love Lottie too,' Victoria admitted, in full agreement with Alice's support for her idol. 'She has taken care of me ever since I was a baby. Do you know what? Mama was jealous of Lottie because she is prettier than she is and—' she added significantly, 'she said Papa couldn't keep his eyes away from her, more than that too but when I told Grandpa he just snorted and said it was a whole load of nonsense.'

'Tell me, Miss Victoria,' Martha coaxed and made Alice catch her breath in dismay. 'Me bein' all grown up Aa'll likely be able t'tell ya.' Quite unconcerned about any ethics involved but very much aware Lottie wouldn't approve and the grapes of wrath could descend upon her if she ever found out. This only got better and better and an innate sense of curiosity knew no bounds, she was more than willing to take a chance.

But it ended, right at that very minute, the words no sooner out of her mouth than a furious voice wrapped around flapping years and she jumped in swift alarm, although the order wasn't barked at her. 'Go to your room, Miss Victoria.' A tone which forbade argument, a flurry of skirts and the girl was off like a shot.

Alarmed, no doubt, but not so easily intimidated, Martha stood her ground, four feet nothing stretched to the limit and a mop capped head tossed high in the air. A laughable stance if the situation hadn't been so serious. 'Never,' Lottie blazed at her, 'never let me hear you mention that terrible day again, it's a closed book,' she snapped, Alice shivering in her size seven boots, Martha if diminutive a different proposition. 'What are y'getting'in such a stew fer?' she retaliated, 'The bairn wanted t'tell the tale an' who are we t'say'er nay, just a pair o'skivvies.' Obviously disgruntled at the failure of her nosiness, cut off in mid stream as it were.

'I don't see Alice Ruddick figuring much in all this,' Lottie scorned, 'and if she has any sense she'll keep well out of it.' Unaware of her friend's support, having heard only the tail end of the conversation but sufficient to warrant strong intervention.

'Well' – Martha snorted, now very much affronted.

'Not well, Martha, far from it.' Lottie was quick to contradict, this had to be nipped in the bud once and for all. 'Bad enough for Miss Victoria to lose father and mother within the matter of weeks, without raking up what is best forgotten. Besides she can't be expected to understand the ravings of a demented mind.' Red faced and very angry.

'Mebbe it suits ya t'keep some things quiet, Lottie Hanson,' Martha retorted nastily, an innuendo which threw her adversary temporarily off balance and she struggled valiantly to regain control, Alice Ruddick swift to ally herself to the person she cared for most devotedly, was undeterred by the possible backlash of Martha's caustic tongue.

'Ye shut up, Martha Connelly, that big mouth o'yours'll be the death o'ya. Lottie could have us both out i' the street i'five minutes flat, a word t'the gaffer is all it would take.' Simple minded she was well aware of how much continued employment in Rothwell House meant to both of them, anxious Martha didn't rock the boat.

Thus reminded of Lottie's superior status, Martha's face fell, to be left without hearth and home would be a veritable disaster. Not another word was spoken, any advantage she held lost in face of such a dreadful prospect. 'Let it rest,' Lottie snapped, absolutely dismayed at this unexpected turn of events and left the kitchen without further ado, afraid what might come out under pressure. The Hanson temper was not so much in evidence nowadays but she was really up tight and to beat a retreat seemed the wisest decision. God knows what might happen should she ever let fly.

Alice didn't hang around for any reprimands from Martha, off to the stables and Tiger's soothing company, more at home with four legged creatures than humans, apart from Lottie, to whom she was absolutely devoted since that long ago day on Fencers' Hill, when their friendship first took root. Hamlet, equally devoted to this big, gawky lass, scrambled to his feet and hurried after her.

The remainder of Victoria's vacation passed without further incident and her eventual departure cast a deep gloom over the occupants of Rothwell House, back to the same dull routine as before, John Coulter's harvest kept Alice busy, any leisure time was spent in the local chapel vestry, where Methodists provided canteen facilities for their own and other Protestant denominations, men billeted in the area before early shipment across the Channel, after the briefest of training periods. To be able to hold and use a gun was the main qualification, the ability to kill came when face to face with the enemy. Most times they would be shot down by some unseen foe with hands on a death dealing machine gun, a matter of pure luck to escape a bullet from the shower which came at them across the the wire.

Martha merely changed one kitchen sink for another, to wash endless dishes after feeding Catholic serving men in the hall of St Aloysius. It was a much livelier atmosphere than that left behind in Rothwell House, as soldiers tried to dispel apprehension with false bravado, raw recruits most of them but after so much fighting and enormous losses they knew what lay ahead.

The gaffer placed few restrictions on either of his servants. 'Let them do their bit,' he told Lottie. 'My needs are easily satisfied and you are always here Charlotte,' as indeed she was, a wan smile her only answer. It seemed everyone had diversions, even the gaffer himself, who made regular pilgrimages to Harrogate, where Felicity lived on in her expensive prison and her father refused to accept the permanency of her condition. 'It's a hard world,' he once remarked, rather quizzical when Lottie said, 'Harder for some than others, sir.' Sympathy or gentle sarcasm, difficult to assess, the latter much nearer the truth. Too many suffered the results of death and deprivation without the compensation of money to lessen the burden. Tod and Mary Wilson were prime examples, Janey's husband was a poor specimen, two lost souls who merely existed under the same roof in close proximity but miles apart in every other way.

Lottie bumped into Mary once or twice on Branton High Street, an embittered woman, left to care for a father whose bigotry robbed her of a man's love in marriage. She was told by Alice after one sortie into the village, about religious instruction from Father Reilly, who still reigned supreme at St Joseph's. A nasty pill for Tod to swallow but he was absolutely dependent upon his waspish spinster daughter, who now held the whip hand and used it wherever it was bound to hurt most.

There were just the two of them left, Tommy Wilson had been lost at the Front, not astute enough it seemed for the cruel gods of war.

Lottie's sympathy did not include Felicity, whose sorry state stemmed from self indulgence, she was more concerned about the sad fate of her beloved Geoffrey, cheated of fatherhood by his wife's frigidity, the child who bore his name with no real claim to it, stolen by the connivance of two evil women, one of them Lottie's own kin.

Madam's upstairs suite remained unoccupied, a shrine to someone still alive, the furniture shrouded in dust sheets. So pitiful to watch a man cling to false hope, it was so very obvious that Rothwell House would never be home to its former mistress again, but there were no feelings of regret from other residents. From time to time, Lottie inspected the room to see no damage occurred, especially in winter, fires were lit to give a measure of warmth to this holy of holies, around which the scent of its former occupant clung to torment her. 'If it was left to me, I would put a match to it,' she often affirmed and really meant what she said, needing no reminder of Geoffrey's drunken wife. Disturbed beyond measure by mental images of a handsome face and strong, manly body, those few passionate kisses still scorched her lips in retrospect, truly spoilt for another man, as Mattie Jackson, so happily married, often grieved. Jake Snowdon was just an unpleasant memory from a long ago past, not worth a single thought.

Another festive season was to come and go before John Starrett accepted the hopelessness of the situation and decided to take action. 'Enter,' he called, in answer to Lottie's knock, summoned to his study one cold, January morning, feeling rather irritated, time she could ill afford with the whole house in chaos, the outcome of freezing weather the reason for this particular upset, water all over the kitchen floor and Jackson not around to bring the turn key into action. 'The plumber's due at any minute,' she told the gaffer, hoping this would expedite whatever he had in mind.

'Forget about the damned plumber, he doesn't need your assistance to do his job. There are important matters I wish to discuss. Sit down, girl,' he ordered brusquely, still inclined to address her thus, instead of by name. In swift obedience she took the seat in front of his desk, right on the edge of the chair, one of her aunt's many instructions, never to relax in the presence of one's superiors. Jessica Finlay's harsh training was still deeply implanted in her niece's mind, if subconsciously.

The man who faced her had shrunk somewhat, that former giant much reduced in size and so forlorn nowadays, only came to life during Victoria's spaced out visits. Not that time stood still for anyone, she was almost thirty three herself and sure she looked it, destined to be an old maid. She was not vain enough to accept the evidence of a bedroom mirror which definitely proved otherwise, a maturer beauty promised in those earlier days now most evident.

John Starrett's eyes appraised her neat, ladylike appearance, it was always a pleasure to behold this comely young woman. 'We are going to Whitegates on Wednesday' he announced without further preamble. 'But, in the meantime I want my daughter's suite completely cleared. Jackson is on night shift, so he can spare you a few hours for a day or two. Store the best of the furniture elsewhere, spread it around the attic rooms. As for personal effects, do what you deem best, I leave everything to your common sense. Consult me if in doubt.' His mind was obviously made up. She wondered at the suddenness of this decision, a much belated one, and didn't relish the idea of going through Felicity's possessions, perhaps there would be some painful reminders of an earlier married life with Geoffrey, from which she shied in horror, the thought of intimacy between them totally abhorrent.

The gaffer kept on talking, unaware of the turmoil his words created. 'My daughter will be staying in Yorkshire permanently,' he went on to inform her. 'Not that I agree but am forced to bow to the wisdom of her doctors, all experienced in their field.' He cleared his throat, husky with emotion. 'This presents me with another problem but first let me acquaint you with what takes me to Whitegates.' Lottie's heart was full at his obvious distress.

'There is a large amount of furniture stored in the east wing,' he explained. 'Some of the better items will be brought here to replace articles of lesser value and the surplus from both houses will go to the sale rooms.' There was a sound of finality in his voice and strong entreaty in piercing grey eyes as he continued. 'Rothwell House will be my only home from now on, even after the war is over. I hope you will stay with me, Charlotte. No danger of some young man waiting to snap you up, I suppose?' A feeble attempt at humour, really quite serious, Lottie's reply was in the negative and most emphatic. 'No danger,' she said and saw him smile in relief.

'As for the other matter,' he stated very solemnly, 'I think we have to accept that my son-in-law didn't survive, although no body was ever found, which makes me Victoria's legal guardian.' It was almost too much to hear her beloved Geoffrey written off like this. 'We do have relatives, of course, but none of them are capable of taking charge if anything should happen to me.' The mention of Victoria's name dragged Lottie out of her mournful reverie. The relatives he spoke of were all old fuddy duddies, no match for a spirited youngster, shocked into even fuller awareness by the significance in his following words. 'I wish to name you as my granddaughter's guardian in the event of my death before she comes of age.'

Lottie's face drained of all colour and she reeled under the impact. 'Oh no, sir, I couldn't,' her protest very real, knocked completely off balance by such an amazing proposal, John Starrett was quick to steady her when she stumbled to her feet. 'Take it easy, girl. All I want is for you to be there for her and make sure she isn't exploited, some wily rascal just after her money. Victoria is headstrong but she trusts you, as I do.'

'Miss Victoria should have someone of her own class,' she put forth vehemently, greatly agitated by the irony of the situation, to actually admit herself unfit to care for her own child. John Starrett refused to take 'No' for an answer. 'Stuff and nonsense,' he snorted, 'Victoria will have all the qualities a young lady of her station needs when she graduates from that damned expensive school. What is required, and you will supply, is someone who really cares and isn't only interested in her financial position.' One argument which outweighed all others, still doubting the wisdom of this decision she reluctantly agreed. 'As you wish, sir, of course, but I sincerely hope you will still be around when she reaches her majority.'

'I hope so too, naturally,' he confessed, genuinely touched, 'Just in case, I shall have the necessary documents drawn up for you to sign. My accountant and solicitor will attend to all other matters but you will be responsible for Victoria's well being and happiness.' Obviously he was determined to have everything properly sewn up. By the time she reached the sanctuary of her own quarters, Alice out of the house and Martha fully occupied with the plumber in the kitchen, Lottie's senses still swam, totally bemused by her employer's latest plan, only herself aware of the true position. She stared idly out of her bedroom window upon a real winter scene, flower beds covered in snow, which like graves, made her think of Geoffrey who had no grave at all and shuddered at the idea of nothing left to bury. Disturbing thoughts which were dramatically dismissed by the sound of her own name, clearly spoken in a deeply sensuous voice. In eager anticpation, she quickly turned, with arms out held, but the space behind was empty of all except familiar articles of furniture. No warm, loving man to clasp her to an eager body, another cruel trick of the imagination, a torment so often endured, always there to haunt her with regret for a love unfulfilled, theirs for the taking, denied because of so many scruples.

But, many miles distant, a man was slowly coming back to life and opened his mouth in an effort to speak, for the first time in months, Lottie the name that croaked through a dry throat. This word was not understood by a buxom, bright faced German nurse who soothed his subsequent agitation in a soft, calming tone, absolutely overjoyed at this present turn of events. A word such as this was insufficient to establish nationality or identity for a patient who had lain almost as dead for so very long, but there were tears in her eyes when she called the attention of a passing doctor. Clever surgery, so much learnt from the thousands of war casualties, assisted greatly in the repair of Geoffrey Cranshawe's body, pulled out of a shell crater, stripped of clothing and any means of identification, his name tag gone with the rest. Dedicated German doctors refused to give up on him, after all he might be one of their own, not of major concern, simply a war victim in need of care. Weeks after he first spoke Lottie's name, before other facts finally came to light, an army number, a name and a likely candidate for repatriation, Geoffrey emerged from a death like trance only to find he could not see and sadly withdrew into the hopelessness of this condition, although now reasonably fit in mind and body.

Completely unaware of even more trauma about to enter her life, Lottie began to merge herself in the distasteful task of clearing Madam's suite. So many painful memories surrounded it and Felicity's remembered presence was still strong enough to plague her, a real *bête-noir* from their very first meeting and impossible to say which of them was the greater casualty. One thing was certain, the gaffer didn't realise how much he continued to ask of her, a determined man accustomed to having his own way had once again succeeded.

* * *

Lottie chanced upon the diaries at the end of a long, tiring day, when every bone in her body ached, her sole desire to close the door of Madam's former abode and never enter it again. Impossible with so much hard work still to be done before all trace of an oppressive regime disappeared, only to bare walls and echoes from the past to remind her of many things she preferred to forget.

Three green, leather bound volumes with gilt filigree clasps lay in the bottom drawer of Felicity Cranshawe's writing bureau, securely locked against prying eyes, the drawer key discovered in one of several pigeon holes and used with trembling fingers. For one breathless moment her heart stood still, unable to move, the likely significance of these books gave rise to a surge of hope, reluctantly relinquished with Jessica Finlay's death, her former mistress the only other person to know the truth. Here now possible proof of her aunt's perfidy.

'She is mine I tell you, they both are,' words spat out in frenzy from a vicious woman's tongue now echoed in her ears, which at the time of utterance confirmed suspicion bur provided no viable proof. That moment long awaited now appeared to be at hand.

Since early morning with Marianne's invaluable help, Lottie had sorted through innumerable articles of clothing, which represented a fortune of John Starrett's money, ever the indulgent father. Most of them were already packed into hampers for distribution to various charitable organisations, some earmarked for impoverished gentlewomen widowed by war. Felicity's discarded day wear would be a God send to those fallen on harder times,, accustomed to such apparel, keeping up appearances being most essential to their pride, now expected to exist on meagre pensions. Alice laughed uproariously when told to choose something for herself. 'Y'must be jokin',' she spluttered, 'Can y'see me muckin' pig styes an' hen crees out in them fancy things,' which did seem rather ludicrous. Some plainer underwear was set aside for Saltersgate folk, to whom Alice still enjoyed playing Lady Bountiful, very careful not to rub it in, a hard lesson once learnt and never forgotten.

Martha's refusal couldn't have been more definite. 'There's nowt that'll fit,' she said abruptly, absolute rejection in dull grey eyes with every right to decline. She wanted no reminder of the woman who despised her deformity, still bitter, she was not known for a forgiving nature. At one stage Marianne pirouetted gaily around the room, a beautiful velvet gown held against her slender body, utterly enraptured by the sensual feel of such luxurious material, a very feminine creation, amazed at the repugnance on Lottie's face when she came to a halt beside her. 'What do you think of this?' she inquired and received a curt reply.

'Not much,' was the answer in a sharper tone than necessary. How could Marianne know of that particular garment's painful connection? But Lottie did, right to the exact date and time of day when Felicity's cruel jibes reached their mark. So much now for that 'unimportant little person' considered fit guardian for Victoria. Fate had really hit back with a vengeance, a very satisfying thought. She deliberately avoided Marianne's questioning eyes and threw the hateful blue gown aside among the rest to be disposed of. 'That thing came out of the ark, Madam hadn't the heart to chuck anything away,' she muttered grimly, her helpmate wise enough not to probe into whys and wherefores of such odd behaviour, just grimaced slightly at the use of such a harsh sounding vowel.

More than five hours later, Marianne gone for two of them, back to her stint in hospital, Lottie stood rooted to the spot, one of the suspected, incriminating diaries in her hand, very much afraid of the serious implications revelation would have for those involved. John Starrett first came to mind, to whom Victoria had become sun, moon and stars, a bitter blow she must harden her heart to deliver. What if he should return from Newcastle, a visit to his accountant and legal advisers, to find the rigmarole totally unnecessary? Painful thoughts which were thrust resolutely aside.

A second key, soon found, was difficult to handle in her present state but it turned without effort, by now she was almost a quivering wreck. Before long there could be an end to the suspicion which had clouded her existence and the validity of Felicity's handwriting was beyond dispute. It was the latest of the diaries, two years of its span still to go but never likely to be completed, its owner in such a sorry state. Her own name leapt from one scribbled page, again on others, the babblings of an insane mind, sheer venom in every single word. Ugly remarks, accusations of adultery between Geoffrey and herself, a man who had not been under the same roof until those days prior to Felicity's banishment, just wicked imaginings, a shot in the dark from a deranged mind. The second book covered a much earlier period but later than the all important time, there were great gaps between entries, Fanny and Charlie Askew viciously maligned. June 1911 missing, blank pages throughout that entire month, no mention of Jessica Finlay's final illness or her demise, banished from her shallow mistress's mind.

Lottie's heart hit rock bottom and she prepared herself for yet another let down, almost afraid to open the third volume, which covered the early years of Felicity's marriage to Geoffrey, so very young both of them, too young maybe, but as she digested the intimate outpourings of a woman's abnormal attitude towards sex, she realised age made no difference. A handsome soldier with a lovely, physically attractive wife, who was utterly devoid of any love for him. One sordid scene after another described to the very last detail, a distasteful condemnation of a red blooded male's natural instincts cruelly denied and derided later in the written word, a warped mind in action.

In sheer agony, Lottie tore the pages out in savage fury, determined nobody else would ever read their nauseating contents, the other two were given the same treament, thrown into the fire and burst into flame, Madam's wicked ramblings were soon no more. The leather covers and filigree clasps were tied into a bundle and hidden among a pile of rubbish. As she thus disposed of them Lottie imagined the sound of empty laughter echoed through the room, hostile as ever it was the first time they came into contact and instantly clashed, Madam's unreasonable animosity never understood.

For days afterwards, she speculated on the fate of the missing diary, one more at least, the most significant of all. Perhaps it had been left at Harrow Square and packed away in one of the huge attics when the Army commandeered the house. Madam and her aunt had covered their tracks well and sadly she decided to close the door for good on this painful chapter of her life, try to accept things as they were. Her claim to Victoria could never be substantiated, Lottie knew without a doubt and wept once more for lost hope, a dream not to be realised.

At last the spacious suite stood empty, badly in need of decoration, distinct patches on walls where mirrors and pictures once hung. John Starrett engaged the services of a local firm called Jordan and Sons, a sad misnomer the two sons lost early in a war which went on and on, no sign of it coming to an end. Although hopes did rise when the Americans joined the Allies in 1917.

'It's all s'pointless,' the senior Jordan said, as Lottie and himself pored over wallpaper and paint samples on the kitchen table. 'There'll be no grand bairns fer me an'the Missis, the lads were all w'had. Even workin' the business seems futile but if Aa didn't have somethin' A'ad go off me rocker.' Such a sad admission but one freely expressed in those terrible times.

The following Wednesday, after lunch, Lottie found herself en route to Whitegates, a rather nostalgic journey, reminding her of so many other trips. Mattie Jackson had stuck in as requested and done well as a furniture remover, a lot of space had been cleared. The gaffer was a distinguished looking travelling companion, attired in well cut tweeds and a deer stalker hat, its flaps pulled down to protect his ears. Bushy whiskers now exchanged for a clean shaven chin and a thick moustache, which took a year or two from his age. A caped coat completed the picture of a well dressed country gentleman, an image he chose to create on this particular day.

Lottie herself was well wrapped up for the journey, her cheeks tingled to a becoming rosy red with the chill of the air, the rest of her warm as toast. They rode in a smaller carriage pulled by a single horse, another animal for Alice to tend but Tiger was still the favourite, used nowadays for shorter journeys only. John Starrett handled the reins well, the roads they travelled free of heavy traffic, just the odd motorised vehicle and horse drawn cart, the latter still part of the rural scene. Ambulances passed them at intervals, marked with that familiar Red Cross, coming from or going to country houses such as

Whitegates, now convalescent homes. With the introduction of tanks at an earlier stage followed by aeroplanes not so long ago the war had become more mechanised, dog fights a new sight above the battlefields, flimsy machines with little between their pilots and death from rapidly firing machine guns to end up on the ground in a burnt out shell. The implements of war may have changed somewhat but they still fulfilled the same deadly purpose one way or another.

A bustling, uniformed figure emerged from the front entrance of the house to greet this very important visitor and Matron ushered the two of them into her own private sitting room, once the gaffer's study. Tea soon appeared, brought by a rosy cheeked country woman, with an easy manner born of long acquaintance. 'God bless me, sir,' she exclaimed in obvious pleasure. 'Yer a sight fer sore eyes, you an' the young Miss.' The laden tray was placed beside Matron, who tried to dismiss her with a flick of the wrist, only to be ignored, the elderly servant anxious to have a word or two with her former master. 'A fine hamper y'sent at Christmas, sir, bonny an' welcome t'be sure. And thanks fer the coal, these old bones take some warmin'up nowadays.' A huge beam on her homely face, John Starrett was definitely embarrassed to be caught out in good works. 'No thanks needed, Mary,' he grunted. 'How is that husband of yours?'

'Fair t'middlin', sir,' she replied and the smile faded, replaced by a look of anxiety. 'It's that chest o'his but Aa reckon he'll pick up when the weather's better.' A hopeful claim but she was none too sure of its validity, her husband a sick man. Matron dispatched the woman kindly but firmly, full of apologies when she left. 'Rather talkative I'm afraid. Let me pour your tea, I can recommend the scones, the cook we inherited is a treasure, but I don't need to tell you that, do I,' she simpered. John Starrett's grey eyes twinkled. 'A treasure indeed. She would have moved with me to Rothwell House if I wasn't blessed with another treasure there. In fact I am surrounded by them.' His eyes on Lottie as he spoke, who wished Martha could have been present to hear the gaffer sing her praises. She was amazed, once more, at the conflicting sides to his nature, so generous towards family servants and yet niggardly where his colliery workers were involved. 'Spoon fed,' he had complained on the journey. 'They should buckle to, instead of moaning on about wages and conditions. A damned sight worse off wallowing in French mud.' Convinced, as always, the miners had no cause for complaint. Lottie was hard pushed not to tell him that living was often harder than dying but the words stuck in her throat as usual, all the old hatreds there to plague her. While the others indulged in conversation, she wandered towards the big windows and watched convalescent officers in the grounds, those able to bear the rigours of a cold winter's day. Some of them minus a leg but quite adept on crutches, soon to be thrown back into a world where crippled ex-servicemen found it hard to survive.

The sight of army great coats over hospital blue brought Geoffrey vividly to mind, the well remembered feel of his buttons as they clung together, the ecstasy of being held in his arms for the very first time, the only time, her breasts aching with desire. She was thankful indeed when John Starrett addressed her directly and brought her back to the present, those few precious memories too agonising to bear but all she would ever have of her beloved man.

'Wool gathering,' he chaffed, 'A penny for them.'

'They aren't worth even that much,' she lied, 'save your money, sir!' Private thoughts, never to be divulged, least of all to Geoffrey's father-in-law.

Matron was obviously delighted at the purpose of their visit, the thought of extra space a wonderful prospect, she expressed a willingness to do anything within her power to help. 'When you are ready, leave the removals to me, transport and manpower present no problem, it's the least we can do when you house us and keep us warm, a real benefactor.'

'Mary Trumble isn't the only one who talks too much,' he grunted when they drove away from the house, Matron's effusive manner was hard to take for any length of time but she did have every reason to be grateful, these other surprising acts of generosity now revealed.

Lottie chuckled at the expression on John Starrett's face, the pit gaffer once again amazed at the pleasure he found in her company, more at ease than ever he was with Felicity, a big disappointment in so many ways. He was prepared to admit he had indulged his daughter too much and vowed not to make the same mistake twice, ruefully aware of his weakness where Victoria was concerned.

They made good time on the homeward journey, diverting from the main road at Fencer's Quarry. 'Business,' the gaffer told Lottie, 'I won't be long,' unconscious of her preoccupation, so many memories surged in upon her on this familiar ground. Maude Elliott passed away in the first year of war and, left without his mainstay, her devoted husband followed soon after, surviving their only son by a few weeks, Billy lost at sea. A touch of irony that Maude's greedily acquired Hanson family possessions were inherited by Robert Elliott's sister, much to Lizzie Ann and Ethel's disappointment, they were quite put out.

Lottie had never set eyes on her younger aunts since the day of Jessica Finlay's funeral, Jimmy Thompson's death on the Somme changed his mother into a religious fanatic, who derived macabre satisfaction from being a dead hero's mother, black worn constantly, even to a black edged hanky on Sundays, pressed to her eyes in chapel for everyone to see. Always a pale reflection of this elder sister, Lizzie Ann followed suit, no son of her own to mourn, only possessed of two daughters, neither of them married and not endowed with their cousin's looks or personality.

This unexpected visit to the big, sandstone quarry was not Lottie's first, local youngsters were forbidden to go near its murky depths, which made it even more attractive. She had been brought here once by Ralph in childhood days and taken right to the edge, clinging fast to her big brother's hand. 'If y'fall in they never find ya,' he whispered in sepulchre tones, making her hang on harder than ever, warned not to divulge where they had been. 'Ye'll get the belt an so will Aa,' he told her, silence thus ensured, close then, sad that this closeness should be lost in the lists of time, not a single word had passed between them for years and never likely to be.

News of the family did reach her, through Alice Ruddick as might be expected, Ralph's wife also helped in the chapel canteen and knowing of the connection seemed to want her husband's sister kept in the picture. Young Robert was almost eighteen and a fine young man according to Alice. Margaret had found her niche in Saltersgate, spoken well of even by Lizzie Phillips, remarried and on the receiving end of many kindnesses, a wee bit 'sackless' to use the vernacular, Lottie's sister-in-law a good manager of the little they had.

'Lottie Hanson'll never be dead as long as young Elizabeth's around,' Alice said in her friend's hearing one day and, curiosity aroused, Lottie paid a visit to The Board School when the bairns trooped out, after walking from the Branton end to avoid the village. Ralph's daughter might have been herself at the same age, except for fly away dark brown hair, easily recognised. She smiled at the ribbons clutched tightly in the lassie's hand. A poignant moment not prolonged in case of discovery but a desperate need emerged to be part of a family again. Not that she belittled that other 'family' in Rothwell House, the folk there were very dear to her heart.

'That's that,' the gaffer announced on his return to the coach breaking into these reflections. 'I shall telephone Jordan this evening, he can start on the rooms at once.' His business at the quarry was over and he was able to switch to the next thing in a trice. 'We can't have furniture arriving and the work not finished. That woman won't be able to get her hands on the east wing quickly enough.' Matron's type was simple enough to read. A nature not unlike his own, Lottie thought in amusement, everything to be done now or sooner. Sam Jordan would be a regular visitor for quite a while, with several other jobs if the gaffer could be cajoled into them, she had sufficient faith in her powers of persuasion, not that she took advantage. John Starrett was so dependent upon this young woman for stability in his life, something all his wealth could never buy. Her father would surely have frowned upon any sort of alliance with the pit gaffer, the thought was very disturbing, there had been a serious battle of loyalties ever since the colliery owner become a big part of her life, a sense of allegiance often stretched to the limit. Speculation as to what would happen if forced to come down on one side or the other, a real clash of interests, she was honest enough to confess she didn't really know, the gaffer had been there when her own kind turned their backs. A definite poser and no mistake, one she hoped never to face but she had a sinking feeling the day of reckoning was sure to come.

* * *

As the upstairs rooms and indeed the entire house took on a new look, rumour began to spread abroad that the war was about to end, a final push in the offing. Most folk were rather sceptical, with so many previous disappointments and caught up as they all were in a conflict now into its fourth year, it was a strange sort of existence to which they had become sadly accustomed and somehow learnt to live with. In the midst of it all, Alice Ruddick alarmed her friends with most unusual behaviour, Martha was first to warn Lottie, 'somethin' was goin' on,' as she put it. 'That lass is up t'no good,' she started emphatically. 'Have y'ever seen'er comb that sandy mane or take a flannel to'er face without a tellin'?' and answered her own questions before Lottie had time to open her mouth. 'No y'haven't an' neither have Aa. Now she's ferever tittivatin'.' Lottie laughed at such concern and said it was all to the good, Alice had to stop being a rag bag sooner or later. 'You should have seen her when I first got to know her properly.' Suddenly reminded of that scarecrow figure in John Coulter's field and a blackberry stained mouth. The memory of it plucked at her heart strings, a strange description for an angel of mercy as the big lass turned out to be. Another lifetime, so long ago.

'It's no laughin' matter,' Martha tutted, There's only one reason fer any lass t'start fussin' over' 'er looks.' This bombshell was dropped with immense satisfaction and immediately rewarded by Lottie's stunned expression. 'A man?' she gasped, absolutely dumbfounded, but every instinct told her it could be true and, if so, a sure road to disaster. Alice's possible involvement with a member of the opposite sex didn't bear thinking about, for obvious reasons.

'An' why not?' came the prompt reply, 'God knows there's plenty o'them on the loose these days. Young Grace widowed wi'a bairn that's not'er man's an'already wi'another chap i'tow,' Martha's tone derisive. 'An' Aa ask ya, what kind o'bloke would go after Alice? Just somebody that's on the hunt fer one thing. An'her wi'all them daft notions in'er head.'

Lottie realised something had to be done but hadn't a clue how to deal with such a delicate matter, she had a complete lack of enthusiasm for this distasteful task, real anxiety written all over her face. Martha was fully aware of this reluctance. 'Leave it t'me,' she said, 'Saltersgate's the place t'find out and it's not exactly your stampin'ground is it?' No hesitation at pushing her nose into their friend's affairs, right up the little busybody's street. But no such action was required, Alice arrived home later that day, very flushed and obviously excited, her plain, homely face wreathed in smiles. 'He wants t'meet ya, Lottie' she burst forth without preamble and took them both by surprise, Martha was speechless for once, which didn't last long. 'Meet who?' she rapped out sharply but eased off when Lottie gave her a stern look. 'Can Aa fetch'im t'the house?' Alice said and received an affirmative answer straight away. 'Anyone you like,' she was told. 'This is your home and we are your family.' Immensely relieved that the man in question wanted to make her acquaintance, one point in his favour at least.

The brawny lass's eyes lit up. 'That's what Aa sayed when'ee asked. Aa'm always on about how good ye've been t'me,' she enthused and Lottie wondered how many confidences had been revealed. What sort of fellow could be serious about a relationship with Alice? 'How about tea on Sunday?' she suggested, Martha's face the picture of disbelief. But this new friend had to be vetted without delay and the affair nipped in the bud if necessary. Sunday was a quiet day around the house and the master would be off to Harrogate, well out of the way.

'Aa'll ask'im when'ee stops by the farm, he's stationed at Branton Park. They come by on sort o'marches,' was the excited reaction, Martha was unable to restrain herself any longer. 'Oh, my God,' she exclaimed, 'some lasses'll go wi'anybody in britches.' Immediately rounded upon, Alice up in arms and ready to do battle. 'Ye've got a nasty mind, Martha Connelly, Joe's a nice lad,' she shot out in anger, red faced, Lottie quickly into calming words. 'Martha didn't mean anything, Alice. She is just worried, we both are,' and a sharp glance defied the offender to utter another word. Feelings were involved and this dear friend musn't be hurt. The Sunday couldn't arrive soon enough. Despite many mutterings and a lot of misgivings, Martha put herself out to make a special tea for Alice's Joe. 'Whatever the chap's like, he is a soldier, an'they don't get home cookin',' she declared, very proud of her culinary expertise and given another occasion to show off, even if she did disapprove of the entire affair.

Joe Simpson proved to be a big surprise, a male edition of Alice herself, someone dragged into service to do menial work, more brawn than brains. After almost four long years medical officers couldn't afford to be choosy about deficiencies, too young or too old it didn't really matter if the applicants were ready to enlist. Alice, really smartened up, blossomed in his company, pathetically pleased to have him there and most anxious for Lottie's approval, who didn't know whether to laugh or cry at times but managed to hide her anxiety, Joe was made to feel very welcome indeed. There were no snide remarks from Martha who revelled in the fellow's appreciation of her baking and he was very polite. It was later in the day after Joe departed and Martha sought an early bed that Alice opened up to provide Lottie with the whole scenario.

'We've done nowt wrong, Lottie, cross me heart. Joe's not like them chaps that hung around Lizzie Street afore you came t'bide, he's different alt'gether. He wants us t'get wed.' Lottie was absolutely overwhelmed but somewhat reassured by Alice's following words. 'Not till the war's over,' she was informed. 'He's off t'France in a couple o'weeks, anyway.' Lottie murmured sympathy at this latter bit of news, sorry to hear Joe was to be so quickly dispatched to the Front. 'You are both very wise,' she said, 'And when he comes back, I shall give you the best wedding a girl ever had.' Hoping the affair would die a natural death in the interim period, Alice not known for anything to last. Promptly they hugged, so reminiscent of the time they laughed and cried after Jessica Finlay's visit to Lizzie Street, her eyes filled with tears. 'You'll be me bridesmaid?' Alice pleaded, off into the realms of white veils and orange blossom, her ordinary features transformed by sheer happiness. Almost thirty four but she was still a girl at heart, who believed in love, marriage and babies, in that order, considered the only worthwhile things in any woman's life. She revelled in the thought of these wonders happening to her and, even if they did come to nothing, would always have her memories.

Lottie's pillows were wet again that night. Alice's joy might easily be short lived but while it lasted she could shout it from the house tops, so unlike her own tragic love never to be spoken of, locked away in an aching heart. If Geoffrey had survived the war, just to be under the same roof would have sufficed, or so she deluded herself, soon to be put to the test and found wanting.

* * *

Geoffrey Cranshawe's repatriation came two months later, first transferred to a British hospital, where thorough examination found no fault in his medical treatment by the enemy, a good job as far as it went, his blindness something else and unaccountable, there were no evident deficiencies.

Lottie clung to her gripping senses when he entered Rothwell House on the arm of his batman, a surly fellow named Stan Hodges, who made it quite plain from the outset that the Major was his concern and nobody else should interfere. There was no answering pressure from Geoffrey's fingers when she took his hand in greeting, just formal acknowledgement between master and servant. Waiting afterwards, with great impatience, for a summons which never came, and as days passed into weeks she was forced to accept he no longer wanted her in his life. The old Geoffrey was gone and a dour, withdrawn stranger had taken his place.

'A fly in the ointment,' was Martha's description of Stan Hodges, detested from the start by one and all. 'This house had more t'recommend it in yer aunt's day an'that's sayin' somethin'. Aa thought we'd seen the last o'snakes wi'Madam gone but he's the daddy o'them all,' very eloquent in voicing her opinions. 'The Major's blind all right if'ee canna see through that slimy toad. What does'ee need'im for, we could manage.' Hodges had the power to make Lottie's flesh creep, with bold admiration in his foxy eyes but she strove not to add fuel to the fire of Martha's antagonism, although much troubled by the upset the man caused among the household staff. Even Hamlet snarled when he was near, usually the friendliest of animals. Hodges made no secret of aversion to Martha's deformity and ridiculed Alice unmercifully, which did nothing for peace and harmony below stairs. An unsolvable situation without Geoffrey's co-operation, unable to approach the man she still loved with every fibre of her being. In sheer desperation she did approach John Starrett, who merely advised her to give it time. 'I appreciate your concern, Charlotte, but my son-in-law would not thank me for meddling. We hardly exchange a word these days. Be patient,' he urged, 'Blindness isn't easy to come to terms with but Geoffrey is too sensible to allow things to go on as they are.' Lottie expected more of him but acceptance of given circumstances had become a sad way of life for everyone, this was just another cross to bear. Alice Ruddick's turn came next, when her intended was killed by an unexploded shell. Joe Simpson one member of a small platoon, had been detailed to collect dead bodies from the battlefield, a grim task, some of the rotting corpses discovered when the mud dried up and often impossible to identify. Not much was left of Joe and his companions when a deadly missile was accidently probed into delayed action.

After just one week of noisy, inconsolable grief, the bereaved lass made a miraculous recovery and basked in her recently acquired status of fiancée to a dead soldier. No longer 'daft Alice' to those who knew her, she constantly flashed the cheap engagement ring which adorned the third finger of her left hand and allowed a vivid, romantic imagination to run riot, the dream in her case probably much better than the reality. Joe became her knight in shining armour, glorified beyond belief, better that way Lottie figured but saddened to think fate had played such a cruel trick with the war on its last legs, according to continuing rumour, which seemed to have more substance than usual.

But other news among them made shattering impact when Marianne announced she was going to have a baby, imparted to Lottie as they walked arm in arm down Branton Road one afternoon. Both were glad to be free of the gloomy atmosphere whivch surrounded the big house, the Jacksons' flat usually the only bolt hole Lottie had but badly in need of fresh air on this particular day.

Knocked speechless, she struggled to take it in, her lack of response unnoticed by an ecstatic Marianne, who babbled on in delight. 'I was certain there must be something wrong with me. We have been married so long and it wasn't for the want of trying,' she admitted candidly. 'I am no spring chicken but we both hoped for a child to complete our marriage. Be happy for us Lottie, please,' her eyes wonderfully alight she completely misunderstood the reason for her companion's lack of response. 'How could I be so thoughtless,' she hastened to say, only to have a neatly gloved hand squeezed reassuringly, as Lottie came to and gathered what she meant. 'Don't fret Marianne, that is all in the past, I don't dwell upon it.' A downright lie which in her euphoric state the expectant mother was prepared to accept as truth.

'Have you seen a doctor?' was the anxious query. 'You will need special care, having a first baby at your age. Let me see, you must be – ?' Smooth brows puckered in thought, soon enlightened. 'Thirty eight in August,' came the prompt reply. 'And I have consulted a doctor, who assures me lots of women have fine, healthy babies at my age. There will be a baby boom after the war ends. If mine is a girl I shall name her Charlotte, Matthew agrees.' Lottie's sharp protest was quite unexpected.

'It won't be a girl,' she hastened to say, 'Jackson always fancied a son and won't be satisfied with anything else.' An attempt at levity which brought forth a giggle of amusement from the mother to be and the tense moment slipped away. Marianne couldn't know how she hated her baptismal name, spoilt for her all those years ago when an envious female derided it out of sheer malice. Only used by the gaffer nowadays, who mostly called her 'girl'. Hardly appropriate for a thirty three year old woman. She chose her time to catch Jackson on his own rather irritated by the fatuous expression on his dear, familiar face, completely overcome by the heady prospect of fatherhood. 'Aa'm old enough t'be the bairn's gran'father' he admitted sheepishly. 'Mebbe a bit set in me ways but Aa'll do me best t'be a good father.' Rather surprised to hear Lottie voice her misgivings. 'Marianne tells me she is four months gone and it is hardly noticeable, you must take care of her,' she urged. 'Make sure she doesn't overdo things, stop working in that hospital for a start. And if you are short of money, you know where to come, I did as you told me and saved all those coppers.' A reference to the past he fully understood and smiled at the memory of that eighteen year old girl. Amusement which soon faded at the melancholy look in her beautiful eyes. 'You were wrong about money, Mattie, it is a necessity and terrible for those without but there are more important things in life.' He sighed as she walked away, with that familiar lift to her slender shoulders and a straightened back. Too many burdens to bear.

As Lottie guessed somehow, Marianne's pregnancy was a difficult one, being almost four months into it before she realised she might be, because of irregular periods and an idea that it was never going to happen. She had worked hard in the hospital during that time, when more care should have been taken and now nothing seemed to go right. 'Don't tell Matthew,' she begged Lottie, after one of many nauseating bouts of sickness, which never seemed to let up. 'He worries. You know how prospective fathers can be' clinging to her for support when the spasm ended and her strength drained, a sorry sight with a pinched, white face. This baby was a mistake, a big mistake, Lottie was worried enough to confide in Martha who shared the same opinion.

'If that lass goes full time it'll be a miracle,' was the gloomy forecast and did her best to tempt an almost non existent appetite with small delicacies, most upset when her efforts were in vain, the food just picked at. 'Sh'should be eatin'fer two,' she argued, a fallacy maybe but the sickly woman took barely enough sustenance for herself, let alone an unborn child. As if all this wasn't enough, Hodges continued to be objectionable and threw his weight around at every opportunity, Geoffrey confined to Felicity's old suite of rooms, now a voluntary prison. She had had no idea when they were refurbished what their ultimate use would be. Fanciful, perhaps, but it seemed that Madam's malignant presence still hung around her blind husband to do him harm. The man servant strove to make himself indispensable in every way, all weighed up in terms of a permanent cushy number, made easy for him by Geoffrey's terrible apathy, no man would be subjected to such coddling against his will. A state which Lottie failed to recognise as self defence, dreadfully afraid of pity from the woman he kept at a distance, whose presence in the same house was an actual torment. Two souls in agony and no apparent solution to their problem. Forced to supplement meagre resources, beggars arrived regularly at the tradesman's entrance to Rothwell House, disabled ex-servicemen who deserved better treatment from a country for which they had fought and suffered, soul destroying for proud men with families to support. 'It's a crying shame,' Lottie raged, after feeding the fourth man in less than a week, all sent off with money in their pockets. 'They shouldn't have to beg,' she flung at Mattie Jackson, who hid his own feelings in a touch of sarcasm. 'Heroes are forgotten when the bands stop playin' an' the flag wavin'comes to an end. This is just the tip of the iceberg. Y'canna help them all lass.' More distressed than he showed by empty sleeves and trousers fastened up from the bottom with safety pins.

Lottie rounded on him furiously. 'The bands haven't stopped playing yet, nor flags flying, men are still being killed and wounded,' she threw at him. 'It isn't like you to be so short on sympathy Mattie Jackson.' An accusation which didn't go unchallenged. 'Aa'm not,' he said, 'An don't say Aa'm havin' it easy i'the shipyard, Aa tried t'join up.' His obvious disgruntlement showed. 'Anyway, charity begins at home, there's plenty needed on yer own doorstep,' An undeniable fact which soon calmed her down.

Reluctant to leave affairs in the hands of underlings, John Starrett spent long hours at his three collieries. Men of Ralph Hanson's ilk did return to the pits, glad to be free of that all pervading stench of death, even if the alternative was underpaid, dangerous work. But old grievances lay just beneath the surface, ready to erupt when the time was right. A world for heroes with a cow and an acre of land was an exploded myth.

Late one evening Lottie overheard a one sided conversation on the telephone, it was not hard to catch the drift. 'Get rid of the fellow!' John Starrett bellowed forth. 'That Reid chap is a confounded trouble maker.' A brief pause then another explosion. 'Union official or not, get rid of him, a lesson to the others, a lot of sheep letting themselves be led by the nose. Think of some pretext to trip him up. If you don't your own job is on the line.' And the receiver was immediately hung up. She wanted to run from her position at the top of the stairs and hurl herself at this autocratic tyrant, to rain heavy blows on him, further angered when he caught sight of her and smiled, his hand raised in acknowledgement when she passed down into the kitchen, seething at such underhand methods to achieve his own ends.

The sad sequel soon came, Alice brought news of Bob Reid's dismissal, the manager had obviously obeyed the gaffer's instructions. A paltry excuse for doing so angered his fellow workmen, who wanted to strike in protest, but were urged to bide their time, coal was essential towards ending a war which had lasted far too long and at such a terrible cost. Bob Reid would never work in mines on the Northumbrian coal field again, nor anywhere else, the old boy's network would see to that, coal owners were ruthless in support of mutual interests.

A few days later, the equivalent of two gold sovereigns arrived by postal order at the Reid home in Theresa Street, sent by an unknown donor to help out. Some of Jessica Finlay's money had been used in a way she would have much deplored, the recipients more than grateful, never to discover to whom they were indebted.

Eviction soon followed and the family crossed the River Tyne into Gateshead, where a sympathetic building contractor in a small family business employed Bob as a navvy, the interim period before accommodation came to hand spent in overcrowded conditions with relatives in the river area, nobody in Saltersgate was foolhardy enough to take them in.

Spring moved into summer with the end of the war a real possibility, civilian starvation and suffering in Germany a relevant factor. In January of that year women over thirty years of age were given the vote, suffragettes were cock-a-hoop but not yet satisfied. Lottie read the print off all radical newspapers purchased secretly, kept well hidden in a Conservative household, and waged constant battle with Mattie Jackson, his liberal allegiance hard to take. 'Both of us working class and you were always a rebel against the establishment like myself,' she remonstrated strongly and often. 'You of all people should vote Labour.' Quite put out by an uncompromising attitude.

'Labour has t'be tried an'this isn't the time. Aa want t'see what they're made of before Aa change me vote. Better the devil y'know,' adding a stern warning. 'An'ye better keep yer mouth shut around the gaffer,' afraid that wayward tongue might run away with her, thankfully more controlled for some time. But this didn't mean the Hanson temper wasn't there waiting to erupt, given sufficient provocation. Marianne stayed out of these heated discussions, only concerned with the problems of pregnancy, not a well woman. 'I don't know why the pair of you argue so much,' she did remark after one stormy session. 'Besides, the woman's vote isn't likely to make much difference.' 'Maybe not yet but when all women have the vote, which they deserve after the man sized jobs they've been doing for four years almost,' Lottie was on her high horse, which she rode continually, really uptight about it all. 'Rubbish,' Marianne countered, 'most women will vote the same way as their husbands or employers, the feudal system still exists. All that forced feeding and tying themselves to the railings for nothing,' she said flatly, much too weary to care.

Despite concern for Marianne's condition, Lottie was appalled by such an attitude especially from the person who taught her so much. 'God forbid that approaching motherhood should make an educated woman into a cabbage.' she retorted, halted by the strained look on her friend's face. The sooner the child was born with a swift return to normality the better, hardly a word to use in connection with Rothwell House, where they went from one crisis to another in quick succession.

The war did look like coming to an end, the civilian population in Kaiser Wilhelm's Germany were on their last legs but there was no sympathy to spare for them, a big enough mess to clear up on the home front, the aftermath likely to be worse than anybody imagined. Politicians were gearing themselves for an early election but Mattie Jackson stopped rising to the bait, determined to keep a low profile, aware of her strong feelings. His main concern was the gentle woman who meant so much to him and whose failing strength continued to be a great worry to them all.

* * *

John Starrett's new automobile and Mattie Jackson's son arrived upon the scene within three days of one another, the war now two months from its end. Due to the gaffer's wealth, and connections in the right circles, it was the first magnificent vehicle of its kind to appear on the streets of Oakfields, almost to the sound of trumpets. Jackson was like a child with a new toy, the gaffer delighted his former coachman had learnt to drive. Martha's prediction of a premature birth was very likely but there was no sign of it happening when the household staff gathered around to inspect and duly admire this latest acquisition. Only Marianne was absent from the scene, resting as she was so often obliged to do, a poorly soul.

'If Mattie Jackson carries on like this over a blessed contraption, God help us all when that bairn arrives,' Martha was suspicious of any innovation, a great believer in the status quo whether good or bad, very wary of change and this shining monster represented that to no small degree.

Lottie regarded it with rather mixed feelings, more of them were soon to appear in such an affluent neighbourhood, to which war had brought a number of changes. Long established residents were gone for various reasons, older occupants of fine residences in the area had passed away with no family to succeed them, their homes acquired by a new breed of folk with money to burn but lacking the gentility of their predecessors and having to strive for acceptance into a charmed circle. The nouveau riche had made fortunes out of war and it was the beginning of a vastly different era.

Alice flatly refused to look at the new car, terribly upset to see Tiger transferred to a small outhouse, the other horse already sold, their stables converted into a roomy garage. She was rather perturbed about John Starrett's plans for the dear old pony which, never one to drag his feet, were soon divulged.

'I have spoken to Reuben Strange,' he informed Lottie when she attended for her daily instructions, a routine never varied unless out of town on periodic visits to Harrogate. 'Reuben is quite prepared to put Tiger out to pasture on his farm. Don't worry he won't be overworked, just rides for his grandchildren when they visit.' A long time friend who owned land adjacent to Whitegates. 'Alice can deliver him, trap and all,' a human touch which endeared him once again but small comfort to the heartbroken lass who tended the pony so devotedly.

'What'll Aa do wi'no horses t'mind?' she wailed like a banshee, an answer soon forthcoming. 'Get stuck in wi'work yer supposed t'do,' Martha said abruptly, 'There's plenty o'chores in this house fer when yer in from the farm, which isn't all that often. Ye've had it easy far too long, me lass.' A sad misjudgement of affairs, farm work not being a piece of cake, she was given a reproachful look but no verbal retaliation. Alice didn't get into conflict with Martha unless it couldn't be avoided.

After numerous hugs and a tearful farewell, she left her former charge at Glebe Farm and travelled back to Rothwell House in an army ambulance, laid on by Matron at Whitegates, which still housed casualties of war, soon to be sent elsewhere and the grand mansion sold, a wonderful buy for anyone with sufficient money. Fortunes were already being made by sale of surplus army equipment, backhanders not unheard of to expedite such nefarious transactions.

Jackson's first official duty was to collect Victoria from Newcastle Central, three weeks of this summer vacation already spent with a friend in Wales. He now wore a smart black uniform with silver buttons and a peaked cap, a returned serviceman glad of his job in the shipyard, disabled but not badly so, strings pulled by the gaffer as might be supposed. With a polishing cloth in his hands before setting off, he failed to notice Lottie's disappointment when told there would be no room for an extra passenger on the return journey, with all the luggage their young mistress was certain to bring. 'Aa reckon the gaffer should o'bought a lorry,' he commented drily, the car a welcome diversion from anxiety and his over the top enthusiasm thus encouraged.

Lottie sincerely hoped Victoria might arouse Geoffrey from his terrible lethargy, restore some semblance of life which, from the moment she breezed into the house and sought her father out seemed highly possible. Stan Hodges was treated with haughty disdain by a self assured teenager, Martha's opinion of Geoffrey's batman already revealed and so forewarned, ready to dig her heels in.

'Good gracious, Papa,' she exclaimed in disgust on entering his stuffy quarters. 'Why are you sitting huddled up in that chair. A lovely autumn day and not a window open. This place is like a mausoleum.' Striding across the room to pull down a sash window. 'There, no draughts, just good fresh air to circulate.' She took her father's hands and pulled him to his feet, secretly appalled at the sight before her. 'I know you can't see but you can feel and should know your way around this room like the back of your hand. Now,' she said in her light, young voice, 'here begins the first lesson. I am standing near the window, come and find me, the way is clear. You stay where you are Hodges,' she snapped and took no pains to hide her immediate dislike for this creep of a man.

Geoffrey seemed reluctant to obey but, after slight hesitation and further persuasion moved slowly towards the input of fresh air and the direction of his daughter's voice gently coaxing. 'I am much too old to play games, Victoria,' he protested but kept moving nevertheless when she persisted. 'Nonsense, Papa, this is a bid for independence, long overdue,' and glared at Hodges who hovered in the background, inwardly seething. 'Bossy little madam,' he smarted, very much aware his master's daughter might easily upset his well made plans. 'It's all right, sir, I am here,' he placated, as if to a child, Victoria's blue eyes dangerously alight, prepared to do battle. 'Then maybe it would be better if you were somewhere else,' she barked, deliberately cutting him down to size. 'My father can do without your services at the moment, I am here.' As indeed she was and very much in control of the situation. Hodges didn't demur and moved to another spot, not too far away but out of sight, ready to intrude upon the scene if the opportunity arose, absolutely livid but too wise to interfere.

'Just a few more steps, Papa,' Victoria persuaded, Geoffrey was soon rewarded by two loving arms wrapped around him when he reached his target. 'That wasn't too difficult was it. You must get Hodges to try more of it when I am gone,' and knowing fine well the man was within earshot said very deliberately. 'But not while I am here.' An antagonism was born at that moment between herself and Geoffrey's batman which coloured their entire relationship from then onwards.

When Victoria related this little episode later in the day, renewed hope awakened in Lottie's heart, delighted to see father and daughter walking in the grounds arm in arm, hearing the girl's lively chatter and the odd chuckle at what she was saying, a wonderful sound. Geoffrey was more animated than he had been in months, Victoria a great tonic, but it was still impossible for Lottie to reconcile this man with the handsome soldier who went to war, into whose strong arms she once melted with such urgency, her own desire reciprocated, easily recognised by the hardness of his manhood pressed against an eagerly responsive body. Feelings she wanted to experience again but she was unable to break down the barriers he had so successfully erected to keep them apart.

After their stroll, Victoria returned her father into Hodges' suffocating care, Geoffrey sorely in need of rest, unused to even such simple exercise for so long a time. 'We are driving to the coast tomorrow,' she announced to Lottie indoors, 'Grandpa will let us use the car if I ask.' A mere formality, the one person who found it impossible to deny this young whirlwind anything. 'Martha will pack a luncheon basket for us and we shall picnic in the car, close to the sea. Papa musn't catch cold and it can be a bit nippy,' she said. 'Hodges can have the day off, he isn't included.' Quick to observe the uneasy expression on Lottie's face. 'I don't know why you let him ride rough shod over all of you. Why doesn't Grandpa give the man his marching orders?' The solution to the problem was quite simple in this young girl's decided opinion. Just what Lottie thought, still annoyed at John Starrett's refusal to take action, usually such a dominant personality. But she was forced to admit, in all fairness, that Geoffrey himself represented the main drawback, difficult to explain this to Victoria, whose own tactics seemed to be working. If only the influence lasted after she left and Hodges tried to resume full control without success, something Lottie prayed for but didn't believe possible.

Victoria was a pretty teenager, not so beautiful as Lottie at the same age but she had all the makings of a very attractive woman. Soft, silky blonde hair cascaded around slim shoulders, gorgeous blue eyes a very distinctive feature in a pert young face. A daughter any mother could be proud of, the hope of ever being acknowledged as such never totally abandoned, although where proof could be discovered was now impossible to ascertain. They had no idea of how they complimented one another, two enchanting examples of absolute femininity, Lottie's rich auburn hair and hazel eyes more fascinating than ever, a great attraction to admiring males when she walked abroad on Branton High Street. Sad that the only man whose admiration she really desired should be unable to see either Victoria or herself.

Mattie Jackson could have been a stumbling block to these picnic plans but Marianne persuaded him to go, secretly tired of his constant fussing, reluctant to leave her side for any length of time. 'Babies are women's work,' she told him, 'And ours isn't due yet.' Her words were endorsed by Lottie who would rather have been included in the outing but consoled herself with Hodge's obvious disgruntlement at his exclusion.

'All this belongs t'yer gran'father,' Jackson pointed out as they drove through Studley, only one of many mining villages en route to the north east coast, all monotonous in their similarity. The whole area was dominated by distinctive winding wheels and slack heaps. Rows of drab houses all led towards the pit head, colliery life lived and breathed thereabouts. So many poorly clad youngsters roamed the streets, some bare footed, staring at the motor car as it drove past, an unusual sight. Victoria's eyes observed them with keen interest, faced with the real image of poverty for the second time in a sheltered existence. That first, brief encounter with Robert Hanson completely forgotten, the war years and more between than and now, she had been too young when it happened to stay with her for long. 'Why are their clothes so worn and some without shoes?' she asked, very disturbed by it all. 'Y'need money t'buy them,' was Jackson's dry retort, his eyes firmly fixed on the road ahead, in case one of the bairns darted in front of the car. 'But their fathers must work,' she insisted and it was Geoffrey who answered, this time in a rather sarcastic tone. 'They do work, my dear, very hard indeed, but honest toil doesn't always provide such luxuries as footwear.'

'But they work for Grandpa,' she exclaimed in surprise, reluctant to let the matter drop. 'Yes, most of them go down the mine,' Geoffrey replied in gentler tone and realised by her silence that an inquiring mind had been given food for thought. He did not see her face suddenly light up, the problem solved. 'Then grandfather must pay them more wages and I shall tell him so. He can't possibly know these children run around so poorly clad.' Jackson's grim smile matched by her father's wry twist of the mouth, both wondering how John Starrett would talk himself out of this situation. Would Victoria soften his heart, where others had failed? A very debatable point. Jackson wasn't into speed, he sat in the driving seat, proud as a peacock, moving through countryside scarred by coal mines and their accompanying paraphernalia. Five or six miles of this before they came to a long avenue of young saplings, fringing the road at both sides of the last lap, likely to be an impressive landmark when they reached maturity, all deciduous of varied species. Not leafy enough yet to obscure Delaval Hall, a stately home only half a mile from the sea at Seaton Sluice, one owned by the so called mad Delavals but now in other hands, their escapades legendary almost, when told in Mattie Jackson's broad Geordie dialect very entertaining indeed. Before long the companionable trio pulled in at the roadside near the dunes, beyond which rolled the Great North Sea. Jackson hailed a passing army officer to make sure it was all right to park. The man leant towards the car and expressed agreement but suddenly caught sight of Geoffrey. 'Captain Cranshawe,' he exclaimed in surprise. 'I heard –' he began then hesitated, 'You heard I was a gonna,' Geoffrey finished for him, 'I almost was … But you have me at a disadvantage and it's a long time since I held that rank. I ended up as Major before the war, Who are you may I ask?'

'Don't you recognise me, sir. I knew you at once,' the officer stated, now with the rank of captain himself. 'My father is blind,' Victoria broke in to ease the situation, 'Perhaps if you gave him your name?'

'Pendleton, sir, I was a subaltern on the Frontier. Maybe you don't remember but I brought a present home for your daughter's fifth birthday this is she, I suppose, quite grown up,' Gazing at Victoria's youthful beauty quite admiringly. Geoffrey was delighted to be recognised, despite his gaunt appearance. But he did have distinctive features which obviously struck a chord of memory. 'Sorry about the blindness, sir. It must be hell. I never made France, rather prone to malaria, so when I returned from India, the Front was out. I'm on coastal defence in this area, a bit of a snip compared with what those other poor devils are getting over there.'

'I remember now,' Victoria said quickly, when she saw her father's mouth tighten in memory. 'It was a sari you brought, it took me ages to grow into it but I was quite small. I don't know what happened to it, I'm afraid.'

'I delivered it to your mother in London, a very beautiful lady. How is she, sir?'

'My wife is no longer with us,' was the brusque reply and Pendleton naturally assumed Felicity was dead and didn't pursue the subject.

Mattie Jackson could have told them the beautiful garment's ultimate fate, destroyed by madam in one of her fits of drunken rage. Lottie in tears when she came down to the kitchen with the torn shreds in her hands.

Nothing more was said and the officer made his departure with a smart salute, Geoffrey quite elated to be remembered after so long a time, knowing without being told how dreadful he must look. There was khaki everywhere and just a few civilians, some walking dogs, the beaches were wired and had to be avoided. The three of them soon fell to and made short shrift of Martha's more than ample provisions, sea air obviously stimulated the appetite, even Geoffrey's which needed a lot of tempting. But, for once, he felt glad to be alive, Victoria's lively chatter was an absolute tonic, a heartwarming sight Jackson wished Lottie were there to see.

After a homeward detour by way of Hepscott and other small Northumbrian hamlets, some coal mining villages in the midst of agricultural land, they reached Rothwell House later than intended to find its occupants in a sorry state. Marianne's premature labour had begun, Jackson was thrown into immediate panic and flew into the flat to be at her side. There was a long, hard struggle before her son came into the world, a world whose future was impossible to envisage. Fortunately both mother and child survived but Marianne never fully recovered her strength and none of the joy so eagerly anticipated actually materialised.

The war came to an end at 11 a.m. on November 11th 1918 to a great deal of flag waving this time in rejoicing but rather subdued in many cases, relieved of course, but some had lost their all and prospects for survivors were none too favourable in its aftermath. The number eleven figured quite largely in important events at the time, that number of days after the armistice when the country went to the polls, Lloyd George returned to Downing Street as Prime Minister of a coalition government, which many believed would not be in office very long, most people badly affected by four years of sheer hell and much too war weary to care.

* * *

A war, supposedly to end all wars was over at last and the hope of everlasting peace between nations unlikely to be realised. Old hatreds still remained and that inherent trait in man towards power and self seeking was guaranteed to rise to the surface again with disastrous results. Treaties were just sheets of paper with scribbled signatures, and an excuse was always to be found to invalidate them if expedient. The assassination of some important personage and the balloon goes up, used as an excuse but seldom the real reason for reneging on the pledged word and nobody to say who held the gun. In the meantime there were pieces to be picked up, an abundance of them in all countries, allied and enemy alike, no easy task for victor or vanquished, if indeed there were a victor in such a horrendous conflict which wasted so many young lives. Mattie Jackson's son quickly thrived but his mother never fully recovered and David, as they named him, became more or less Lottie's responsibility, with assistance from Martha and Alice, all three of them wrapped up in this new addition to the wider family. Jackson became obsessed with guilt for the pregnancy which almost took his wife's life, and previously overjoyed at the prospect of fatherhood, now stood back from the role, Marianne his sole concern.

Appalled at this state of affairs, Lottie knew that sooner or later he must be faced with his responsibility and didn't look forward to being the one to do it. David, cruelly deprived of a frail mother's wholehearted attention needed the security of his father's total awareness and Mattie Jackson failed miserably in this direction, so much out of character, Marianne was much too weak to realise what was happening.

The time leading up to David's third birthday saw great disturbance in the coal fields, the Parish Relief man was often seen around Saltersgate's cobbled lanes, vetting homes for the least sign of luxury when families were obliged to apply for benefit, the word luxury given a very wide definition. A system which cried out to be thwarted, poor folk became quite adept in dealing with it, united in their efforts. This unpopular visitor's presence was soon made known, as if by bush telegraph and combined measures were taken towards concealment of the few pitiful treasures folk possessed, everything of value hurried next door in a jiffy, front door or back, whichever the situation warranted. This public servant was only there to do his job but was severely ostracised because of it.

On May 21st 1921, Marianne Jackson passed away, a day to be remembered by coal miners thereafter as Black Friday, left alone in a strike meant to include men of other industries, thirteen weeks of it, this desertion a sore point for years to come. Of no consequence to Mattie Jackson, sadly bereft by the loss of his beloved wife. 'How shall Aa manage without'er?' he groaned in anguish, a lifeless body held close in his arms. 'Wi' all the useless buggars i'this world not worth their salt, why did'ee have t'take her,' he raged against the Almighty. 'What's left fer me wi'her gone?'

'Your son,' Lottie told him in some impatience. 'You do have one, Marianne's child. God knows she suffered plenty to have him. Take care of David as his mother would have wished, make something of the lad.' And hardened her heart at the agony on his well loved face. 'A bairn needs a mother,' he shot out in his grief, cutting short the other words which hovered on her tongue, quick to add, 'Oh aye, Aa can work fer'im an'see'ee gets a good education but there's more t'fetchin'up a bairn than that.' Very despondent and ready to throw in the towel, an attitude totally alien to Lottie Hanson's nature, a fighter against adversity, this fact had been proven times without number.

The Hanson temper flew into action and she lashed out, Jackson had to be forced out of such negative thinking. 'All right,' she admitted, 'It won't be easy but you don't have to shoulder it alone. There are three grown women in Rothwell House, all prepared to lend a hand. Not the same as having his own mother but he won't go short on love, or anything else come to that,' her impatience was quite evident, hardly the time or place but it had to be said. 'Yer fergettin'the gaffer. Bairns get i'the way,' he stated gloomily but did begin to brighten up a little, his spirits lifted even further as Lottie carried on, determined to make him see sense. 'Don't give the gaffer a second thought. Be what he may, a black hearted devil sometimes, he has never refused any reasonable request where his household staff was concerned. Think about Grace Jennings and how he allows Alice to work at the farm,' and she pressed on relentlessly, now sure of his full attention.

'David spends a lot of time in the kitchen, that's where he is now.' Too kind to remind him Marianne had never been able to cope with such a spirited youngster, always grateful to have him taken off her hands, Jackson had been kept in ignorance of a lot, to save him anxiety. Young David, like all children, transferred his affection to those who gave him most attention, never aware of his delicate mother as a creature of flesh and blood, more the angel she had undoubtedly become.

'Well – if yer sure?' he queried with some hesitation. 'Aa was gonna contact me sister i'South Shields.' 'Over my dead body,' Lottie thought and inwardly cringed, imagining Marianne's reaction to such a dreadful idea. Jackson's sister was a kindly soul but semi literate and no desire to be anything else. Absolutely horrifieed she assured him they could cope if they all pulled together. 'David's old enough to stay in the coach house with you at night, Mattie, good company for you, but we'll attend to his needs throughout the day. If he should be sick at any time, I'll take him with me,' Martha and Alice's willingness to co-operate was not in question, both devoted to the little lad. Jackson's face crumpled. 'Yer a fine lass, Lottie Hanson,' he choked out, her hands clasped in the fervour of gratitude, tears in his tired eyes, weary from many sleepless hours over the last few weeks. 'Who was always there to give me a helping hand?' she said, deep emotion hidden in brusqueness, reminded of this man's staunch friendship through the years and the great debt she owed the still figure on the bed, whose hard graft in hospital had eventually taken its toll, strong only in spirit.

A few days later, Marianne was laid to rest in a sheltered spot near the west wall in South Branton cemetery, the new part as it was known, already filling up as the area became more populated. Few were there to witness the brief internment at the graveside, Saltersgate folk otherwise occupied and Jackson's wife not one of them, a lady to her finger tips but a true friend to those who knew her well, none more than Lottie Hanson, to whom she gave the great gift of learning, a rich legacy.

* * *

The usual bravado existed at the beginning of the present strike but it didn't take long to bite with disastrous effect, it was the women who suffered most, the little there was usually going to bairns and menfolk, in that order. 'Aa had mine afore y'come in,' the well worn excuse, which fooled nobody. Nothing was ever said but something was always left on husband's plates, which they could have nicely licked as clean as a whistle. Kept well informed by farm labourers who lived in the village, Alice passed news on, wise enough on this occasion to keep her visits down, the horror of that previous experience never completely forgotten, deeming it better not to aggravate the situation, although relationships had improved since then. When she did venture forth it was never empty handed and Lottie didn't question as to the wherewithal, nor check the store cupboard. What the eye didn't see the heart didn't grieve over, a good policy.

John Starrett insisted on police protection and Martha railed incessantly at the inconvenience but still supplied the men on duty with numerous cups of tea, thriving upon snippets of information gleaned from loose tongues. 'Ye lot should think shame,' she accused on one occasion, 'them pit lads are workin' class the same as yerselves,' strong criticism in her words, one scarlet faced copper was quick to defend his actions, 'Aa'm just doin' me job, Missis. When y'take on this uniform yet sworn t'uphold the law.' Martha straight into the fray, no hesitation. 'An' who is it makes the blessed laws?' she said, going on to answer her own question. 'Them wi'money an'power, that's who. The rest of us are just mugs that have t'toe the line or end up i'jail.' She spat out, very formidable when aroused, despite her lack of inches. After which the men quickly downed their mugs of tea and made a hasty retreat.

The gaffer spent little time at home, idle pits were a huge responsibility, pumps to be manned and other safety measures to follow if mines were to be workable when the strike ended, the outcome inevitable but not without a struggle. Wages, as usual, were the main reason for this dispute. A lot of patience was required to deal with John Starrett in his disgruntled moods, Lottie was used as a confidante. He was so wrapped up in his own biased opinions her lack of response went unnoticed, silence taken as a sign of agreement. Stan Hodges deliberately incited Martha whenever possible, scathing in his opposition to the miners' cause, cock-a-hoop whenever the law took a hand. 'What d'ye know about it anyway?' she flung at him one morning. 'Ye've got yersel a nice cushy number, lickin' a blind man's boots.' A barb which reached its mark, his face red with anger. 'Take a good look at yerself. Not many folk would have y'round them with a humpy back starin' them i' the face for good an' constant.' Halted from further comment by Lottie's swift retaliation, truly incensed by such a cruel jibe, she let herself go, abandoning that cool, aloof manner to scorch him with her tongue.

'Take what you came for, Hodges, and leave this kitchen. Martha is a long serving, well respected member of the household staff, if I hear any more of such talk, I shall speak to Mr Starrett and have you dismissed.' Hodges was not slow to remind her that Major was his employer and might think otherwise.'

'Your employer, maybe, but in someone else's house. Don't push your luck,' she blazed, infuriated by the fellow's insolence. Hodges' bold, calculating eyes raked her shapely figure from top to toe with sheer impudence, reminiscent of Cud Matthews the same lecherous type, who tried to strip a woman naked with one all embracing glance. Although terribly disturbed she stared him out just as she did with Jake Snowdon at Jessica Finlay's funeral, Hodges was first to look away. Partial victory, at least, but she was left with a nasty taste in her mouth, knowing she had made an enemy, a dangerous one at that.

'Good riddance t'bad rubbish,' Martha erupted when he left the kitchen. 'Aa could stick a knife i' that slimy creature's guts an' watch'im bleed t'death. But ye look out Lottie, Aa see the way'ee eyes ya at times. Not the sort t'meet in a dark alley. Trouble, mark my words,' she snorted and gave the fire a hefty poke to vent her spleen. 'Here all this time an'no sign of 'im takin' his hook. Miss Victoria's the only one that can fettle 'im,' she stated in truth. Lottie said no more but thought a great deal, Hodges was a real thorn in the flesh and not to be underestimated.

None of them knew how much their friend grieved at Geoffrey Cranshawe's refusal to accept his condition and find compensations, learn

Braille, walk Hamlet but most of all to take comfort from her loving arms, lower the barriers he had erected between them. 'I would do anything,' she vowed and meant it, so much happiness had been thrown away because Geoffrey could not face up to life. She was totally unconscious of how his heart leapt at the sound of her voice, alert to every footstep when she passed his door on her way downstairs. And the smell of lavender that lingered in parts of the house he sometimes frequented, always with Hodges at his back. 'Oh Lottie,' he so often agonised in despair, never able to forget the warmth of her body in his arms and those eagerly responsive lips. His life was an empty void that only she could fill but vowed he would never allow her to sacrifice herself for him, not realising it would be no sacrifice at all. The following weeks saw many ugly scenes in and around the area, police obliged to use force when the odd black leg or two were set upon as they tried to reach the pit, their familieis ostracised, even children in school. Alice's stories became ever more alarming as time dragged on, starting to visit Saltersgate quite regularly. 'Aa'm i' the good books,' she stated smugly, 'Wi' me workin' odd times at the farm, Aa can lay me hands on a thing or two t'help out. The boss doesn't know how many eggs the hens lay, an' a few taties out of each bag'll never be missed,' she gloated triumphantly, Lottie was hard pushed to hide a smile.

'And the rest,' she sighed, thinking of the store cupboards in Rothwell House, but some sort of reprimand was needed and she felt bound to deliver it. 'There's jail for anyone caught stealing. And that's what it is, my girl, whatever you might say,' secretly proud of Alice's ingenuity for taking just a little at a time, never too much. A guilty look exchanged with Martha showed she was a partner in crime. 'Perhaps I should check around this house more often,' she put in drily and watched her words go home. 'But that might be bolting the stable door when the horse is gone.' No word of protest from either of her companions, real proof of guilt.

She didn't pursue the matter further, it was rough justice if John Starrett's food found its way into hungry bellies, he could well afford the loss. He trusted her implicitly, rather a wry thought, she was surprised how little it bothered her, definitely anti establishment at the present time. But one disturbing item of news came too close for comfort, Alice burst into the kitchen, straight to the point. 'Your Ralphie's been nobbled,' she gasped. 'Him an' Boxer Smith, Tom Curran an' all,' babbling almost incoherently. Lottie was absolutely transfixed. No time for senseless animosity, it was all gone by now on her part at least. She knew the capers striking miners got involved in, the heavy penalties if caught, and her anxiety deepened as Alice prattled on.

'They tipped the heavy brewery wagon over, at the end o'Chapel Street. They'd been hidin' behind the Catholic School wall till it got there. Beer was runnin' down the gutters,' she finished gleefully.

Martha grunted her disgust. 'Aa bet some o'them were on their hands an'knees lickin'it up. Me mother used t'say some men would drink ale through a shitten clout.' Crude as ever and she exploded into ribald laughter, immediately chastised. Lottie saw no humour in her brother's possible imprisonment. 'Be quiet,' she rapped out, 'And stop that silly cackling.' Going on to demand of Alice, if this were the whole story, which she knew fine well it couldn't be.

'They've been taken t'Newcastle i'the Black Maria. Annie Macey sayed there was coppers swarmin' all over the street in no time at all. Folk reckon they'd been keepin' watch in Pearson's front room since afore daylight.' Full of it and delighted to be at the centre of attention.

'That figures,' Lottie said, tight lipped, 'Billy Pearson's a blackleg and must have kept his ear to the ground. It all adds up.' The picture now became clear. 'It's a pity they get so carried away with their antics and don't credit the police with any brains. Get my coat, please, I am going to Maria Street.'

'Yer what?' Martha choked out, quite taken aback, Alice too, who breathed incredulously. 'Y'haven't been near Saltersgate fer donkeys years.' Unaware of that surreptitious visit to the Board School to see Elizabeth. But she dashed off to Lottie's room and soon returned with a grey serge coat draped across her arm, quite put out.

'Aa'm not sure how folk'll take it, y'couldn't o'picked a worse time,' she moaned, nevertheless she helped Lottie on with the coat, a very plain but smart garment.

'If the gaffer sends for me, say you don't know where I am. Not that he's in yet and won't be I guess with so much going on.' Lottie was so determined nothing would stop her. 'Wait a minute,' Martha said, 'Aa'm comin' wi'ya. No tellin'what might happen.' The idea of the of the little woman in the role of protector rather ridiculous, her strongest weapon a sharp tongue. 'No Martha, this is something I must do alone,' was the firm reply, as Lottie made her way towards the outside stairway, shoulders lifted and back straightened as usual, ready for whatever might occur. The two occupants left behind in the room could only stare anxiously as they watched her retreating figure through the basement window, no easy task in front of her.

* * *

There were no shades of darkness to cloak Lottie Hanson's long delayed return to Maria Street, instead it was a fine summer evening, the sort when Saltersgate women sat on their doorsteps to escape the stifling atmosphere inside the house and a grand opportunity to get all the local gossip, or to have the satisfaction of passing a juicy bit of it on. An excursion into her past for John Hanson's daughter, a mind immediately besieged by memories especially that eventful day when she turned her back on the village forever, a forever which was ending right at that very minute, as she turned past Cud Matthews' smallholding towards Lizzie Street and Alice's old home. There was no sign of Cud, Jake Snowdon and himself spared the rigours of the trenches, dark whispers in Jake's case, venereal disease not virulent in colliery villages but he mixed with city prostitutes and it might well have been that. As for Cud, nobody was quite sure why he wasn't taken, food production maybe but his acreage hardly lent itself to much in that direction, perhaps he was unfit for some reason or other, never divulged. The two men certainly weren't the pals they used to be, perhaps Cud had wised up, there were signs of it the day of Jessica Finlay's funeral, consorting with the Devil a sure way to hell.

Lottie's name reached the ears from all sides as she made her way towards Maria Street, many unfamiliar faces, some known as youngsters now mothers with families, no shortage of bairns running the streets, mostly barefooted. But all in whispers, no loud name calling and no violence, so much the lady in manner and bearing, far removed from the frightened lass banished by cruel tongues, that momentous Friday afternoon so long ago.

She soon began to doubt the wisdom of her mission, a foolish impulse maybe, filled with apprehension as she neared her destination, mixed feelings at the idea of coming face to face with her family but immensely relieved Ralph would not be among them, although distressed at the circumstances which took him away. No back lane, the front door on this occasion and a young giant who opened it in answer to her knock, a head taller than his father and a real Hanson, apart from that copper coloured hair, her own crowning glory. She was willing to bet he hated it.

Robert Hanson stared at her through bright blue eyes, their likeness to Victoria's almost uncanny. He stood there and forced his aunt to make the first approach. 'Hello Robert,' she said, 'I believe you know who I am, a long time since we met. Will you ask your mother if I am allowed to cross the threshold, if not perhaps she will come to the door?' He shuffled awkwardly, from one foot to the other, obviously taken aback. 'Me father's not here,' he stammered self consciously, strangely reluctant to call his mother, who suddenly appeared of her own accord and hazel eyes met dull blue in sharp assessment, not for the first time. Margaret was astounded at the identity of her visitor, each aware of changes in the other. Lottie improved with maturity, a beautiful woman, but her sister-in-law's former prettiness was faded beyond belief. Only the quiet dignity remained, no sign of fluster, just the briefest of hesitation before she decided to invite Lottie into the house.

Once inside, her caller wasted no time, 'What can I do to help?' she queried, tremendous effort was required to keep her composure, assailed by sheer nostalgia, which threatened to destroy any confidence she possessed. Margarget's answer came, straight to the point. 'Ralph won't accept help from you.' A plain statement of fact. 'He doesn't forget,' she said obviously disturbed by this unexpected encounter.

'Nor forgive,' was the retort to this. 'I understand, it took some time to soften towards him. I am not here to offer charity, Aunt Jessica left money, some of it rightly his. Should it be a case of paying a fine or going to prison, surely he won't allow stupid pride to stand in the way.'

'That's what ye think,' Robert broke in, full of indignation. 'Me father'll not come out if the others have t'bide inside, an' who'll pay their fines? They haven't got two ha'pennies t'rub again one another, none o'them and the contingency fund's had it.'

'I'm afraid he is right,' Margaret said in support. 'Even if Ralph wanted to accept the money, he wouldn't desert his friends. My husband is loyal through and through.' Pride in her voice and love shining out of tired eyes, obviously not long since they were full of tears.

'You aren't telling me anything I don't already know but he does have loyalty towards his wife and family.' Her nephew was soon into attack. 'We're all in this t'gether, every Man Jack an' Aa'm here t'look after me mother an' our Liz, if they keep'im 'n jail. Anyway ye work fer the gaffer.' Condemnation in those brilliant blue eyes. John Starrett the whiskered gentleman who wanted to give him money, his identity not discovered until later, the anagonism now felt part of being a miner like his father and the rest.

Margaret was quick to chastise his rudeness. 'Be quiet Robert, you know how much we are already indebted towards your aunt. If it wasn't for her you wouldn't have a sister,' and saw her son flush, lapsing into a sulky silence.

'Don't feel you must apologise for him,' Lottie said, 'I have seen the day when I would have reacted exactly the same, tolerance is something we all have to learn,' now uneasy and anxious to be off. 'Let me know what Ralph decides. You will mention it?' she asked, his answer a forgone conclusion but worth a try. He might listen if Margaret found the right approach but whether she would another matter altogether.

'Of course,' ashamed not to offer her sister-in-law a cup of tea but certain she had ventured far enough against Ralph's wishes. He was certain to hear of Lottie's visit from nosy neighbours, reaching him even behind bars. Lottie hesitated, not sure how to approach another delicate matter without giving offence, young Robert on the defensive and all ears. 'And you?' she inquired of Ralph's wife, 'How are you managing?' None too well by the look of things, evidence of malnutrition written all over Margaret's pinched face and painfully thin body. 'About the same as everyone else after ten weeks without a penny coming into the house. Miners are treated like lepers by most charitable organisations. We can't go to the Parish Relief, every stick of furniture would have to be sold first and these things belonged to Ralph's mother.'

'My mother too,' Lottie wanted to shout, Bessie Hanson's treasured possessions must never be allowed to fall into the hands of strangers, sold off willy nilly for next to nothing, every single item hard come by.

'There is tea in the house and half a loaf of bread. I spent my last coppers on the bread this morning and the butcher gave me some fat to render down for dripping. The money I had in the Co-op went ages ago. Some of the local farmers and shopkeepers are very kind. Not exactly high living but we survive.'

Robert found his tongue again. 'There's the soup kitchen in the Store Hall,' he defended hotly 'The poor helpin' the poor.' His ladylike aunt relegated to where he thought she belonged, ready to discount any connection, bitterly sarcastic.

Lottie ignored the jibes and delved into the bottom of her bone handled bag to produce several silver coins, laid on the bamboo table near the front window. 'It isn't much, I know,' she apologised, 'But it will help,' and half expected the money to be swept aside in anger. 'Take it,' she pleaded, 'Silly pride doesn't fill empty bellies and someone has to live to tell the tale. Go on,' she urged, 'It is my own money, I really earned it, Aunt Jessica was an old bitch, she led me a not so merry dance for years.' Pleased to see a faint smile on her sister-in-law's lips.

Margaret's eyes misted over. 'One point on which Ralph and yourself do agree, he hasn't a good word to say for his mother's sister. I won't see my family starve, I took money from you before Elizabeth was born and I'm doing it again.' She sighed rather ruefully. 'Thank you but God help me if your brother ever finds out.'

Robert's hostility towards the gesture knew no bounds, 'Me mother has no right takin'money from ya,' he spat out furiously and flung himself out of the room, Margaret was full of apologies. 'The Hanson temper,' Lottie accepted with raised eyebrows, thankful to have learnt a measure of control. 'He won't tell his father anything I don't want him to know,' she was assured, 'I think it works both ways.' A need to convey the strong affinity between father and son, equally devoted to both parents.

'We all do what we must and most of us have something to regret,' Lottie said, the last words exchanged before Ralph's wife opened the front door and watched a slim, graceful figure walk away from the house, impervious to curious glances thrown her way. Lottie's offer was guaranteed to take the wind out of Ralph's sails but refusal was a racing certainty. No mention would be made of the handful of florins picked up from the occasional table and hidden away, Margaret Hanson's pride came a poor second to the welfare of her family and it was easier to cover up with her husband behind bars. Care was taken in the spending of it, spread around to avoid comment on any sudden surfeit of money, when all were as poor as church mice.

Ralph Hanson and his comrades were sent down for three months, the option of a fine flatly refused. 'Sh'should know better than t'offer,' he complained of Lottie, 'W'all stick t'gether whatever happens.' No fiery tirade as expected nor an explosion against ancient sins, just the sharp command. 'An' mind y'take nowt from'er, not a single penny piece. She'll not get the chance t'chuck that back i'me face when it suits'er.' The high colour on his wife's cheeks was not attributed to guilt. 'Yer hot lass, it's stuffy in here,' he said and squeezed her hand in affectionate concern. 'It'll pass, jail and the strike. Nowt lasts ferever, good or bad.' This conversation before the men were transferred to Durham and Margaret walked the four mile journey home after her fleeting visit to Newcastle, that same four miles already walked to get there.

Ralph came out of prison late October to find the men back at work, weeks of hardship for nothing and dozens of men victimised for involvement, himself included. Robert kept the roof over their heads, no issue of that made by the gaffer, young muscle was needed if pits were to continue operation and he was keen to retrieve some of his losses. The lad's pay was insufficient to keep three adults and a growing lassie but was infinitely better than nothing at all.

Lottie's resentment showed in a cool manner towards her employer, master and servant relationship and no more. After two weeks of such chilling treatment, John Starrett could stand it no longer and faced her with it. 'Tell me what I have done to offend you, Charlotte, and we might return to our former footing.' Humble behaviour for such a proud man.

Lottie trembled apprehensively, one thing to act the way she had done but impossible to explain why. What could she say? Very conscious of those grey eyes which regarded her rather quizzically then hit the nail right on the head as usual. 'I suppose you think I have treated your brother unfairly. Do you wish me to reinstate him? Our long acquaintance does afford you some privilege, Charlotte.'

'My brother is a proud man, like yourself, sir, he wouldn't want me to intercede on his behalf. He won't seek favours and neither will I. Besides –' she began to say and took a deep breath she added hurriedly, 'he wouldn't accept the offer of work unless his friends were re-employed also.' Amazed at her own audacity.

'Then it appears we have deadlock?'

'I am afraid so, sir.'

John Starrett's calm suddenly vanished. 'Don't look at me with those expressive eyes of yours, as if I were the villain of the piece. Those damned stubborn miners aren't always right, even if they are your own kind.'

'No sir,' she snapped involuntarily, astounded to see a slow smile wreathe his rugged face. 'That's better girl, I like a bit of spirit, far better than being chilled to the bone. Let's call a truce, shall we?'

She laughed in spite of herself. 'Yes sir, I was wrong to act so childishly, it won't happen again.'

'Don't spoil it by changing into a timid kitchen maid,' he muttered self consciously, delighted to be back on good terms with this young woman, so refreshing in her honesty, the only totally sincere friend he actually possessed.

The following morning John Starrett told his colliery manager to wait at least a month before reinstating Ralph Hanson and the others. 'But don't make it easy for them when they do start,' he ordered. 'If you do the damned idiots will be fired with enthusiasm for another go, believing me to be soft in the head. God knows I must be, they cost me a fortune in lost production.' The attitude of a man who didn't know the first thing about poverty or how much a thirteen week strike took out of workers and their families, his wage bill was now less, what was wanted in the first place, an all round reduction in pay.

Lottie received the news four weeks later via Alice, wise enough not to mention the subject again. It was a great effort for someone of the gaffer's calibre to unbend to this extent and he had no desire to be reminded of his weakness.

The miners, beaten but unbowed, began to plan ahead for future action, a strong determination to improve their miserable lot, no matter the cost, for any concession would be dearly bought. Deeply embedded in their minds were seeds of resentment against men in other industries, a situation employers were quick to manipulate to their own advantage, a policy of 'divide and rule' which they used with great expertise, long experience in the art of suppression. 'Know thine enemy' was an excellent maxim and more education for the lower classes the only answer, to become knowledgeable enough to recognise all the moves and use them to their own advantage.

* * *

'Heaven's above Martha, you are old fashioned. This is 1925 and women are becoming more emancipated every day.' A statement from Victoria which was greeted with a hoot of derision. 'If bein' what y'say means wearin' frocks right up t'yer backside, Aa'll bide the way Aa am, thanks. That thing leaves nowt t'the imagination. Anyway it's not ladylike sittin' i' that fashion.' A waste of breath as Martha knew only too well, nothing perturbed her self possessed young mistress who, according to the little servant went far beyond the bounds of decency in what she chose to wear.

Victoria giggled at the obvious disapproval on Martha's face, the older woman aghast at the particular garment she had on, a long waisted creation which ended just above the knees, to reveal a pair of shapely legs, too much for a sense of propriety that went back to Queen Victoria's day.

For the past fifteen minutes or so, the twenty year old had been seated, cross legged, on the kitchen table, revealing details of the latest brush with her grandfather, she was given undivided attention until too much leg was shown and Martha felt obliged to speak out. It was no secret to anyone in Rothwell House that John Starrett and this self willed girl often clashed head on, despite the strong affection between them, Victoria was not easy to browbeat. This present issue was only one among many, the honours usually going to the young rebel.

'There's nowt wrong in havin' a comin' out ball,' Martha insisted, returning to the matter in question before a show of legs got in the way. 'Yer gran'father wants folk t'see what a bonny lass y'are an' fer ya t'meet some nice young chaps.' Not in the least discouraged by the scornful look thrown at her, Victoria's silky bobbed hair swung back, a blonde head tossed in defiance. 'An' y'needn't go all hoity toity on me, madam. High time y'were thinkin' o'gettin' hitched.' Martha was not afraid of speaking her mind where the young mistress was concerned. Lottie had allowed the conversation to drift along until Martha overstepped the mark, strangely unwilling to think of Victoria and marriage. Where would they find someone good enough for her precious girl? A very special person to keep her under control and still be happy, there were too many with an eye to the main chance.

'When I marry, and it won't be for ages, I want a real man, not one of the chinless wonders Grandpa trots out every now and again. A man like Papa used to be or even Grandpa in his prime, the stubborn old darling.'

A spirited tussle between two equally strong wills had gone on since before Christmas when the celebration for her coming of age was first mentioned, finishing school behind her and now in permanent residence, Victoria was a joy to all except Stan Hodges, who resented the influence she had on her blind father, afraid of his own position. Not that Victoria had so much luck nowadays. Geoffrey was more of a recluse than ever.

Lottie's hazel eyes misted at this reference to that man of former years, still hopelessly in love, and did her best to steer talk away from such painful memories. 'What do you want for your birthday celebration?' she asked, Victoria's reply was very definite.

'A small select party of my nearest and dearest. That is what I mean to have.' Full red lips set in firm lines. 'Everyone in this house, apart from Hodges, rather like Jackson's wedding.' Here she stopped very sad faced. 'It won't be the same without Marianne but David will represent her, I love David.' Jackson's son was almost seven years old and a great favourite, at school in the village now and showing signs of wanting to learn, no pit work for his son Mattie Jackson determined, another year or two to see in which direction the lad might be inclined, he was saving hard to further his education when the time arrived.

How could it be the same, Lottie thought? Marianne gone, Geoffrey so introvert and Mattie Jackson a pale shadow of his earlier self, fine healthwise but some of that former spirit had gone out of him. As for herself, almost forty years old and still a spinster, her heart given forever to a man who didn't want it. Not a single word of love had crossed his lips since his return to the fold, he scarcely exchanged words with her at all.

And on top of that Victoria declared, 'I want every school child in Saltersgate to have a present. Not a silly mug with my name on it, money perhaps to buy boots or shoes.' An astounding suggestion but one Mattie Jackson or her father may have fully understood, had they been present. An indelible impression had been made upon a young girl's mind when she saw children without shoes or poorly shod, neither man aware of the sequel when she confronted her grandfather as promised, full of false illusion.

'There is so much you don't understand, Victoria,' he tried to explain. 'Most working class woes are of their own making.' He was very upset by the youngster's fiery disapproval of his deeply inherent ideas. 'If you don't do something now, I shall when I am older,' she vowed, already half way out of the room and refused to be called back, two bright red splashes of anger on soft, young cheeks and tears of disappointment in those vivid blue eyes, a sad feeling of having been well and truly let down. That feeling was never forgotten nor the vow she made. Absolutely stunned by Victoria's apparent concern for those less fortunate than herself, Lottie found it difficult to offer advice but felt she must, there were problems involved in such a scheme. 'If that is what you really want and your grandfather agrees, it would be preferable if the footwear was bought for them' she ventured to propose. 'They could find other uses for money.' This was not condemnation just woeful acceptance of human frailty, she was loathe to add that footwear might easily find its way to the pawnshop week after week, in on Monday, redeemed on Friday, if funds were available, a sad way of life.

Too built up on her proposal, Victoria wouldn't be willing to accept the obvious snags, it was only left to John Starrett to foot the bill, if the gaffer gave in to his granddaughter's wheedling ways, she was quite adept at getting around him shades of his attitude towards Felicity which ended in disaster and made Lottie very apprehensive indeed. But this was one matter on which he might stand his ground, never soft where his work force was concerned.

The birthday girl reiterated firmly that Stan Hodges wouldn't be invited. 'I shall tell Papa,' so very definitely determined to succeed on all counts and who to say she wouldn't.

'The man's a creep, Papa,' she said on return from Switzerland, prepared to take the enture situation in hand. 'I hate the way he babies you and he's a real Uriah Heap.' She was terribly upset by her father's apparent withdrawal from any sort of existence. It was one reason she refused a season in London but also she was appalled at the thought of being in charge of some elderly dowager to be presented at court, for a handsome fee of course.

'I am home where I belong,' she stated. 'Send me away and I shall kick over the traces and disgrace the family name.' No idle threat, she meant every word, that firm lift of the chin which always meant business, even John Starrett was not immune to Victoria's strength of will which more than equalled his own. When two dinosaurs clash, one of them must always accept defeat. She won that argument without a great deal of effort, it might be said, her grandfather was secretly delighted to have her cheery presence continually around the house, especially on those grim days when he returned from Harrogate, Felicity still alive in her own mad world, one fact his enormous wealth could not alter.

'She'll win,' Martha prohesied with regard to the party. 'An'them boots are as good as on the bairns' feet already.' She was proved right on both counts, despite the gaffer's initial reaction, he was unable to say her nay, a devoted slave to this lively young miss, who wrapped them all around her little finger, both upstairs and down. William Dowling, master sadler and footwear specialist, with premises on Branton High Street was absolutely astounded when the gaffer placed the order, chits to be issued to parents, no money to exchange hands. 'Good brass chucked down the drain,' Dowling said, long enough acquainted to be outspoken. 'Most o' them'll be across there by the followin' Monday mornin'.' His finger pointed over the road towards another shop, with three brass balls above its door. 'Usually Sunday suits,' he stated laconically, articles pawned at the beginning of each week and redeemed before the next Sunday, should funds permit. If not men were missing from church on one pretext or another.

Ralph Hanson wanted to refuse the gaffer's bounty. 'Nowt but charity,' he grunted. 'Ye'll not be standin' in any queue with a chitty in yer hand,' he warned, only to find his gentle wife unusually defiant, prepared to do battle on this occasion. 'Take a good look at Elizabeth's feet and then say she doesn't need shoes.' An air of quiet determination which won the day but not the last word on the subject. 'It's my job t'provide fer me family. Tell that old skinflint t'give us all a livin' wage an' keep his charity,' he stormed in frustration, off to his allotment to work out badly outraged feelings, wounded pride hard to swallow.

Victoria's party came next on the agenda with Martha fully prepared to make it very special. 'Even if sh'isn't havin' the grand affair the gaffer wanted, there'll be no scrimpin',' she vowed, completely unbashed at the number of times the grocer's lad staggered under the weight of provisions ordered by Lottie at her request.

Alice was taken into Newcastle by tram to purchase a dress for the occasion and returned home after a three hour session with the best of a limited choice, there had been a great difference of opinion between Lottie and herself. 'Aa liked that one wi'all the frills,' the big lass grumbled incessantly, the frock they finally settled upon was much more suitable but didn't appeal to Alice's romantic fancy, she had no idea of how incongruous she looked in fussy attire.

Stan Hodges watched the hectic preparations with keen interest, broad hints and toadying to Victoria, enough to make Lottie sick to her stomach. 'Fishin' fer an invitation he's not likely t'get,' Martha gloated. 'If'ee has the bloomin' nerve t'ask, Miss Victoria'll soon put 'im in his place.' All thoughts of the common enemy were cast aside to give full attention to more pressing matters, she was absolutely in her element.

Saltersgate miners and others countrywide were enjoying a brief respite, their wages pegged by the Baldwin administration for nine months, this was not what they really wanted but it gave time to gather strength for the next conflict, which the government realised was inevitable as working class folk became increasingly impatient for a fairer share of the cake. A wholesale clash was on the agenda sooner or later and the authorities meant to be prepared. John Starrett took the opportunity for a journey to Harrogate and insisted Victoria should accompany him, Lottie was absolutely aghast at such stupidity. 'God knows what the sight of Miss Victoria might trigger off in that deranged mind. Why does he have to cast such gloom on her coming of age?' And Lottie wondered as Jackson did, if Geoffrey knew of this enforced pilgrimage or if he was too submerged in his lethargic condition to care, unresponsive now to his daughter's light hearted chivvying, Hodges seemingly given the clear field he had striven to so hard to achieve.

Four days before the celebration was due to take place the travellers boarded a train at Newcastle Central, not expected to return until the following day, booked in for one night at a luxurious hotel near the Harrogate clinic. Victoria was none too happy at the prospect of coming face to face with her mother once more, hardly surprising.

Jackson drove them to the station, beset by memories of the day he set out on that same journey, with coach and horses, to pick up the woman who became the light of his life, sorely missed, although he was very conscious of his duty as a father, David was now the centre of this good fellow's existence. Lottie's words had certainly reached their mark and the lad fitted into a life around three caring women, a young lady who played games and made a fuss of him, everything just as Aunt Lottie predicted. Only from Stan Hodges did David keep his distance, despite the man's efforts to ingratiate himself, there was an evil in him that even a seven year old boy recognised, with that uncanny instinct youngsters and animals seem to possess. An underlying sense of mistrust pervaded the entire household, apart from Geoffrey who appeared to have no feeling one way or another.

With almost three days to finalise arrangements for the small celebration Victoria wanted and was going to have, the whole house shone with all the spit and polish it received. Snack meals were the order of the day amid a host of grumbles from Alice, whose mind dwelt on the host of goodies stashed away but she was forbidden to go near. 'Keep yer greedy hands off that lot,' Martha warned, 'Or ye'll wish ye'd never been born,' saying wearily, 'Wi' all the graft that's gone inta this place w'could nicely eat off the floor.' Tired but secretly proud of their preparations towards the great day, a tiredness which soon disappeared when Alice and herself were given the evening off to attend a Guild meeting in the Co-op Hall. It was not Lottie's idea of pleasure but the other two enjoyed the gossip over a cup of tea, what the speaker had to say of much less importance, right above their heads as might be expected.

An hour after they left the house, Jackson forcibly removed David from Lottie's knee where the laddie had been curled up for some time. 'I shall come and tuck you in,' she promised, her cheeks wet from spontaneous kisses, any ploy to delay bedtime, an expression in his young eyes reminded her of Marianne and she hugged him close. There was a dearth of conversation nowadays with her friend no longer there, Mattie and herself talked, of course, but not in any real depth, the spark had gone out of him, lost without a devoted wife and companion, who didn't live long enough to be any sort of mother to their son.

'Three bedtimes an' it's the party,' the excited laddie exclaimed for the umpteenth time, he had no wish to leave the place where everything seemed to be happening, imagining it might suddenly vanish if he didn't keep a watchful eye on all proceedings, he was as high as a kite and wouldn't be easy to settle down for the night.

'A good job when it's all over an' done wi',' Jackson groaned, the seven year old hoisted across the stable yard, where Lottie joined them in the flat as promised. A hot drink and half an hour with an old friend, this habit had been cultivated after Marianne's death, well aware it was the hardest part of day for Mattie Jackson, when the door closed behind her and he felt the miss of his beloved wife, cuddled into him in bed. He didn't miss the sexual side of their marriage, non existent for some time before David's birth, just the togetherness, the wonderful feeling they had always shared.

Lottie was lonely too, when she locked the basement door, lonely for the man on an upper floor of the house, who wanted none of her, and deserted even by Hamlet, the faithful beast probably upstairs at Geoffrey's feet, which signified Hodges must be out, always given a wide berth by the family pet.

She jumped when someone fumbled at the latch but gathered it must be Geoffrey's servant and moved to open it, appalled when he almost fell into the room. One look at glassy eyes and bloated features told her he was much the worse for drink and her heart missed a beat. 'You are drunk,' she threw at him contemptuously. 'It might be better if you went straight to your own quarters,' fearful as he lurched towards her.

'Better fer who?' his thick slobbering lips curled in derision. 'Aa'm not good enough fer ya, is that it? No worse than some ye've lain wi',' the objectionable lout spluttered and she stepped away from him. 'There was this chap Aa met i' the pub sayed his name was Jake Snowdon an' y' knew'im well at one time.' Significant words, obviously he was well informed, Jake not the sort to let sleeping dogs lie. The passing of time had brought Stan Hodges an opportunity to avenge himself for that cutting down to size, all those years ago, an ego bashing never forgotten.

Although terribly disturbed, Lottie made sure none of it registered on her face, nothing apart from disgust, she had had plenty of practice at hiding her feelings, her youthful indiscretion now back to haunt her and Hodges out to extract every ounce out of the filth he had been filled with, Jake had no doubt been in excellent from and revelled in it.

That loathsome tongue rambled on. 'There was some mention of a place called Batey's field. A bit o'all right was how'ee put it, went inta great detail.' His coarse mind was not hard to read, Hodges believed he had her in his power at last.

'If you don't go, I shall,' she spat out angrily, it was not easy to appear unconcerned at what he had just brought into the open, and she turned towards the inside stairway, her exit soon blocked by a swaying figure, none too steady on his feet. She decided to try different tactics, to lure this beastly man into a false sense of oneupmanship. 'Black coffee is what you need,' and moved to the stove. There was a smirk of satisfaction on his repulsive face. 'That's more like it,' he drawled. 'Let you an'me get nice an'cosy. Yer a fine lookin' woman, just my type. We should get better acquainted an'now's as good a time as ever wi'that humpy backed midget an'daft Alice out o'the way.' Lottie was furious at this insulting reference to her absent friends.

The polite veneer had vanished, no begrudging respect, dismissed by the sordid tale he had recently heard. Hodges and Jake were two of a kind and the scales probably tipped in Jake's favour, no recommendation. Fearful now to no small degree, she took the coffee pot from the stove and poured some of the steaming liquid into a large mug. 'Milk an' two sugars,' he demanded rudely, the last words to leave his mouth as the scalding liquid splashed in his face to a loud bellow of pain, thrown off balance long enough for her to reach the door, which unfortunately opened inwards. Precious seconds were lost before a numb body plunged upstairs into a darkened passage, intent on flight but God knows where or to whom. 'Geoffrey, oh Geoffrey,' came out in strangled tone from her dry mouth, panic stricken with a compelling need to reach he beloved's side, where sense of survival in Rothwell House might stop Hodges short in his evil purpose, she had no illusions as to what he was after.

Weighed down by terror she pushed ahead, one foot on the first stair of the main flight when a rough hand grabbed at her ankle and pulled her backwards. She struggled, how desperately Lottie struggled, a mind bedevilled by the fate awaiting her but was soon pinned to the floor by a heavy, repulsive body.

Now all predatory male and panting with lust and overdue exertion, Hodges' blistering tongue let fly. 'Think yer clever, playin' hard t'get when ye've already lain wi'one man an' had'is bairn. Aa'll sharp prove Aa'm more of a lover than Jake Snowdon ever was, y'might enjoy it more second time round.' His mouth was on hers in a kiss that stank of ale, absolutely odious, the last straw, and she tore her lips away in absolute hysteria, praying someone would miraculously appear before Jake's vengeance was ultimately complete.

Some cruel fate threw the two men together, Jake discovering who Hodges was and his interest in her, no doubt plied the other fellow with beer and his venomous tongue did the rest. It took one rogue to recognise another, she scorned, her mind in turmoil but, firmly resolved to make rape no picnic, she lifted one knee sharply between her assailant's legs, a vicious dig where it was bound to hurt, maimed for life she sincerely hoped in savage rage.

Hodges still smarted from the scalding coffee and yelled again in sheer agony, one of Lottie's wrists was released to instinctively handle this new source of pain. The finger nails of her loosened hand ripped at his twisted face and dug in deep, making sure he would bear the mark for some considerable time if nothing else, hard to explain away.

'Y'bloody bitch, y'little hell cat,' he cursed, bleeding profusely and still tortured by that upward thrust of her knee. 'Y'might as well bide still, cause Aa'm havin'ya, my God Aa'm havin'ya. There's nobody i'this house but a blind man an'he's as good as nowt.' The words spat out in unrestrained venom, no thought in a mind befuddled by drink that this whole affair would not be easily swept under the rug, perhaps relying on her shame to keep quiet.

That refinement instilled in Lottie by Marianne went by the board, now she was no lady just a frantic, terrified woman, who uttered the same threat made in Alice Ruddick's bed. 'Aa'll swing fer ya, that Aa will. Damn yer rotten soul t'hell,' she shrieked and wished the bread knife was in her hand to do him lethal damage, her strength almost gone.

Hodges forced her legs part and his reeking mouth sought hers while exploratory fingers groped around soft breasts. 'God help me,' Lottie groaned in despair and hoped to die rather than suffer degradation, never to be taken in love just pure lust, in full knowledge this time what it was all about. She was no innocent lass skilfully seduced by an experienced lecher, rape and no mistake, far worse to endure. Her assailant fumbled with his trouser buttons, soon hard and bare between her legs as she thrashed from side to side to prevent that final thrust. Scalding tears poured down her cheeks for what seemed a lost cause, until a door creaked on the floor above, Geoffrey's door, and she prayed for him to appear. But all she heard was her own name in a husky voice and a sharp order to Hamlet, from a blind man who cursed his own inadequacy.

Hamlet needed no word of command, Lottie's cries were enough to alert the faithful beast, a friend in danger. Just seconds later canine teeth embedded themselves in a bare buttock and roars of anguish filled the air. A welcome sound to the man groping his way along the landing towards the head of the stairs. 'Get this bloody animal off me,' the sufferer shrieked in terror and rolled away from Lottie, who scrambled to her feet but made no attempt to restrain the dog, furious enough to allow her dumb rescuer to do his worst.

With the angry beast still hanging on, Hodges dragged himself towards the hall stand in search of a weapon, forestalled by a whirling dervish who made sure she got there first, grabbing one of the gaffer's silver topped canes, she lifted above Hodges' head in all seriousness, even if it killed him and 'swing fer ya' might well have been in the final reckoning.

Now, almost at the top of the first floor stairs Geoffrey shouted Lottie's name repeatedly but taking one step too many, he hurtled into space, a sickening thud when he reached the bottom and lay there dreadfully still. 'Get out,' Lottie hissed, calling Hamlet to heel and placed herself between Hodges and the inert body of his master, when he moved forward to help. 'Get out of here while you can,' she railed at him, 'or I'll set the dog on you again.' Hamlet snarling, was quite willing to have another go but 'Stay, Hamlet,' she ordered as Hodges thought better of it and beat a hasty retreat. He knew his reign in Rothwell House was over, he had been instrumental in his own dismissal. Geoffrey Cranshawe might well be dead and John Starrett's reaction whether or not very predictable, he was anxious now to put as much distance as possible between himself and inevitable retribution. A boat out of the Tyne maybe the best means of escape. He wasn't without money, the 'cushy number' had definitely paid off, and a berth would be found quite easily, no questions asked if somebody's palm was sufficiently greased, he was desperate enough to try anything.

* * *

Lottie still had presence of mind to phone the doctor, despite a trembling in every limb and absolutely distraught as she did so, her eyes fixed on that beloved figure on the floor, there was no sign of movement, so very still. She didn't go into detail, not at this stage, hoping it wouldn't be necessary to rake up all the dirt, relieved to see Martha and Alice emerge from the basement area. 'Get Mattie,' she ordered and the younger woman needed no second bidding, taking swiftly to her heels, the sign of her master and Lottie's wild, dishevelled state more than sufficient incentive for immediate action.

'Where's Hodges?' Martha demanded. 'Don't say anythin', Aa can tell. That bloody bastard, Aa reckoned somethin' had t'happen an' Aa guess it did.' But totally out of character she didn't wait for an answer, just knelt beside Geoffrey and felt for a pulse, then gave a deep sigh of relief. 'He's not dead,' she stated bluntly and put her arms around Lottie, who got down on the floor, they were both there when Jackson came upon them, in shirt sleeves and braces dangling, the latter hastily slipped over his shoulders. Ye'll have phoned the doctor, Aa reckon? We'd better not move'im Aa've left Alice t'keep an eye on David.' He took in Lottie's torn, bloodstained clothing and Hamlet's watchful stance but questions could wait. 'Fetch a rug t'keep 'im warm,' he ordered, Martha rushing to obey. 'An'ye lass, tidy yerself up, y'canna let the doctor see ya in that state, take too much explainin'.'

Jackson was right, the use of soap and water and a quick change into a clean blouse and skirt worked wonders with outward signs of her ordeal and made Lottie feel a lot better, but the smell of Hodge's revolting body still lingered in her nostrils. At this time, however, Geoffrey was her main concern, she couldn't get back to him quickly enough and arrived only seconds before Mattie opened the door to Angus MacLean, the family physician, who lost no time in running experienced hands over the whole of the unconscious man's body.

'Amazing,' he pronounced, after careful scrutiny. 'It probably happened before he had time to think, he made no effort to save himself. No broken bones but he will certainly feel his sores when he comes to. We should know in a few hours if his concussion needs hospital care, his pulse is quite steady considering. I'll help you get him to bed,' he said to Mattie Jackson and between them they carefully lifted Geoffrey from the floor and carried him upstairs, while Lottie brought up the rear. Martha watched the slow procession from the bottom hallway until they disappeared from view then made her way to the kitchen, there was spilt coffee to mop up and a broken mug to be disposed of also. She tutted the while and tried to visualise what happened before Alice and herself returned from Saltersgate, those imaginings not so far from the awful truth. 'Bloody bastard,' repeated more than once, her hatred for Stan Hodges given full rein. The doctor insisted someone should sit with his patient, he had actually been called to a difficult confinement, his next port of call. 'If I'm needed, call the house and my wife will get hold of me.' Lottie was quick to offer her services. 'Jackson has a small boy at home,' she explained, 'He should get back to the coach house.' Her offer was accepted and told the practitioner would call by in the morning unless wanted beforehand. 'If the concussion is mild, as I believe it to be, Major Cranshawe will propbably come to then lapse into natural sleep. That is what I am hoping for.'

'What did happen?' Jackson asked when the doctor left. 'The master slipped and fell,' Lottie answered evasively, pretending not to understand. 'Go home now, Mattie, I can manage,' she murmured wearily, reaction about to set in and she wanted him out of the way. Jackson's irritation showed. 'Stop playin'games lass, y'know fine what Aa'm getting'at. Y'didn't get the way ye were wi'the Major fallin'downstairs, no blood on him, not that Aa could see. An' where is the mighty Hodges in all this?' He looked hard at her and took a deep breath. 'My God, what's that slimy toad been up to?' His answer was in the shamed look on a face drained of all colour. 'Please Mattie, it's over, let it rest,' she pleaded wearily, visions of him in full pursuit of her aggressor like an avenging angel and Hodges well away by now, she was thankful to have escaped with no harm done to her person but all aquiver at the horrific memory of her terrible experience.

'All right,' he conceded, none too willingly, 'It can bide fer now but it's not finished, not by a long chalk.' He gave her hand a reassuring squeeze. 'There's plenty o'coal t'keep the fire goin'. Give'is a shout if y'need owt. God bless ya, lass,' and received a tremulous smile for his concern on her behalf. Lottie took up position close to the bed where Geoffrey lay, her hand on his, wakened from a fretful sleep in the early hours by a fluttering sigh. She saw her beloved's eyelids lift for a brief moment or two, then relax into the natural sleep the doctor expected. Relief eased the tension in her own aching body and she climbed onto the bed, the closeness longed for and denied her for seven years now hers, she was soon fast asleep.

In the first light of a grey dawn, the fire almost burnt out, Lottie slowly emerged from slumber and made a move to replenish it, although the room was quite warm. Caressing fingers loosened the pins at the nape of her neck, to spread rich, auburn tresses across the pillow, pulled gently backwards to do so. A tender voice whispered in her ear, endearments she had yearned to hear, all part of a wonderful dream from which she hoped never to awaken an in pure bliss cuddled closer. 'Your hair is still the colour of burnished copper my darling, darling Lottie,' the voice went on to murmur, so enthralled that the significance of these words failed to penetrate bemused senses, prepared to bask in the luxury of such sensuous feelings before the dream vanished. Then she suddenly jerked into awareness, the implication mind shattering, almost impossible to believe.

'You can see,' she gasped and tried to raise herself up, held firm by the weight of an arm laid across her prone body. 'You can see,' she repeated, astounded that such a miracle had been born out of near disaster, a joy almost too much to bear.

The voice had little strength, that of a man who had lived in a darkened world so long, mostly silent, but full of love and so very tender. 'Yes, I can see, not too clearly I'm afraid, your dear face is a blur but not the colour of your hair. How often I have longed to wrap it around my fingers. Don't cry Lottie, don't cry.' The dampness of a soft cheek pressed lovingly against his unshaven chin. So much emotion kept suppressed for what seemed an eternity.

'They did tell me in Germany and again in England there was no apparent defect, my sight could return as my speech did, but I lost hope. Perhaps it is too soon to rejoice, even now.' This doubt was quickly dispelled. 'That is defeatist talk,' Lottie gently scolded. 'Doctor Maclean is due later this morning, he will know what you must do. Meanwhile don't expose your eyes to strong light,' very confident and highly elated.

'What happened down there?' he groaned, becoming conscious of his sores. 'I heard your screams and felt so helpless. Hamlet seemed to be the only solution,' the faithful beast was immediately astir at the sound of his name, Lottie's companion throughout the night.

'The right solution, he arrived just in time,' she murmured, reluctant to talk about it, her involuntary shudders felt by the man who lay so close to her. 'Tell me, what did happen?' Geoffrey persisted and the sorry tale was revealed in faltering tone. He had the right to know what prompted Hodge's attempt at rape, painful no doubt but necessary. 'He met Jake Snowdon in a public house, who told him I – –' here she broke off, then added tremulously 'Told him I was easy game,' her head now buried against him in shame.

'Don't,' Geoffrey begged, 'I only know what Felicity chose to tell me and remember how young you looked with my child in your arms. You fed her, I know,' barely able to hear a softly spoken 'Yes'. 'I could kill both those men for what they did to you. Thank God Hodges failed. He has gone, I suppose?' 'I sent him packing, threatened to set Hamlet on him again and he wasn't too keen on that idea. Now I have told you all this, you see what sort of a woman I am, a real wanton, even with the bedclothes between us you had better watch out.' A feeble attempt at humour.

Geoffrey realised Lottie's mental agony went far beyond any physical hurt she was feeling. 'Let that young girl go, my darling, Jake Snowdon had nothing of the woman you really are. I adore you Lottie, but I won't reduce you to that same level, some hole in the corner affair, clandestine meetings, a web of deceit. Felicity could live for years.'

'If that is the only way we can be together, then so be it,' she told him, willing to grasp the joy of fulfilment whatever the cost. Their lips met, her quivering mouth parted in the giving and receiving of a passionate kiss, the first after so many love starved years, ready for complete surrender, a glorious experience she never expected to be hers.

But Geoffrey's battered body took over, white with pain he drew back and lay against his pillows, absolutely drained, 'Sorry, my dearest, of all the damned things to happen. I am a poor specimen of a lover but I want you – God, how I want you.'

'Darling,' she soothed, her desire quickly suppressed to ease him into a more comfortable position. 'We can wait until you recover and become the man you used to be.' A loud groan was his immediate response, regret and physical pain a powerful combination. 'I must have seemed a right swine to you, my darling,' he admitted ruefully but a light kiss told him all was forgiven, Lottie's heart and hazel eyes aglow. Just as well, amid such euphoria, she did not know Geoffrey actually welcomed a chance to collect himself, with this loved one so very close, his feelings for her overwhelming and relieved that severely aching bones pulled him back from the very edge of a temptation too strong to resist in his normal state. A dangerous situation, much too dangerous, a merciful reprieve, his wife locked away in a mental institution he could not be divorced, but was too honourable a man to make Lottie his mistress. Exactly what she would be if they surrendered to their mutual love for one another, what was termed a 'light of love'. How could he let her sink to that level when she was his whole world, a queen among women. Lottie had no conception of her power to arouse him without even trying, still somewhat of an innocent despite having given birth to a child. What would happen if she ever discovered she had this power and chose to use those womanly wiles? He was honest enough to confess that not too far below the surface within himself lay a hope that this might take place and bid goodbye to all those noble principles, catastrophic no doubt but an enticing prospect.

* * *

The reconciled pair spent the best part of that day in one another's company, the holding of hands and tender kisses from time time, a strong urge in both of them to take their relationship to its natural conclusion but Geoffrey was determined and, unaware of his firm resolution not to make her his mistress, Lottie was too solicitous for his condition to make any demands. She revelled in these precious moments, fully convinced they would soon be united in fulfilment of a love so long denied them. Her close attendance on the young master caused no raised eyebrows, not even Martha's 'Didn't Aa tell ya Hodges was trouble?' she gloated, overjoyed to have him out of their lives and saved Lottie any embarrassment by not asking a host of questions. For once that avid curiosity was held in firm control, a great relief to the person most involved.

Alice, never so quick to catch on, just inquired what happened to 'that bloke', when Hodges didn't make an appearance, and was just told he had hopped it and no reason given. 'The Major'll not need'im anyway,' informed Geoffrey's sight had returned and, before long, below stairs, it seemed as if someone named Stan Hodges never even existed.

Late in the day, a very subdued young lady arrived home, the visit to Felicity had been a most harrowing experience, dramatic happenings not confined to the big house. Not a single word crossed Madam's lips until they rose to depart, when a torrent of oaths blasted forth, expletives which would have done justice to the foulest mouth anywhere. Dragged out of the room screeching her head off, a terrible sight for Victoria to witness, John Starrett was a deeply disturbed man. Never again, he vowed, sadly determined to limit his own visits which, according to the clinic's medical staff, served no real purpose.

Jackson picked them up at the station as arranged but said no more than the Major had fallen downstairs, he was badly bruised and shaken, the good news worth waiting for. A flash of shapely legs and Victoria leapt from the car, when they reached home, time then to put John Starrett in the picture. 'Thank God,' the brusque exclamation, which hid some real emotion, Lottie's ordeal was not mentioned at this stage. 'The bruises will heal. We shall have a drink to my son-in-law's recovery after dinner,' he promised before he strode indoors.

'The best birthday present a girl ever had,' Victoria said in pure delight, quite overcome when she discovered her father could see, Geoffrey's greeting an instant clue. 'I like you in that blue dress,' he told her, 'it matches your eyes,' overwhelmed to have such a beautiful daughter, no longer the teenager he last saw, that image held in his mind's eye but not supplanted by the vision of loveliness she had grown to be.

The penny took only seconds to drop and the effect was electrifying, her arms around him in stranglehold until Geoffrey begged for mercy. 'Hold on,' he pleaded, 'I am labelled fragile, handle with care,' as happy as she was with their wonderful reunion but sore enough to grimace with pain. 'Sorry, Papa but that excuse won't last forever, your days of idleness will soon be over. Lottie and I must find something to occupy your mind, take you firmly in hand,' Victoria babbled on, those glorious blue eyes alight, the previous day's sordid experience completely erased, her despondency dismissed and the person she knew as mother along with it, Geoffrey was now his daughter's main consideration and gallantly quipped he couldn't be taken in hand by two more beautiful women. The younger of them was so engrossed in future plans, she failed to notice the way her father's eyes devoured Lottie, as if to absorb every single detail, a look more eloquent than words. 'Everything will be splendid from now on,' Victoria enthused, ecstatic to hear Hodges had gone but didn't ask for reasons, too much occupied with her own ideas, the fact that the man she detested had actually left Rothwell House was all that seemed to register. John Starrett raised his eyebrows when told of Stan Hodge's departure but wasn't prepared to be fobbed off with lame excuses and tackled Lottie when he managed to get her alone, no wish to upset Geoffrey or involve Victoria in further unpleasantness. Lottie knew only the truth would suffice and stepped back from the rage on the gaffer's face when he heard the sordid tale, the main part of it anyway.

'I'll find him,' he threatened, 'If I have to hire every detective agency in England, I'll root out the bastard.' Suddenly alarmed at the pallor of Lottie's face. 'Please sir, please don't,' she implored, appalled at the thought of what might arise from such measures. 'Damn it girl,' he exploded, 'You surely aren't going to let a man get away with that!' his voice so harsh she trembled and groped her way into a chair. 'I couldn't bear to set eyes upon him again and would certainly have to if it went to court, you know that.' Tears streaming down her cheeks.

The gaffer bent down and raised her from the chair into the comfort of his arms. 'All right girl, all right. It's finished, I hope he rots in hell and never knows a minute's peace from now on, but you won't have to bear any more, that's a promise,' and held her as he never comforted his own daughter, except in early childhood. It felt right and very good indeed, just a few moments then back to normal, 'Now wipe those damned eyes, I'm famished. Can a man not be fed in his own house,' he barked and Lottie laughed through her tears. 'Yes sir, of course, sir, in two shakes of a lamb's tail,' off like a shot to the kitchen, an enormous load lifted from her mind and touched by his concern to no small degree, the side of John Starrett which drew her to him never more evident.

The birthday party went with a swing, shared together by both the upstairs and downstairs family, plus Mattie Jackson and young David. Geoffrey was forced to be content with second hand knowledge of the affair. One or other of them popped in from time to time with food or to chat, Lottie being careful not to appear too eager to take more than her fair share of turns at his bedside.

It was a struggle to suppress pangs of jealousy at Geoffrey's instant rapport with Victoria and she chided herself for such stupidity, it was a voyage of discovery for both of them, learning to be father and daughter all over again, so much of the girl's life he had missed for one reason or another. Dangerous times were ahead, Victoria's sharp eyes would be quick to notice any impropriety, careful always to call him 'sir' as usual, there would be no touching in her presence or over fond glances.

On one occasion, in the room with them, she made some feeble excuse to leave, her departure barely acknowledged, so absorbed were they in each other and what they were doing. A family unit in their own minds and in the eyes of those around them. Ironic, come to think of it, her daughter and the man she loved, huddled together in shared interest, she was still unable to lay claim to either of them.

Despair hit her right between the eyes as she flew downstairs where she belonged, only a servant in Rothwell House after all. A pity she did not see Geoffrey look up as the door closed behind her, missed already, never able to see enough of her, that elfin face and delightfully curved body a joy to behold, somehow afraid she might disappear altogether from his life and he wondered just how long his avowed restraint would last or if he really wanted it to.

* * *

By late summer of that same year, Geoffrey Cranshawe's sight was fully restored. On his arrival the morning after the accident, Angus MacLean lost no time in making an appointment with a London eye specialist for a couple of weeks ahead, which gave his patient sufficient time to recover from the fall, delighted it should have such a marvellous consequence. He recommended dark glasses, meantime, with the added advantage that Geoffrey's eyes were behind them not visible to others and he was able to gaze at Lottie with his heart in them, eloquent looks she couldn't see either but only to have his head turned her way made the imagination run riot.

Numerous discussions took place with regard to his future. 'The Army is definitely out,' he informed Lottie one day when they were alone. 'I could take up a staff position probably but I've been out of things so long, I am bound to have lost touch' After eight years it would be a different set up altogether. 'Besides, I don't think I really want that.' 'What about the coal industry?' she suggested, rather half hearted, knowing John Starrett would be pleased to have a male member of the family involved. 'Not on your life,' Geoffrey hooted, well aware of her feelings. 'I've seen your expression when my father-in-law gets tough with his men. You are very transparent darling,' highly amused at her discomfort. 'If I ever became one of the hated bosses you would surely make me suffer. Apart from which the idea holds no appeal. So what else is there for a broken old war horse. Maybe I am too old to be taught new tricks,' he stated ruefully, now in his mid forties, the word old about to be hotly denied when Victoria came into the room, one of her frequent unheralded appearances, rather disconcerting. She caught the tail end of her father's speech but not the endearment, very fortuitous indeed. 'Try politics,' the sprightly young madam proposed 'with your social and army backgrounds they would snap you up. I can just visualise your campaign literature. Vote for Cranshawe. Blind hero returns to life and so forth,' her blue eyes alive with mischief but actually quite serious. 'By the way, what are you?'

Her father laughed. 'That is for both of us to find out, myself first,' he sighed. 'Eight years is a long time in a country's political life and it passed me by. A soldier isn't supposed to have any politics, just obedience for whatever those in power decree. I shall use this coming winter to catch up with some reading and try to find my bearings.'

'Not too much reading, sir,' Lottie hastened to advise, careful to keep her place in Victoria's presence but she had to issue this word of caution. She found the thought of Geoffrey and politics very disturbing, their opinions were certain to differ and enough barriers were erected already, truly dismayed by his flat refusal to consummate their love and the reason for it.

'Get yourself round and about, Papa,' Victoria urged. 'Go to some Party meetings, you would find them very stimulating, especially on the opposition side. You should hear the hecklers at the back of the halls,' and stopped abruptly, aware of saying more than intended. Geoffrey's head lifted and eyebrows raised above the dark glasses he still chose to wear at times. 'And there was I thinking some young man was on the horizon. So that is where you spend your evenings?' thoroughly amused to see her disconcerted, not at all usual. She laughed self consciously and a tell tale flush suffused her delicate skin. More to this than met the eye, Lottie thought, time for some discreet enquiries, beginning with Martha, always a fount of knowledge in such matters but who seemed rather surprised when approached. 'No lad that Aa know of. Not that there shouldn't be at her age, high time sh'settled down, not gallivantin' wi'all an sundry.'

'All and sundry?' Lottie gulped. Now she was getting somewhere, quite horrified by the implication, protective as always she hoped Victoria wasn't embroiled in something improper, if not a young fellow, whom or what?

'Well – accordin't'Alice, sh'does get t'some funny places. What's a fine lady like Miss Victoria doin' at the Labour Party meetin' hall i' Newcastle fer a start. God ferbid sh'gets mixed up wi'somebody there,' absolutely aghast at the very idea. Not the sort of behaviour for the pit gaffer's granddaughter and should be nipped in the bud straight away, she warned Lottie, whose feelings ran along those same lines. Victoria was a law unto herself and capable of anything. When it was possible to pin the miscreant down long enough, she broached the subject and didn't mince words, ending up with 'What would your gandfather have to say?' No mention of Geoffrey's feelings, she was not entirely sure what they might be, he being much more liberal minded about his headstrong daughter's goings on but who knows? Realising how easily she accepted him as Victoria's father, a bit of wishful thinking no doubt.

Immediately on the defensive, Victoria didn't deny a thing. 'So what?' She said, 'Grandpa'a an old stick in the mud but I expected a more open view from you, Lottie. The only way to discover the opinions of others is to listen to what they have to say and that is what I am doing. His generation is on the way out, there has to be change.' Bright blue eyes full of enthusiasm, a shame to dampen it but a sort of brake had to be used to stop such fervour getting out of hand.

'You can't sit in two corners at once, young lady. The people you are consorting with hate your grandfather's kind and all they represent. Confrontation on a large scale has to come sooner or later and where will you stand then, when loyalties come into conflict. Old feelings die hard, if at all, which I have often found to my cost.'

'I don't know, I really don't know,' Victoria was obliged to confess. 'Grandfather is good to me but his ways don't have to be mine. If he were to die tomorrow, God forbid, I wouldn't want his collieries, too many problems. Men shouldn't have to work for so little.' Quite earnest in her beliefs.

One part of Lottie silently applauded this attitude, how could it be otherwise, but she thought of the man who had been her friend for years and rose to his defence. 'Keep such notions to yourself, change must come as you say, but let him carry on in the belief that his life's work will be carried on after him.' And she wondered even as she said it, why she should be the devil's advocate. John Starrett was regarded as the Devil Incarnate by his employees with good reason.

Victoria kept a still tongue but still continued to attend Labour Party meetings in the area and leant more and more towards Socialism. At one of these meetings she met Robert Hanson for the second time, too young on that first occasion to remember him now but immediately attracted to the strapping young man he had grown into during the intervening years. Robert felt stirrings of recognition when he set eyes on her again, a lovely young lady, obviously out of her class among those gathered there. The bright blue eyes, corn coloured hair and bonny face had matured obviously but some strange instinct told him who she must be, amazed to find the gaffer's grandaughter in such unexpected surroundings.

'Slummin' a bit aren't ya?' he taunted, anything to offset the devastating effect she had upon him. 'A far cry from your neck of the woods. Does the gaffer want a spy i'the enemy camp?' This was right below the belt and absolutely unjustified, those startling eyes soon ablaze with anger, her golden head tossed high.

'Whatever you may think of my grandfather, he wouldn't use me for such tactics, nor would I allow him to do so. Who are you and why do you hate him so much?'

Rather piqued that she had no remembrance of him, Robert lashed out in scorn and ignored the fact she was just a small child. 'So, y'don't know me, why should ya. Y'were a snobby little bitch when w'met anyway. Aa'm Robert Hanson an'you asked yer grandfather t'buy me a pair o'boots.'

A vague memory touched her mind but no clear recollection. 'Oh,' she said, reminded that this must be Lottie's nephew, the same colour hair, a shock of it.

'Oh,' he mocked in repetition, 'The answer t'yer question's easy. Y'canna sit i' these meetin's an' not realise why Polrigg miners have no room fer John Starrett. A few hundred at Belsford an' Studly an'all that feel the same.' Momentarily contrite when he saw the look of hurt on her face. 'All right Aa'll keep off the subject o'yer precious grandfather,' unable to resist a final dig. 'Somebody loves the old skinflint it seems.'

Victoria bristled but stifled an urge for further retaliation and asked instead about the speakers for the evening, her companion was instantly diverted. 'A man an'woman,' he told her, 'Both prospective candidates. They'll get in the next time if the lackies stop votin' like their masters. Be sure an' keep them upper class ears open, they're educated an' talk a lot o'common sense,' exciting her with his obvious fervour.

There was something very likeable about the young fellow at her side, squeaky clean, scrubbed almost and quite presentable, even if a neatly pressed suit shone from too much wear and constant brushing. Margaret Hanson was very particular with the few clothes her son possessed. It was a lively meeting, so many strong minded individuals in this one room, those who would make socialism a force to be reckoned with in the future but somewhat at odds in the way and the speed in which they wanted things done. Victoria's head buzzed in total confusion when it came to an end and the gathering dispersed, still in Robert Hanson's company when they walked to the tram stop near the Handyside Arcade in Percy Street. 'What?' he quipped, 'No chauffer driven car t'fetch ya?' Amazed at the attraction this blue eyed beauty held for him. Reluctant to part so soon, he counted his coppers to see if he had enough for two tram fares, smiling at her efforts to keep up with his long strides he slackened off a bit, an excitement in him not engendered by the meeting they had recently left. 'Jackson drove me into town and dropped me at the Haymarket, I told him not to bother coming back, I would take a tram. He didn't exactly approve,' she said with asn impish grin. 'I walk from the tram stop on High Street. I do have two legs, I am not exactly incapable.'

'So I've noticed – – the legs I mean,' delighted to see her blush. 'A fair stretch from Branton High Street t'Nob Hill. Mebbe Aa'd better walk that way wi'ya an'go home by the wall. See the bogey man doesn't get ya.' Her laughter was quite infectious but rather self conscious, taken aback by the suggestion.

'Perhaps you had,' she accepted shyly, elated to think Robert desired more of her company. His forthright manner was so refreshing after casual boyfriends among her own set, sons of the gentry introduced at odd intervals, John Starrett so anxious for her to make a suitable marriage, he wouldn't approve of this association, that was for sure.

They strolled, haphazardly, along side streets and lanes which led away from the Great North Road, where they alighted from the rackety Low Fell tram, the longest route possible to delay the moment of parting. There was no awkwardness between them, although Robert's shabby attire compared most unfavourably with his companion's well cut clothes, simple but very expensive. Robert's strong local dialect was in marked contrast to Victoria's refined manner of speech. Conversation never slackened, both good talkers and willing listeners, indulging a little in the age old art of flirtation and soon they found themselves within yards of Rothwell House, with no excuse to linger, it was dark by now. 'This is where Aa say good night,' Robert mumbled, rather self conscious, overawed now by his surroundings, the old barriers back in place. 'Aa can just imagine me aunt's eyebrows liftin' at the sight o' Miss Victoria hobnobbin' wi' the likes o'me,' he mocked, deliberate emphasis on the word 'Miss', the whole mood of the evening suddenly changed. 'You are afraid,' Victoria triumphed. 'You don't want anyone to know you walked the pit gaffer's grandaughter home. That makes you more of the snob you think I am,' her bonny face alive with mischief. 'How d'ya know what Aa think?' he muttered. 'See ya around sometime.' A parting shot before the darkness swallowed him up, too far away to hear Victoria's soft laughter or what she said. 'You will Robert Hanson,' she whispered, 'I'll make sure of that.' She was possessed of feelings never experienced before and hard to understand.

'I'm home,' she shouted down to the kitchen and hurried upstairs, fully convinced her flushed face and shining eyes would be an absolute give away, Lottie always too perceptive where she was concerned, not to know the reason why. Besides, what was there to tell, she argued and knew she lied, a vital spark had kindled between Robert and herself the sort that might easily burst into flame.

They met several times during the next few weeks, sometimes by accident, more often by design. Victoria became very astute at that but was rather disturbed by the fact that Robert drew his own line, over which he didn't intend to cross. Lottie's nephew struggled hard to keep this relationship on purely platonic terms, Victoria was not helping in the least. He fought the attraction she had for him, so comfortable to be with and to share confidences, once told of his burning ambition to emigrate to Australia.

'It's a young country,' he enthused, 'Cryin' out for my kind t'settle an'make somethin o' theirselves. Given half a chance Aa'd be off like a shot. There's nowt i' this God forsaken hole.' Unaware of the effect his words had upon her, how much this latter statement hurt.

'If you go to Australia, I shall never see you again,' she said without thinking and caught an apprehensive look in his blue eyes, quick to cover up this unfortunate faux pas. 'Who shall I have to argue with?' she added lightly, and warned herself to tread more warily in future.

Lottie's own emotional entanglement tended to occupy her thoughts to the exclusion of all else and Victoria's even more irrational behaviour passed right over her head, attention was drawn towards it by Martha, who missed nothing and remarked one day there might be romance in the offing. 'All the signs,' she added knowingly and Lottie groaned inwardly, this long time friend was too perceptive for words. Highly improbable her love for Geoffrey was any secret either but she was too wise to risk further trouble after that strong hint of dismissal years before, forgotten by Alice within days but Martha had a long memory.

Alice pricked her ears at the mere hint of romance, there was no gossip in Saltersgate about Robert and the gaffer's granddaughter, they were too adept at covering their tracks. Victoria had been so long away from home in educational establishments and was unknown to most of them in any case. 'Miss Victoria and a lad.' Alice exclaimed in rapture. 'That's champion isn't it? D'ya remember what a fine chap my Joe was?'

'How could anybody ferget?' was the tart reply. 'It's time y'stopped resurrectin' the poor fella, let'im rest in peace. It's the livin, w'need t'bother about.' Her words followed by a fit of sulks, along with a firm resolution never to speak to Martha again, this solemn vow made at least twice every week.

The mystery remained unsolved but a much more serious worry took its place, John Starrett was found slumped across his desk one morning, unconscious. 'I'm not surprised', Angus MacLean declared, after a thorough examination. 'Overdoing things. Those collieries of yours will be the death of you,' he told the gaffer who had soon come round. 'Stuff and nonsense,' he barked out but lacked the usual bite. 'I am not dead yet and if I am likely to be in the near future tell me straight, none of your shilly shallying. Not that anything you say will make any difference, I would rather die in harness.' Never a day's illness since Lottie first knew him, a man who seemed invincible somehow, was now confined to bed under strong protest.

'He must be made to take things easy,' Angus MacLean warned Geoffrey before he left the house. 'And see that he cuts down on the rich living, he carries too much weight. A holiday away from all this would do him good,' said with a huge grin on his strong looking face. 'Not the best of patients, I know, but try to keep him in bed for a day or two at least. The attack was slight but a warning, nevertheless, which shouldn't be ignored.' The gaffer did not take kindly to his enforced rest, nor did he obey instructions to the letter. 'Poppycock,' he muttered, when Lottie tried to remonstrate, 'And you can take that muck away,' when she proposed a plateful of scrambled eggs for lunch. 'MacLean is a proper old woman.' He was most insistent that a telephone be installed at his bedside, his colliery managers were contacted a number of times each day. Long conversations, guaranteed to raise his blood pressure, being the man he was. 'We must get him out of this house, away from the area,' Geoffrey sighed but knew it would be no easy task to persuade this stubborn man to do anything his will. 'Victoria,' he exclaimed, as an idea suddenly occurred to him. 'If anyone can get him to do it, she can. Besides, she could do with a holiday herself, always mooning around the house nowadays.'

An ideal solution, to kill two birds with one stone, hardly an apt expression under the circumstances but very opportune should Victoria be able to remove John Starrett and herself at the same time, an end to political meetings and disturbing influences, Lottie was not to know her own nephew figured very largely in this latter category. Apart from which, there was wild talk in the village about a general strike being imminent, men from all industries and occupations. Victoria's great affection for her grandfather tipped the scales in the plotters' favour. 'I need a break and so do you,' she persisted when John Starrett dithered. 'We can both relax and forget about everything for a while, be good company for each other. And you choose where to go, perhaps some nice seaside resort in the south,' was the suggestion. Forget about Robert Hanson too, she hoped, her feelings in such a turbulent state. A persuasive tongue did the trick, the gaffer hard to convince his colliery wheels could possibly turn without his overriding presence and bothered about the likelihood of a general strike but, at last, decided he needed to be fit to deal with such when it came and he could be back within a day if necessary. 'Aa'll be busy, anyway,' was all Robert said when told of the arrangements, Victoria silently pleading for him to beg her not to go or at least admit she would be a miss. 'Ye'll be better out o'the way,' he added significantly but didn't expand and left her rather peeved at such easy acceptance of her departure from the scene. Not even a goodbye kiss, she thought, steeped in misery, unaware of Robert's overwhelming desire to hold her close but he couldn't trust himself, this beautiful young woman had come to mean too much to him and it wouldn't do, they definitely had no future together. He left with the image of a disconsolate slump to her slender shoulders and an unhappy face as they parted company.

Sad, maybe, but Victoria was optimistic enough to believe a four week separation might work wonders for a love Robert refused to acknowledge, he had a wise head on his young shoulders, much wiser than the woman who adored him almost to distraction. Trouble lay ahead, big trouble, to place them firmly on opposite sides of an unsurmountable fence and love for the pit gaffer's granddaughter was a luxury this humble collier couldn't afford.

* * *

The fashionable hotel chosen in Lyme Regis was deadly dull till Richard Barrington and his father arrived upon the scene, whether by accident or design was hard to assess, Richard was was surprised but obviously relieved to see a younger face among such a surplus of elderly patrons, wealthy old ladies looked after by middle aged spinsters, the latter's sole purpose to run after them hand and foot, relatives or employers permanent residents for spring, summer and autumn of the year. Not enough men left to go round after the war, Victoria estimated sadly, sweethearts killed perhaps and didn't want anyone else. Was this what fate had in store for her? Painfully reminded of Robert Hanson she was so much in love with the aggravating fellow, it had to be him or nobody.

The elderly Barrington was a contemporary of her grandfather and a colliery owner. Not a close friend by any means but his only son an eligible bachelor and in the mining business with his father, which made Victoria wonder how much her grandfather had to do with them being there, it was too much of a coincidence. A plot was hatched between William Barrington and himself, owner of Legwood and Roguehill, Richard a so called ideal match, which would serve the ends of both parties, with eyes to the main chance. John Starrett had no male heir and Barrington wouldn't say no to some influence in the running of another three pits, this was her inheritance but one she didn't want. If she did, Victoria couldn't see herself playing second fiddle to Richard or his father, a young lady who had a very definite mind of her own.

The younger man appeared to agree with her assessment of the situation, an unpretentious human being and she liked him, a rather tepid feeling set against the heat Robert stirred within her. Certainly he was under his pompous father's thumb, whom she utterly disliked from the moment they met.

'Those two old codgers are decidedly throwing us together, let's give them a run for their money,' Victoria proposed and spent lots of time in Richard's company from then on but found it very odd he never made a pass at her. Not that it mattered, her heart belonged to someone else, even if that special person seemed unwilling for anything of a romantic nature to develop. Victoria had heaps of time to reflect upon her relationship with Lottie's nephew, never a single kiss, and imagined how marvellous it would be to be kissed by him, really kissed, no lukewarm peck just unbridled passion, melting as that attractive mouth took its fill from hers, no end to the way her thoughts ran amok.

With the added satisfaction that his scheming had borne fruit, the young pair right in their assumption, John Starrett's health improved, the sea air, excellent cuisine and the contents of a good cellar all heightened his spirits, not that over indulgence in the latter two was a good idea. But Victoria and Richard decided to keep up the pretence and let the rascals wallow in their illusions, careful not to upset the apple cart.

The colliery owners read the print off every Conservative controlled newspaper and itched to be back in harness, the contents most disturbing.

Reports daily of consultation between Trade Unions and government ministers to avoid an all out stoppage, clever politicians prepared to go to any lengths to keep the wheels of industry turning, once successful in setting miners apart from other work men, colliers were the real thorn in their flesh. Divide and rule was their slogan, another strike in isolation would be unlikely to succeed.

Still inclined towards Socialism, Victoria's reading matter would not have pleased her grandfather, with two of the men in her life in opposite camps and her father's views none too evident, this was sufficient to cause great confusion in an impressionable young mind.

Victoria debated with herself at great length. Did she really want a different life style? Brought up in the same sort of luxury as her present surroundings she had never known anything else. Robert's was a completely opposite existence and love meant sharing but who would share what with whom? Maybe not much give in either of them if it came to the crunch. Lottie was obviously aware of the difficulties, her opinion mattered quite a lot, but she was not so willing to get into discussion nowadays, obviously taught discretion with the passing of time and, in any case, couldn't be told about the connection with her own nephew.

'May as well go home, Barrington,' John Starrett suggested one morning at breakfast, their meals taken together by mutual consent. 'Better do it before the railway system grinds to a halt. A damned inconvenience, no thought for others,' William Barrington said, both men cut from the same cloth. All this as they tucked into an enormous meal, the gaffer barely recovered from one attack and going the right way towards another. 'You will eat yourself into an early grave' Victoria remonstrated, not for the first time, but wasted her breath as usual, nothing was likely to turn her grandfather from the habits of a lifetime, regardless of the consequences. 'Stop fussing girl,' he muttered in disgust. 'Better dead than a life not worth living.' An understandable philosophy but over indulgence was one of his greatest weaknesses and probably the death of him. What he digested in one go was sufficient to eke out for a working class family's main meal of the day.

At another breakfast table, more than four hundred miles to the north, Geoffrey Cranshawe perused that day's issue of the only newspapers allowed in Rothwell House, other points of view had to be sought elsewhere, no so called radical literature permitted under this roof, 'Not even good enough to light fires,' the gaffer scorned, absolutely convinced of the infallibility of Conservative doctrines.

'A nasty business,' Geoffrey commented sadly. 'The outcome will be much worse than anyone imagines because of hard liners on both sides. But the diehards have it best,' he said to Lottie, 'They don't give an inch. It can be most disturbing to see the other fellow's point of view. You and I are sufferers in this respect.' Heartwarming to know some of his beliefs coincided with her own. They had spent more time together during Victoria's absence, spared her sudden, unannounced appearances and sharp scrutiny from those keen blue eyes, often rather disconcerting. Treasured moments but painful with so much longing in body and mind, the only solution being to part company until these urges passed. Lottie was sorely tempted to use the feminine wiles Geoffrey knew she possesed to ignite flames of passion but managed to control the impulse out of respect for his wishes. She believed herself perfectly willing to accept what being his mistress would entail, a life of pretence, hole in the corner, whatever, but deep down lay the thought of Victoria and the effect it would have upon her, a big stumbling block not easy to dismiss. Contingency plans were well under way in Saltersgate and elsewhere, as men got ready for the anticipated struggle, some rather sceptical about support from other industries. 'The buggars let 'is down the last time,' came from many tongues, miners still sore at the former betrayal. 'Not this time,' was the confident argument from young, eager beavers, who saw it all as a great crusade and certain of ultimate victory. 'Nowt 'l get past the picket lines this time,' Ralph Hanson vowed with intense feeling, those months in jail plenty to temper his enthusiasm to some degree, the indignity of life behind bars never forgotten but still willing to risk more of the same for the justice of their cause. With all the workers in the country coming out together, it had to be a short, sharp fight, he maintained, and gave a thought to men of Jackie Phillips' ilk, long dead but always prepared to get stuck in regardless of the cost. 'Fer ye Jackie an'all them like ya,' he vowed, so many fallen by the wayside in his lifetime and before, a long struggle. Lots of faces were missing after the war and too many mining accidents which could have been avoided, A continual battle for the rights of poorer folk, money and power always in the hands of a small minority.

Men in Robert Hanson's age group were brimful of youthful fervour for a confrontation expected to bring the hated establishment to its knees. An attitude which brought scathing indictment from his sister, now into her teens, Elizabeth was a little firebrand and scornful of the antics men employed, always ready to take on both male members of her family, no holds barred, and proudly indulged by her father who idolised his family. Sadly Ralph couldn't see how much she resembled his sister, that same sort of spirit he disparaged in Lottie. 'Don't worry Mam, there'll be some money comin' inta the house, Aa'm workin', aren't Aa.' Elizabeth smug in her own importance as an only wage earner, her job unlikely to be affected by the strike, the grocery shop in Branton patronised mainly by an upper class clientele.

Tightened belts once again, Margaret grieved, her precious Co-op dividend drawn for numerous purposes since the last futile effort. But dried goods such as tea, sugar and a few tins of this and that stashed away were a drop in the ocean if the strike dragged on interminably. Margaret missed Janey Wilson at such times, her friendship had been amply repaid during the woman's lengthy illness, Mary very grateful. Nothing but continued bitterness against her father, Ralph unforgiving too, his only sister denied inclusion in the family circle. A sad trait in these north country folk but she was always quick to remind herself of numerous good ones to offset the bad.

Meanwhile, in Rothwell House, Martha's grumbles began before it even started, anticipating invasion of her kitchen yet again, the police certain to be called upon to guard the premises. Not in the least mellowed by age, nobody knew how old she was, her tongue was as tart as ever. 'Years have nowt t'do with it,' she argued strongly when conversation touched upon someone of their acquaintance being too old for work. 'Aa'm just as good as Aa was twenty years ago,' she proudly boatsed and bustled into action to prove the point, just as sprightly and almost an institution according to Lottie, who couldn't imagine the big house without her.

'Them two want t'get theirselves home or they'll be stuck down there,' she proclaimed, her concern for Victoria, the gaffer well able to take care of himself in Martha's opinion. Lottie fretted about the whole nasty business, trouble surely between her and John Starrett, if Victoria was still of the same mind, the gaffer's views were rock solid, one of the diehards Geoffrey spoke of, her own loyalties liable to be severely tested once more. However open minded her beloved seemed to be, the inherent sense of ancestry in both of them could rise to the fore, two vastly different blood lines.

Late one evening the telephone in the lower hallway jerked her suddenly into awareness and alarmed to be called so late she threw a warm dressing gown on and ran to answer it, moving by instinct, accustomed to every nook and cranny, a fleeting memory of that other time she ran in desperation thrust firmly aside.

'Miss Victoria,' she gasped into the mouthpiece when she discovered who the caller was. 'What a time to ring. Has something happened to your grandfather?' soon reassured. 'No, nothing like that, it is only eleven thirty. Did I disturb your beauty sleep?' Victoria sounded very amused. 'Is that all it is?' Lottie said, 'We all retired early. I thought it must be at least two in the morning.' A quick look at the grandfather clock, illuminated by moonlight, told her there was no mistake. 'I won't keep you,' Victoria promised, 'Besides, there is a long queue for the phones. Just to tell you we are travelling home tomorrow, we should be in Newcastle by seven in the evening, ask Jackson to come to the station. I must run, everyone here is making preparations to leave. Bye.' 'Bye,' Lottie answered in bemused fashion to a dead line and replaced the receiver. A busy day ahead, beds to air, dinner menu to arrange, an end to the lighter meals Geoffrey preferred, the gaffer's appetite a different kettle of fish.

'And what was all that about?' a deep voice from behind and the exhilarating sense of a warm, masculine body so close sent a shiver of expectation down her spine, close enough to touch. A quick turn and she would be in Geoffrey's arms where she longed to be, shaken into trembling by a surge of desire, an urgent need for him in every fibre of her being. 'Miss Victoria is coming home tomorrow,' she stammered, the prefix used to put herself firmly in place, so much aware of his nearness and she wondered if that same fire burned inside him also and if she should encourage it, show how very much he was wanted. Geoffrey needed no encouragement, Victoria was furthest from his mind at that moment, very much alive to the fresh, well remembered scent of lavendar always associated with this beloved woman from the very first feel of her in his arms. Willpower, exercised to his torment for what seemed an eternity, suddenly vanished and he moved towards forbidden joys. Their bodies merged, Lottie melted into his arms and a hungry mouth found hers, which opened to meet it in great urgency of desire.

'It wouldn't be right,' he groaned, when they stopped to take a breath, but the flood gates of passion were open at last. 'No it wouldn't be right,' she murmured without conviction, pressing ever closer, able to feel the need in Geoffrey's responsive body. The time for fulfilment had come, no retreat, anything else they might have said denied utterance, when two mouths met again and they forgot their scruples, carried along in a deluge of unbridled passion, soon in Lottie's bed, with no sure knowledge afterwards as to how they got there.

Some time later, she awoke to the feel of Geoffrey's arms around her slender body, their limbs lovingly entwined. No shame just absolute content, a coming together after so many wasted years of hopeless longing, kept apart by a mutual sense of right and wrong. She was quite willing to admit Geoffrey's strength of mind in this respect, ready to succumb to her own feelings on many occasions. No lustful taking of pleasure, something far beyond that, and no awkwardness as might well have been, her lover's apology for hurting her totally unnecessary. A woman now past the first flush of youth had been taken into realms of rapture, often dreamt of but never experienced. She nestled closer, reluctant to awaken her sleeping partner to the cruel reality of so little time before Martha and Alice came downstairs to start their day, an idyllic interlude which soon must end. Geoffrey's dark eyes opened slowly and gazed straight into hers, celibate for so long and immediately anxious. 'It was wonderful my darling, wonderful,' she hastened to assure him, in answer to that unspoken question, such strong affinity between them. 'How does it feel to be an abandoned woman?' he teased and pressed tantalising lips against her soft breasts, already peaked in response, a heady sensation for both of them, eager to give further satisfaction to love starved bodies and they proceeded to do so in great ecsatasy.

'It feels – – -you know how it feels,' came a much delayed reply, when they lay back blissfully replete, suddenly quite shy, full of gratitude as sordid memories slipped away. Geoffrey's hard to control passion had taken her to heights hitherto unknown, the past banished forever, as of no account. This was love not lust, the difference so obvious and absolutely overwhleming. He turned towards her in a last, warm embrace. A pity they couldn't stay there locked in the security of this marvellous feeling for one another, but the world was about to intrude again, never sympathetic to their sort of relationship. Where did they go from here? A question neither of them was able to answer with any certainty.

* * *

The tedious journey homeward, with numerous diversions, did nothing to contain John Starrett's temper, immensely irritated by the inconvenience, even more scathing than usual in his strongly expressed indictment of the working classes, supported wholeheartedly by William Barrington. Victoria and Richard kept silent, secretly ashamed of their respective relatives but knew any intervention could only cause further embarrassment. Their first class travelling companions were in the same situation as themselves, forced to alter arrangements before the entire railway network dragged to a halt, only concerned about the trouble it was causing them and they vented their spleen upon those employees forced to look after their needs.

Mattie Jackson trod the station platform for almost two hours, upset to be absent at David's bedtime, a nightly ritual enjoyed by man and boy. Marianne would never be dead when his son's eyes regarded him with the same trusting expression, he was careful to keep his wife's image alive in the lad's mind. But with a sick mother known to him for so short a time, the boy had no visual remembrance at all, apart from a wedding photograph which scarcely did her justice, a studio portrait taken after the wedding, a very stiff pose in bride and groom.

None too happy about the imminent strike, certain to be an outcast from the beginning because of his connection with the pit gaffer, Jackson worried lest David suffered too, if local youngsters chose to take spite out of him, convinced this present confrontation would be long and bitter, everyone expected to be for or against, with no room for neutrality.

When at last the travellers appeared Victoria's heart lifted at the sight of him, always a veritable tower of strength, perhaps not so much since Marianne died but in childhood days the servants in Rothwell House had represented the stability in her life. That same heart was sore at the thought of Robert and her grandfather, both staunch advocates of very opposite beliefs, which meant nothing but grief, truly dismayed to be in such an invidious position. In no mood for decision making but sadly convinced that, sooner or later, she would have to support one or the other and none too sure who it would be.

Dinner was very much delayed that evening and not a happy meal, serving dishes passed around by Lottie, who listened to the conversation but took no part in it, which soon became heated when Geoffrey ventured to say working class folk were due to a better deal. 'Stuff and nonsense,' John Starrett rapped at him and almost choked on a piece of prime sirloin, medium rare as he liked it. 'There is a decided plan to life, some men are born to rule and others to serve. Ever since those damned Trades Unions came into being there has been nothing but trouble. This strike won't last, most of them haven't the stomach for it,' he disparaged, oozing confidence. 'The miners lasted thirteen weeks on their own in 1921, it might be your turn to climb down grandfather,' Victoria remarked, immediately pounced upon, the gaffer red in the face. 'When I was young, women didn't have so much to say for themselves,' never pleased when crossed, 'I'm off to my bed,' already on his feet, pushing his chair away from the table. 'Radicals under my own roof but quite prepared to eat the food I provide,' he finished nastily.

Victoria gasped and Geoffrey's lips tightened. 'Your dinner, sir,' Lottie put in hurriedly, his meal barely touched, food wilfully wasted when soon so many would be on the bread line. 'My appetite has been taken away,' he growled, a baleful glace in Victoria's direction, to whom he apportioned most of the blame, further protest was useless.

'I suppose you agree with all this silly nonsense, Charlotte?' John Starrett turned to her and said before leaving the room. 'A fine thing when my entire household is against me,' and sounded just like a petulant child. 'I could never be against YOU, sir,' strong emphasis on this one particular word, which made her actual feelings quite plain. A direct look from those steely grey eyes as he departed, absolute silence in his wake. Any good derived from the recent holiday had been jeopardised by a family argument, the General Strike not yet begun and they were already at loggerheads.

The supposed all out stoppage, when it did come, lasted a mere nine days, the miners left to carry on alone as before, a sense of betrayal engendered then to reach out far into the future years, a great source of bitterness. But these were determined men, made so by the very nature of their work, with no illusions about the hardship facing them, wives and families were solid in support, fully resolved not to go down without giving it their best effort. A few days after her return, Victoria bumped into Robert on Branton High Street, elation at the sight of him was soon dampened. 'Miss Victoria Cranshawe. Back among the riff raff after mixin wi'the la-de-da. How's the old man? Bloomin' Aa expect.' And watched her rise to the bait as intended, blue eyes ablaze, this cheeky banter the only defence against her undeniable attraction.

'As if you cared,' she snapped, 'Your manners certainly haven't improved,' furious at the way her heart raced and realising how much she cared for this handsome devil, she had a strong urge to throw her arms around his neck in fond embrace, so glad to set eyes on him again. Robert laughed, soon uneasy at the odd looks they received from passers by, none of them known to him, thank goodness. 'Yer right bonny when yer mad,' he teased, indeed no lie, those soft red lips, blue eyes and golden hair had a devastating effect upon him, hard to shake off. 'Aa'll be takin' a walk across the Moor round about three o'clock, if y'should happen t'be passin' that way.' An obvious invitation couched in a careless manner. 'Don't expect me,' she flung after him when he touched his cap in sheer impudence and walked away, afraid to linger in such an open place, Victoria seemingly oblivious of the fact, furious at his offhand manner but knew she would meet him. Robert only needed to crook his little finger for her to follow, to the ends of the earth if necessary. Australia could be the answer, a new beginning on equal terms and money would be no problem. All obstacles were ignored, Robert's pride and an attack of tight fistedness on John Starrett's part, her father an unknown factor in the equation. 'What's wrong, kitten?' Geoffrey inquired after being rounded on three times in quick succession, astounded to see her young mouth quiver. 'It's a mess, daddy, the whole thing is a mess.' The word 'daddy' used for the first time in years, a sure indication it was something of a very personal nature that troubled her. 'I can always lend a shoulder to cry on,' he offered gently, astounded to be taken at his word, robbed of such demonstrations for most of her younger life and enormously touched.

'Victoria is uptight,' he confided in Lottie. 'But I can't make a twenty two year old bare her soul if she doesn't want to. You talk to her,' he suggested, and was informed at once she could easily be told to mind her own business, still convinced some man was involved, obviously unsuitable if Victoria chose not to mention him. The situation was soon banished from her mind when Jackson and the gaffer came back from Polrigg. 'Scab written all over the car,' Mattie complained and had never sounded so upset, except when Marianne died. 'In bright yella paint. The gaffer's hoppin' mad but not half s'much as me. Aa'm handin' in me notice. That stuff'll not rub off in a month o'Sundays.'

Jackson's pride and joy was cruelly defaced, an absolute wreck, and no amount of elbow grease would remove the crude words without irreparable damage to its surface. Lottie's immediate task was to soothe outraged feelings. 'Forget it,' she advised, although equally distressed. 'The work of youngsters, no doubt, with nothing better to do.' But she knew deep down no bairn was guilty of this offence. 'Don't think of leaving because of senseless vandalism, the place wouldn't be the same without you and David,' she pleaded, dismayed by the wounded expression on this dear, familiar face. 'Aa canna carry on like this Lottie,' he burst out, almost at the end of his tether. 'Aa've even stopped poppin' out fer a drink at night, men Aa've supped wi'fer years turnin'their backs.' She realised now why she hadn't been called upon to babysit of late. 'It won't last forever,' she said. 'Somebody has to see sense. The men's cause is right even if methods of retaliation leave much to be desired. But how else do they claim what is rightfully theirs?' No answer to such a vexed question.

'How do Aa know,' Jackson snorted contemptuously. 'Aa'm not a pit man, just a coal owner's lackey. Aa'll have a go at the car but don't expect t'make much impression. They've done fer it good an'proper.' Lottie was quick to offer encouragement. 'You can try,' she said and hoped some hard graft might work the hurt out of his system. 'I'll take David off your hands for a while. A walk across the Moor might blow the cobwebs away and I've been promising long enough.' Desperate to put all the upheaval behind her for while, a seven year old would be the ideal companion, no hang ups in that direction.

Under strict instructions to be a good lad, David clung tightly to Lottie's hand through the streets of Oakfields, no distance from the Town Moor, almost past himself with excitement when he saw the wide open space. 'Can w'go right t'the other side, Aunt Lottie? It's ever such a long way but Aa'm big now,' he proudly claimed, the broadness of his vowels very noticeable, with no Marianne to help eradicate it with patient determination, definitely Mattie Jackson's son, his refined mother not being around to rub off those rough edges.

'Miles and miles,' she assured him, knowing what he wanted to hear, 'And yes, we will go right to the other side and back.' The Town Moor, Newcastle's lung, belonged to the Freemen of this big industrial town, mostly flat ground, except for one slightly undulating area, a hollow filled with deciduous trees, the only shade on any bright summer's day.

Lottie's incredulous eyes spotted two familiar figures en route to this leafy copse, no mistaking the man's tall, loose limbed form or that shock of bright auburn hair, glinting in the sun. The blonde tresses of the girl at his side were easy to distinguish and a lissom body reaching just above her companion's shoulder. 'Victoria!' she gasped. 'And Robert!' scarcely able to believe the evidence of her own eyes, shaken by the impact of discovery, this was the explanation for her daughter's recent mood swings. She musn't be seen, the only solution was to turn tail immediately, which brought the expected cries of protest from young David. 'Y'sayed w'would walk miles an'miles, Aunt Lottie, that's what y'sayed. What are w'goin' back fer?' he kept on wailing all the way to Rothwell House, so unlike this favourite person break a promise.

Mattie Jackson, perspiring heavily, lifted his eyes from the car and stared in amazement at his son's blotched face. 'Have ye been a bad lad?' he asked, a quick glance to see if the boy was all in one piece, no damage done, 'No,' came Lottie's swift disclaimer and the tearful youngster found himself packed off to Martha, with the promise of home made lemonade and biscuits. 'Now lass,' Jackson demanded, reminded by the expression on her face of those stormy sessions long ago. 'Somethin's happened, y'were as right as rain when the pair o'ya set off. If it's owt t'do wi'David Aa'll tan the hide off 'im.' An unlikely punishment and they both knew it. 'Nothing to do with David,' she hastened to assure him. 'But things couldn't be worse.' A comforting hand was thrust irritably aside, which signified she intended to tackle the problem alone. There was some strange sort of irony in the fact that they they stood almost on the same spot where she refused his help after that fateful meeting with Jake Snowdon. Eighteen years old and her back straight as a ramrod, just as it was now as she walked towards the house without another word. In the sanctuary of her own sitting room, Lottie fretted over this recent discovery, not to be shared with anyone, especially Geoffrey, wondering how far the impossible relationship had progressed. Full cousins, blood related, a torturous thought and nothing to ease it. One more cruel trick of fate in a life plagued with them and she forced to suffer in silence as always.

Not knowing which way to turn, she wept as she had done so many times in the past, unaware of the scene being enacted among that small clump of trees, near the Moor's edge, convinced the fault was hers, a case of sinfulness biding its time to exact payment in this heartbreaking fashion. One sin added to another by consummation of her love for Geoffrey, a man whose life was still alive. And, well accustomed to indulging in self condemnation, Lottie Hanson did the usual excellent job of tearing herself apart.

* * *

That stubborn streak in Victoria lost the battle of whether to meet Robert or not and she left Rothwell House a short while before Lottie and David, the sight of him just beyond the turnstile beside the big gate enough to make her eyes light up in anticipation, angry at her own weakness but fully determined to force a show down, no more dangling on a string.

'Aa didn't reckon ye'd come,' he said by way of greeting but his blue eyes absorbed every inch of her, as pretty as a picture she should gave a big sign displayed 'Danger – Forbidden Territory' to be taken notice of if he had any sense, which seemed to have deserted him for once. This meeting was a mistake and one he could well regret.

'I almost didn't,' she admitted, tagging along beside him as he trod the path, then in typical Victoria outspokeness took the bull by the horns. 'Do you have any feeling for me at all?' came the blunt question, totally unprepared for the hoot of derision which escaped his lips, he rather taken aback, both of them inclined towards the unpredictable.

'What sort o'question is that? Yer a bonny lass an'w'get on all right most o'the time but that doesn't mean Aa'm pining away wi'love fer ya,' he spat out vehemently, a bit too emphatic in rejection, at great pains to avoid the startled blue eyes gazing up at him and wondering how he would cope if she burst into tears.

'Well –' she exclaimed in utter disbelief. Most girls would have slapped his face or done something equally feminine but not this one, who flung back her head and laughed, 'What's s'funny?' he shot out, rather piqued at her attitude, tears much easier to understand, even more surprised when the laughter turned to anger, pin points of it in those gorgeous eyes, plus an expression difficult to analyse. 'Just who do you imagine you are, Robert Hanson? If you had spent so much time with any Saltersgate girl, you would have kissed her by now, at least, wouldn't you?' A disturbing niggle warned him to be wary, not at all sure what she was up to. This was no half educated lass, a very intelligent young woman capable of almost anything, he guessed, and put himself on guard.

Delighted to see signs of discomposure, Victoria didn't wait for an answer. 'So –' she went on to say. 'What makes me so different? I do have the necessary equipment. Perhaps you are afraid to kiss me?' Deliberate provocation, her full red lips raised in invitation, impossible for any red blooded male to resist and Robert didn't. 'Damn ya,' he groaned and pulled her towards him in savage fury, a fiercely demanding kiss told her all she wanted to know, her lips parted in willing surrender but she was suddenly fearful of what she may have released.

Lottie witnessed none of this, just those first steps along the path, already on her way back to Rothwell House with a protesting youngster, her mind in absolute turmoil, left wondering what was going on but nothing that represented any danger until now. 'You are hurting me,' Victoria accused, pulling herself out of his arms, flushed and trembling. 'Somebody wants t'hurt ya,' Robert blazed, his blood on fire, kicking the turf beneath his feet, now off the pathway onto the grass, not far from the hollow of trees. His hands were dug deep into trouser pockets to curb the impulse to drag her back into his arms, he took refuge in anger, totally out of control. 'Aa love ya, is that what y'want t'hear? A fat lot o'good it'll do either of us,' and strode away to fling himself to the ground in misery, an admission reluctantly torn from him, utterly demoralised by that all revealing kiss. Victoria fell to her knees beside him, on the grass among the trees, her soft golden hair cascading forward. 'I am sorry Robert, so very sorry,' she murmured, almost in tears. 'Please forgive me but I had to know, it has been eating me up for ages. I love you too or think I do,' so utterly confused, a faltering confession.

His reply was explosive. 'Y'think y'do. That's the whole damned thing in a nutshell. Grow up lass, this is no game we are playin'.' Still on her knees, much too close, a sweet appealing young woman, infinitely more dangerous than the Victoria who proved more than a match in many arguments. 'Perhaps if you kissed me again, I might know for sure,' she whispered, 'and weren't so mad at me,' she added softly. Robert was completely disarmed by her nearness, an absolute innocent who didn't realise what she was doing, not entirely, conscious only of unfamiliar urges in her own body, too strong to deny.

'Damn ya,' Robert cursed again, a sharp twist to his mouth, pinning her to the ground with the weight of arousal, lips harshly demanding then gentled, an agonised moan deep inside. 'Y'should o'left well alone, Victoria, ye an' me are poles apart in all ways,' he murmured against her welcoming lips, too far gone to cry halt.

She felt as if she was tumbling down a deep well, eager to drown in its depths, no resistance in either of them as they surrendered to a mutual rush of feeling, nothing between them now but clothing, soon thrust aside to allow warm flesh to bond, hard male and receptive female. Instinct took over, no strength of will left to resist temptation. Robert's calloused hands cupped her soft breasts but his mouth soon replaced them, ardent but caressing, trying not to hurt or scare her in any way. But some hurt was inevitable and she cried out involuntarily, making him hold back, Victoria was well past restraint and wrapped her legs around him, soon urgently interwined and before long they were close as man and woman can ever be, locked in ecstasy, until a feeling of absolute release swept through them and they fell away exhausted. Their eyes met, questioning but unashamed, no sign of regret, not in the immediate wake of such glorious repletion.

'Oh God, Victoria, Aa love ya, Aa love ya,' and suddenly she shrugged into her partly discarded clothing, seeking a state of normality but quick to reassure him of her own love. 'And I am not sorry – – – not one little bit,' rosy cheeked and very beautiful in the culmination of all she had desired for so long a time.

He kissed her again, 'Y'mebbe should be,' he muttered woefully, 'W'might both be sorry after this. 'Y' realise what might have happened?' Now quite solemn.

'Made a child, you mean?' straight to the point.

'It has been known,' he said drily. 'Aa never meant t'go s'far but right now how could Aa feel sorry. Victoria Aa – –' Her fingers silenced him, across his lips in gentle caress. 'The woman tempted me,' she said and laughed, 'I guess I did,' her face close enough to kiss, which he did very thoroughly. 'He didn't take much temptin'.' Robert acknowledged regretfully. 'But it was madness. What sort of future d'we have? Yer grandfather would have me shot an' Aa'd deserve it. But Aa'm glad Aa was the first.' A feeling of warmth flooded right through Victoria's aching body at this latter admission, which needed no confirmation, easy for any man to know.

The firm pressure of his fingers made her wince with pain and he held her small hand against tender lips to soothe them. They had surrendered to passion and now must return to very different worlds. Robert realised Victoria did not fully realise the enormity of what they had done, the thought of inevitable opposition from their separate camps unbearable. No more of this, he vowed, and prayed there would be no unfortunate outcome from their foolishness, although the idea of Victoria having his child would have been wonderful under different circumstances. He loved her and mentally unbraided himself for the whole situation, presumptuous ever to imagine he had anything to offer the pit gaffer's granddaughter. Hours later, in her daintily furnished bedroom, surrounded by luxury, Victoria basked in remembrance of every single moment in his arms and blushed furiously, although quite alone. She wanted more, much more, but only with Robart, darling Robert, a tiny niggle amid all the elation. 'See ya sometime,' he said with his parting kiss, a fierce onslaught on a receptive mouth, tongue sought tongue before renunciation of a love which must not be, the last they would share. No mention of any further meeting just a rueful smile. 'An' ye'll be sure t'let'is know if – ?' And she knew what he meant, the sight of that tall, upright figure tore at her heart strings as he walked away.

Suddenly, she flung herself across the bed and wept, unable to stay the tears or banish an uneasiness from her mind. Victoria, the headstrong girl had disappeared and only a subdued young woman remained, uncertain of her future and dreadfully afraid, but not sorry for the rapture she found in Robert Hanson's arms. If there were to be a child then so be it, they would face it together and to hell with her grandfather's outdated ideas, change in the air and scandal only a nine days wonder, she was far off beam in this belief. No wonder she felt half convinced, the pit gaffer's granddaughter considering, for the very first time, those others directly involved, bound to be badly affected by their actions. As for the timing, with a bitter strike in process, it couldn't have been worse.

* * *

'If that girl is in love, it certainly isn't making her happy,' Geoffrey Cranshawe bemoaned, fully convinced some young fellow to be responsible for his daughter's misery, usually so vivacious, full of life. 'It could be a dustman, for all I care,' he proclaimed once in sheer desperation and hoped Lottie might get to the bottom of it, as she so often did in the past, but not in the present circumstances or so it seemed. Lottie accepted that Geoffrey truly believed his daughter's choice unimportant against her happiness and Robert was a fine, upstanding young fellow, handsome enough to make any girl's heart beat faster. But they were full cousins, marriage impossible, no likelihood of it happening in any case, with John Starrett to uphold the law of class. She hoped a gloomy face signified an end to the affair, prepared to let the matter ride in the cowardly hope this might be the fact, of so nothing needed to be said or done

Two weeks after that ecstatic interlude on the Town Moor, Victoria knew there was to be no child, it was difficult to define her feelings. Robert had removed himself right out of her sphere, what they shared a one off experience. But she still carried a torch for him, he was seldom out of her thoughts and sometimes filled her dreams, where nothing separated them, she was soon reminded on awakening of the stern reality, over which she held no control.

Victoria's unhappiness distracted Lottie from Geoffrey, a purely platonic relationship by mutual consent, even able to convince herself that the girl's unenviable position lay at her own door, because she had sinned and revelled in it. Not that the need in either of them lessened, only making matters worse, should the opportunity arise it could happen again.

It never entered Victoria's head that something else might be to blame for Robert's absence, a man often had other irons in the fire, in his case absolute dedication to the miners' cause and he was up to his neck in all that went on. One of many young hotheads caught up in a battle of wits with authority he was prepared to take incalculable risks, even more reckless as time wore on and desperation entered the game. Being so involved kept his mind away from the love of his life, except in erotic dreams, which were full of her.

Margaret Hanson worried the whole time Robert was out of sight, scarcely at home except to sleep there and sometimes not even then. Never a hint to where he was going and she was so inclined to vent her frustration on Ralph, whose role in this present conflict took on much milder form, begging expeditions, seeking vegetables and other ingredients for the village soup kitchen and organising picket duties. 'Ye've been sent down afore,' his fellow workmen reminded him, 'The devils would throw the book at ya, if y'got nicked again.' A great relief to Margaret to have one of her men out of danger, both very dear to her heart. Some farmers were sympathetic and gave what they could spare but others suffered lightning raids under cover of darkness, odd sacks of this and that from barns and outhouses, the edges of fields robbed of their crops. Poaching was rife too for rabbits and game birds, all of which represented danger, heavy penalties if caught. Cloak and dagger stuff carried out by Robert's age group and even younger, with no thought of consequences. 'So much energy to spare.' Margaret despaired, after yet another stormy session with her son, who stormed out of the house in high dudgeon. 'If those young chaps aren't playing pitch and toss for halfpennies down The Lonnen, they are up to far worse, any of which could land them in jail,' she sadly lamented, Robert's erratic moods were hard to deal with. She was totally unaware of the added complication of her son's love for the colliery owner's granddaughter. He tried his damndest to put Victoria out of his mind but once tasted the joy of love's consummation is hard to forget, even worse if denial is self inflicted.

'Jail would be somethin' he'd remember fer the rest of'is life.' Ralph stated, the fetid smell of prison often in his nostrils. 'But he's a man an' only doin' what Aa did afore'im.' A comforting arm around his wife's lean shoulders, the feel of her bones hard to bear. 'There's nowt on ya, bonny lass, but the gaffer'll see us in hell afore'ee parts wi' a single penny. Mebbe w'ask more o'women than w'have a right.' A silencing finger soon against his mouth. 'Don't ever talk that way,' Margaret gently chastened. 'It can't be wrong to fight for what should be yours. We shall come through this as always, win or lose.'

Ralph Hanson's heart swelled with love for his faithful wife, a veritable tower of strength when needed. No Saltersgate lass was a better helpmate to her man in troubled times than this beloved woman, always there to support him. She saw the look in his eyes and planted a tiny kiss on the top of a fastly balding head. 'I made it after all, didn't I?' she said and found herself closely enveloped in strong arms. 'Aye, y'did at that,' he freely admitted, not usually so demonstrative, these words and signs of affection so precious to a woman who had achieved the nigh impossible, never easy for any incomer to gain acceptance from mining folk.

John Starrett paid daily visits to his three collieries, completely against doctor's orders, now resplendent in a brand new car. The timing of its purchase, although necessary, was sufficient to further incense those on the bread line. 'He shoves 'is bloody wealth down their throats,' Jackson bristled, still in the gaffer's service, his threat of resignation although genuine never carried out with a laddie to fetch up and educate. He hated these regular excursions, not the sort to be at odds with his own kind, and done in silent protest.

Geoffrey avoided discussion with his father-in-law whenever possible, unwilling to worsen a relationship already strained by an adamant refusal to visit his estranged wife. 'He knows the situation,' Lottie was his confidante, 'Even if she were sane I would be the last person Felicity wanted to see. Our marriage ended long before this happened to her. I am no hypocrite. Thank God he has given up on Victoria.' He felt so angry at being tied for life to such a hopeless wreck, with the woman he truly loved his for the taking but only in marriage, firmly resolved on this. Lottie refrained from comment, it had all been said so many times, one night of fulfilment and nothing since, the odd stolen embrace but no calculated adultery. 'There might have been a child,' he fretted after that one and only lapse, a coming together of two people in love, spontaneous not premeditated, furious at himself for putting her at risk. 'Some day, perhaps,' he said, his heart in his eyes, sadly aware how easily Felicity could outlive him and Lottie's child bearing years might soon be at an end. They often spoke about the strike, very down to earth in assessment of the situation. 'They won't win,' Geoffrey prophesied and Lottie had to agree. 'The odds are against them. If the others had stuck it out, maybe, but they have only right and courage to sustain them in the fight and these seldom weigh in their favour.'

'Plenty of courage,' Lottie stated proudly, sickened by daily bulletins from Alice, men jailed for trivial offences, her friend's activities still a source of worry, she was quite willing to purloin John Coulter's farm produce to help Saltersgate folk.

'That lass will end up in prison,' she said to Martha, who shrugged her concern aside. 'Stop yer fussin', wife. Alice has more aloft than w'give'er credit fer.' Quite an admission, never generous with her praise, especially towards their ungainly friend. Not changed a whit, the same untidy creature she was before that brief acquaintance with Joe Simpson, his cheap ring still on her finger, dulled by time but likely to go with her to the grave.

The strike dragged on unmercifully, youngsters scratted on the old pit heap for coal, a warren of deeper holes, always on sharp look out for the colliery 'poliss' who turned a blind eye unless faced with blatant defiance. After a train derailment at Cramlington, an unfortunate affair, the constabulary in mining areas were ordered to keep revolvers on hand and be prepared to use them. An injunction which was frowned upon by wiser heads on the bosses' side, sad indeed for a force which prided itself on keeping the peace unarmed, Martha's opinion was very scathing and naturally given voice.

'Turnin' guns on yer own kind,' she hotly accused the young constable on duty at Rothwell House, cups of tea given rather more begrudgingly than of yore, John Starrett's orders carried out to the letter and no more. 'Shovin' men i' jail fer nowt hardly,' she ranted on, up in arms at this new development.

'Aa've got no gun, Missis,' the man defended, sick of the whole ugly business and anxious to be back to normal duty, he had no stomach for some of the things he had to do. Despite increased anxiety for his health, the gaffer refused to alter this daily routine, Polrigg was always first on the list, at exactly the same time every day, the height of stupidity. 'Come with me?' he asked Victoria one morning at breakfast, where he devoured his usual substantial meal. 'When I die,' he stated continually, 'it won't be on an empty stomach,' hell bent on indulgence. Sherry before dinner, wine with it, port or claret afterwards, sometimes Napoleon brandy with expensive Havana cigars, all against Angus MacLean's precise instructions.

Geoffrey hoped Victoria would have the sense to refuse, which she tried to do without giving offence. 'Stay at home for once,' she pleaded. 'What point is there in visiting idle pits, you employ managers to see safety measures are carried out. There are pickets and mobs everywhere, one of these days you'll run into trouble.'

John Hanson's colour heightened and his grey eyes flashed fire. 'Nonsense, girl, I must show the flag, let them know I can't be intimidated. Besides, I need to keep my eye on things or they don't get done,' he grunted and looked so woebegone Victoria relented, much to her father's dismay.

'Do you think it is any place for a woman?' he had the temerity to ask, soon rounded upon. 'This particular young woman happens to be my granddaughter and old enough to please herself. I am not likely to expose her to danger,' the gaffer barked and Victoria's beseeching look begged for an end to any further argument. 'My daughter,' the words on the tip of Geoffrey's tongue, which Lottie immediately sensed, strongly disposed to claim, 'Neither your kin nor his,' taut with anger at this unfortunate turn of events.

'Don't go near Saltersgate,' Victoria said in undertone to Jackson before John Starrett joined them at the car, more sense than to take the short cut through the village. 'Aa'll go by the North Road and turn off at Branton Park. There'll be a right collection at the pit gates,' he told her, ''e should change the visitin' times, it could save a whole lot o'bother.' Convinced something had to happen sooner of later, the men were unlikely to accept deliberate provocation forever without retaliation.

Victoria saw her grandfather coming and cautioned Jackson, quick to give her a last bit of hurried advice. 'Don't let'is feet touch the ground till we're through them gates, it's safer there.' Sure the old man had lost his marbles, Victoria's presence could be the last straw. There were lots of women around and easily incited by sight of a beautiful, well dressed young lady, the picture of health, she could stir up a host of ill feeling and God knows what might ensue. Victoria shouldn't be subjected to any of it, the women were often more vicious than their menfolk.

Way back in the days of coach and horses, the gaffer usually mounted and dismounted in the stable yard, only for Madam was the grand entrance and exit, but since his heart attack the car had been driven to the front door and he didn't demur, wise enough in this respect at least. He soon joined them and off they went.

Two pairs of eyes watched them go, Lottie's lovely hazel ones full of anxiety and Geoffrey's none the less. 'You should have stopped her,' she accused him, rather heatedly, quite unfair. 'If her grandfather is determined to antagonise the men, she shouldn't be in the thick of trouble if it comes.' The reprimand was accepted with a tolerant smile. 'Perhaps, but a tall order my dear. Tell Victoria not to do something and she is most likely to do the opposite. My daughter has a mind of her own. Come to think of it she reminds me of you,' he said with the utmost affection.

Lottie's heart jumped, an icy band around it, too near the bone for comfort. 'Do you really believe I am stupid enough to walk into a den of lions?' She responded furiously, immediately contrite when Geoffrey's finely chiselled mouth tightened in hurt, quick to apologise. 'My poor love,' he sympathised and stopped any further words with his lips, a gentle kiss. 'Living under the same roof can be both heaven and hell. Sometimes I think we are mad not to flout convention as so many do. The house in Harrow Square is still mine, let on short, renewable lease, the Askews kept on by my tenants. Something I can call my own and pass on to Victoria from the paternal side of her family. 'Perhaps we could – –' he was not allowed to finish.

'Victoria,' Lottie stammered, 'She musn't be hurt,' burying a tearful face in the roughness of his tweed jacket. The whole thing was ludicrous, her daughter's biological father without a penny to his name. The kiss too gentle, when she wanted to lose herself in passionate embrace. Again she must keep up the pretence, let him imagine any irritation stemmed mainly from concern for Victoria's safety, kept unaware of the complexity of it all.

Geoffrey held his loved one close, dreadfully afraid to touch that tremulous mouth but sorely tempted. 'Don't fret, my dearest, and try not to worry too much, Victoria is a very resourceful young lady, well able to take care of herself.' Trying to instil a confidence he himself did not feel, his daughter's ability to cope was soon to be put under very great strain.

* * *

The well trodden track to the colliery gates was lined at both sides with grim faced men, official pickets on duty at the actual entrance to the yard, well acquainted with the timing of the gaffer's regular visits. 'Silly old buggar,' Jackson muttered under his breath, fully convinced John Starrett sought confrontation so police could be called in and heads would roll, any ploy used to bring the men to their senses, his own never questioned by such a self opinionated man.

It wasn't just the gaffer himself in danger, Jackson was dreadfully concerned about the safety of the young woman obliged to drive with them, blackmailed by fondness for the old reprobate. Anyone could be made a fool of to obtain advantage, even the granddaughter he idolised so much and who was fully expected to share his own views, prepared to go along with them whatever it might entail. Not a nice thought and he decided to give John Starrett the benefit of the doubt. Surely not, he deliberated, but the belief persisted, a disturbing niggle which refused to go away.

Victoria's bright blue eyes dimmed as they absorbed the whole miserable scene, very upset at what they beheld. 'They all look so pinched,' she exclaimed in distress, even more bothered by the ragged state of bairns who darted hither and thither, to them it was somewhat of a game as yet but their time would surely come if this effort produced negative results. Women, young and not so young, in drab woollen shawls hugged closely to their bodies, it was not a cold day by any means but so little nourishing food meant thin blood, in which respect women suffered most, unselfishness an inherent trait.

'It doesn't have to be this way,' John Starrett grunted, his heavy brows furrowed in anger, not entirely devoid of feeling but he was a hard headed business man and strikes cost money, his entire life geared to the making of it. 'Work is there for those who want it, they don't understand the economics of the situation. The women should encourage them to return to their jobs instead of egging them on.' Instantly alert when he caught sight of a lorry load of goods coming up behind them, no likelihood of pickets allowing it through.

'Put your foot down Jackson, they'll open the gates,' he blustered 'If the driver waits until we move, he can follow. The idiots won't chance being run over.' It was accepted procedure for the chauffeur to be allowed entry, usually amid ripe language and catcalls but they had never stopped before. 'Is that a wise move, sir?' he ventured, very much relieved to hear Victoria echo support. 'No it isn't, have some sense grandfather, apparently they won't stop us but other transport is a different matter altogether.' The men stood silent, caps doffed in mock respect, determination written all over their faces, any deviation and the whole thing could erupt into violence of which John Starrett was completely aware. 'Those are spare parts the fellow is delivering, for the pumps, no blacksmiths to make them and I'll be damned if I'll allow a servant or slip of a girl to govern how I deal with the matter,' he bellowed into the back of Mattie's neck. Stiffened in resentment, John Starrett's own veins thickened into unsightly cords, his face purple with rage, no good for him in his condition, he was foolhardy without a doubt.

Thrusting Victoria's restraining hands aside, the gaffer pushed his way out of the car and strode forward into battle, like some Roman gladiator, afraid of nothing or nobody, totally out of control. The old man had guts, Jackson reluctantly admitted and gazed after the retreating figure, not even his worst enemy could say otherwise and he was surrounded by them, men whose hatred festered deep within, courage no defence if the crowd turned nasty. 'What should we do, Miss Victoria?' he turned to ask but she was gone, swift on John Starrett's heels, ever impulsive and an immediate target for the female element, her very appearance an affront to their femininity, a vast difference between themselves and this fashionably dressed woman, even more ferocious in their fury than the gaffer himself. Now he was surrounded by a clamorous mob, who shouted obscenities but never laid a hand on him, just a solid barrier of bodies to keep him at bay, only his head visible, greater in stature than most. Completely unhinged, his silver topped cane flayed left and right, making connection now and again to yelps of agony.

Trailed by screeching females, Victoria struggled to reach him, absolutely terrified and about to fall to the ground when Robert Hanson rushed to her rescue, white faced and furious at this unfortunate twist to that morning's happenings. 'My grandfather, help him, please,' she implored, not realising how much she asked of him. Robert was prepared to defy the wrath of his own kind to save the girl he loved, the gaffer a different proposition altogether. Silly old fool.

The furious women soon transferred their anger to someone who dared interfere. 'Buggar off,' he roared above the commotion. 'If yer that keen on usin' yer hands stop that damned lorry from gettin' through the gate. Turn the bloody thing over if y'have ta,' and dragged Victoria onto the grass verge as the women flew off like screaming banshees to do what he ordered, worse than men when fully aroused.

'Ferget about the stupid idiot,' he yelled above the uproar, 'He's doin' a great job wi' that damned cane, a few cracked skulls Aa reckon. What possessed'im t'fetch y'here the day, dafter than Aa thowt.'

Now inflamed beyond all reason, Victoria let fly, mindless with fear. 'If you don't help him Robert Hanson, I swear to God I'll never forgive you, never. The sooner you get on that ship to Australia the better, you won't be any great miss.' A downright lie which should have choked her there and then but she was past herself with anxiety and rags.

'Shut up,' he stormed and drew her roughly behind a hedge, out of sight, her arms held in fearsome grip. Beyond caring how much he hurt, Robert kissed her hard on the mouth, and even in such a distraught state she recognised the finality in this passionate embrace. 'Now d'ya see why there canna be owt atween us?' He shot at her but still held fast. 'Bide still, Aa'm not lettin' that bonny face getting' spoilt fer nobody. Yer old man started it, let' 'im finish. God knows the old buggar's tough enough.' Nobody outside Rothwell House was aware of that previous heart attack, a well kept secret, but there was begrudging respect in a tense young voice.

Mattie Jackson pushed his way towards them, surprised to discover the existence of a relationship and anticipated a fine how d'ya do, if the gaffer got wind of it. 'Take'er t'the car an' keep'er there, everybody's otherwise occupied. Sit on the little spitfire if y'have ta,' Robert growled. 'They'll not do'im any real harm, he's the one wi' the stick. Serve the old bastard right if they do, anyway,' deliberately offensive, his blue eyes fixed on Victoria's face, full of undisguised contempt. So be it, the rift had to be complete. 'An' don't look at me lass. It takes some doin' lettin' an old tyrant go at ya wi' a stick an' do nowt t'defend yerself.'

Her anger spilt over. 'Not a single man among you, they are animals, you are all animals,' she spat at him and protested all the way to the car, Jackson was quite unmoved. 'Sorry Miss, best wait till it calms down a bit.' 'If anything happens to my grandfather the pits will be mine and I shall blacklist them all over the country – when they come out of prison,' she added vindictively, relieved to see police transport appear and uniformed figures swarm onto the roadway, batons raised. 'Poor beggars,' Jackson sympathised, as men were caught and held by the scruff of the neck, women too, then hauled into the Black Maria, screaming defiance. But many had disappeared, as if by magic through nearby houses, doors open front and back, a quick means of escape to fields beyond, well known terrain. Robert Hanson was among them, his cap pulled well down to hide that distinctive, auburn hair, a right give away.

John Starrett stood alone in the lane, all fight gone out of him, a pathetic sight. Victoria, released from the car, rushed forward to help this beloved old man, who swayed from side to side in drunken fashion, then fell to the hard earth, one hand clutched to his throat. 'Grandpa, Grandpa,' she screamed in horror, already down on her knees beside his still form. 'He's dead, Jackson, they've killed him,' Mattie close behind. 'No, Miss Victoria,' he comforted, fingers on the gaffer's wrist. 'Aa can feel a pulse, faint but still there. We'll get'im home an'call the doctor. He'd sooner be in'is own bed Aa reckon.' And might have added 'to die', fully convinced the master was on his last legs.

A burly police inspector soon joined them, some of his men were knocked about a bit and several of the miners had concussion, there was blood on the gaffer's cane to ascertain the cause, lying on the ground close beside him. Sick and tired of such scenes, the officer said he would need a statement from both of them later and Jackson saw Victoria's mouth tighten. 'And ye'll get it, sir, the whole story,' was the spontaneous reply and her eyebrows lifted. 'Even if it costs me job,' he might have added, fully resolved the gaffer's part in this would not be swept under the carpet as so often occurred, the bosses and their cronies in high places were dab hands at whitewash.

Victoria travelled in a police ambulance, fretting the while at the slowness of the journey, her grandfather's still body and a first aid man for company, still mentally berating Robert's refusal to help, she had no idea how much he had risked to rescue her. Here was the conflict of love and loyalty Lottie warned of and she had no hesitation as to whether her duty lay, in no mood to be magnanimous, not even fair minded. All she saw at that time was the finger of death on a well loved face, filled with hatred towards those she considered responsible but hard pushed to dismiss the sight of her grandfather going into battle, wielding that lethal object so indiscriminately, with no restraint.

Jackson took the short cut towards Saltersgate and went through the village itself, few around to be interested in his passing, news had not yet travelled this far. Rothwell House had been alerted by phone and Lottie rushed to meet him, her face ashen. 'They're fetchin'the gaffer back now,' he told her and put her in the picture, making her quail at what might lie ahead. 'The way Aa see it, he's not long fer this world,' was the grim announcement.

'And Victoria?' Geoffrey inquired fearfully, close behind. 'Safe but in a state and not prepared t'accept things as they actually happened. That nephew o'yours saved'er bacon but sh' didn't thank 'im fer it,' Jackson informed Lottie. 'He could be in big trouble, manhandlin'er t'stop'er runnin' inta danger an' getting hurt.' A look in Lottie's eyes betrayed the fact that she knew of their association. 'Mebbe 'ee should be got out o'the way fer a bit,' which at once caused anxiety and gave her food for thought, perhaps a use here for some of Aunt Jessica's money, if there was time to get hold of it before he scarpered. Angus MacLean arrived just minutes after the ambulance trundled to the front of the house, summoned by Geoffrey when the news first came through. 'It had to happen,' he said. 'The stubborn old fool couldn't take orders. Don't let them move him until I get there,' now into the vehicle in no time at all, grave faced when he at last emerged. 'Take him to his room and mind how you go' he ordered brusquely, the ambulance men and Mattie Jackson quick to obey, supervised every step of the way by a man who had been friend and physician for many years.

Victoria stood by in a complete stupor as they bore John Starrett into the house and it was Geoffrey who laid a comforting arm around her shoulders, Lottie having preceded the solemn procession indoors. He escorted the stunned girl, silent now and all tears gone, too worn out emotionally to weep any more at present. Strange as it may seem, given the nature of their parting, it was Robert's arms she needed but how could that be? She hated him and never wanted to see him again, reprimanding herself strongly for this sign of weakness, but in such a befuddled state of mind she forgot that hatred is so often akin to love and the latter doesn't die so easily.

* * *

It took several pairs of hands and a great amount of effort to divest the gaffer of his outer clothing, much simpler to cut some of it off Angus Maclean advised. A strong advocate for continued use of the old fashioned night shirt, John Starrett was at last robed in one, an oversized edition for comfort, although he was still a big man. No pyjamas for him, despite numerous attempts by his granddaughter to bring him up to date. Damned uncomfortable things he derided and couldn't be persuaded to make the change, so very much set in his ways. 'How long?' Lottie ventured to ask when Jackson escorted his fellow helpers to the kitchen for a bite to eat and a welcome cup of tea, Martha had already prepared in that direction. 'Difficult to say,' Angus Maclean admitted, with no attempt at evasion, he had had dealings with Lottie before today and gave her credit for obvious common sense. 'Perhaps quite soon, another day, who knows, his sort doesn't give up without a struggle, your employer is a strong minded individual. Someone should sit with him, phone me when the end comes.'

Geoffrey soon made an appearance, Victoria went off to her room to brood in solitude. He knew Lottie would bear the brunt of it all, they all depended upon her so much, too much he acknowledged ruefully. 'Don't grieve,' he said, no stranger to death himself, so close to it for many a long month. 'My father-in-law lived his life to the full,' calmly reassuring, her small hand clasped in his, so cold to the touch.

'I hope there will be someone to grieve for me,' she whispered, now drawn into his loving arms and almost expected a roar of disapproval from the bed but nothing came, no sound except John Starrett's laboured breathing, the gaffer's life was slipping away as they stood there in comforting embrance, which hardly seemed fitting under existing circumstances.

Suddenly ill at ease, she moved away. 'I'll stay with him through the night, if Jackson and yourself will share the rest of today. We must keep Victoria out of it.' So very protective towards this twenty two year old. 'You can make some preliminary arrangements while Mattie is doing his stint. There are written instructions in his safe.' She was conscious at that moment of how much the dying man had confided in her. When told of her grandfather's imminent decease and of how the other three were to share the vigil, Victoria didn't offer to take part. 'I haven't seen anyone die before,' she murmured and looked so pathetic, surprising when she suddenly erupted into condemnation. 'Grandpa shouldn't be dying, those dreadful men are to blame, women too.' Lottie's reaction was not what she expected.

'Even animals tend to bite if they are beaten, it was a foolish thing to do. There were no bruises on the master's body when Doctor MacLean examined him, we can't allow a miscarriage of justice.' She had been fully briefed by Mattie and was determined to defend the innocent. When her friend enlarged upon Robert's intervention, she admitted knowledge of his association with Victoria. 'Finished now, thank heaven,' she sighed in relief, ashamed of her own feelings, well acquainted with unrequited love.

The upper class lady Victoria was brought up to be rose to the surface and her blue eyes flashed fire. 'I might have known what you would say, Lottie, you are one of them after all. Why don't you live among them if you think they are so perfect?' the answer when it came was very direct. 'Because I need to earn a living, Miss Victoria. Your grandfather –' she said almost choking on the word but pulled herself together to continue. 'Your grandfather has always been a good employer to those under his roof, from whom he received, in return, unstinted loyalty and service, all working class folk have to give. Twenty three years is a long time to work for the same person, I must have done something right.' Pleased now for the gift of self expression bestowed upon her by Marianne and with an air of quiet dignity, she turned away to begin her night time vigil. Geoffrey was just relieved there was no one to witness this little scene or see Victoria flounce out of the room, the rift Lottie had anticipated from the outset now upon them.

This painful encounter with her daughter gave much food for thought during the long night hours, with only the faithful Hamlet for company, still reasonably agile, hopefully a few years in him yet and even closer to Lottie since his part in her rescue from Stan Hodges. She looked hard at the man on the bed, a friend for more than two decades, it was impossible to imagine Rothwell House without his imposing presence. The end of an era, with few to really mourn his passing, he had so many enemies among the mining community and others of his own kind merely business acquaintances.

The thought did cross her mind that Victoria might feel disposed to sell Rothwell House when it came to her, she was thankful that guardianship was no longer an issue, she had never been comfortable with the idea. No house meant the loss of homes for Martha, Alice and herself, Victoria's recent outburst was most disconcerting. She visualised providing shelter for all three of them, Mattie Jackson and David too, if he wanted stability for the lad. Geoffrey's place was with his daughter, she was almost glad, no avenue remained to prove Victoria belonged to her. The love they shared would have to be sacrificed for these unforeseen circumstances, left with only a few precious memories to sustain her for the rest of her life. In the midst of it all she conceived a use for Aunt Jessica's money at last, sufficient to put a roof over her head and those of her closest friends, rough justice indeed, which gave some satisfaction in the midst of it all, but she was sorry she wouldn't be able to withdraw money for Robert in time. The slightest of movement in the cold hand she was holding jolted a bemused mind into instant awareness and her eyes travelled across the Alhambra quilt and upwards towards the gaffer's drawn face, there was mute appeal in his sunken eyes. Perhaps he wanted to share these final conscious moments with others close to him? But his head moved from side to side in agitation and John Starrett's index finger flexed towards a big, mahogany chest of drawers, brought from Whitegates towards the end of the war, magnificent in its highly polished state. What did he want? Some memento from the past maybe, his younger life with wife and child before it all turned sour. A shot in the dark but worth a try. Intent on humouring a dying man and in full view, so he could see, Lottie touched each of the drawers in turn until she reached the bottom and caught an almost imperceptible nod of the head, glazed eyes closed in obvious relief, the effort nearly too much for fast fading strength. Now to open the drawer and find what the gaffer was so anxious for her to discover.

The very last thing she expected and withdrew from the sight of it in horror, her body rigid, truly astounded. Right before her astonished eyes lay a green, leather bound diary, with a gilt filigree clasp, a replica of those others burnt in anger and disappointment so long ago. Its existence, here in this room, told Lottie all she wanted to know and the truth struck home so forcibly, she was filled with a deep sense of betrayal. Never had she envisaged John Starrett's hand in the cruel deception perpetrated upon her, a man she trusted, capable of the same infamous behaviour as his own daughter and Jessica Finlay.

Through the mists of approaching death, the gaffer saw Lottie's back stiffen as she rose from the floor, the all revealing book held tight, too late now to tell of his outraged feelings when he read the diaries, Felicity's true nature laid bare to a devoted father. Sadly disillusioned but unable to turn from his only child, he digested the terrible tale of that exchange of babies in Harrow Square, a despicable crime against a poor, defenceless girl. Then came the realisation of all it meant, relinquishment of any claim to Victoria, the apple of his eye, her real mother a humble servant who had become a true friend.

John Starrett's dilemma was soul destroying, the arguments used to convince himself the child had a better future with him were pure self deception. Too proud to expose the family to such adverse publicity, that later decision to make Lottie Victoria's guardian was a sop to his conscience, easily silenced. He never knew why he kept the incriminating diary and left the others where she was sure to find them. Perhaps he had some secret hope at the back of a troubled mind that revelation might be forced upon him, afraid now to meet his Maker with such a terrible burden of guilt. Fearful also of the look he was certain to see on Lottie's face when she turned towards the bed.

But a calm, collected woman walked across the room, firm decision in every line of her slender form, the book in her hand unopened. How could she lay claim to Victoria after all this time? Enough to have the truth confirmed at last, a truth which came more than twenty years too late. Just a dying man to take the fire of any anger she still felt, whose only sin was to love her daughter as much as she did herself, the real criminals were beyond the power of earthly justice. Left to the wrath of the Lord and definitely in hell if there were any such place, Felicity was alone in a hell of her own making. No satisfaction was to be found in sending John Starrett to whatever awaited him without forgiveness.

She raised the diary chest high, unlocked as she expected, and tore out the pages without reading a single line. The built up fire soon made them into a charred mess, the leather binding and gilt clasp to be disposed of elsewhere. A faint sigh of relief came from the bed, John Starrett knew that the collier's daughter, who had become so great a part of his life had just made the final sacrifice, Victoria would always remember him as her grandfather and with this consoling thought, the pit gaffer closed his eyes to die in peace.

Shaken to the core, Lottie returned to keep vigil but the peaceful look on a dearly loved face told her death had come quietly, as she would have wished, the dampness on his waxen cheeks confirmed he had recognised the forgiveness in her heart before his life ebbed away.

Lottie Hanson's beautiful hazel eyes were awash as she bade farewell to a friendship, an up and down relationship which had lasted twenty two years. It was an irony to think her daughter would inherit so much of this man's huge fortune, the actual size of it impossible to imagine. Three prosperous collieries, many acres of good farming land and goodness knows what else. Victoria would never know of her humble ancestry. Their recent conflict of opinion hopefully to be sorted out, gave her an uneasy feeling, she was none too sure how her daughter would act when it came to the crunch. An intelligent mind, free of that first agonising grief, could make her view the situation in its perspective and their mutual affection was strong enough to endure, shades of her stormy self when young. Victoria would need support until the funeral was over and long afterwards.

The strike was now on its last legs and the bitterness in its aftermath must be weathered by all of them, suddenly struck by the strange fact that after years of torment, she too had found a measure of peace, the uncertainly which had haunted her soon to be buried in John Starrett's grave. She bent low to kiss the gaffer's cold cheek, a fond farewell, time to inform the others of his passing and, for some reason hard to understand her own heart felt lighter somehow as she left the dead man's room, closing the door behind her, a symbolic end to so many chapters of a tempestuous life.

* * *

The colliery owner's funeral was the ostentatious affair one might expect, his last Will and Testament yet to be read but full instructions had been left as to how both should be conducted. Not surprising that these arrangements were a final demonstration of wealth and influence, everyone of any importance thereabouts was in attendance, top brass of all description. William Barrington and his son were among the chief mourners, a gleam of anticipation in this shrewd man's eyes, easy to guess upon whom and what his thoughts were centred, Victoria was already envisaged as a prospective daughter-in-law and Richard was guaranteed to do as he was told. His father's interest was mainly in the gaffer's three collieries, which in alliance with his own would make him a force to be reckoned with among his contemporaries. The idea of stepping into John Starrett's shoes held great appeal, he was not big enough to fill them, of much lesser stature in all ways. Victoria was only thought of as a means to an end.

Local miners, still on strike, lined the route from Oakfields, in evidence also at various points between this upper class area and John Coulter's farmhouse, along that same road the gaffer travelled so often to Stamfordham, where he had chosen to be laid to rest. Some men doffed their caps in respect for their natural adversary, mostly of the old school, there were few young men in attendance, either on principle or too busy elsewhere with strike affairs. The mining community, as a whole, was rather anxious to know what might lie head of them 'under new management', all eyes on a tearful Victoria, in the first mourning car with her father and several of her grandfather's kin, few of them met previously.

'Ride with us,' father and daughter both said to Lottie. 'He would have wanted it.' But she had no desire to make tongues wag and preferred to remain in Rothwell House to keep an eye on preparations for a buffet meal, only a select few were invited after the internment, others had been provided for in a country hotel, close to the cemetery.

Alice, bathed in tears as usual, received constant scolding from Martha, who berated the poor lass unmercifully, Lottie in the unenviable role of peacemaker as usual, was rather irritated on this day of all days. But the gaffer's death didn't go deep with either of her friends, Martha's only comment that the master had been a pleasure to cook for, there was no sentiment in the little woman's make up and Alice's copious tears were quite superficial, neither of them had got so far as to think how this might affect their own lives.

The funeral cortege actually passed Whitegates en route to the Parish Church, where the mourners gathered and Harold Peabody's successor took the funeral service, also the committal at the graveside, the gaffer was laid among his ancestors beside his wife, a place for Felicity when she died, no sign of that as yet, she was disgustingly healthy except in mind. An excellent source of income for those responsible for her welfare, they had every reason to keep her alive. Several of the gaffer's former employees were in attendance but kept in the background to allow the upper crust centre stage as it were, regarded as their right. With Geoffrey's permission Mattie Jackson accompanied by young David and three colliery managers, drove John Starrett's own car but kept well to the rear, in a vehicle brightly polished as a mark of respect for his long time employer. The lengthy ride in a posh motor car, was the youngster's main concern.

When the splendid buffet meal in Rothwell House was over, this latest of Martha's culinary efforts much appreciated, the reading of the will took place, just the occupants of the big house and Mattie Jackson present, at the gaffer's request. This was taken, by the few relatives who reluctantly departed, as a bad sign as far as they were concerned. Martha and Alice were completely out of their depth but proud as peacocks to actually sit in the upstairs drawing room, in the presence of their betters, an honour hitherto undreamt of.

'The gaffer knew how t'do things proper,' Martha proclaimed, delighted not to be ignored, Jessica Finlay's exclusion of them from her funeral still rankled. 'Breedin' always tells,' she declared sanctimoniously, rather hypocritical but always able to justify anything she said or did, she had never changed one iota in this direction as long as they had known her.

Victoria's anger ran its course in the few days between her grandfather's death and his funeral, no indictment was made against those she formerly held responsible. Mattie Jackson's account of what happened at the colliery gates, supported by doctor's evidence, cleared those in prison awaiting trial, they were just fined for disturbance of the peace, a small contingency fund was available in such cases, built up since the last strike but getting dangerously low. Her daughter's dignified behaviour made Lottie's heart swell with pride, her strength of character attributed to the working class blood in her veins, the polish added with education and advantage. Positive proof that, given the same opportunities, many poorer folk would be able to carve out a better place for themselves in the general scheme of things. 'Forgive me, please,' Victoria begged of Lottie, amid a host of tears, 'I was beastly to you, dreadful of me when you have always been so good, the nearest to a mother I have ever known.' Words which filled the recipient with unbelievable joy, her own cup full and running over. If only Geoffrey and herself could be together, she sighed inwardly, but that was an impossible dream with little chance of ever coming true.

John Starrett's will held few surprises, there were the expected legacies to those who served him in Rothwell House and Whitegates. Martha and Alice to receive one hundred pounds each and they gasped at the amount, a real fortune. To Mary Trumble, now widowed, a similar amount and also his former Whitegate's coachman. Mattie Jackson was to have twice this sum and money invested for David's education. A swift image of a smiling Marianne came into her head as Lottie absorbed this welcome piece of news.

'To my son-in-law Geoffrey Cranshawe, I bequeath Rothwell House and an annual income for its upkeep, the interest from monies invested for this purpose. The capital is not to be touched and to revert to my estate on the beneficiary's demise.' None were more astonished than Geoffrey himself, who felt the firm pressure of his daughter's hand and glimpsed a look of approval on Lottie's lovely face, delighted to know he was now master of the old house. Legacies too for the Askews, not forgotten by a man who had every reason to be grateful to this loyal pair, Felicity had been an enormous handful to them for quite some time.

Sufficient money was set aside to keep his daughter in comfortable incarceration for the rest of her life, no stipulation was made about regular visits by husband or daughter, the futility of such finally accepted. Other bequests also, all pointed to the enormity of the gaffer's estate. Money to Stamfordham Parish Church and other charitable organisations, all from a man considered by his miners to be a tight fisted old so and so and not without cause.

After a cough to clear his throat and a sip of water, the solicitor droned on. 'To my dear granddaughter Victoria Cranshawe I leave the residue of my estate and all monies held in my name after compliance with other bequests, apart from the ownership of my three collieries, Polrigg, Belsford and Studley, the stock of which I wish apportioned in the following manner.'

Lottie held her breath and wondered what was to come, the ownership of these pits vital to so many people. 'Forty nine per cent to the aforementioned Victoria Cranshawe,' the voice continued, 'twenty seven percent to my son-in-law Geoffrey Cranshawe, in the hope that he will play some part in the running of the mines. The remainder to my devoted friend and servant, Charlotte Hanson, if still in my employment at the time of my death. No colliery to be sold without the consent of all three stockholders.'

Victoria threw back her blonde head and laughed, much to the solicitor's disapproval, Geoffrey's smile was rather rueful, so well tuned to Lottie's thoughts and feelings to realise the invidious position in which she found herself, the expression on her face was one of complete bewilderment. Mattie Jackson was amazed also but over the moon on Lottie's behalf as well as his own. Martha and Alice were not on the same wave length and only concerned with the wonder of their sudden affluence. 'He can't do this to me,' Lottie raged afterwards when she and her fellow stockholders were alone. 'I won't accept it. You can have my share between you and welcome.' So angry she could scarcely contain herself, John Starrett's purpose was impossible to fathom.

Victoria was highly amused. 'He has done it and you can't alter a single thing. You, my dear Lottie, whether you like the idea or not, are part owner of all three collieries. But don't imagine you can stop the strike by giving everyone a rise in wages, Papa and I can soon put paid to that. Besides you heard the proviso grandfather made, someone appointed to give sensible advice on mining affairs.'

'Someone exactly like himself, I suppose. Our hands will be tied somehow or other and you both know it.' Lottie muttered furiously.

'Be fair, what do any of us know about coal mining, he had to cover our backs.' Geoffrey told her and hoped she would simmer down, still fuming. 'As for you, my darling daughter, remember Lottie and I own fifty one per cent between us, you can't out vote us on any issue.'

Lottie's reply was very terse. 'And just think, you and Victoria in cahoots would leave me no say whatsoever.' Quite peevish.

'He knew neither of us would do that but he made it so the pair of you can keep me in order. He has bound us together hand and foot, the crafty old devil,' Victoria breathed admiringly.

Geoffrey spoke up. 'Your grandfather knew how headstrong and impulsive you are, my dear, and where Lottie's sympathies lie. He was counting on my common sense and affection for both of you to keep the balance. He always wanted me to take an interest in his damned pits. As you say, a crafty old devil,' he finished ruefully.

'I shan't take a single penny out of it. You can pay me my wage as housekeeper, as always. An increase, of course.' Lottie insisted and imagined she heard John Starrett's deep throated chuckle at her consternation but didn't wait for the protests she expected to come. 'If you can see me sitting around like a lady, while someone else manages this house, you are sadly mistaken,' and almost finished by adding 'So there.' Then, as an afterthought added, 'sir.'

'Business partners now, Lottie, you can dispense with the "sir",' Geoffrey said but failed to reckon with her strength of will. 'There will be no difference. Apart from the solicitor and members of this household nobody else knows of this, Martha and Alice haven't a clue what it means. In any case, they have both sympathised with me already for not receiving any money. Terribly unfair in Martha's opinion, not exactly how she put it, naturally. Alice has offered me a half share of her legacy.' Smiling as she recalled Martha's exact words.

'After all y'did fer him an'that barmy daughter o'his. D'ya reckon'ee just fergot or somethin',' the little woman tried to console, both servants absolutely flabbergasted by their sudden wealth. 'Just the total amount of the estate will be noted in the press. Prepare yourself for a host of suitors, Victoria.' Geoffrey teased and got the sharp end of his daughter's tongue. 'Let anyone come after me for my money and I shall soon send them packing,' she retorted, blue eyes alive with temper, quite a formidable young lady when aroused, as her two companions both knew only too well. It would take a strong man to deal with her. Her father wasn't done, however. 'William Barrington has you earmarked for his son. Not a bad young fellow but hardly the right one for you my dear and, as we all know, his father rules the roost. I bet he has an amalgamation of collieries in mind. A wife's property becomes her husband's, you do realise that, I hope.'

'Then all I can say, Papa, is he is in for a shock when he discovers I am not the sole owner,' Victoria exulted, quite tickled at the whole idea.

'Who is likely to tell him, if we keep a low profile?' Geoffrey quipped and Lottie, listening to their banter, hoped that when it came to marriage, her daughter would recognise gold from dross, forced to acknowledge that in choosing Robert, as Victoria obviously did, a fine young man but it was an ill starred affair from the outset, like Geoffrey and herself. She wondered if John Starrett somehow sensed his son-in-law's interest and tried to bridge the gap, reparation for the wrong done to her in the past. Soon she dismissed this as a load of rubbish, it was not in his nature to go against the rules of class, some redress maybe but in such an unfortunate way, bound to create an ocean of difficulties, and she prayed nobody need ever know the full contents of the gaffer's will.

John Starrett had left her something else, a letter handed over by his solicitor, her name on the envelope in his copper plate handwriting, not yet opened. A loophole, she guessed, if she needed ever to tell Victoria after all. Should she open it now or keep it safely hidden until after her own death, when Victoria was sure to read it? Her intention was now to leave a will, something to bequeath apart from what remained of Jessica Finlay's legacy, this was quite a sum accruing interest all the time. But every instinct urged her to refuse the colliery stock, no matter what her partners had to say.

Geoffrey drew her attention to household affairs, to be discussed with him daily instead of John Starrett, pleased and sad at the same time. While they talked, Victoria wandered towards the window looking out but seeing nothing, besieged by images of Robert, that tall, loose limbed figure as it strode away from her on the Town Moor, the memory of that passionate interlude so fresh in her mind. The ugliness lingered of their last meeting at the pit head and a farewell kiss which still scorched her lips in retrospect. 'Damn you, Robert Hanson!' came from the depths of an aching heart, the loss of grandfather and lover almost simultaneous, parting from the latter in so much anger. Suitors, her father said, but it would take someone very special to wipe all trace of Robert from both mind and heart. A couple of days earlier Lottie mentioned her nephew may have emigrated to Australia, not to know it was a deliberate attempt to cry 'finis' to an impossible situation, nobody really knew where Robert had vanished to. He had thought it wiser to sling his hook before the law descended upon him, unaware of subsequent happenings, even the gaffer's death. Victoria was in furious enough mood to be instrumental in sending him to jail, he was also ignorant of her eventual fair assessment of the whole rotten business.

She stood there, idly contemplating the possibility of marriage at some future date and actually considered Richard Barrington. Not that she believed him capable of passionate love but he was a good friend and many a sound marriage was built on such. She did want to bear a child some day, for which purpose she needed a husband. There was no doubt in a confident young mind that she could deal with William Barrington, her grandfather's collieries well out of this avaricious man's reach.

But Robert's copper coloured head and devasting blue eyes continued to give her no peace and it took considerable willpower to shake herself free and she resorted to flippancy to ease the pain. 'Just a thought, Lottie, you could marry Papa and wouldn't have to call him, sir,' she joked, with no idea of the impact her words created, her father and Lottie absolutely stunned.

'Miss Victoria,' Lottie gasped in horror, 'Your grandfather's ridiculous will and now this silly nonsense. More than enough for one day,' her face drained of all colour.

Full of mischief, Victoria ignored their obvious dismay. 'Well, it isn't such a bad idea,' unaware of the bombshell she had dropped and found the whole thing amusing, in dire need of humour, after such serious goings on.

'Downright stupidity,' Lottie snapped, 'Please keep your daughter under control, sir.' None too sure what had triggered this train of thought and most uneasy. 'But I haven't time to waste on such absurdity. If I don't get back to the kitchen there won't be any dinner this evening, Martha had already drunk one glass of sherry too many before I left,' she stammered lamely and not in full control of her emotions hurried out of the room. The instigator of this unfortunate happening stared open mouthed. 'Why is Lottie so upset, she usually knows when I am making a joke about something?' very distressed at the outcome. Geoffrey was a loss for the right approach. 'Well –' he began and speedily collected his thoughts. 'It has been quite a day one way and another, especially for Lottie, worried about the terms of your grandfather's will. To be made a capitalist in one stroke and married off with the next might be rather too much for anyone to absorb all at once.' He showed a calmness he certainly did not feel but convinced it was just teasing and his daughter did not know of his feelings for Lottie nor the reciprocation of them.

'I shall pop downstairs this very minute and apologise to her.' She was on her way to the door when her father cried halt. 'No, my dear, not advisable, one of those occasions when the least said soonest mended. Besides, I am not free to marry anyone,' he stated solemnly and saw a shadow cross her pretty face.

'Oh yes, of course, there is Mama,' she faltered, very subdued, Felicity almost written off in her mind, never really any part of her life as Lottie was. Geoffrey was of the firm opinion that his daughter would be no obstacle should marriage ever become a possibility, but was fully convinced his wife would live to a ripe old age, John Starrett's daughter still very much in the reckoning.

* * *

Lottie deliberately avoided the kitchen area and her own quarters, much too dangerous in her present mood, with Martha's mind and eyes razor sharp. Instead, she beat a hasty retreat to that other room on the second floor landing, where John Starrett once insisted she slept to be near Victoria. Overwhelmed by a need for solitude she locked herself in, her daughter's flippant remark too close for comfort and an enormous jolt to her nervous system. To touch on something so vital, even in jest, showed how much of a tightrope they walked day after day but she was made to realise what they were missing, truly dismayed at the thought of slipping into old age without the intimacy and sexual fulfilment her body so often craved. Take life by the horns, an inner voice cajoled, it surely owes you something for what it has stolen from you. Get rid of that stupid tendency to deny yourself lest someone else be hurt. No need for such sacrifice, the persistent voice urged and how she longed to take heed of its bidding, which on sudden impulse she decided to obey.

Her feet gained impetus and bore her swiftly towards the door, ready to run down two flights of stairs into Geoffrey's loving arms, where she yearned to be, his scruples given their marching orders along with her own. She was reminded of those first passionate kisses in the stable yard and a war weary soldier denied the solace of love in all its fullness, before going back to the horrors awaiting him, and of his return sunk deep in the slough of utter despondency. Thinking more so of that one night of glorious fulfilment years afterwards and nothing since, when there was so much to share.

Catching sight of herself in the full length mirror near the door, she stopped in her tracks to behold a woman forty three years old, still young in heart and body, not allowed to go to seed like so many of her class. Modesty forbade listing other attributes, the beauty she had always possessed, certain to fade into mediocrity without the fulfilment of love to keep it alive. Would denial eventually turn it sour? A risk she wasn't prepared to take, determined to break down Geoffrey's defences, come together in every sense of the word.

Filled with new resolve, Lottie turned the key, ready to open the door into a wonderful future, highly elated at the prospect, a heady sensation soon dismissed by the sobering reminder of John Starrett only hours in his grave. It was hardly an appropriate time to put such a wild scheme into action, hesitation her immediate undoing and exhilaration soon replaced by weariness of body and soul as events of the past few days caught up with her and now made themselves seriously felt. Tomorrow, she promised herself in half hearted fashion, running past the downstairs room where Geoffrey was still ensconced with Victoria, she could hear their voices. She went straight into the kitchen where nothing ever changed and plunged at once onto the sharp end of a typical Martha outburst.

'About time an' all, where've y'been? Dallyin' as if the morra'lldo, an'me waitin't'see what's wanted fer the night's dinner.' Excitement engendered by the impact of a hundred pound legacy gone for a while, practicality to the fore, a creature of habit drunk or sober and with a decided leaning towards the former on this occasion.

Alice gave a lopsided grin and whispered behind their friend's back. 'She's a bit tiddly, Lottie, but it's been a grand day, hasn't it?' No matter that the former master of the house was dead and buried, even the saddest of occasions were red letter days on Alice's calendar. 'An' we'll be bidin'here the same as always,' the big lass declared, her plain face alight at this pleasing prospect. Lottie represented her security, the role accepted from the very beginning of a long standing friendship.

'The same as always, Alice,' she echoed reassuringly, with the sinking feeling that this might apply in other ways also. Her resolution had soon begun to crumble, the story of her life somehow, tomorrow eagerly anticipated but it never seemed to live up to expectations, so why should the following day prove any different? 'I'll sleep on it,' she promised herself and with enormous effort turned her mind to affairs of the moment, the future not hers to control. With that familiar lift to her shoulders and straightened back she sought strength amid her weariness to handle Martha, that irascible creature still rabbiting on, halted momentarily when a light young voice carried down from the floor above. 'Lottie – Lottie,' came the urgent cry and Martha muttered under her breath, quite out of sorts. 'It's Miss Victoria,' Alice said unnecessarily, only to receive an irritable earful. 'W'know fine who it is. What does'er ladyship want now?' Martha snapped, her young mistress obviously out of favour for some unknown reason. The beginnings of a hangover were about to be felt by one and all.

'Her mother,' Lottie had the strongest inclination to shout in reply, precisely who she was, Victoria's mother, a fact known only by herself and two others, both in their graves, Felicity no longer in the reckoning in this respect. An indisputable truth, the person she had been all along, doing those things a mother does for twenty two years. The feeding of Victoria as a baby, a comfort in those early days of grief when a tiny mouth took its fill from her full, warm breasts. Soothing a crying infant through many sleepless nights, when teething and nursed in the throes of the usual childhood illnesses. Always there for her and still was, would be into an unforeseeable future, God willing. A mother in every conceivable way and by her daughter's recent admission regarded as such. No dream just pure reality. As for those other dreams, who knows? Life was a waiting game, something she excelled in the cynical thought, plenty of practice throughout the years.

'Coming,' she cried and ran upstairs to see what her daughter required of her, Martha's snort of disapproval completely ignored and the tart remark thrown after her retreating figure. 'Aa still don't know what's fer dinner an' Aa'm not a mind reader,' this to the clatter of pots and pans. She accepted the fact that neither Martha nor Alice understood her devotion and never would, the secret of Victoria's true identity held close to an ever loving maternal heart, hers and hers alone. John Starrett's letter was locked safely away, there if ever needed but she couldn't envisage the gaffer's confession being brought to light, not by her. Victoria might well take such a revelation in her stride but Geoffrey's manhood would receive a devastating blow, years of his life wasted in a disastrous marriage, no swift end to it in sight, the joy of fathering a daughter his only compensation. There was too much love in her heart to destroy this image with the almost unbelievable truth.

Lover and daughter both awaited her in the hallway, anxiety written all over their beloved faces, not surprising after that earlier angry departure. She smiled and Victoria flew into her arms, 'I love you, Lottie, really I do,' she said in muffled tone, hugged even closer for this heart stirring admission, and across the golden head buried into her shoulder, her own eyes and Geoffrey's met and held, so much love in them, the smile that wreathed his handsome face indeed a joy to behold and she prayed for satisfaction in what she undoubtedly possessed, without that agonising craving for something she might never have.

* * *

S S *Ballantyne* was three days out of Aden, well into the Indian Ocean, when Robert Hanson stood on her upper deck, careful to avoid contact with any of the paying passengers, immigrants like himself but affluent enough to hire berths aboard this medium sized cargo ship. Most of his time had been spent in the boiler room, he was glad to be free for a while from the stench of sweating bodies, his own much sweeter after a wash down in a bucket of sea water, using the privacy of a dark recess between two life boats. There had been no opportunity for total immersion since that last dip in the sea at the Suez port of call, he was not supposed to be in this part of the ship but its passengers were at dinner and those on watch could be relied upon to turn a blind eye.

John Starrett was still alive when Robert dashed into 24, Maria Street, absolutely breathless and almost to the point of exhaustion, despite his youth. Just time for hurried explanations and to cram a few articles of clothing into a bag, his mother handing over her last few coppers and hurriedly wrapped the little food available in a familiar red and white, gypsy like handkerchief. Then off to Newcastle across the Town Moor, his feet heavy as lead and a heart to match, the sight of that hollow of trees a strong reminder of his lost love. Hiding around the station area until undercover of darkness he hopped aboard a goods train and rode freight to Liverpool on more than one train and after weeks of waiting, sleeping rough and taking any work available he got the necessary papers, Australia a young country, badly needing an influx of men after the loss of so many Diggers in the Fourteen-Eighteen War.

He signed aboard the *Ballantyne* as a stoker, ironic to think the coal he shovelled into her boilers may have been hewed in one of the gaffer's collieries, stockpiled and sold before the strike got off the ground, coal owners had been astute enough to cover all contingencies. Reminded of that wicked old devil wherever he seemed to be, he was sorry John Starrett and Victoria shared the same blood, not to know how wrong he was in this assumption, bitterly resentful of any connection.

There had been no contact with home since his hasty departure, even a postmark could send the law to hunt him out, he was careful not to disclose his whereabouts and had no idea what to do when the ship docked in Sydney Harbour. The coal mining area was north of there, or so he was informed, not that he intended to finish up hewing coal but to get started he might have to do the job he knew best.

Several Saltersgate families had emigrated since the Great War ended but very irregular letters home suggested conditions were no better than in the old country, they had little hope of ever setting foot in England again. But Robert had youth on his side and single status, both a definite plus, spurred on by burning ambition and the determination to go back home some day, with the sole intention of rubbing a few noses in the muck, show those upper class bastards a thing or two. He had a gut feeling, despite youthful optimism, that it could be a long haul.

Victoria's vivid blue eyes and corn coloured hair haunted his dreams, tormented continually by the might have been, so grateful for a wonderful sexual experience he would never forget and in no way regarded lightly. Memories were marred to some degree by their last meeting, the burning hatred that blazed from those same eyes, once aglow with love for him. He had deliberately burnt his boats, too much in love to leave her hankering after him for years to come, terrible to think of his lovely girl a shrivelled old spinster, too many of those after the war. The thought of her in someone else's arms was a torture he must learn to endure, he had no other option.

Victoria was not the only woman remembered with regret, his mother's face white but composed when they said their goodbyes, fully resolved not to make it harder for him, Elizabeth was left to shed all the tears. 'It's too far,' his young sister wailed, 'We'll never get t'see ya again,' she choked, his reply meant to give her some sort of reassurance. 'Never's a long time,' he told her with a bearlike hug, too emotional to utter another word. Robert Hanson would never know the full extent of his mother's grief, the tears both parents shed the night of his departure, huddled close in their soft, feather bed. 'I knew something had to happen sooner or later.' Margaret sobbed uncontrollably. 'But not this, Ralph, not this, it's too much to bear,' her face buried deep in her husband's shoulder, his flannel shirt soaking wet.

'Aye lass, it's hard but ye'll bear it,' he muttered consolingly, 'W'both will, t'gether, as we've always done,' disturbed by the trembling of her slender body. Well inured against the many griefs and woes in their sort of life, Ralph Hanson had wanted better for the woman who felt so frail in his arms, yet very much aware of that inner strength she possessed, often greater than his own.

Weeks later, his face uplifted to the galaxy of stars in a southern hemisphere sky, their son's thoughts were with them, thousand of miles between. News reached the ship, when it put in at Aden, that the strike was over, the gaffers smelling like roses as usual, while miners returned to the black earth to toil for a mere pittance. He swore then that when he went back things would be different and didn't realise how prophetic this statement would prove to be. He stared, now, at the heavens above, convinced that hell was there on earth, there was some ironic significance in stoking in a ship's boiler room, not much to choose between that and the mines, except that a slow death underground would be much worse than drowning.

He shook himself free of such morbid thinking, he had no idea what awaited him in an unknown country, a bit apprehensive naturally, although unafraid of hard graft. There would be other gaffers at first, no doubt, but he would be his own boss in time, an end to the bowing and scraping, John Starrett's face imprinted on his mind, the epitome of all he detested. Whatever fears he might have must not be allowed to undermine his confidence but a sense of loneliness made itself felt, the *Ballantyne* although fair sized was just a speck on this large ocean, himself even less and he had no family or close friends to support him. New friends would have to be tried and tested and he was bound to make mistakes, often taken for a ride in ignorance. A struggle to rid himself of negative feelings, fully resolved not to drown in the depths of despair.

Victoria's image was never to fade from his mind, there would be other women of course, he was a young man with natural urges which would lead him along thorny paths but still to remain faithful in an odd sort of way. In his dreams she always appeared young and beautiful, those glorious blue eyes soft and luminous in memory and a smile that tore at his guts. He often cursed the fate that threw them together in the first place with no hope of any permanence. Tormented by the well remembered feel of that yielding body in his arms when they surrendered to the uncontrollable force of mutual desire, something he never experienced with any other woman, sex was only indulged in for sheer physical relief and he hated himself afterwards, marriage the furthest thing from his mind.

Why did that miserly old bastard have to be her grandfather, the thought which never ceased to anger him, consumed with hatred for the pit gaffer and others of the same ilk, this feeling was sufficient to galvanise him into renewed effort whenever he wanted to give up. Not to know he heaped curses upon a dead man's head but doubtful if such knowledge would lessen this antagonism. 'Aa'll show the old bastard' a constant threat, a satisfaction already taken out of reach. Much later in life the realisation came that deep hatred of John Starrett was a decided spur to ambition and even then he would be loath to acknowledge the fact.

The hand of fate, with so many vagaries, may well have decreed that Robert and Victoria would meet again and be manipulating the situation to draw them both, inexorably towards the where and when. One thing was certain, if such were predestined, others would be caught up in the mechanisms, its puppet victims already chosen and even now in firm control of the strings, to dangle them at will.